TOLSTOY
SELECTED STORIES

TOLSTOY
SELECTED STORIES

LEO TOLSTOY

This edition published in 2018 by Arcturus Publishing Limited
26/27 Bickels Yard, 151–153 Bermondsey Street,
London SE1 3HA

Cover design: Peter Ridley
Cover illustration: Peter Gray
Design: Dani Leigh

AD006507UK

Printed in the UK

CONTENTS

INTRODUCTION

Leo Tolstoy was born Count Lyov Nikolayevich Tolstoy on 9 September 1828 into an aristocratic Russian family. Death was a constant in his early childhood. His mother, Mariya Nikolayevna, died before he turned two and his father, Nikolay Tolstoy, died when he was only nine years old. His next two guardians, his grandmother and aunt, also died shortly after his father, leaving him and his siblings to live with an aunt in Kazan. Nonetheless, his first work was a dreamy and pleasant autobiography about his early years entitled *Detstvo*, published in 1852 under an alias in the distinguished *Sovremennik* journal.

At the University of Kazan, his reckless behaviour resulted in his leaving before his studies were complete. He returned to Yasnaya Polyana with the hopes of improving his estate and teaching himself. He joined the army alongside his older brother and served in the Crimean War between 1853 and 1856.

It was this experience that began his career as a short story writer. His first short story, 'The Raid' (1853) examined the nature of bravery and was soon followed by three pieces on the Siege of Sevastopol. His short fiction varied greatly, from the exhilarating thriller, 'The Prisoner of the Caucausus' (1872), to the acclaimed psychological novella 'The Death of Ivan Ilych' (1886).

After vainly refusing to join in conversation with other intellectuals, he lost all of his money while gambling in Paris in 1857. As a result, he was forced to return to Russia. He discovered a passion for pedagogy and opened a school for poor children. In 1862, he met and married Sofya Andreyevna Bers, whose father was a respectable doctor in Moscow. With all of his attention now on his marriage and his writing, he was able to publish many works on ethical matters, such as *Otrochestvo* (1854), *Yunost* (1857), and 'Lyutsern' (1857).

Between 1863 and 1877, Tolstoy achieved his greatest success as a novelist. It was during this time that he wrote both *War and Peace* and *Anna Karenina*, two of the most renowned novels of all time. After finishing *Anna Karenina*, he struggled with an intense existential crisis, which caused him to turn to religion. He wrote several pieces between 1880 and 1884, including *An Examination of Dogmatic Theology* in 1880 and *Union and Translation of the Four Gospels* in 1881, in which he criticized religious practices because he believed that they obscured the message of Christ. His newfound religious fervour caused bitter conflict in his marriage. In 1910, Tolstoy left his wife, dying soon after from pneumonia and heart failure at a railroad station in Astapovo.

GOD SEES THE TRUTH, BUT WAITS

In the town of Vladímir lived a young merchant named Iván Dmítritch Aksyónof. He had two shops and a house of his own.

Aksyónof was a handsome, fair-haired, curly-headed fellow, full of fun, and very fond of singing. When quite a young man he had been given to drink, and was riotous when he had had too much; but after he married he gavet up drinking, except now and then.

One summer Aksyónof was going to the Nízhny Fair, and as he bade goodbye to his family his wife said to him, 'Iván Dmítritch, do not start today; I have had a bad dream about you.'

Aksyónof laughed, and said, 'You are afraid that when I get to the fair I shall go on the spree.'

His wife replied: 'I do not know what I am afraid of; all I know is that I had a bad dream. I dreamt you returned from the town, and when you took off your cap I saw that your hair was quite grey.'

Aksyónof laughed. 'That's a lucky sign,' said he. 'See if I don't sell out all my goods, and bring you some presents from the fair.'

So he said goodbye to his family, and drove away.

When he had travelled halfway, he met a merchant whom he knew, and they put up at the same inn for the night. They had some tea together, and then went to bed in adjoining rooms.

It was not Aksyónof's habit to sleep late, and, wishing to travel while it was still cool, he aroused his driver before dawn, and told him to put in the horses.

Then he made his way across to the landlord of the inn (who lived in a cottage at the back), paid his bill, and continued his journey.

When he had gone about twenty-five miles, he stopped for the horses to be fed. Aksyónof rested awhile in the passage of the inn, then he stepped out into the porch, and, ordering a samovár[1] to be heated, got out his guitar and began to play.

Suddenly a *tróyka*[2] drove up with tinkling bells, and an official alighted, followed by two soldiers. He came to Aksyónof and began to question him, asking him who he was and whence he came. Aksyónof answered him fully, and said, 'Won't you have some tea with me?' But the official went on cross-questioning him and asking him, 'Where did you spend last night? Were you alone, or with a fellow merchant? Did you see the other merchant this morning? Why did you leave the inn before dawn?'

Aksyónof wondered why he was asked all these questions, but he described all that had happened, and then added, 'Why do you cross-question me as if I were a thief or a robber? I am travelling on business of my own, and there is no need to question me.'

Then the official, calling the soldiers, said, 'I am the police officer of this district, and I question you because the merchant with whom you spent last night has been found with his throat cut. We must search your things.'

They entered the house. The soldiers and the police officer unstrapped Aksyónof's luggage and searched it. Suddenly the officer drew a knife out of a bag, crying, 'Whose knife is this?'

Aksyónof looked, and seeing a blood-stained knife taken from his bag, he was frightened.

---

1   *The samovár ('self-boiler') is an urn in which water can be heated and kept on the boil.*
2   *A tróyka is a three-horse conveyance.*

'How is it there is blood on this knife?'

Aksyónof tried to answer, but could hardly utter a word, and only stammered: 'I – I don't know – not mine.'

Then the police officer said, 'This morning the merchant was found in bed with his throat cut. You are the only person who could have done it. The house was locked from inside, and no one else was there. Here is this blood-stained knife in your bag, and your face and manner betray you! Tell me how you killed him, and how much money you stole?'

Aksyónof swore he had not done it; that he had not seen the merchant after they had had tea together; that he had no money except eight thousand roubles of his own, and that the knife was not his. But his voice was broken, his face pale, and he trembled with fear as though he were guilty.

The police officer ordered the soldiers to bind Aksyónof and to put him in the cart. As they tied his feet together and flung him into the cart, Aksyónof crossed himself and wept. His money and goods were taken from him, and he was sent to the nearest town and imprisoned there. Enquiries as to his character were made in Vladímir. The merchants and other inhabitants of that town said that in former days he used to drink and waste his time, but that he was a good man. Then the trial came on: he was charged with murdering a merchant from Ryazán, and robbing him of twenty thousand roubles.

His wife was in despair, and did not know what to believe. Her children were all quite small; one was a baby at her breast. Taking them all with her, she went to the town where her husband was in gaol. At first she was not allowed to see him; but, after much begging, she obtained permission from the officials, and was taken to him. When she saw her husband in prison-dress and in chains, shut up with thieves and criminals, she fell down, and did not come to her senses for a long time. Then she drew her children to her, and sat down near him. She told him of things at home, and asked about what had happened to him. He told her all, and she asked, 'What can we do now?'

'We must petition the Tsar not to let an innocent man perish.'

His wife told him that she had sent a petition to the Tsar, but that it had not been accepted.

Aksyónof did not reply, but only looked downcast.

Then his wife said, 'It was not for nothing I dreamt your hair had turned grey. You remember? You should not have started that day.' And passing her fingers through his hair, she said: 'Ványa dearest, tell your wife the truth; was it not you who did it?'

'So you, too, suspect me!' said Aksyónof, and, hiding his face in his hands, he began to weep. Then a soldier came to say that the wife and children must go away; and Aksyónof said goodbye to his family for the last time.

When they were gone, Aksyónof recalled what had been said, and when he remembered that his wife also had suspected him, he said to himself, 'It seems that only God can know the truth; it is to Him alone we must appeal, and from Him alone expect mercy.'

And Aksyónof wrote no more petitions; gave up all hope, and only prayed to God.

Aksyónof was condemned to be flogged and sent to the mines. So he was flogged with a knout, and when the wounds made by the knout were healed, he was driven to Siberia with other convicts.

For twenty-six years Aksyónof lived as a convict in Siberia. His hair turned white as snow, and his beard grew long, thin and grey. All his mirth went; he stooped; he walked slowly, spoke little, and never laughed, but he often prayed.

In prison Aksyónof learnt to make boots, and earned a little money, with which he bought *The Lives of the Saints*. He read this book when there was light enough in the prison; and on Sundays in the prison church he read the lessons and sang in the choir; for his voice was still good.

The prison authorities liked Aksyónof for his meekness, and his fellow prisoners respected him: they called him 'Grandfather,' and 'The Saint'. When they wanted to petition the prison authorities about anything, they always made Aksyónof their spokesman, and when there were quarrels among the prisoners they came to him to put things right and to judge the matter.

No news reached Aksyónof from his home, and he did not even know if his wife and children were still alive.

One day a fresh gang of convicts came to the prison. In the evening the old prisoners collected round the new ones and asked them what towns or villages they came from, and what they were sentenced for. Among the rest Aksyónof sat down near the newcomers, and listened with downcast air to what was said.

One of the new convicts, a tall, strong man of sixty, with a closely cropped grey beard, was telling the others what he had been arrested for.

'Well, friends,' he said, 'I only took a horse that was tied to a sledge, and I was arrested and accused of stealing. I said I had only taken it to get home quicker, and had then let it go; besides, the driver was a personal friend of mine. So I said, "It's all right." "No," said they, "you stole it." But how or where I stole it they could not say. I once really did something wrong, and ought by rights to have come here long ago, but that time I was not found out. Now I have been sent here for nothing at all... Eh, but it's lies I'm telling you; I've been to Siberia before, but I did not stay long.'

'Where are you from?' asked someone.

'From Vladímir. My family are of that town. My name is Makár, and they also call me Semyónitch.'

Aksyónof raised his head and said: 'Tell me, Semyónitch, do you know anything of the merchants Aksyónof, of Vladímir? Are they still alive?'

'Know them? Of course I do. The Aksyónofs are rich, though their father is in Siberia: a sinner like ourselves, it seems! As for you, Gran'dad, how did you come here?'

Aksyónof did not like to speak of his misfortune. He only sighed, and said, 'For my sins I have been in prison these twenty-six years.'

'What sins?' asked Makár Semyónitch.

But Aksyónof only said, 'Well, well – I must have deserved it!'

He would have said no more, but his companions told the newcomer how Aksyónof came to be in Siberia: how someone had killed a merchant, and had put a knife among Aksyónof's things, and Aksyónof had been unjustly condemned.

When Makár Semyónitch heard this, he looked at Aksyónof, slapped his own knee, and exclaimed, 'Well, this is wonderful! Really wonderful! But how old you've grown, Gran'dad!'

The others asked him why he was so surprised, and where he had seen Aksyónof before; but Makár Semyónitch did not reply. He only said: 'It's wonderful that we should meet here, lads!'

These words made Aksyónof wonder whether this man knew who had killed the merchant; so he said, 'Perhaps, Semyónitch, you have heard of that affair, or maybe you've seen me before?'

'How could I help hearing? The world's full of rumours. But it's long ago, and I've forgotten what I heard.'

'Perhaps you heard who killed the merchant?' asked Aksyónof.

Makár Semyónitch laughed, and replied, 'It must have been him in whose bag the knife was found! If someone else hid the knife there, "He's not a thief till he's caught," as the saying is. How could anyone put a knife into your bag while it was under your head? It would surely have woke you up?'

When Aksyónof heard these words, he felt sure this was the man who had killed the merchant. He rose and went away. All that night Aksyónof lay awake. He felt terribly unhappy, and all sorts of images rose in his mind. There was the image of his wife as she was when he parted from her to go to the fair. He saw her as if she were present; her face and her eyes rose before him; he heard her speak and laugh. Then he saw his children, quite little, as they were at that time: one with a little cloak on, another at his mother's breast. And then he remembered himself as he used to be – young and merry. He remembered how he sat playing the guitar in the porch of the inn where he was arrested, and how free from care he had been. He saw, in his mind, the place where he was flogged, the executioner, and the people standing around; the chains, the convicts, all the twenty-six years of his prison life, and his premature old age. The thought of it all made him so wretched that he was ready to kill himself.

'And it's all that villain's doing!' thought Aksyónof. And his anger was so great against Makár Semyónitch that he longed for vengeance, even if he himself should perish for it. He kept repeating prayers all night, but could get no peace. During the day he did not go near Makár Semyónitch, nor even look at him.

A fortnight passed in this way. Aksyónof could not sleep at nights, and was so miserable that he did not know what to do.

One night as he was walking about the prison he noticed some earth that came rolling out from under one of the shelves on which the prisoners slept. He stopped to see what it was. Suddenly Makár Semyónitch crept out from under the shelf, and looked up at Aksyónof with frightened face. Aksyónof tried to pass without looking at him, but Makár seized his hand and told him that he had dug a hole under the wall, getting rid of the earth by putting it into his high boots, and emptying it out every day on the road when the prisoners were driven to their work.

'Just you keep quiet, old man, and you shall get out too. If you blab they'll flog the life out of me, but I will kill you first.'

Aksyónof trembled with anger as he looked at his enemy. He drew his hand away, saying, 'I have no wish to escape, and you have no need to kill me; you killed me long ago! As to telling of you – I may do so or not, as God shall direct.'

Next day, when the convicts were led out to work, the convoy soldiers noticed that one or other of the prisoners emptied some earth out of his boots. The prison was searched, and the tunnel found. The Governor came and questioned all the prisoners to find out who had dug the hole. They all denied any knowledge of it. Those who knew, would not betray Makár Semyónitch, knowing he would be flogged almost to death. At last the Governor turned to Aksyónof, whom he knew to be a just man, and said:

'You are a truthful old man; tell me, before God, who dug the hole?'

Makár Semyónitch stood as if he were quite unconcerned, looking at the Governor and not so much as glancing at Aksyónof. Aksyónof's lips and hands trembled, and for a long time he could not utter a word. He thought, 'Why should I screen him who ruined my life? Let him pay for what I have suffered. But if I tell, they will probably flog the life out of him, and maybe I suspect him wrongly. And, after all, what good would it be to me?'

'Well, old man,' repeated the Governor, 'tell us the truth: who has been digging under the wall?'

Aksyónof glanced at Makár Semyónitch, and said, 'I cannot say, your honour. It is not God's will that I should tell! Do what you like with me; I am in your hands.'

However much the Governor tried, Aksyónof would say no more, and so the matter had to be left.

That night, when Aksyónof was lying on his bed and just beginning to doze, someone came quietly and sat down on his bed. He peered through the darkness and recognized Makár.

'What more do you want of me?' asked Aksyónof. 'Why have you come here?'

Makár Semyónitch was silent. So Aksyónof sat up and said, 'What do you want? Go away, or I will call the guard!'

Makár Semyónitch bent close over Aksyónof, and whispered, 'Iván Dmítritch, forgive me!'

'What for?' asked Aksyónof.

'It was I who killed the merchant and hid the knife among your things. I meant to kill you too, but I heard a noise outside; so I hid the knife in your bag and escaped out of the window.'

Aksyónof was silent, and did not know what to say. Makár Semyónitch slid off the bed-shelf and knelt upon the ground. 'Iván Dmítritch,' said he, 'forgive me! For the love of God, forgive me! I will confess that it was I who killed the merchant, and you will be released and can go to your home.'

'It is easy for you to talk,' said Aksyónof, 'but I have suffered for you these twenty-six years. Where could I go to now? ... My wife is dead, and my children have forgotten me. I have nowhere to go...'

Makár Semyónitch did not rise, but beat his head on the floor. 'Iván Dmítritch, forgive me!' he cried. 'When they flogged me with the knout it was not so hard to bear as it is to see you now ... yet you had pity on me, and did not tell. For Christ's sake forgive me, wretch that I am!' And he began to sob.

When Aksyónof heard him sobbing he, too, began to weep.

'God will forgive you!' said he. 'Maybe I am a hundred times worse than you.' And at these words his heart grew light, and the longing for home left him. He no longer had any desire to leave the prison, but only hoped for his last hour to come.

In spite of what Aksyónof had said, Makár Semyónitch confessed his guilt. But when the order for his release came, Aksyónof was already dead.

A PRISONER
IN THE CAUCASUS

I

An officer named Zhílin was serving in the army in the Caucasus.

One day he received a letter from home. It was from his mother, who wrote: 'I am getting old, and should like to see my dear son once more before I die. Come and say goodbye to me and bury me, and then, if God pleases, return to service again with my blessing. But I have found a girl for you, who is sensible and good and has some property. If you can love her, you might marry her and remain at home.'

Zhílin thought it over. It was quite true, the old lady was failing fast and he might not have another chance to see her alive. He had better go, and, if the girl was nice, why not marry her?

So he went to his Colonel, obtained leave of absence, said goodbye to his comrades, stood the soldiers four pailfuls of vódka[3] as a farewell treat, and got ready to go.

It was a time of war in the Caucasus. The roads were not safe by night or day. If ever a Russian ventured to ride or walk any distance away from his fort, the Tartars killed him or carried him off to the hills. So it had been arranged that twice every week a

---

3 *Vódka is a spirit distilled from rye. It is the commonest form of strong drink in Russia.*

body of soldiers should march from one fortress to the next to convoy travellers from point to point.

It was summer. At daybreak the baggage train got ready under shelter of the fortress; the soldiers marched out; and all started along the road. Zhílin was on horseback, and a cart with his things went with the baggage train. They had sixteen miles to go. The baggage train moved slowly; sometimes the soldiers stopped, or perhaps a wheel would come off one of the carts, or a horse refuse to go on, and then everybody had to wait.

When by the sun it was already past noon, they had not gone half the way. It was dusty and hot, the sun was scorching and there was no shelter anywhere: a bare plain all round – not a tree, not a bush, by the road.

Zhílin rode on in front, and stopped, waiting for the baggage to overtake him. Then he heard the signal-horn sounded behind him: the company had again stopped. So he began to think: 'Hadn't I better ride on by myself? My horse is a good one: if the Tartars do attack me, I can gallop away. Perhaps, however, it would be wiser to wait.'

As he sat considering, Kostílin, an officer carrying a gun, rode up to him and said:

'Come along, Zhílin, let's go on by ourselves. It's dreadful; I am famished, and the heat is terrible. My shirt is wringing wet.'

Kostílin was a stout, heavy man, and the perspiration was running down his red face. Zhílin thought awhile, and then asked: 'Is your gun loaded?'

'Yes it is.'

'Well, then, let's go, but on condition that we keep together.'

So they rode forward along the road across the plain, talking, but keeping a lookout on both sides. They could see afar all round. But after crossing the plain the road ran through a valley between two hills, and Zhílin said: 'We had better climb that hill and have a look round, or the Tartars may be on us before we know it.'

But Kostílin answered: 'What's the use? Let us go on.'

Zhílin, however, would not agree.

'No,' he said; 'you can wait here if you like, but I'll go and look round.' And he turned his horse to the left, up the hill. Zhílin's horse was a hunter, and carried him up the hillside as if it had wings. (He had bought it for a hundred roubles as a colt out of a herd, and had broken it in himself.) Hardly had he reached the top of the hill, when he saw some thirty Tartars not much more than a hundred yards ahead of him. As soon as he caught sight of them he turned round, but the Tartars had also seen him, and rushed after him at full gallop, getting their guns out as they went. Down galloped Zhílin as fast as the horse's legs could go, shouting to Kostílin: 'Get your gun ready!'

And, in thought, he said to his horse: 'Get me well out of this, my pet; don't stumble, for if you do it's all up. Once I reach the gun, they shan't take me prisoner.'

But, instead of waiting, Kostílin, as soon as he caught sight of the Tartars, turned back towards the fortress at full speed, whipping his horse now on one side now on the other, and its switching tail was all that could be seen of him in the dust.

Zhílin saw it was a bad lookout; the gun was gone, and what could he do with nothing but his sword? He turned his horse towards the escort, thinking to escape, but there were six Tartars rushing to cut him off. His horse was a good one, but theirs were still better; and besides, they were across his path. He tried to rein in his horse and to turn another way, but it was going so fast it could not stop, and dashed on straight towards the Tartars. He saw a red-bearded Tartar on a grey horse, with his gun raised, come at him, yelling and showing his teeth.

'Ah,' thought Zhílin, 'I know you, devils that you are. If you take me alive, you'll put me in a pit and flog me. I will not be taken alive!'

Zhílin, though not a big fellow, was brave. He drew his sword and dashed at the red-bearded Tartar, thinking: 'Either I'll ride him down, or disable him with my sword.'

He was still a horse's length away from him, when he was fired at from behind, and his horse was hit. It fell to the ground with all its weight, pinning Zhílin to the earth.

He tried to rise, but two ill-savoured Tartars were already sitting on him and binding his hands behind his back. He made an effort and flung them off, but three others jumped from their horses and began beating his head with the butts of their guns. His eyes grew dim, and he fell back. The Tartars seized him, and, taking spare girths from their saddles, twisted his hands behind him and tied them with a Tartar knot. They knocked his cap off, pulled off his boots, searched him all over, tore his clothes, and took his money and his watch.

Zhílin looked round at his horse. There it lay on its side, poor thing, just as it had fallen; struggling, its legs in the air, unable to touch the ground. There was a hole in its head, and black blood was pouring out, turning the dust to mud for a couple of feet around.

One of the Tartars went up to the horse and began taking the saddle off, it still kicked, so he drew a dagger and cut its windpipe. A whistling sound came from its throat, the horse gave one plunge, and all was over.

The Tartars took the saddle and trappings. The red-bearded Tartar mounted his horse, and the others lifted Zhílin into the saddle behind him. To prevent his falling off, they strapped him to the Tartar's girdle, and then they all rode away to the hills.

So there sat Zhílin, swaying from side to side, his head striking against the Tartar's stinking back. He could see nothing but that muscular back and sinewy neck, with its closely shaven, bluish nape. Zhílin's head was wounded: the blood had dried over his eyes, and he could neither shift his position on the saddle nor wipe the blood off. His arms were bound so tightly that his collar-bones ached.

They rode up and down hills for a long way. Then they reached a river which they forded, and came to a hard road leading across a valley.

Zhílin tried to see where they were going, but his eyelids were stuck together with blood, and he could not turn.

Twilight began to fall; they crossed another river, and rode up a stony hillside. There was a smell of smoke here, and dogs were barking. They had reached an Aoul (a Tartar village). The Tartars got off their horses; Tartar children came and stood round Zhílin, shrieking with pleasure and throwing stones at him.

The Tartar drove the children away, took Zhílin off the horse, and called his man. A Nogáy[4] with high cheekbones, and nothing on but a shirt (and that so torn that his breast was all bare), answered the call. The Tartar gave him an order. He went and fetched shackles: two blocks of oak with iron rings attached, and a clasp and lock fixed to one of the rings.

They untied Zhílin's arms, fastened the shackles on his leg, and dragged him to a barn, where they pushed him in and locked the door.

Zhílin fell on a heap of manure. He lay still awhile then groped about to find a soft place, and settled down.

II

That night Zhílin hardly slept at all. It was the time of year when the nights are short, and daylight soon showed itself through a chink in the wall. He rose, scratched to make the chink bigger, and peeped out.

Through the hole he saw a road leading downhill; to the right was a Tartar hut with two trees near it, a black dog lay on the threshold, and a goat and kids were moving about wagging their tails. Then he saw a young Tartar woman in a long, loose, bright-coloured gown, with trousers and high boots showing from under it. She had a coat thrown over her head, on which she carried a large metal jug filled with water. She was leading by the hand a small, closely shaven Tartar boy, who wore nothing but a shirt; and as she went along balancing herself, the muscles of her back quivered. This woman carried the water into the hut, and, soon

4 *One of a certain Tartar tribe.*

after, the red-bearded Tartar of yesterday came out dressed in a silk tunic, with a silver-hilted dagger hanging by his side, shoes on his bare feet, and a tall black sheepskin cap set far back on his head. He came out, stretched himself, and stroked his red beard. He stood awhile, gave an order to his servant, and went away.

Then two lads rode past from watering their horses. The horses' noses were wet. Some other closely shaven boys ran out, without any trousers, and wearing nothing but their shirts. They crowded together, came to the barn, picked up a twig, and began pushing it in at the chink. Zhílin gave a shout, and the boys shrieked and scampered off, their little bare knees gleaming as they ran.

Zhílin was very thirsty: his throat was parched, and he thought: 'If only they would come and so much as look at me!'

Then he heard someone unlocking the barn. The red-bearded Tartar entered, and with him was another, a smaller man, dark, with bright black eyes, red cheeks and a short beard. He had a merry face and was always laughing. This man was even more richly dressed than the other. He wore a blue silk tunic trimmed with gold, a large silver dagger in his belt, red morocco slippers worked with silver, and over these a pair of thick shoes, and he had a white sheepskin cap on his head.

The red-bearded Tartar entered, muttered something as if he were annoyed, and stood leaning against the doorpost, playing with his dagger, and glaring askance at Zhílin, like a wolf. The dark one, quick and lively, and moving as if on springs, came straight up to Zhílin, squatted down in front of him, slapped him on the shoulder, and began to talk very fast in his own language. His teeth showed, and he kept winking, clicking his tongue and repeating, 'Good Russ, good Russ.'

Zhílin could not understand a word, but said, 'Drink! give me water to drink!'

The dark man only laughed. 'Good Russ,' he said, and went on talking in his own tongue.

Zhílin made signs with lips and hands that he wanted something to drink.

The dark man understood, and laughed. Then he looked out of the door, and called to someone: 'Dina!'

A little girl came running in: she was about thirteen, slight, thin, and like the dark Tartar in face. Evidently she was his daughter. She, too, had clear black eyes, and her face was good-looking. She had on a long blue gown with wide sleeves, and no girdle. The hem of her gown, the front, and the sleeves, were trimmed with red. She wore trousers and slippers, and over the slippers stouter shoes with high heels. Round her neck she had a necklace made of Russian silver coins. She was bareheaded, and her black hair was plaited with a ribbon and ornamented with gilt braid and silver coins.

Her father gave an order, and she ran away and returned with a metal jug. She handed the water to Zhílin and sat down, crouching so that her knees were as high as her head; and there she sat with wide-open eyes watching Zhílin drink, as though he were a wild animal.

When Zhílin handed the empty jug back to her, she gave such a sudden jump back, like a wild goat, that it made her father laugh. He sent her away for something else. She took the jug, ran out, and brought back some unleavened bread on a round board, and once more sat down, crouching, and looking on with staring eyes.

Then the Tartars went away and again locked the door.

After a while the Nogáy came and said: '*Ayda*, the master, *Ayda*!'

He, too, knew no Russian. All Zhílin could make out was that he was told to go somewhere.

Zhílin followed the Nógay, but limped, for the shackles dragged his feet so that he could hardly step at all. On getting out of the barn he saw a Tartar village of about ten houses, and a Tartar church with a small tower. Three horses stood saddled before one of the houses; little boys were holding them by the reins. The dark Tartar came out of this house, beckoning with his hand for Zhílin to follow him. Then he laughed, said something in his own language, and returned into the house.

Zhílin entered. The room was a good one: the walls smoothly

plastered with clay. Near the front wall lay a pile of bright-coloured feather beds; the side walls were covered with rich carpets used as hangings, and on these were fastened guns, pistols and swords, all inlaid with silver. Close to one of the walls was a small stove on a level with the earthen floor. The floor itself was as clean as a thrashing ground. A large space in one corner was spread over with felt, on which were rugs, and on these rugs were cushions stuffed with down. And on these cushions sat five Tartars, the dark one, the red-haired one, and three guests. They were wearing their indoor slippers, and each had a cushion behind his back. Before them were standing millet cakes on a round board, melted butter in a bowl, and a jug of *buza*, or Tartar beer. They ate both cakes and butter with their hands.

The dark man jumped up and ordered Zhílin to be placed on one side, not on the carpet but on the bare ground, then he sat down on the carpet again, and offered millet cakes and *buza* to his guests. The servant made Zhílin sit down, after which he took off his own overshoes, put them by the door where the other shoes were standing, and sat down nearer to his masters on the felt, watching them as they ate, and licking his lips.

The Tartars ate as much as they wanted, and a woman dressed in the same way as the girl – in a long gown and trousers, with a kerchief on her head – came and took away what was left, and brought a handsome basin, and a ewer with a narrow spout. The Tartars washed their hands, folded them, went down on their knees, blew to the four quarters, and said their prayers. After they had talked for a while, one of the guests turned to Zhílin and began to speak in Russian.

'You were captured by Kazi-Mohammed,' he said, and pointed at the red-bearded Tartar. 'And Kazi-Mohammed has given you to Abdul Murat,' pointing at the dark one. 'Abdul Murat is now your master.'

Zhílin was silent. Then Abdul Murat began to talk, laughing, pointing to Zhílin, and repeating, 'Soldier Russ, good Russ.'

The interpreter said, 'He orders you to write home and tell

them to send a ransom, and as soon as the money comes he will set you free.'

Zhílin thought for a moment, and said, 'How much ransom does he want?'

The Tartars talked awhile, and then the interpreter said, 'Three thousand roubles.'

'No,' said Zhílin, 'I can't pay so much.'

Abdul jumped up and, waving his arms, talked to Zhílin, thinking, as before, that he would understand. The interpreter translated: 'How much will you give?'

Zhílin considered, and said, 'Five hundred roubles.' At this the Tartars began speaking very quickly, all together. Abdul began to shout at the red-bearded one, and jabbered so fast that the spittle spurted out of his mouth. The red-bearded one only screwed up his eyes and clicked his tongue.

They quietened down after a while, and the interpreter said, 'Five hundred roubles is not enough for the master. He paid two hundred for you himself. Kazi-Mohammed was in debt to him, and he took you in payment. Three thousand roubles! Less than that won't do. If you refuse to write, you will be put into a pit and flogged with a whip!'

'Eh!' thought Zhílin, 'the more one fears them the worse it will be.'

So he sprang to his feet, and said, 'You tell that dog that if he tries to frighten me I will not write at all, and he will get nothing. I never was afraid of you dogs, and never will be!'

The interpreter translated, and again they all began to talk at once.

They jabbered for a long time, and then the dark man jumped up, came to Zhílin, and said: '*Dzhigit Russ, dzhigit Russ!*' (*Dzhigit* in their language means 'brave.') And he laughed, and said something to the interpreter, who translated: 'One thousand roubles will satisfy him.'

Zhílin stuck to it: 'I will not give more than five hundred. And if you kill me you'll get nothing at all.'

The Tartars talked awhile, then sent the servant out to fetch something, and kept looking, now at Zhílin, now at the door. The servant returned, followed by a stout, bare-footed, tattered man, who also had his leg shackled.

Zhílin gasped with surprise: it was Kostílin. He, too, had been taken. They were put side by side, and began to tell each other what had occurred. While they talked, the Tartars looked on in silence. Zhílin related what had happened to him; and Kostílin told how his horse had stopped, his gun misfired, and this same Abdul had overtaken and captured him.

Abdul jumped up, pointed to Kostílin, and said something. The interpreter translated that they both now belonged to one master, and the one who first paid the ransom would be set free first.

'There now,' he said to Zhílin, 'you get angry, but your comrade here is gentle; he has written home, and they will send five thousand roubles. So he will be well fed and well treated.'

Zhílin replied: 'My comrade can do as he likes. Maybe he is rich; I am not. It must be as I said. Kill me, if you like – you will gain nothing by it; but I will not write for more than five hundred roubles.'

They were silent. Suddenly up sprang Abdul, brought a little box, took out a pen, ink, and a bit of paper, gave them to Zhílin, slapped him on the shoulder, and made a sign that he should write. He had agreed to take five hundred roubles.

'Wait a bit!' said Zhílin to the interpreter; 'tell him that he must feed us properly, give us proper clothes and boots, and let us be together. It will be more cheerful for us. And he must have these shackles taken off our feet,' and Zhílin looked at his master and laughed.

The master also laughed, heard the interpreter, and said: 'I will give them the best of clothes: a cloak and boots fit to be married in. I will feed them like princes; and if they like they can live together in the barn. But I can't take off the shackles, or they will run away. They shall be taken off, however, at night.' And he jumped up and slapped Zhílin on the shoulder, exclaiming: 'You good, I good!'

Zhílin wrote the letter, but addressed it wrongly, so that it should not reach its destination, thinking to himself: 'I'll run away!'

Zhílin and Kostílin were taken back to the barn and given some maize straw, a jug of water, some bread, two old cloaks and some worn-out military boots – evidently taken from the corpses of Russian soldiers. At night their shackles were taken off their feet, and they were locked up in the barn.

III

Zhílin and his friend lived in this way for a whole month. The master always laughed and said: 'You, Iván, good! I, Abdul, good!' But he fed them badly, giving them nothing but unleavened bread of millet flour baked into flat cakes, or sometimes only unbaked dough.

Kostílin wrote home a second time, and did nothing but mope and wait for the money to arrive. He would sit for days together in the barn sleeping, or counting the days till a letter could come.

Zhílin knew his letter would reach no one, and he did not write another. He thought: 'Where could my mother get enough money to ransom me? As it is she lived chiefly on what I sent her. If she had to raise five hundred roubles, she would be quite ruined. With God's help I'll manage to escape!'

So he kept on the lookout, planning how to run away.

He would walk about the Aoul whistling; or would sit working, modelling dolls of clay, or weaving baskets out of twigs: for Zhílin was clever with his hands.

Once he modelled a doll with a nose and hands and feet and with a Tartar gown on, and put it up on the roof. When the Tartar women came out to fetch water, the master's daughter, Dina, saw the doll and called the women, who put down their jugs and stood looking and laughing. Zhílin took down the doll and held it out to them. They laughed, but dared not take it. He put down the doll and went into the barn, waiting to see what would happen.

Dina ran up to the doll, looked round, seized it, and ran away.

In the morning, at daybreak, he looked out. Dina came out of the house and sat down on the threshold with the doll, which she had dressed up in bits of red stuff, and she rocked it like a baby, singing a Tartar lullaby. An old woman came out and scolded her, and, snatching the doll away, she broke it to bits and sent Dina about her business.

But Zhílin made another doll, better than the first, and gave it to Dina. Once Dina brought a little jug, put it on the ground, sat down gazing at him, and laughed, pointing to the jug.

'What pleases her so?' wondered Zhílin. He took the jug thinking it was water, but it turned out to be milk. He drank the milk and said: 'That's good!'

How pleased Dina was! 'Good, Iván, good!' said she, and she jumped up and clapped her hands. Then, seizing the jug, she ran away. After that, she stealthily brought him some milk every day.

The Tartars make a kind of cheese out of goat's milk, which they dry on the roofs of their houses; and sometimes, on the sly, she brought him some of this cheese. And once, when Abdul had killed a sheep, she brought Zhílin a bit of mutton in her sleeve. She would just throw the things down and run away.

One day there was a heavy storm, and the rain fell in torrents for a whole hour. All the streams became turbid. At the ford, the water rose till it was seven feet high, and the current was so strong that it rolled the stones about. Rivulets flowed everywhere, and the rumbling in the hills never ceased. When the storm was over, the water ran in streams down the village street. Zhílin got his master to lend him a knife, and with it he shaped a small cylinder, and cutting some little boards, he made a wheel to which he fixed two dolls, one on each side. The little girls brought him some bits of stuff, and he dressed the dolls, one as a peasant, the other as a peasant woman. Then he fastened them in their places, and set the wheel so that the stream should work it. The wheel began to turn and the dolls danced.

The whole village collected round. Little boys and girls, Tartar men and women, all came and clicked their tongues.

'Ah, Russ! Ah, Iván!'

Abdul had a Russian clock, which was broken. He called Zhílin and showed it to him, clicking his tongue.

'Give it me, I'll mend it for you,' said Zhílin.

He took it to pieces with the knife, sorted the pieces, and put them together again, so that the clock went all right.

The master was delighted, and made him a present of one of his old tunics which was all in holes. Zhílin had to accept it. He could, at any rate, use it as a coverlet at night.

After that Zhílin's fame spread; and Tartars came from distant villages, bringing him now the lock of a gun or of a pistol, now a watch to mend. His master gave him some tools – pincers, gimlets and a file.

One day a Tartar fell ill, and they came to Zhílin saying, 'Come and heal him!' Zhílin knew nothing about doctoring, but he went to look, and thought to himself, 'Perhaps he will get well anyway.'

He returned to the barn, mixed some water with sand, and then in the presence of the Tartars whispered some words over it and gave it to the sick man to drink. Luckily for him, the Tartar recovered.

Zhílin began to pick up their language a little, and some of the Tartars grew familiar with him. When they wanted him, they would call: 'Iván! Iván!' Others, however, still looked at him askance, as at a wild beast.

The red-bearded Tartar disliked Zhílin. Whenever he saw him he frowned and turned away, or swore at him. There was also an old man there who did not live in the Aoul, but used to come up from the foot of the hill. Zhílin only saw him when he passed on his way to the Mosque. He was short, and had a white cloth wound round his hat. His beard and moustaches were clipped, and white as snow; and his face was wrinkled and brick-red. His nose was hooked like a hawk's, his grey eyes looked cruel, and he had no teeth except two tusks. He would pass, with his turban on his head, leaning on his staff, and glaring round him like a wolf. If he saw Zhílin he would snort with anger and turn away.

Once Zhílin descended the hill to see where the old man lived. He went down along the pathway and came to a little garden surrounded by a stone wall; and behind the wall he saw cherry and apricot trees, and a hut with a flat roof. He came closer, and saw hives made of plaited straw, and bees flying about and humming. The old man was kneeling, busy doing something with a hive. Zhílin stretched to look, and his shackles rattled. The old man turned round, and, giving a yell, snatched a pistol from his belt and shot at Zhílin, who just managed to shelter himself behind the stone wall.

The old man went to Zhílin's master to complain. The master called Zhílin, and said with a laugh, 'Why did you go to the old man's house?'

'I did him no harm,' replied Zhílin. 'I only wanted to see how he lived.'

The master repeated what Zhílin said.

But the old man was in a rage; he hissed and jabbered, showing his tusks and shaking his fists at Zhílin.

Zhílin could not understand all, but he gathered that the old man was telling Abdul he ought not to keep Russians in the Aoul, but ought to kill them. At last the old man went away.

Zhílin asked the master who the old man was.

'He is a great man!' said the master. 'He was the bravest of our fellows; he killed many Russians, and was at one time very rich. He had three wives and eight sons, and they all lived in one village. Then the Russians came and destroyed the village, and killed seven of his sons. Only one son was left, and he gave himself up to the Russians. The old man also went and gave himself up, and lived among the Russians for three months. At the end of that time he found his son, killed him with his own hands, and then escaped.

After that he left off fighting, and went to Mecca to pray to God; that is why he wears a turban. One who has been to Mecca is called "Hadji" and wears a turban. He does not like you fellows. He tells me to kill you. But I can't kill you. I have paid money for you and, besides, I have grown fond of you, Iván. Far from killing you, I would not even let you go if I had not promised.' And he laughed, saying in Russian, 'You, Iván, good; I, Abdul, good!'

IV

Zhílin lived in this way for a month. During the day he sauntered about the Aoul or busied himself with some handicraft, but at night, when all was silent in the Aoul, he dug at the floor of the barn. It was no easy task digging, because of the stones; but he worked away at them with his file, and at last had made a hole under the wall large enough to get through.

'If only I could get to know the lay of the land,' thought he, 'and which way to go! But none of the Tartars will tell me.'

So he chose a day when the master was away from home, and set off after dinner to climb the hill beyond the village, and to look around. But before leaving home the master always gave orders to his son to watch Zhílin, and not to lose sight of him. So the lad ran after Zhílin, shouting: 'Don't go! Father does not allow it. I'll call the neighbours if you won't come back.'

Zhílin tried to persuade him, and said: 'I'm not going far; I only want to climb that hill. I want to find a herb – to cure sick people with. You come with me if you like. How can I run away with these shackles on? Tomorrow I'll make a bow and arrows for you.'

So he persuaded the lad, and they went to look at the hill. It did not seem far to the top; but it was hard walking with shackles on his leg. Zhílin went on and on, but it was all he could do to reach the top. There he sat down and noted how the land lay. To the south, beyond the barn, was a valley in which a herd of horses was pasturing and at the bottom of the valley one could see another

Aoul. Beyond that was a still steeper hill, and another hill beyond that. Between the hills, in the blue distance, were forests, and still further off were mountains, rising higher and higher. The highest of them were covered with snow, white as sugar; and one snowy peak towered above all the rest. To the east and to the west were other such hills, and here and there smoke rose from Aouls in the ravines. 'Ah,' thought he, 'all that is Tartar country.' And he turned towards the Russian side. At his feet he saw a river, and the Aoul he lived in, surrounded by little gardens. He could see women, like tiny dolls, sitting by the river rinsing clothes. Beyond the Aoul was a hill, lower than the one to the south, and beyond it two other hills well wooded; and between these, a smooth bluish plain, and far, far across the plain something that looked like a cloud of smoke. Zhílin tried to remember where the sun used to rise and set when he was living in the fort, and he saw that there was no mistake: the Russian fort must be in that plain. Between those two hills he would have to make his way when he escaped.

The sun was beginning to set. The white, snowy mountains turned red, and the dark hills turned darker; mists rose from the ravine, and the valley, where he supposed the Russian fort to be, seemed on fire with the sunset glow. Zhílin looked carefully. Something seemed to be quivering in the valley like smoke from a chimney, and he felt sure the Russian fortress was there.

It had grown late. The Mullah's cry was heard. The herds were being driven home, the cows were lowing, and the lad kept saying, 'Come home!' But Zhílin did not feel inclined to go away.

At last, however, they went back. 'Well,' thought Zhílin, 'now that I know the way, it is time to escape.' He thought of running away that night. The nights were dark – the moon had waned. But as ill luck would have it, the Tartars returned home that evening. They generally came back driving cattle before them and in good spirits. But this time they had no cattle. All they brought home was the dead body of a Tartar – the red one's brother – who had been killed. They came back looking sullen, and they all gathered together for the burial. Zhílin also came out to see it.

They wrapped the body in a piece of linen, without any coffin, and carried it out of the village, and laid it on the grass under some plane trees. The Mullah and the old men came. They wound clothes round their caps, took off their shoes, and squatted on their heels, side by side, near the corpse.

The Mullah was in front: behind him in a row were three old men in turbans, and behind them again the other Tartars. All cast down their eyes and sat in silence. This continued a long time, until the Mullah raised his head and said: 'Allah!' (which means God). He said that one word, and they all cast down their eyes again, and were again silent for a long time. They sat quite still, not moving or making any sound.

Again the Mullah lifted his head and said, 'Allah!' and they all repeated: 'Allah! Allah!' and were again silent.

The dead body lay immovable on the grass, and they sat as still as if they too were dead. Not one of them moved. There was no sound but that of the leaves of the plane trees stirring in the breeze. Then the Mullah repeated a prayer, and they all rose. They lifted the body and carried it in their arms to a hole in the ground. It was not an ordinary hole, but was hollowed out under the ground like a vault. They took the body under the arms and by the legs, bent it, and let it gently down, pushing it under the earth in a sitting posture, with the hands folded in front.

The Nogáy brought some green rushes, which they stuffed into the hole, and, quickly covering it with earth, they smoothed the ground, and set an upright stone at the head of the grave. Then they trod the earth down, and again sat in a row before the grave, keeping silence for a long time.

At last they rose, said 'Allah! Allah! Allah!' and sighed.

The red-bearded Tartar gave money to the old men; then he too rose, took a whip, struck himself with it three times on the forehead, and went home.

The next morning Zhílin saw the red-bearded Tartar, followed by three others, leading a mare out of the village. When they were beyond the village, the red-bearded Tartar took off his tunic and turned up his sleeves, showing his stout arms. Then he drew a dagger and sharpened it on a whetstone. The other Tartars raised the mare's head, and he cut her throat, threw her down, and began skinning her, loosening the hide with his big hands. Women and girls came and began to wash the entrails and the inwards. The mare was cut up, the pieces taken into the hut, and the whole village collected at the red Tartar's hut for a funeral feast.

For three days they went on eating the flesh of the mare, drinking *buza*, and praying for the dead man. All the Tartars were at home. On the fourth day at dinner-time Zhílin saw them preparing to go away. Horses were brought out, they got ready, and some ten of them (the red-bearded one among them) rode away; but Abdul stayed at home. It was new moon, and the nights were still dark.

'Ah!' thought Zhílin, 'tonight is the time to escape.' And he told Kostílin; but Kostílin's heart failed him.

'How can we escape?' he said. 'We don't even know the way.'

'I know the way,' said Zhílin.

'Even if you do,' said Kostílin, 'we can't reach the fort in one night.'

'If we can't,' said Zhílin, 'we'll sleep in the forest. See here, I have saved some cheeses. What's the good of sitting and moping here? If they send your ransom – well and good; but suppose they don't manage to collect it? The Tartars are angry now, because the Russians have killed one of their men. They are talking of killing us.'

Kostílin thought it over.

'Well, let's go,' said he.

V

Zhílin crept into the hole, widened it so that Kostílin might also get through, and then they both sat waiting till all should be quiet in the Aoul.

As soon as all was quiet, Zhílin crept under the wall, got out, and whispered to Kostílin, 'Come!' Kostílin crept out, but in so doing he caught a stone with his foot and made a noise. The master had a very vicious watchdog, a spotted one called Oulyashin. Zhílin had been careful to feed him for some time before. Oulyashin heard the noise and began to bark and jump, and the other dogs did the same. Zhílin gave a slight whistle, and threw him a bit of cheese. Oulyashin knew Zhílin, wagged his tail, and stopped barking.

But the master had heard the dog, and shouted to him from his hut, 'Hayt, hayt, Oulyashin!'

Zhílin, however, scratched Oulyashin behind the ears, and the dog was quiet, and rubbed against his legs, wagging his tail.

They sat hidden behind a corner for awhile. All became silent again, only a sheep coughed inside a shed, and the water rippled over the stones in the hollow. It was dark, the stars were high overhead, and the new moon showed red as it set, horns upward, behind the hill. In the valleys the fog was white as milk.

Zhílin rose and said to his companion, 'Well, friend, come along!'

They started; but they had only gone a few steps when they heard the Mullah crying from the roof, 'Allah, Beshmillah! Ilrahman!' That meant that the people would be going to the Mosque. So they sat down again, hiding behind a wall, and waited a long time till the people had passed. At last all was quiet again.

'Now then! May God be with us!' They crossed themselves, and started once more. They passed through a yard and went down the hillside to the river, crossed the river, and went along the valley.

The mist was thick, but only near the ground; overhead the stars shone quite brightly. Zhílin directed their course by the stars. It was cool in the mist, and easy walking; only their boots were uncomfortable, being worn out and trodden down. Zhílin took his off, threw them away, and went barefoot, jumping from stone to stone, and guiding his course by the stars. Kostílin began to lag behind.

'Walk slower,' he said, 'these confounded boots have quite blistered my feet.'

'Take them off!' said Zhílin. 'It will be easier walking without them.'

Kostílin went barefoot, but got on still worse. The stones cut his feet, and he kept lagging behind. Zhílin said: 'If your feet get cut, they'll heal again; but if the Tartars catch us and kill us, it will be worse!'

Kostílin did not reply, but went on, groaning all the time.

Their way lay through the valley for a long time. Then, to the right, they heard dogs barking. Zhílin stopped, looked about, and began climbing the hill, feeling with his hands.

'Ah!' said he, 'we have gone wrong, and have come too far to the right. Here is another Aoul, one I saw from the hill. We must turn back and go up that hill to the left. There must be a wood there.'

But Kostílin said: 'Wait a minute! Let me get breath. My feet are all cut and bleeding.'

'Never mind, friend! They'll heal again. You should spring more lightly. Like this!'

And Zhílin ran back and turned to the left up the hill towards the wood.

Kostílin still lagged behind, and groaned. Zhílin only said 'Hush!' and went on and on.

They went up the hill and found a wood as Zhílin had said. They entered the wood and forced their way through the brambles, which tore their clothes. At last they came to a path and followed it.

'Stop!' They heard the tramp of hoofs on the path, and waited, listening. It sounded like the tramping of a horse's feet, but then ceased. They moved on, and again they heard the tramping. When they paused, it also stopped. Zhílin crept nearer to it, and saw something standing on the path where it was not quite so dark. It looked like a horse, and yet not quite like one, and on it was something queer, not like a man. He heard it snorting. 'What can it be?' Zhílin gave a low whistle, and off it dashed from the path into the thicket, and the woods were filled with the noise of crackling, as if a hurricane were sweeping through, breaking the branches.

Kostílin was so frightened that he sank to the ground. But Zhílin laughed and said: 'It's a stag. Don't you hear him breaking the branches with his antlers? We were afraid of him, and he is afraid of us.'

They went on. The Great Bear was already setting. It was near morning, and they did not know whether they were going the right way or not. Zhílin thought it was the way he had been brought by the Tartars, and that they were still some seven miles from the Russian fort; but he had nothing certain to go by, and at night one easily mistakes the way. After a time they came to a clearing. Kostílin sat down and said: 'Do as you like, I can go no farther! My feet won't carry me.'

Zhílin tried to persuade him.

'No, I shall never get there; I can't!'

Zhílin grew angry, and spoke roughly to him.

'Well, then, I shall go on alone. Goodbye!'

Kostílin jumped up and followed. They went another three miles. The mist in the wood had settled down still more densely; they could not see a yard before them, and the stars had grown dim.

Suddenly they heard the sound of a horse's hoofs in front of them. They heard its shoes strike the stones. Zhílin lay down flat, and listened with his ear to the ground.

'Yes, so it is! A horseman is coming towards us.'

They ran off the path, crouched among the bushes, and waited. Zhílin crept to the road, looked, and saw a Tartar on horseback driving a cow and humming to himself. The Tartar rode past. Zhílin returned to Kostílin.

'God has led him past us; get up and let's go on!'

Kostílin tried to rise, but fell back again.

'I can't; on my word I can't! I have no strength left.'

He was heavy and stout, and had been perspiring freely. Chilled by the mist, and with his feet all bleeding, he had grown quite limp.

Zhílin tried to lift him, when suddenly Kostílin screamed out: 'Oh, how it hurts!'

Zhílin's heart sank.

'What are you shouting for? The Tartar is still near; he'll have heard you!' And he thought to himself, 'He is really quite done up. What am I to do with him? It won't do to desert a comrade.'

'Well, then, get up, and climb up on my back. I'll carry you if you really can't walk.'

He helped Kostílin up, and put his arms under his thighs. Then he went out on to the path, carrying him.

'Only, for the love of heaven,' said Zhílin, 'don't throttle me with your hands! Hold on to my shoulders.'

Zhílin found his load heavy; his feet, too, were bleeding, and he was tired out. Now and then he stooped to balance Kostílin better, jerking him up so that he should sit higher, and then went on again.

The Tartar must, however, really have heard Kostílin scream. Zhílin suddenly heard someone galloping behind and shouting in the Tartar tongue. He darted in among the bushes. The Tartar seized his gun and fired, but did not hit them, shouted in his own language, and galloped off along the road.

'Well, now we are lost, friend!' said Zhílin. 'That dog will gather the Tartars together to hunt us down. Unless we can get a couple of miles away from here we are lost!' And he thought to himself, 'Why the devil did I saddle myself with this block? I should have got away long ago had I been alone.'

'Go on alone,' said Kostílin. 'Why should you perish because of me?'

'No I won't go. It won't do to desert a comrade.'

Again he took Kostílin on his shoulders and staggered on. They went on in that way for another half mile or more. They were still in the forest, and could not see the end of it. But the mist was already dispersing, and clouds seemed to be gathering; the stars were no longer to be seen. Zhílin was quite done up. They came to a spring walled in with stones by the side of the path. Zhílin stopped and set Kostílin down.

'Let me have a rest and a drink,' said he, 'and let us eat some of the cheese. It can't be much farther now.'

But hardly had he lain down to get a drink, when he heard the sound of horses' feet behind him. Again they darted to the right among the bushes, and lay down under a steep slope.

They heard Tartar voices. The Tartars stopped at the very spot where they had turned off the path. The Tartars talked a bit, and then seemed to be setting a dog on the scent. There was a sound of crackling twigs, and a strange dog appeared from behind the bushes. It stopped, and began to bark.

Then the Tartars, also strangers, came climbing down, seized Zhílin and Kostílin, bound them, put them on horses, and rode away with them.

When they had ridden about two miles, they met Abdul, their owner, with two other Tartars following him. After talking with the strangers, he put Zhílin and Kostílin on two of his own horses and took them back to the Aoul.

Abdul did not laugh now, and did not say a word to them.

They were back at the Aoul by daybreak, and were set down in the street. The children came crowding round, throwing stones, shrieking, and beating them with whips.

The Tartars gathered together in a circle, and the old man from the foot of the hill was also there. They began discussing; and Zhílin heard them considering what should be done with him and Kostílin. Some said they ought to be sent farther into the mountains; but the old man said: 'They must be killed!'

Abdul disputed with him, saying: 'I gave money for them, and I must get ransom for them.' But the old man said: 'They will pay you nothing, but will only bring misfortune. It is a sin to feed Russians. Kill them, and have done with it!'

They dispersed. When they had gone, the master came up to Zhílin and said: 'If the money for your ransom is not sent within a fortnight, I will flog you; and if you try to run away again, I'll kill you like a dog! Write a letter, and write properly!'

Paper was brought to them, and they wrote the letters. Shackles were put on their feet, and they were taken behind the Mosque to a deep pit about twelve feet square, into which they were let down.

VI

Life was now very hard for them. Their shackles were never taken off, and they were not let out into the fresh air. Unbaked dough was thrown to them as if they were dogs, and water was let down in a can.

It was wet and close in the pit, and there was a horrible stench. Kostílin grew quite ill, his body became swollen and he ached all over, and moaned or slept all the time. Zhílin, too, grew downcast; he saw it was a bad lookout, and could think of no way of escape.

He tried to make a tunnel, but there was nowhere to put the earth. His master noticed it, and threatened to kill him.

He was sitting on the floor of the pit one day, thinking of freedom and feeling very downhearted, when suddenly a cake fell into his lap, then another, and then a shower of cherries. He looked up, and there was Dina. She looked at him, laughed, and ran away. And Zhílin thought: 'Might not Dina help me?'

He cleared out a little place in the pit, scraped up some clay, and began modelling toys. He made men, horses and dogs, thinking, 'When Dina comes I'll throw them up to her.'

But Dina did not come next day. Zhílin heard the tramp of horses; some men rode past, and the Tartars gathered in council near the Mosque. They shouted and argued; the word 'Russians' was repeated several times. He could hear the voice of the old man. Though he could not distinguish what was said, he guessed that Russian troops were somewhere near, and that the Tartars, afraid they might come into the Aoul, did not know what to do with their prisoners.

After talking awhile, they went away. Suddenly he heard a rustling overhead, and saw Dina crouching at the edge of the pit, her knees higher than her head, and bending over so that the coins of her plait dangled above the pit. Her eyes gleamed like stars. She drew two cheeses out of her sleeve and threw them to him. Zhílin took them and said, 'Why did you not come before? I have made some toys for you. Here, catch!' And he began throwing the toys up, one by one.

But she shook her head and would not look at them.

'I don't want any,' she said. She sat silent for awhile, and then went on, 'Iván, they want to kill you!' And she pointed to her own throat.

'Who wants to kill me?'

'Father; the old men say he must. But I am sorry for you!'

Zhílin answered: 'Well, if you are sorry for me, bring me a long pole.'

She shook her head, as much as to say, 'I can't!'

He clasped his hands and prayed her: 'Dina, please do! Dear Dina, I beg of you!'

'I can't!' she said, 'they would see me bringing it. They're all at home.' And she went away.

So when evening came Zhílin still sat looking up now and then, and wondering what would happen. The stars were there, but the moon had not yet risen. The Mullah's voice was heard; then all was silent. Zhílin was beginning to doze, thinking: 'The girl will be afraid to do it!'

Suddenly he felt clay falling on his head. He looked up, and saw a long pole poking into the opposite wall of the pit. It kept poking about for a time, and then it came down, sliding into the pit. Zhílin was glad indeed. He took hold of it and lowered it. It was a strong pole, one that he had seen before on the roof of his master's hut.

He looked up. The stars were shining high in the sky, and just above the pit Dina's eyes gleamed in the dark like a cat's. She stooped with her face close to the edge of the pit, and whispered,

'Iván! Iván!' waving her hand in front of her face to show that he should speak low.

'What?' said Zhílin.

'All but two have gone away.'

Then Zhílin said, 'Well, Kostílin, come; let us have one last try; I'll help you up.'

But Kostílin would not hear of it.

'No,' said he, 'It's clear I can't get away from here. How can I go, when I have hardly strength to turn round?'

'Well, goodbye, then! Don't think ill of me!' and they kissed each other. Zhílin seized the pole, told Dina to hold on, and began to climb. He slipped once or twice; the shackles hindered him. Kostílin helped him, and he managed to get to the top. Dina, with her little hands, pulled with all her might at his shirt, laughing.

Zhílin drew out the pole and said, 'Put it back in its place, Dina, or they'll notice, and you will be beaten.'

She dragged the pole away, and Zhílin went down the hill. When he had gone down the steep incline, he took a sharp stone and tried to wrench the lock off the shackles. But it was a strong lock and he could not manage to break it, and besides, it was difficult to get at. Then he heard someone running down the hill, springing lightly. He thought: 'Surely, that's Dina again.'

Dina came, took a stone, and said, 'Let me try.'

She knelt down and tried to wrench the lock off, but her little hands were as slender as little twigs, and she had not the strength. She threw the stone away and began to cry. Then Zhílin set to work again at the lock, and Dina squatted beside him with her hand on his shoulder.

Zhílin looked round and saw a red light to the left behind the hill. The moon was just rising. 'Ah!' he thought, 'before the moon has risen I must have passed the valley and be in the forest.' So he rose and threw away the stone. Shackles or no, he must go on.

'Goodbye, Dina dear!' he said. 'I shall never forget you!'

Dina seized hold of him and felt about with her hands for a

place to put some cheeses she had brought. He took them from her.

'Thank you, my little one. Who will make dolls for you when I am gone?' And he stroked her head.

Dina burst into tears, hiding her face in her hands. Then she ran up the hill like a young goat, the coins in her plait clinking against her back.

Zhílin crossed himself, took the lock of his shackles in his hand to prevent its clattering, and went along the road, dragging his shackled leg, and looking towards the place where the moon was about to rise. He now knew the way. If he went straight he would have to walk nearly six miles. If only he could reach the wood before the moon had quite risen! He crossed the river; the light behind the hill was growing whiter. Still looking at it, he went along the valley. The moon was not yet visible. The light became brighter, and one side of the valley was growing lighter and lighter, and shadows were drawing in towards the foot of the hill, creeping nearer and nearer to him.

Zhílin went on, keeping in the shade. He was hurrying, but the moon was moving still faster; the tops of the hills on the right were already lit up. As he got near the wood the white moon appeared from behind the hills, and it became light as day. One could see all the leaves on the trees. It was light on the hill, but silent, as if nothing were alive; no sound could be heard but the gurgling of the river below.

Zhílin reached the wood without meeting anyone, chose a dark spot, and sat down to rest.

He rested, and ate one of the cheeses. Then he found a stone and set to work again to knock off the shackles. He knocked his hands sore, but could not break the lock. He rose and went along the road. After walking the greater part of a mile he was quite done up, and his feet were aching. He had to stop every ten steps. 'There is nothing else for it,' thought he. 'I must drag on as long as I have any strength left. If I sit down, I shan't be able to rise again. I can't reach the fortress; but when day breaks

I'll lie down in the forest, remain there all day, and go on again at night.'

He went on all night. Two Tartars on horseback passed him; but he heard them a long way off, and hid behind a tree.

The moon began to grow paler, the dew to fall. It was getting near dawn, and Zhílin had not reached the end of the forest. 'Well,' thought he, 'I'll walk another thirty steps, and then turn in among the trees and sit down.'

He walked another thirty steps, and saw that he was at the end of the forest. He went to the edge; it was now quite light, and straight before him was the plain and the fortress. To the left, quite close at the foot of the slope, a fire was dying out, and the smoke from it spread round. There were men gathered about the fire.

He looked intently, and saw guns glistening. They were soldiers – Cossacks!

Zhílin was filled with joy. He collected his remaining strength and set off down the hill, saying to himself: 'God forbid that any mounted Tartar should see me now, in the open field! Near as I am, I could not get there in time.'

Hardly had he said this when, a couple of hundred yards off, on a hillock to the left, he saw three Tartars.

They saw him also and made a rush. His heart sank. He waved his hands, and shouted with all his might, 'Brothers, brothers! Help!'

The Cossacks heard him, and a party of them on horseback darted to cut across the Tartars' path. The Cossacks were far and the Tartars were near; but Zhílin, too, made a last effort. Lifting the shackles with his hand, he ran towards the Cossacks, hardly-knowing what he was doing, crossing himself and shouting, 'Brothers! Brothers! Brothers!'

There were some fifteen Cossacks. The Tartars were frightened, and stopped before reaching him. Zhílin staggered up to the Cossacks.

They surrounded him and began questioning him. 'Who are you? What are you? Where from?'

But Zhílin was quite beside himself, and could only weep and repeat, 'Brothers! Brothers!'

Then the soldiers came running up and crowded round Zhílin – one giving him bread, another buckwheat, a third vódka: one wrapping a cloak round him, another breaking his shackles.

The officers recognized him, and rode with him to the fortress. The soldiers were glad to see him back, and his comrades all gathered round him.

Zhílin told them all that had happened to him.

'That's the way I went home and got married!' said he. 'No. It seems plain that fate was against it!'

So he went on serving in the Caucasus. A month passed before Kostílin was released, after paying five thousand roubles ransom. He was almost dead when they brought him back.

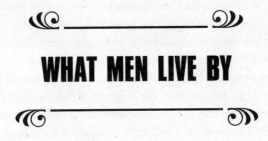

WHAT MEN LIVE BY

'**We know that we have** passed out of death into life, because we love the brethren. He that loveth not abideth in death.' – (1 John 3:14) 'Whoso hath the world's goods, and beholdeth his brother in need, and shutteth up his compassion from him, how doth the love of God abide in him? My little children, let us not love in word, neither with the tongue; but in deed and truth.' – (1 John 3:17-18). 'Love is of God; and everyone that loveth is begotten of God, and knoweth God. He that loveth not knoweth not God; for God is love.' – (1 John 4:7-8). 'No man hath beheld God at any time; if we love one another, God abideth in us.' – (1 John 4:12). 'God is love; and he that abideth in love abideth in God, and God abideth in him.' – (1 John 4:16). 'If a man say, I love God, and hateth his brother, he is a liar; for he that loveth not his brother whom he hath seen, how can he love God whom he hath not seen?' – (1 John 4:20).

I

A shoemaker named Simon, who had neither house nor land of his own, lived with his wife and children in a peasant's hut, and earned his living by his work. Work was cheap, but bread was dear, and what he earned he spent for food. The man and his wife had but one sheepskin coat between them for winter wear, and even that was torn to tatters, and this was the second year he had been wanting to buy sheepskins for a new coat. Before winter Simon saved up a little money: a three-rouble note lay hidden in his wife's box, and five roubles and twenty kopeks[5] were owed him by customers in the village.

So one morning he prepared to go to the village to buy the sheepskins. He put on over his shirt his wife's wadded nankeen jacket, and over that he put his own cloth coat. He took the three-rouble note in his pocket, cut himself a stick to serve as a staff, and started off after breakfast. 'I'll collect the five roubles that are due to me,' thought he, 'add the three I have got, and that will be enough to buy sheepskins for the winter coat.'

He came to the village and called at a peasant's hut, but the man was not at home. The peasant's wife promised that the money should be paid next week, but she would not pay it herself. Then Simon called on another peasant, but this one swore he had no money, and would only pay twenty kopeks which he owed for a pair of boots Simon had mended. Simon then tried to buy the sheepskins on credit, but the dealer would not trust him.

'Bring your money,' said he, 'then you may have your pick of the skins. We know what debt-collecting is like.'

So all the business the shoemaker did was to get the twenty kopeks for boots he had mended, and to take a pair of felt boots a peasant gave him to sole with leather.

Simon felt downhearted. He spent the twenty kopeks on vódka, and started homewards without having bought any skins. In the morning he had felt the frost; but now, after drinking the vódka, he felt warm, even without a sheepskin coat. He trudged along, striking his stick on the frozen earth with one hand, swinging the felt boots with the other, and talking to himself.

'I'm quite warm,' said he, 'though I have no sheepskin coat. I've had a drop, and it runs through all my veins. I need no sheepskins. I go along and don't worry about anything. That's the sort of man I am! What do I care? I can live without sheepskins.

5   *One hundred kopeks make a rouble.*

I don't need them. My wife will fret, to be sure. And, true enough, it *is* a shame; one works all day long, and then does not get paid. Stop a bit! If you don't bring that money along, sure enough I'll skin you, blessed if I don't. How's that? He pays twenty kopeks at a time! What can I do with twenty kopeks? Drink it – that's all one can do! Hard up, he says he is! So he may be – but what about me? You have house, and cattle, and everything; I've only what I stand up in! You have corn of your own growing; I have to buy every grain. Do what I will, I must spend three roubles every week for bread alone. I come home and find the bread all used up, and I have to fork out another rouble and a half. So just pay up what you owe, and no nonsense about it!'

By this time he had nearly reached the shrine at the bend of the road. Looking up, he saw something whitish behind the shrine. The daylight was fading, and the shoemaker peered at the thing without being able to make out what it was. 'There was no white stone here before. Can it be an ox? It's not like an ox. It has a head like a man, but it's too white; and what could a man be doing there?'

He came closer, so that it was clearly visible. To his surprise it really was a man, alive or dead, sitting naked, leaning motionless against the shrine. Terror seized the shoemaker, and he thought, 'Someone has killed him, stripped him, and left him here. If I meddle I shall surely get into trouble.'

So the shoemaker went on. He passed in front of the shrine so that he could not see the man. When he had gone some way, he looked back, and saw that the man was no longer leaning against the shrine, but was moving as if looking towards him. The shoemaker felt more frightened than before, and thought, 'Shall I go back to him, or shall I go on? If I go near him something dreadful may happen. Who knows who the fellow is? He has not come here for any good. If I go near him he may jump up and throttle me, and there will be no getting away. Or if not, he'd still be a burden on one's hands. What could I do with a naked man? I couldn't give him my last clothes. Heaven only help me to get away!'

So the shoemaker hurried on, leaving the shrine behind him – when suddenly his conscience smote him, and he stopped in the road.

'What are you doing, Simon?' said he to himself. 'The man may be dying of want, and you slip past afraid. Have you grown so rich as to be afraid of robbers? Ah, Simon, shame on you!'

So he turned back and went up to the man.

II

Simon approached the stranger, looked at him, and saw that he was a young man, fit, with no bruises on his body, only evidently freezing and frightened, and he sat there leaning back without looking up at Simon, as if too faint to lift his eyes. Simon went close to him, and then the man seemed to wake up. Turning his head, he opened his eyes and looked into Simon's face. That one look was enough to make Simon fond of the man. He threw the felt boots on the ground, undid his sash, laid it on the boots, and took off his cloth coat.

'It's not a time for talking,' said he. 'Come, put this coat on at once!' And Simon took the man by the elbows and helped him to rise. As he stood there, Simon saw that his body was clean and in good condition, his hands and feet shapely, and his face good and kind. He threw his coat over the man's shoulders, but the latter could not find the sleeves. Simon guided his arms into them, and drawing the coat well on, wrapped it closely about him, tying the sash round the man's waist.

Simon even took off his torn cap to put it on the man's head, but then his own head felt cold, and he thought: 'I'm quite bald, while he has long curly hair.' So he put his cap on his own head again. 'It will be better to give him something for his feet,' thought he; and he made the man sit down, and helped him to put on the felt boots, saying, 'There, friend, now move about and warm yourself. Other matters can be settled later on. Can you walk?'

The man stood up and looked kindly at Simon, but could not say a word.

'Why don't you speak?' said Simon. 'It's too cold to stay here; we must be getting home. There now, take my stick, and if you're feeling weak, lean on that. Now step out!'

The man started walking, and moved easily, not lagging behind.

As they went along, Simon asked him, 'And where do you belong to?'

'I'm not from these parts.'

'I thought as much. I know the folks hereabouts. But, how did you come to be there by the shrine?'

'I cannot tell.'

'Has someone been ill-treating you?'

'No one has ill-treated me. God has punished me.'

'Of course God rules all. Still, you'll have to find food and shelter somewhere. Where do you want to go to?'

'It is all the same to me.'

Simon was amazed. The man did not look like a rogue, and he spoke gently, but yet he gave no account of himself. Still Simon thought, 'Who knows what may have happened?' And he said to the stranger: 'Well then, come home with me, and at least warm yourself awhile.'

So Simon walked towards his home, and the stranger kept up with him, walking at his side. The wind had risen and Simon felt it cold under his shirt. He was getting over his tipsiness by now, and began to feel the frost. He went along sniffling and wrapping his wife's coat round him, and he thought to himself: 'There now – talk about sheepskins! I went out for sheepskins and come home without even a coat to my back, and what is more, I'm bringing a naked man along with me. Matryóna won't be pleased!' And when he thought of his wife he felt sad; but when he looked at the stranger and remembered how he had looked up at him at the shrine, his heart was glad.

III

Simon's wife had everything ready early that day. She had cut wood, brought water, fed the children, eaten her own meal, and now she sat thinking. She wondered when she ought to make bread: now or tomorrow? There was still a large piece left.

'If Simon has had some dinner in town,' thought she, 'and does not eat much for supper, the bread will last out another day.'

She weighed the piece of bread in her hand again and again, and thought: 'I won't make any more today. We have only enough flour left to bake one batch. We can manage to make this last out till Friday.'

So Matryóna put away the bread, and sat down at the table to patch her husband's shirt. While she worked she thought how her husband was buying skins for a winter coat.

'If only the dealer does not cheat him. My good man is much too simple; he cheats nobody, but any child can take him in. Eight roubles is a lot of money – he should get a good coat at that price. Not tanned skins, but still a proper winter coat. How difficult it was last winter to get on without a warm coat. I could neither get down to the river, nor go out anywhere. When he went out he put on all we had, and there was nothing left for me. He did not start very early today, but still it's time he was back. I only hope he has not gone on the spree!'

Hardly had Matryóna thought this, when steps were heard on the threshold, and someone entered. Matryóna stuck her needle into her work and went out into the passage. There she saw two men: Simon, and with him a man without a hat, and wearing felt boots.

Matryóna noticed at once that her husband smelt of spirits. 'There now, he has been drinking,' thought she. And when she saw that he was coatless, had only her jacket on, brought no parcel, stood there silent, and seemed ashamed, her heart was ready to break with disappointment. 'He has drunk the money,' thought she, 'and has been on the spree with some good-for-nothing fellow whom he has brought home with him.'

Matryóna let them pass into the hut, followed them in, and saw that the stranger was a young, slight man, wearing her husband's coat. There was no shirt to be seen under it, and he had no hat. Having entered, he stood neither moving, nor raising his eyes, and Matryóna thought: 'He must be a bad man – he's afraid.'

Matryóna frowned, and stood beside the oven looking to see what they would do.

Simon took off his cap and sat down on the bench as if things were all right.

'Come, Matryóna; if supper is ready, let us have some.'

Matryóna muttered something to herself and did not move, but stayed where she was, by the oven. She looked first at the one and then at the other of them, and only shook her head. Simon saw that his wife was annoyed, but tried to pass it off. Pretending not to notice anything, he took the stranger by the arm.

'Sit down, friend,' said he, 'and let us have some supper.'

The stranger sat down on the bench.

'Haven't you cooked anything for us?' said Simon.

Matryóna's anger boiled over. 'I've cooked, but not for you. It seems to me you have drunk your wits away. You went to buy a sheepskin coat, but come home without so much as the coat you had on, and bring a naked vagabond home with you. I have no supper for drunkards like you.'

'That's enough, Matryóna. Don't wag your tongue without reason. You had better ask what sort of man—'

'And you tell me what you've done with the money?'

Simon found the pocket of the jacket, drew out the three-rouble note, and unfolded it.

'Here is the money. Trífonof did not pay, but promises to pay soon.'

Matryóna got still more angry; he had bought no sheepskins, but had put his only coat on some naked fellow and had even brought him to their house.

She snatched up the note from the table, took it to put away in safety, and said: 'I have no supper for you. We can't feed all the naked drunkards in the world.'

'There now, Matryóna, hold your tongue a bit. First hear what a man has to say—'

'Much wisdom I shall hear from a drunken fool. I was right in not wanting to marry you – a drunkard. The linen my mother gave me you drank; and now you've been to buy a coat – and have drunk it, too!'

Simon tried to explain to his wife that he had only spent twenty kopeks; tried to tell how he had found the man – but Matryóna would not let him get a word in. She talked nineteen to the dozen, and dragged in things that had happened ten years before.

Matryóna talked and talked, and at last she flew at Simon and seized him by the sleeve.

'Give me my jacket. It is the only one I have, and you must needs take it from me and wear it yourself. Give it here, you mangy dog, and may the devil take you.'

Simon began to pull off the jacket, and turned a sleeve of it inside out; Matryóna seized the jacket and it burst its seams. She snatched it up, threw it over her head and went to the door. She meant to go out, but stopped undecided – she wanted to work off her anger, but she also wanted to learn what sort of a man the stranger was.

IV

Matryóna stopped and said: 'If he were a good man he would not be naked. Why, he hasn't even a shirt on him. If he were all right, you would say where you came across the fellow.'

'That's just what I am trying to tell you,' said Simon. 'As I came to the shrine I saw him sitting all naked and frozen. It isn't quite the weather to sit about naked! God sent me to him, or he would have perished. What was I to do? How do we know what may have happened to him? So I took him, clothed him, and brought him along. Don't be so angry, Matryóna. It is a sin. Remember, we all must die one day.'

Angry words rose to Matryóna's lips, but she looked at the

stranger and was silent. He sat on the edge of the bench, motion-less, his hands folded on his knees, his head drooping on his breast, his eyes closed, and his brows knit as if in pain. Matryóna was silent: and Simon said: 'Matryóna, have you no love of God?'

Matryóna heard these words, and as she looked at the stranger, suddenly her heart softened towards him. She came back from the door, and going to the oven she got out the supper. Setting a cup on the table, she poured out some *kvass*[6]. Then she brought out the last piece of bread, and set out a knife and spoons.

'Eat, if you want to,' said she.

Simon drew the stranger to the table.

'Take your place, young man,' said he.

Simon cut the bread, crumbled it into the broth, and they began to eat. Matryóna sat at the corner of the table, resting her head on her hand and looking at the stranger.

And Matryóna was touched with pity for the stranger, and began to feel fond of him. And at once the stranger's face lit up; his brows were no longer bent, he raised his eyes and smiled at Matryóna.

When they had finished supper, the woman cleared away the things and began questioning the stranger. 'Where are you from?' said she.

'I am not from these parts.'

'But how did you come to be on the road?'

'I may not tell.'

'Did someone rob you?'

'God punished me.'

'And you were lying there naked?'

'Yes, naked and freezing. Simon saw me and had pity on me. He took off his coat, put it on me and brought me here. And you have fed me, given me drink and shown pity on me. God will reward you!'

Matryóna rose, took from the window Simon's old shirt she

6   *A non-intoxicating drink usually made from rye malt and rye flour.*

had been patching, and gave it to the stranger. She also brought out a pair of trousers for him.

'There,' said she, 'I see you have no shirt. Put this on, and lie down where you please, in the loft or on the oven[7].'

The stranger took off the coat, put on the shirt, and lay down in the loft. Matryóna put out the candle, took the coat, and climbed to where her husband lay.

Matryóna drew the skirts of the coat over her and lay down, but could not sleep; she could not get the stranger out of her mind.

When she remembered that he had eaten their last piece of bread and that there was none for tomorrow, and thought of the shirt and trousers she had given away, she felt grieved; but when she remembered how he had smiled, her heart was glad.

Long did Matryóna lie awake, and she noticed that Simon also was awake – he drew the coat towards him.

'Simon!'

'Well?'

'You have had the last of the bread, and I have not put any to rise. I don't know what we shall do tomorrow. Perhaps I can borrow some of neighbour Martha.'

'If we're alive we shall find something to eat.'

The woman lay still awhile, and then said, 'He seems a good man, but why does he not tell us who he is?'

'I suppose he has his reasons.'

'Simon!'

'Well?'

'We give; but why does nobody give us anything?'

Simon did not know what to say; so he only said, 'Let us stop talking,' and turned over and went to sleep.

---

7 *The brick oven in a Russian peasant's hut is usually built so as to leave a flat top, large enough to lie on, for those who want to sleep in a warm place.*

V

In the morning Simon awoke. The children were still asleep; his wife had gone to the neighbour's to borrow some bread. The stranger alone was sitting on the bench, dressed in the old shirt and trousers, and looking upwards. His face was brighter than it had been the day before.

Simon said to him, 'Well, friend; the belly wants bread, and the naked body clothes. One has to work for a living. What work do you know?'

'I do not know any.'

This surprised Simon, but he said, 'Men who want to learn can learn anything.'

'Men work, and I will work also.'

'What is your name?'

'Michael.'

'Well, Michael, if you don't wish to talk about yourself, that is your own affair; but you'll have to earn a living for yourself. If you will work as I tell you, I will give you food and shelter.'

'May God reward you! I will learn. Show me what to do.'

Simon took yarn, put it round his thumb and began to twist it.

'It is easy enough – see!'

Michael watched him, put some yarn round his own thumb in the same way, caught the knack, and twisted the yarn also.

Then Simon showed him how to wax the thread. This also Michael mastered. Next Simon showed him how to twist the bristle in, and how to sew, and this, too, Michael learned at once.

Whatever Simon showed him he understood at once, and after three days he worked as if he had sewn boots all his life. He worked without stopping, and ate little. When work was over he sat silently, looking upwards. He hardly went into the street, spoke only when necessary, and neither joked nor laughed. They never saw him smile, except that first evening when Matryóna gave them supper.

VI

Day by day and week by week the year went round. Michael lived and worked with Simon. His fame spread till people said that no one sewed boots so neatly and strongly as Simon's workman, Michael; and from all the district round people came to Simon for their boots, and he began to be well off.

One winter day, as Simon and Michael sat working, a carriage on sledge runners, with three horses and with bells, drove up to the hut. They looked out of the window; the carriage stopped at their door, a fine servant jumped down from the box and opened the door. A gentleman in a fur coat got out and walked up to Simon's hut. Up jumped Matryóna and opened the door wide. The gentleman stooped to enter the hut, and when he drew himself up again his head nearly reached the ceiling, and he seemed quite to fill his end of the room.

Simon rose, bowed, and looked at the gentleman with astonishment. He had never seen anyone like him. Simon himself was lean, Michael was thin, and Matryóna was dry as a bone, but this man was like someone from another world: red-faced, burly, with a neck like a bull's, and looking altogether as if he were cast in iron.

The gentleman puffed, threw off his fur coat, sat down on the bench, and said, 'Which of you is the master bootmaker?'

'I am, your Excellency,' said Simon, coming forward.

Then the gentleman shouted to his lad, 'Hey, Fédka, bring the leather!'

The servant ran in, bringing a parcel. The gentleman took the parcel and put it on the table.

'Untie it,' said he. The lad untied it.

The gentleman pointed to the leather.

'Look here, shoemaker,' said he, 'do you see this leather?'

'Yes, your honour.'

'But do you know what sort of leather it is?'

Simon felt the leather and said, 'It is good leather.'

'Good, indeed! Why, you fool, you never saw such leather before in your life. It's German, and cost twenty roubles.'

Simon was frightened, and said, 'Where should I ever see leather like that?'

'Just so! Now, can you make it into boots for me?'

'Yes, your Excellency, I can.'

Then the gentleman shouted at him: 'You *can*, can you? Well, remember whom you are to make them for, and what the leather is. You must make me boots that will wear for a year, neither losing shape nor coming unsewn. If you can do it, take the leather and cut it up; but if you can't, say so. I warn you now if your boots become unsewn or lose shape within a year, I will have you put in prison. If they don't burst or lose shape for a year I will pay you ten roubles for your work.'

Simon was frightened, and did not know what to say. He glanced at Michael and nudging him with his elbow, whispered: 'Shall I take the work?'

Michael nodded his head as if to say, 'Yes, take it.'

Simon did as Michael advised, and undertook to make boots that would not lose shape or split for a whole year.

Calling his servant, the gentleman told him to pull the boot off his left leg, which he stretched out.

'Take my measure!' said he.

Simon stitched a paper measure seventeen inches long, smoothed it out, knelt down, wiped his hands well on his apron so as not to soil the gentleman's sock, and began to measure. He measured the sole, and round the instep, and began to measure the calf of the leg, but the paper was too short. The calf of the leg was as thick as a beam.

'Mind you don't make it too tight in the leg.'

Simon stitched on another strip of paper. The gentleman twitched his toes about in his sock, looking round at those in the hut, and as he did so he noticed Michael.

'Whom have you there?' asked he.

'That is my workman. He will sew the boots.'

'Mind,' said the gentleman to Michael, 'remember to make them so that they will last me a year.'

Simon also looked at Michael, and saw that Michael was not looking at the gentleman, but was gazing into the corner behind the gentleman, as if he saw someone there. Michael looked and looked, and suddenly he smiled, and his face became brighter.

'What are you grinning at, you fool?' thundered the gentleman. 'You had better look to it that the boots are ready in time.'

'They shall be ready in good time,' said Michael.

'Mind it is so,' said the gentleman, and he put on his boots and his fur coat, wrapped the latter round him, and went to the door. But he forgot to stoop, and struck his head against the lintel.

He swore and rubbed his head. Then he took his seat in the carriage and drove away.

When he had gone, Simon said: 'There's a figure of a man for you! You could not kill him with a mallet. He almost knocked out the lintel, but little harm it did him.'

And Matryóna said: 'Living as he does, how should he not grow strong? Death itself can't touch such a rock as that.'

VII

Then Simon said to Michael: 'Well, we have taken the work, but we must see we don't get into trouble over it. The leather is dear, and the gentleman hot-tempered. We must make no mistakes. Come, your eye is truer and your hands have become nimbler than mine, so you take this measure and cut out the boots. I will finish off the sewing of the vamps.'

Michael did as he was told. He took the leather, spread it out on the table, folded it in two, took a knife and began to cut out.

Matryóna came and watched him cutting, and was surprised to see how he was doing it. Matryóna was accustomed to seeing boots made, and she looked and saw that Michael was not cutting the leather for boots, but was cutting it round.

She wished to say something, but she thought to herself:

'Perhaps I do not understand how gentlemen's boots should be made. I suppose Michael knows more about it – and I won't interfere.'

When Michael had cut up the leather, he took a thread and began to sew not with two ends, as boots are sewn, but with a single end, as for soft slippers.

Again Matryóna wondered, but again she did not interfere. Michael sewed on steadily till noon. Then Simon rose for dinner, looked around, and saw that Michael had made slippers out of the gentleman's leather.

'Ah,' groaned Simon, and he thought, 'How is it that Michael, who has been with me a whole year and never made a mistake before, should do such a dreadful thing? The gentleman ordered high boots, welted, with whole fronts, and Michael has made soft slippers with single soles, and has wasted the leather. What am I to say to the gentleman? I can never replace leather such as this.'

And he said to Michael, 'What are you doing, friend? You have ruined me! You know the gentleman ordered high boots, but see what you have made!'

Hardly had he begun to rebuke Michael, when 'rat-tat' went the iron ring that hung at the door. Someone was knocking. They looked out of the window; a man had come on horseback, and was fastening his horse. They opened the door, and the servant who had been with the gentleman came in.

'Good day,' said he.

'Good day,' replied Simon. 'What can we do for you?'

'My mistress has sent me about the boots.'

'What about the boots?'

'Why, my master no longer needs them. He is dead.'

'Is it possible?'

'He did not live to get home after leaving you, but died in the carriage. When we reached home and the servants came to help him alight, he rolled over like a sack. He was dead already, and so stiff that he could hardly be got out of the carriage. My mistress sent me here, saying: "Tell the bootmaker that the gentleman who ordered boots of him and left the leather for them no longer needs the boots, but that he must quickly make soft slippers for the corpse. Wait till they are ready, and bring them back with you." That is why I have come.'

Michael gathered up the remnants of the leather; rolled them up, took the soft slippers he had made, slapped them together, wiped them down with his apron, and handed them and the roll of leather to the servant, who took them and said: 'Goodbye, masters, and good day to you!'

VIII

Another year passed, and another, and Michael was now living his sixth year with Simon. He lived as before. He went nowhere, only spoke when necessary, and had only smiled twice in all those years – once when Matryóna gave him food, and a second time when the gentleman was in their hut. Simon was more than pleased with his workman. He never now asked him where he came from, and only feared lest Michael should go away.

They were all at home one day. Matryóna was putting iron pots in the oven; the children were running along the benches and looking out of the window; Simon was sewing at one window, and Michael was fastening on a heel at the other.

One of the boys ran along the bench to Michael, leant on his shoulder, and looked out of the window.

'Look, Uncle Michael! There is a lady with little girls! She seems to be coming here. And one of the girls is lame.'

When the boy said that, Michael dropped his work, turned to the window, and looked out into the street.

Simon was surprised. Michael never used to look out into the street, but now he pressed against the window, staring at something. Simon also looked out, and saw that a well-dressed woman was really coming to his hut, leading by the hand two little girls in fur coats and woolen shawls. The girls could hardly be told one from the other, except that one of them was crippled in her left leg and walked with a limp.

The woman stepped into the porch and entered the passage. Feeling about for the entrance she found the latch, which she lifted, and opened the door. She let the two girls go in first, and followed them into the hut.

'Good day, good folk!'

'Pray come in,' said Simon. 'What can we do for you?'

The woman sat down by the table. The two little girls pressed close to her knees, afraid of the people in the hut.

'I want leather shoes made for these two little girls, for spring.'

'We can do that. We never have made such small shoes, but we can make them; either welted or turnover shoes, linen lined. My man, Michael, is a master at the work.'

Simon glanced at Michael and saw that he had left his work and was sitting with his eyes fixed on the little girls. Simon was surprised. It was true the girls were pretty, with black eyes, plump, and rosy-cheeked, and they wore nice kerchiefs and fur coats, but still Simon could not understand why Michael should look at them like that – just as if he had known them before. He was puzzled, but went on talking with the woman, and arranging the price. Having fixed it, he prepared the measure. The woman lifted the lame girl on to her lap and said: 'Take two measures from this little girl. Make one shoe for the lame foot and three for the sound one. They both have the same sized feet. They are twins.'

Simon took the measure and, speaking of the lame girl, said: 'How did it happen to her? She is such a pretty girl. Was she born so?'

'No, her mother crushed her leg.'

Then Matryóna joined in. She wondered who this woman was, and whose the children were, so she said: 'Are not you their mother then?'

'No, my good woman; I am neither their mother nor any relation to them. They were quite strangers to me, but I adopted them.'

'They are not your children and yet you are so fond of them?'

'How can I help being fond of them? I fed them both at my own breasts. I had a child of my own, but God took him. I was not so fond of him as I now am of them.'

'Then whose children are they?'

IX

The woman, having begun talking, told them the whole story.

'It is about six years since their parents died, both in one week: their father was buried on the Tuesday, and their mother died on the Friday. These orphans were born three days after their father's death, and their mother did not live another day. My husband and I were then living as peasants in the village. We were neighbours of theirs, our yard being next to theirs. Their father was a lonely man; a woodcutter in the forest. When felling trees one day, they let one fall on him. It fell across his body and crushed his bowels out. They hardly got him home before his soul went to God; and that same week his wife gave birth to twins – these little girls. She was poor and alone; she had no one, young or old, with her. Alone she gave them birth, and alone she met her death.'

'The next morning I went to see her, but when I entered the hut, she, poor thing, was already stark and cold. In dying she had rolled on to this child and crushed her leg. The village folk came to the hut, washed the body, laid her out, made a coffin, and buried her. They were good folk. The babies were left alone. What was to be done with them? I was the only woman there who had a baby at the time. I was nursing my first-born – eight weeks old. So I took them for a time. The peasants came together, and thought and thought what to do with them; and at last they said to me: "For the present, Mary, you had better keep the girls, and later on we will arrange what to do for them." So I nursed the sound one at my breast, but at first I did not feed this crippled one. I did not suppose she would live. But then I thought to myself, why should the poor innocent suffer? I pitied her, and began to feed her. And so I fed my own boy and these two – the three of them – at my own breast. I was young and strong, and had good food, and God gave me so much milk that at times it even overflowed. I used sometimes to feed two at a time, while the third was waiting. When one had enough I nursed the third. And God so ordered it that these grew up, while my own was buried before he was two years old. And I had no more children, though we prospered. Now my husband is working for the corn merchant at the mill. The pay is good, and we are well off. But I have no children of my own, and how lonely I should be without these little girls! How can I help loving them! They are the joy of my life!'

She pressed the lame little girl to her with one hand, while with the other she wiped the tears from her cheeks.

And Matryóna sighed, and said: 'The proverb is true that says, "One may live without father or mother, but one cannot live without God."'

So they talked together, when suddenly the whole hut was lighted up as though by summer lightning from the corner where Michael sat. They all looked towards him and saw him sitting, his hands folded on his knees, gazing upwards and smiling.

X

The woman went away with the girls. Michael rose from the bench, put down his work, and took off his apron. Then, bowing low to Simon and his wife, he said: 'Farewell, masters. God has forgiven me. I ask your forgiveness, too, for anything done amiss.'

And they saw that a light shone from Michael. And Simon rose, bowed down to Michael, and said: 'I see, Michael, that you are no common man, and I can neither keep you nor question you. Only tell me this: how is it that when I found you and brought you home, you were gloomy, and when my wife gave you food you smiled at her and became brighter? Then when the gentleman came to order the boots, you smiled again and became brighter still? And now, when this woman brought the little girls, you smiled a third time, and have become as bright as day? Tell me, Michael, why does your face shine so, and why did you smile those three times?'

And Michael answered: 'Light shines from me because I have been punished, but now God has pardoned me. And I smiled three times, because God sent me to learn three truths, and I have learnt them. One I learnt when your wife pitied me, and that is why I smiled the first time. The second I learnt when the rich man ordered the boots, and then I smiled again. And now, when I saw those little girls, I learnt the third and last truth, and I smiled the third time.'

And Simon said, 'Tell me, Michael, what did God punish you for? and what were the three truths? that I, too, may know them.'

And Michael answered: 'God punished me for disobeying Him. I was an angel in heaven and disobeyed God. God sent me to fetch a woman's soul. I flew to earth, and saw a sick woman lying alone, who had just given birth to twin girls. They moved feebly at their mother's side, but she could not lift them to her breast. When she saw me, she understood that God had sent me for her soul, and she wept and said: "Angel of God! My husband has just been buried, killed by a falling tree. I have neither sister, nor aunt, nor mother: no one to care for my orphans. Do not take my soul! Let me nurse my babes, feed them, and set them on their feet before I die. Children cannot live without father or mother." And I hearkened to her. I placed one child at her breast and gave the other into her arms, and returned to the Lord in heaven. I flew to the Lord, and said: "I could not take the soul of the mother. Her husband was killed by a tree; the woman has twins, and prays that her soul may not be taken. She says: 'Let me nurse and feed my children, and set them on their feet. Children cannot live without father or mother.' I have not taken her soul." And God said: "Go – take the mother's soul, and learn three truths: *Learn what dwells in man, what is not given to man,* and *what men live by.*

When thou hast learnt these things, thou shalt return to heaven."
So I flew again to earth and took the mother's soul. The babes
dropped from her breasts. Her body rolled over on the bed and
crushed one babe, twisting its leg. I rose above the village, wishing
to take her soul to God; but a wind seized me, and my wings
drooped and dropped off. Her soul rose alone to God, while I
fell to earth by the roadside.'

XI

And Simon and Matryóna understood who it was that had lived
with them, and whom they had clothed and fed. And they wept
with awe and with joy. And the angel said: 'I was alone in the
field, naked. I had never known human needs, cold and hunger,
till I became a man. I was famished, frozen, and did not know
what to do. I saw, near the field I was in, a shrine built for God,
and I went to it hoping to find shelter. But the shrine was locked,
and I could not enter. So I sat down behind the shrine to shelter
myself at least from the wind. Evening drew on. I was hungry,
frozen, and in pain. Suddenly I heard a man coming along the
road. He carried a pair of boots, and was talking to himself. For
the first time since I became a man I saw the mortal face of a
man, and his face seemed terrible to me and I turned from it.
And I heard the man talking to himself of how to cover his body
from the cold in winter, and how to feed wife and children. And
I thought: "I am perishing of cold and hunger, and here is a man
thinking only of how to clothe himself and his wife, and how to
get bread for themselves. He cannot help me. When the man saw
me he frowned and became still more terrible, and passed me by
on the other side. I despaired; but suddenly I heard him coming
back. I looked up, and did not recognize the same man: before,
I had seen death in his face; but now he was alive, and I recognized
in him the presence of God.

He came up to me, clothed me, took me with him, and brought
me to his home. I entered the house; a woman came to meet us

and began to speak. The woman was still more terrible than the man had been; the spirit of death came from her mouth; I could not breathe for the stench of death that spread around her. She wished to drive me out into the cold, and I knew that if she did so she would die. Suddenly her husband spoke to her of God, and the woman changed at once. And when she brought me food and looked at me, I glanced at her and saw that death no longer dwelt in her; she had become alive, and in her too I saw God.

'Then I remembered the first lesson God had set me: "*Learn what dwells in man.*" And I understood that in man dwells Love! I was glad that God had already begun to show me what He had promised, and I smiled for the first time. But I had not yet learnt all. I did not yet know "*What is not given to man*", and "*What men live by*".

'I lived with you, and a year passed. A man came to order boots that should wear for a year without losing shape or cracking. I looked at him, and suddenly, behind his shoulder, I saw my comrade – the angel of death. None but me saw that angel; but I knew him, and knew that before the sun set he would take that rich man's soul. And I thought to myself, "The man is making preparations for a year, and does not know that he will die before evening." And I remembered God's second saying, "*Learn what is not given to man*".

'What dwells in man I already knew. Now I learnt what is not given him. It is not given to man to know his own needs. And I smiled for the second time. I was glad to have seen my comrade angel – glad also that God had revealed to me the second saying.

'But I still did not know all. I did not know "*What men live by*". And I lived on, waiting till God should reveal to me the last lesson. In the sixth year came the girl twins with the woman; and I recognized the girls, and heard how they had been kept alive. Having heard the story, I thought, "Their mother besought me for the children's sake, and I believed her when she said that children cannot live without father or mother; but a stranger has nursed them, and has brought them up." And when the woman showed her love for the children that were not her own, and wept over them, I saw in her the living God and understood *"What men live by"*. And I knew that God had revealed to me the last lesson, and had forgiven my sin. And then I smiled for the third time.'

XII

And the angel's body was bared, and he was clothed in light so that eye could not look on him; and his voice grew louder, as though it came not from him but from heaven above. And the angel said:

'I have learnt that all men live not by care for themselves but by love.

'It was not given to the mother to know what her children needed for their life. Nor was it given to the rich man to know what he himself needed. Nor is it given to any man to know whether, when evening comes, he will need boots for his body or slippers for his corpse.

'I remained alive when I was a man, not by care of myself, but because love was present in a passerby, and because he and his wife pitied and loved me. The orphans remained alive not because of their mother's care, but because there was love in the heart of a woman, a stranger to them, who pitied and loved them. And all men live not by the thought they spend on their own welfare, but because love exists in man.

'I knew before that God gave life to men and desires that they should live; now I understood more than that.

'I understood that God does not wish men to live apart, and therefore he does not reveal to them what each one needs for himself; but he wishes them to live united, and therefore reveals to each of them what is necessary for all.

'I have now understood that though it seems to men that they live by care for themselves, in truth it is love alone by which they live. He who has love, is in God, and God is in him, for God is love.'

And the angel sang praise to God, so that the hut trembled at his voice. The roof opened, and a column of fire rose from earth to heaven. Simon and his wife and children fell to the ground. Wings appeared upon the angel's shoulders, and he rose into the heavens.

And when Simon came to himself the hut stood as before, and there was no one in it but his own family.

A SPARK NEGLECTED BURNS THE HOUSE

'**Then came Peter, and said** to him, "Lord, how oft shall my brother sin against me, and I forgive him? Until seven times?" Jesus saith unto him, "I say not unto thee, until seven times; but, until seventy times seven. Therefore is the kingdom of heaven likened unto a certain king, which would make a reckoning with his servants. And when he had begun to reckon, one was brought unto him, which owed him ten thousand talents. But forasmuch as he had not wherewith to pay, his lord commanded him to be sold, and his wife, and children, and all that he had, and payment to be made. The servant therefore fell down and worshipped him, saying, Lord, have patience with me, and I will pay thee all. And the lord of that servant, being moved with compassion, released him, and forgave him the debt. But that servant went out, and found one of his fellow servants, which owed him a hundred pence: and he laid hold on him, and took him by the throat saying, "Pay what thou owest." So his fellow servant fell down and besought him, saying, "Have patience with me, and I will pay thee." And he would not: but went and cast him into prison, till he should pay that which was due. So when his fellow servants saw what was done, they were exceeding sorry, and came and told unto their lord all that was done. Then his lord called him unto him, and saith to him, "Thou wicked servant, I forgave thee all that debt, because thou besoughtest me: shouldest not thou also have had mercy on thy fellow servant, even as I had mercy on thee?" And his lord was wroth, and delivered him to the tormentors, till he should pay all that was due. So shall also my heavenly Father do unto you, if ye forgive not everyone his brother from your hearts.' (Matthew 18: 21–35)

There once lived in a village a peasant named Iván Stcherbakóf. He was comfortably off, in the prime of life, the best worker in the village, and had three sons all able to work. The eldest was married, the second about to marry, and the third was a big lad who could mind the horses and was already beginning to plough. Iván's wife was an able and thrifty woman, and they were fortunate in having a quiet, hard-working daughter-in-law. There was nothing to prevent Iván and his family from living happily. They had only one idle mouth to feed; that was Iván's old father, who suffered from asthma and had been lying ill on the top of the brick oven for seven years. Iván had all he needed: three horses and a colt, a cow with a calf, and fifteen sheep. The women made all the clothing for the family, besides helping in the fields, and the men tilled the land. They always had grain enough of their own to last over beyond the next harvest and sold enough oats to pay the taxes and meet their other needs. So Iván and his children might have lived quite comfortably had it not been for a feud between him and his next-door neighbour, Limping Gabriel, the son of Gordéy Ivánof.

As long as old Gordéy was alive and Iván's father was still able to manage the household, the peasants lived as neighbours should. If the women of either house happened to want a sieve or a tub, or the men required a sack, or if a cart-wheel got broken and could not be mended at once, they used to send to the other house, and helped each other in neighbourly fashion. When a calf strayed into the neighbour's thrashing ground they would just drive it out, and only say, 'Don't let it get in again; our grain is lying there.' And such things as locking up the barns and outhouses, hiding things from one another, or backbiting were never thought of in those days.

That was in the fathers' time. When the sons came to be at the head of the families, everything changed.

It all began about a trifle.

Iván's daughter-in-law had a hen that began laying rather early in the season, and she started collecting its eggs for Easter. Every day she went to the cart shed, and found an egg in the cart; but one day the hen, probably frightened by the children, flew across the fence into the neighbour's yard and laid its egg there. The woman heard the cackling, but said to herself: 'I have no time now; I must tidy up for Sunday. I'll fetch the egg later on.' In the evening she went to the cart, but found no egg there. She went and asked her mother-in-law and brother-in-law whether they had taken the egg. 'No,' they had not; but her youngest brother-in-law, Tarás, said: 'Your Biddy laid its egg in the neighbour's yard. It was there she was cackling, and she flew back across the fence from there.'

The woman went and looked at the hen. There she was on the perch with the other birds, her eyes just closing ready to go to sleep. The woman wished she could have asked the hen and got an answer from her.

Then she went to the neighbour's, and Gabriel's mother came out to meet her.

'What do you want, young woman?'

'Why, Granny, you see, my hen flew across this morning. Did she not lay an egg here?'

'We never saw anything of it. The Lord be thanked, our own hens started laying long ago. We collect our own eggs and have no need of other people's! And we don't go looking for eggs in other people's yards, lass!'

The young woman was offended, and said more than she should have done. Her neighbour answered back with interest, and the women began abusing each other. Iván's wife, who had been to fetch water, happening to pass just then, joined in too. Gabriel's wife rushed out, and began reproaching the young woman with things that had really happened and with other things that had never happened at all. Then a general uproar commenced, all shouting at once, trying to get out two words at a time, and not choice words either.

'You're this!' and 'You're that!' 'You're a thief!' and 'You're a slut!' and 'You're starving your old father-in-law to death!' and 'You're a good-for-nothing!' and so on.

'And you've made a hole in the sieve I lent you, you jade! And it's our yoke you're carrying your pails on – you just give back our yoke!'

Then they caught hold of the yoke, and spilt the water, snatched off one another's shawls, and began fighting. Gabriel, returning from the fields, stopped to take his wife's part. Out rushed Iván and his son and joined in with the rest. Iván was a strong fellow; he scattered the whole lot of them, and pulled a handful of hair out of Gabriel's beard. People came to see what was the matter, and the fighters were separated with difficulty.

That was how it all began.

Gabriel wrapped the hair torn from his beard in a paper, and went to the District Court to have the law of Iván. 'I didn't grow my beard,' said he, 'for pockmarked Iván to pull it out!' And his wife went bragging to the neighbours, saying they'd have Iván condemned and sent to Siberia. And so the feud grew.

The old man, from where he lay on the top of the oven, tried from the very first to persuade them to make peace, but they would not listen. He told them, 'It's a stupid thing you are after, children, picking quarrels about such a paltry matter. Just think! The whole thing began about an egg. The children may have taken it – well, what matter? What's the value of one egg? God sends enough for all! And suppose your neighbour did say an unkind word – put it right; show her how to say a better one! If there has been a fight – well, such things will happen; we're all sinners, but make it up, and let there be an end of it! If you nurse your anger it will be worse for you yourselves.'

But the younger folk would not listen to the old man. They

thought his words were mere senseless dotage. Iván would not humble himself before his neighbour.

'I never pulled his beard,' he said, 'he pulled the hair out himself. But his son has burst all the fastenings on my shirt, and torn it... Look at it!'

And Iván also went to law. They were tried by the Justice of the Peace and by the District Court. While all this was going on, the coupling pin of Gabriel's cart disappeared. Gabriel's women-folk accused Iván's son of having taken it. They said: 'We saw him in the night go past our window, towards the cart; and a neighbour says he saw him at the pub, offering the pin to the landlord.'

So they went to law about that. And at home not a day passed without a quarrel or even a fight. The children, too, abused one another, having learnt to do so from their elders; and when the women happened to meet by the riverside, where they went to rinse the clothes, their arms did not do as much wringing as their tongues did nagging, and every word was a bad one.

At first the peasants only slandered one another; but afterwards they began in real earnest to snatch anything that lay handy, and the children followed their example. Life became harder and harder for them. Iván Stcherbakóf and Limping Gabriel kept suing one another at the Village Assembly, and at the District Court, and before the Justice of the Peace until all the judges were tired of them. Now Gabriel got Iván fined or imprisoned; then Iván did as much to Gabriel; and the more they spited each other the angrier they grew – like dogs that attack one another and get more and more furious the longer they fight. You strike one dog from behind, and it thinks it's the other dog biting him, and gets still fiercer. So these peasants: they went to law, and one or other of them was fined or locked up, but that only made them more and more angry with each other. 'Wait a bit,' they said, 'and I'll make you pay for it.' And so it went on for six years. Only the old man lying on the top of the oven kept telling them again and again: 'Children, what are you doing? Stop all this paying back;

keep to your work, and don't bear malice – it will be better for you. The more you bear malice, the worse it will be.'

But they would not listen to him.

In the seventh year, at a wedding, Iván's daughter-in-law held Gabriel up to shame, accusing him of having been caught horse-stealing. Gabriel was tipsy, and unable to contain his anger, gave the woman such a blow that she was laid up for a week; and she was pregnant at the time. Iván was delighted. He went to the magistrate to lodge a complaint. 'Now I'll get rid of my neighbour! He won't escape imprisonment, or exile to Siberia.' But Iván's wish was not fulfiled. The magistrate dismissed the case. The woman was examined, but she was up and about and showed no sign of any injury. Then Iván went to the Justice of the Peace, but he referred the business to the District Court. Iván bestirred himself: treated the clerk and the Elder of the District Court to a gallon of liquor and got Gabriel condemned to be flogged. The sentence was read out to Gabriel by the clerk: 'The Court decrees that the peasant Gabriel Gordéyef shall receive twenty lashes with a birch rod at the District Court.'

Iván too heard the sentence read, and looked at Gabriel to see how he would take it. Gabriel grew as pale as a sheet, and turned round and went out into the passage. Iván followed him, meaning to see to the horse, and he overheard Gabriel say, 'Very well! He will have my back flogged: that will make it burn; but something of his may burn worse than that!'

Hearing these words, Iván at once went back into the Court, and said: 'Upright judges! He threatens to set my house on fire! Listen: he said it in the presence of witnesses!'

Gabriel was recalled. 'Is it true that you said this?'

'I haven't said anything. Flog me, since you have the power. It seems that I alone am to suffer, and all for being in the right, while he is allowed to do as he likes.'

Gabriel wished to say something more, but his lips and his cheeks quivered, and he turned towards the wall. Even the officials were frightened by his looks. 'He may do some mischief to himself or to his neighbour,' thought they.

Then the old Judge said: 'Look here, my men; you'd better be reasonable and make it up. Was it right of you, friend Gabriel, to strike a pregnant woman? It was lucky it passed off so well, but think what might have happened! Was it right? You had better confess and beg his pardon, and he will forgive you, and we will alter the sentence.'

The clerk heard these words, and remarked: 'That's impossible under Statute 117. An agreement between the parties not having been arrived at, a decision of the Court has been pronounced and must be executed.'

But the Judge would not listen to the clerk.

'Keep your tongue still, my friend,' said he. 'The first of all laws is to obey God, who loves peace.' And the Judge began again to persuade the peasants, but could not succeed. Gabriel would not listen to him.

'I shall be fifty next year,' said he, 'and have a married son, and have never been flogged in my life, and now that pockmarked Iván has had me condemned to be flogged, and am I to go and ask his forgiveness? No; I've borne enough... Iván shall have cause to remember me!'

Again Gabriel's voice quivered, and he could say no more, but turned round and went out.

It was seven miles from the Court to the village, and it was getting late when Iván reached home. He unharnessed his horse, put it up for the night, and entered the cottage. No one was there. The women had already gone to drive the cattle in, and the young fellows were not yet back from the fields. Iván went in, and sat down, thinking. He remembered how Gabriel had listened to the sentence, and how pale he had become, and how he had turned to the wall; and Iván's heart grew heavy. He thought how he himself would feel if he were sentenced, and he pitied Gabriel. Then he heard his old father up on the oven cough, and saw him sit up, lower his legs, and scramble down. The old man dragged himself slowly to a seat and sat down. He was quite tired out with the exertion, and coughed a long time till he had cleared his throat. Then, leaning against the table, he said: 'Well, has he been condemned?'

'Yes, to twenty strokes with the rods,' answered Iván.

The old man shook his head.

'A bad business,' said he. 'You are doing wrong, Iván! Ah! it's very bad – not for him so much as for yourself! ... Well, they'll flog him: but will that do you any good?'

'He'll not do it again,' said Iván.

'What is it he'll not do again? What has he done worse than you?'

'Why, think of the harm he has done me!' said Iván. 'He nearly killed my wife, and now he's threatening to burn us up. Am I to thank him for it?'

The old man sighed, and said: 'You go about the wide world, Iván, while I am lying on the oven all these years, so you think you see everything, and that I see nothing... Ah, lad! It's you that don't see; malice blinds you. Others' sins are before your eyes, but your own are behind your back. "He's acted badly!" What a thing to say! If he were the only one to act badly, how could strife exist? Is strife among men ever bred by one alone? Strife is always between two. His badness you see, but your own you don't. If he were bad, but you were good, there would be no strife. Who pulled the hair out of his beard? Who spoilt his haystack? Who dragged him to the law court? Yet you put it all on him! You live a bad life yourself, that's what is wrong! It's not the way I used to live, lad, and it's not the way I taught you. Is that the way his old father and I used to live? How did we live? Why, as neighbours should! If he happened to run out of flour, one of the women would come across: "Uncle Trol, we want some flour." "Go to the barn, dear," I'd say: "take what you need." If he'd no one to take his horses to pasture, "Go, Iván," I'd say, "and look after his horses." And if I was short of anything, I'd go to him. "Uncle Gordéy," I'd say, "I want so-and-so!" "Take it Uncle Trol!" That's how it was between us, and we had an easy time of it. But now? ... That soldier the other day was telling us about the fight at Plevna[8]. Why, there's war between you worse than at Plevna! Is that living? ... What a sin it is! You are a man and master of the house; it's you who will have to answer. What are you teaching the women and the children? To snarl and snap? Why, the other day your Taráska – that greenhorn – was swearing at neighbour Irena, calling her names; and his mother listened and laughed. Is that right? It is you will have to answer. Think of your soul. Is this all as it should be? You throw a word at me, and I give you two in return; you give me a blow, and I give you two. No, lad! Christ, when He walked on earth, taught us fools something very different... If you get a hard word from anyone, keep silent, and his own conscience will accuse him. That is what our Lord taught. If you get a slap, turn the other cheek. "Here, beat me, if that's what I deserve!" And his own conscience will rebuke him. He will soften, and will listen to you. That's the way He taught us, not to be proud! ... Why don't you speak? Isn't it as I say?'

Iván sat silent and listened.

The old man coughed, and having with difficulty cleared his throat, began again: 'You think Christ taught us wrong? Why, it's all for our own good. Just think of your earthly life; are you better off, or worse, since this Plevna began among you? Just reckon up what you've spent on all this law business – what the driving backwards and forwards and your food on the way have cost you! What fine fellows your sons have grown; you might live and get on well; but now your means are lessening. And why? All because of this folly; because of your pride. You ought to be ploughing with your lads, and do the sowing yourself; but the fiend carries you off to the judge, or to some pettifogger or other. The ploughing is not done in time, nor the sowing, and mother earth

8 *A town in Bulgaria, the scene of fierce and prolonged fighting between the Turks and the Russians in the war of 1877.*

can't bear properly. Why did the oats fail this year? When did you sow them? When you came back from town! And what did you gain? A burden for your own shoulders... Eh, lad, think of your own business! Work with your boys in the field and at home, and if someone offends you, forgive him, as God wished you to. Then life will be easy, and your heart will always be light.'

Iván remained silent.

'Iván, my boy, hear your old father! Go and harness the roan, and go at once to the Government office; put an end to all this affair there; and in the morning go and make it up with Gabriel in God's name, and invite him to your house for tomorrow's holiday' (it was the eve of the Virgin's Nativity). 'Have tea ready, and get a bottle of vódka and put an end to this wicked business, so that there should not be any more of it in future, and tell the women and children to do the same.'

Iván sighed, and thought, 'What he says is true,' and his heart grew lighter. Only he did not know how, now, to begin to put matters right.

But again the old man began, as if he had guessed what was in Iván's mind.

'Go, Iván, don't put it off! Put out the fire before it spreads, or it will be too late.'

The old man was going to say more, but before he could do so the women came in, chattering like magpies. The news that Gabriel was sentenced to be flogged, and of his threat to set fire to the house, had already reached them. They had heard all about it and added to it something of their own, and had again had a row, in the pasture, with the women of Gabriel's household. They began telling how Gabriel's daughter-in-law threatened a fresh action: Gabriel had got the right side of the examining magistrate, who would now turn the whole affair upside down; and the schoolmaster was writing out another petition, to the Tsar himself this time, about Iván; and everything was in the petition – all about the coupling pin and the kitchen-garden – so that half of Iván's homestead would be theirs soon. Iván heard what they were saying, and his heart grew cold again, and he gave up the thought of making peace with Gabriel.

In a farmstead there is always plenty for the master to do. Iván did not stop to talk to the women, but went out to the threshing-floor and to the barn. By the time he had tidied up there, the sun had set and the young fellows had returned from the field. They had been ploughing the field for the winter crops with two horses. Iván met them, questioned them about their work, helped to put everything in its place, set a torn horse collar aside to be mended, and was going to put away some stakes under the barn, but it had grown quite dusk, so he decided to leave them where they were till next day. Then he gave the cattle their food, opened the gate, let out the horses Tarás was to take to pasture for the night, and again closed the gate and barred it. 'Now,' thought he, 'I'll have my supper, and then to bed.' He took the horse collar and entered the hut. By this time he had forgotten about Gabriel and about what his old father had been saying to him. But, just as he took hold of the door handle to enter the passage, he heard his neighbour on the other side of the fence cursing somebody in a hoarse voice: 'What the devil is he good for?' Gabriel was saying. 'He's only fit to be killed!' At these words all Iván's former bitterness towards his neighbour re-awoke. He stood listening while Gabriel scolded, and, when he stopped, Iván went into the hut.

There was a light inside; his daughter-in-law sat spinning, his wife was getting supper ready, his eldest son was making straps for bark shoes, his second sat near the table with a book, and Tarás was getting ready to go out to pasture the horses for the night. Everything in the hut would have been pleasant and bright, but for that plague – a bad neighbour!

Iván entered, sullen and cross; threw the cat down from the bench, and scolded the women for putting the slop-pail in the wrong place. He felt despondent, and sat down, frowning, to mend the horse collar. Gabriel's words kept ringing in his ears: his threat at the law court, and what he had just been shouting in a hoarse voice about someone who was 'only fit to be killed'.

His wife gave Tarás his supper, and, having eaten it, Tarás put on an old sheepskin and another coat, tied a sash round his waist, took some bread with him, and went out to the horses. His eldest brother was going to see him off, but Iván himself rose instead, and went out into the porch. It had grown quite dark outside, clouds had gathered, and the wind had risen. Iván went down the steps, helped his boy to mount, started the foal after him, and stood listening while Tarás rode down the village and was there joined by other lads with their horses. Iván waited until they were all out of hearing. As he stood there by the gate he could not get Gabriel's words out of his head: 'Mind that something of yours does not burn worse!'

'He is desperate,' thought Iván. 'Everything is dry, and it's windy weather besides. He'll come up at the back somewhere, set fire to something, and be off. He'll burn the place and escape scot-free, the villain! ... There now, if one could but catch him in the act, he'd not get off then!' And the thought fixed itself so firmly in his mind that he did not go up the steps but went out into the street and round the corner. I'll just walk round the buildings; who can tell what he's after?' And Iván, stepping softly, passed out of the gate. As soon as he reached the corner, he looked round along the fence, and seemed to see something suddenly move at the opposite corner, as if someone had come out and disappeared again. Iván stopped, and stood quietly, listening and looking. Everything was still; only the leaves of the willows fluttered in the wind, and the straws of the thatch rustled. At first it seemed pitch dark, but, when his eyes had grown used to the darkness, he could see the far corner, and a plough that lay there, and the eaves. He looked a while, but saw no one.

'I suppose it was a mistake,' thought Iván; 'but still I will go round,' and Iván went stealthily along by the shed. Iván stepped so softly in his bark shoes that he did not hear his own footsteps. As he reached the far corner, something seemed to flare up for a moment near the plough and to vanish again. Iván felt as if struck to the heart; and he stopped. Hardly had he stopped, when something flared up more brightly in the same place, and he clearly saw a man with a cap on his head, crouching down, with his back towards him, lighting a bunch of straw he held in his hand. Iván's heart fluttered within him like a bird. Straining every nerve, he approached with great strides, hardly feeling his legs under him. 'Ah,' thought Iván, 'now he won't escape! I'll catch him in the act!'

Iván was still some distance off, when suddenly he saw a bright light, but not in the same place as before, and not a small flame. The thatch had flared up at the eaves, the flames were reaching up to the roof, and, standing beneath it, Gabriel's whole figure was clearly visible.

Like a hawk swooping down on a lark, Iván rushed at Limping Gabriel. 'Now I'll have him; he shan't escape me!' thought Iván. But Gabriel must have heard his steps, and (however he managed it) glancing round, he scuttled away past the barn like a hare.

'You shan't escape!' shouted Iván, darting after him.

Just as he was going to seize Gabriel, the latter dodged him; but Iván managed to catch the skirt of Gabriel's coat. It tore right off, and Iván fell down. He recovered his feet, and shouting, 'Help! Seize him! Thieves! Murder!' ran on again. But meanwhile Gabriel had reached his own gate. There Iván overtook him and was about to seize him, when something struck Iván a stunning blow, as though a stone had hit his temple, quite deafening him. It was Gabriel who, seizing an oak wedge that lay near the gate, had struck out with all his might.

Iván was stunned; sparks flew before his eyes, then all grew dark and he staggered. When he came to his senses Gabriel was no longer there: it was as light as day, and from the side where his homestead was, something roared and crackled like an engine at work. Iván turned round and saw that his back shed was all ablaze, and the side shed had also caught fire, and flames and smoke and bits of burning straw mixed with the smoke, were being driven towards his hut.

'What is this, friends? …' cried Iván, lifting his arms and striking his thighs. 'Why, all I had to do was just to snatch it out from under the eaves and trample on it! What is this, friends? ...' he kept repeating. He wished to shout, but his breath failed him; his voice was gone. He wanted to run, but his legs would not obey him, and got in each other's way. He moved slowly, but again staggered and again his breath failed. He stood still till he had regained breath, and then went on. Before he had got round the back shed to reach the fire, the side shed was also all ablaze; and the corner of the hut and the covered gateway had caught fire as well. The flames were leaping out of the hut, and it was impossible to get into the yard. A large crowd had collected, but nothing could be done. The neighbours were carrying their belongings out of their own houses, and driving the cattle out of their own sheds. After Iván's house, Gabriel's also caught fire, then, the wind rising, the flames spread to the other side of the street and half the village was burnt down.

At Iván's house they barely managed to save his old father; and the family escaped in what they had on; everything else, except the horses that had been driven out to pasture for the night, was lost; all the cattle, the fowls on their perches, the carts, ploughs, and harrows, the women's trunks with their clothes, and the grain in the granaries – all were burnt up!

At Gabriel's, the cattle were driven out, and a few things saved from his house.

The fire lasted all night. Iván stood in front of his homestead and kept repeating, 'What is this? ... Friends! ... One need only have pulled it out and trampled on it!' But when the roof fell in, Iván rushed into the burning place, and seizing a charred beam, tried to drag it out. The women saw him, and called him back; but he pulled out the beam, and was going in again for another when he lost his footing and fell among the flames. Then his son made his way in after him and dragged him out. Iván had singed his hair and beard and burnt his clothes and scorched his hands, but he felt nothing. 'His grief has stupefied him,' said the people. The fire was burning itself out, but Iván still stood repeating:

'Friends! ... What is this? ... One need only have pulled it out!'

In the morning the village Elder's son came to fetch Iván.

'Daddy Iván, your father is dying! He has sent for you to say goodbye.'

Iván had forgotten about his father, and did not understand what was being said to him.

'What father?' he said. 'Whom has he sent for?'

'He sent for you, to say goodbye; he is dying in our cottage! Come along, daddy Iván,' said the Elder's son, pulling him by the arm; and Iván followed the lad.

When he was being carried out of the hut, some burning straw had fallen on to the old man and burnt him, and he had been taken to the village Elder's in the farther part of the village, which the fire did not reach.

When Iván came to his father, there was only the Elder's wife in the hut, besides some little children on the top of the oven. All the rest were still at the fire. The old man, who was lying on a bench holding a wax candle[9] in his hand, kept turning his eyes towards the door. When his son entered, he moved a little. The old woman went up to him and told him that his son had come. He asked to have him brought nearer. Iván came closer.

'What did I tell you, Iván?' began the old man. 'Who has burnt down the village?'

'It was he, father!' Iván answered. 'I caught him in the act. I saw him shove the firebrand into the thatch. I might have pulled away the burning straw and stamped it out, and then nothing would have happened.'

'Iván,' said the old man, 'I am dying, and you in your turn will have to face death. Whose is the sin?'

Iván gazed at his father in silence, unable to utter a word.

'Now, before God, say whose is the sin? What did I tell you?'

---

9 Wax candles are much used in the services of the Russian Church, and it is usual to place one in the hand of a dying man, especially when he receives unction.

Only then Iván came to his senses and understood it all. He sniffed and said, 'Mine, father!' And he fell on his knees before his father, saying, 'Forgive me, father; I am guilty before you and before God.'

The old man moved his hands, changed the candle from his right hand to his left, and tried to lift his right hand to his forehead to cross himself, but could not do it, and stopped.

'Praise the Lord! Praise the Lord!' said he, and again he turned his eyes towards his son.

'Iván! I say, Iván!'

'What, father?'

'What must you do now?'

Iván was weeping.

'I don't know how we are to live now, father!' he said.

The old man closed his eyes, moved his lips as if to gather strength, and opening his eyes again, said: 'You'll manage. If you obey God's will, you'll manage!' He paused, then smiled, and said: 'Mind, Iván! Don't tell who started the fire! Hide another man's sin, and God will forgive two of yours!' And the old man took the candle in both hands and, folding them on his breast, sighed, stretched out, and died.

Iván did not say anything against Gabriel, and no one knew what had caused the fire.

And Iván's anger against Gabriel passed away, and Gabriel wondered that Iván did not tell anybody. At first Gabriel felt afraid, but after awhile he got used to it. The men left off quarrelling, and then their families left off also. While rebuilding their huts, both families lived in one house; and when the village was rebuilt and they might have moved farther apart, Iván and Gabriel built next to each other, and remained neighbours as before.

They lived as good neighbours should. Iván Stcherbakóf remembered his old father's command to obey God's law, and quench a fire at the first spark; and if anyone does him an injury he now tries not to revenge himself, but rather to set matters right again; and if anyone gives him a bad word, instead of giving a worse in return, he tries to teach the other not to use evil words; and so he teaches his womenfolk and children. And Iván Stcherbakóf has got on his feet again, and now lives better even than he did before.

TWO OLD MEN

I

'The woman saith unto him, "Sir, I perceive that thou art a prophet. Our fathers worshiped in this mountain; and ye say, that in Jerusalem is the place where men ought to worship." Jesus saith unto her, "Woman, believe me, the hour cometh when neither in this mountain, nor in Jerusalem, shall ye worship the Father ... But the hour cometh, and now is, when the true worshippers shall worship the Father in spirit and truth: for such doth the Father seek to be his worshippers."' (John 4: 19-21, 23).

There were once two old men who decided to go on a pilgrimage to worship God at Jerusalem. One of them was a well-to-do peasant named Efím Tarásitch Shevélef. The other, Elisha Bódrof, was not so well off.

Efím was a staid man, serious and firm. He neither drank nor smoked nor took snuff, and had never used bad language in his life. He had twice served as village Elder, and when he left office his accounts were in good order. He had a large family: two sons and a married grandson, all living with him. He was hale, long-bearded and erect, and it was only when he was past sixty that a little grey began to show itself in his beard.

Elisha was neither rich nor poor. He had formerly gone out carpentering, but now that he was growing old he stayed at home and kept bees. One of his sons had gone away to find work, the other was living at home. Elisha was a kindly and cheerful old man. It is true he drank sometimes, and he took snuff, and was fond of singing; but he was a peaceable man, and lived on good terms with his family and with his neighbours. He was short and dark, with a curly beard, and, like his patron saint Elisha, he was quite bald-headed.

The two old men had taken a vow long since and had arranged to go on a pilgrimage to Jerusalem together: but Efím could never spare the time; he always had so much business on hand; as soon as one thing was finished he started another. First he had to arrange his grandson's marriage; then to wait for his youngest son's return from the army, and after that he began building a new hut.

One holiday the two old men met outside the hut and, sitting down on some timber, began to talk.

'Well,' asked Elisha, 'when are we to fulfil our vow?'

Efím made a wry face.

'We must wait,' he said. 'This year has turned out a hard one for me. I started building this hut thinking it would cost me something over a hundred roubles, but now it's getting on for three hundred and it's still not finished. We shall have to wait till the summer. In summer, God willing, we will go without fail.'

'It seems to me we ought not to put it off, but should go at once,' said Elisha. 'Spring is the best time.'

'The time's right enough, but what about my building? How can I leave that?'

'As if you had no one to leave in charge! Your son can look after it.'

'But how? My eldest son is not trustworthy – he sometimes takes a glass too much.'

'Ah, neighbour, when we die they'll get on without us. Let your son begin now to get some experience.'

'That's true enough; but somehow when one begins a thing one likes to see it done.'

'Eh, friend, we can never get through all we have to do. The other day the women-folk at home were washing and housecleaning for Easter. Here something needed doing, there something else, and they could not get everything done. So my eldest daughter-in-law, who's a sensible woman, says: 'We may be thankful the holiday comes without waiting for us, or however hard we worked we should never be ready for it.'

Efím became thoughtful.

'I've spent a lot of money on this building,' he said, 'and one can't start on the journey with empty pockets. We shall want a hundred roubles apiece – and it's no small sum.'

Elisha laughed.

'Now, come, come, old friend!' he said, 'you have ten times as much as I, and yet you talk about money. Only say when we are to start, and though I have nothing now I shall have enough by then.'

Efím also smiled.

'Dear me, I did not know you were so rich!' said he. 'Why, where will you get it from?'

'I can scrape some together at home, and if that's not enough, I'll sell half a score of hives to my neighbour. He's long been wanting to buy them.'

'If they swarm well this year, you'll regret it.'

'Regret it! Not I, neighbour! I never regretted anything in my life, except my sins. There's nothing more precious than the soul.'

'That's so; still it's not right to neglect things at home.'

'But what if our souls are neglected? That's worse. We took the vow, so let us go! Now, seriously, let us go!'

II

Elisha succeeded in persuading his comrade. In the morning, after thinking it well over, Efím came to Elisha.

'You are right,' said he, 'let us go. Life and death are in God's hands. We must go now, while we are still alive and have the strength.'

A week later the old men were ready to start. Efím had money enough at hand. He took a hundred roubles himself, and left two hundred with his wife.

Elisha, too, got ready. He sold ten hives to his neighbour, with any new swarms that might come from them before the summer. He took seventy roubles for the lot. The rest of the hundred roubles he scraped together from the other members of his household, fairly clearing them all out. His wife gave him all she had been saving up for her funeral; and his daughter-in-law also gave him what she had.

Efím gave his eldest son definite orders about everything: when and how much grass to mow, where to cart the manure, and how to finish off and roof the cottage. He thought out everything, and gave his orders accordingly. Elisha, on the other hand, only explained to his wife that she was to keep separate the swarms from the hives he had sold, and to be sure to let the neighbour have them all, without any tricks. As to household affairs, he did not even mention them.

'You will see what to do and how to do it, as the needs arise,' he said. 'You are the masters, and will know how to do what's best for yourselves.'

So the old men got ready. Their people baked them cakes, and made bags for them, and cut them linen for leg-bands.[10] They put on new leather shoes, and took with them spare shoes of platted bark. Their families went with them to the end of the village and there took leave of them, and the old men started on their pilgrimage.

Elisha left home in a cheerful mood, and as soon as he was out of the village forgot all his home affairs. His only cares were how to please his comrade, how to avoid saying a rude word to anyone, how to get to his destination and home again in peace and love. Walking along the road, Elisha would either whisper some prayer to himself or go over in his mind such of the lives of the saints as he was able to remember. When he came across

10 *Worn by Russian peasants instead of stockings.*

anyone on the road, or turned in anywhere for the night, he tried to behave as gently as possible and to say a godly word. So he journeyed on, rejoicing. One thing only he could not do, he could not give up taking snuff. Though he had left his snuff box behind, he hankered after it. Then a man he met on the road gave him some snuff; and every now and then he would lag behind (not to lead his comrade into temptation) and would take a pinch of snuff.

Efím too walked well and firmly; doing no wrong and speaking no vain words, but his heart was not so light. Household cares weighed on his mind. He kept worrying about what was going on at home. Had he not forgotten to give his son this or that order? Would his son do things properly? If he happened to see potatoes being planted or manure carted, as he went along, he wondered if his son was doing as he had been told. And he almost wanted to turn back and show him how to do things, or even do them himself.

III

The old men had been walking for five weeks; they had worn out their home-made bark shoes, and had to begin buying new ones when they reached Little Russia.[11] From the time they left home they had had to pay for their food and for their night's lodging, but when they reached Little Russia the people vied with one another in asking them into their huts. They took them in and fed them, and would accept no payment; and more than that, they put bread or even cakes into their bags for them to eat on the road.

The old men travelled some five hundred miles in this manner free of expense, but after they had crossed the next province, they

11 *Little Russia is situated in the south-western part of Russia, and consists of the Governments of Kiev, Poltava, Tchernigov, and part of Kharkov and Kherson.*

came to a district where the harvest had failed. The peasants still gave them free lodging at night, but no longer fed them for nothing. Sometimes, even, they could get no bread: they offered to pay for it, but there was none to be had. The people said the harvest had completely failed the year before. Those who had been rich were ruined and had had to sell all they possessed; those of moderate means were left destitute, and those of the poor who had not left those parts, wandered about begging, or starved at home in utter want. In the winter they had had to eat husks and goosefoot.

One night, the old men stopped in a small village; they bought fifteen pounds of bread, slept there, and started before sunrise, to get well on their way before the heat of the day. When they had gone some eight miles, on coming to a stream they sat down, and, filling a bowl with water, they steeped some bread in it, and ate it. Then they changed their leg-bands, and rested for a while. Elisha took out his snuff box. Efím shook his head at him.

'How is it you don't give up that nasty habit?' said he.

Elisha waved his hand. 'The evil habit is stronger than I,' he said.

Presently they got up and went on. After walking for nearly another eight miles, they came to a large village and passed right through it. It had now grown hot. Elisha was tired out and wanted to rest and have a drink, but Efím did not stop. Efím was the better walker of the two, and Elisha found it hard to keep up with him.

'If I could only have a drink,' said he.

'Well, have a drink,' said Efím. 'I don't want any.'

Elisha stopped.

'You go on,' he said, 'but I'll just run in to the little hut there. I will catch you up in a moment.'

'All right,' said Efím, and he went on along the high road alone, while Elisha turned back to the hut.

It was a small hut plastered with clay, the bottom a dark colour, the top whitewashed; but the clay had crumbled away. Evidently it was long since it had been re-plastered, and the thatch was off the roof on one side. The entrance to the hut was through the yard. Elisha entered the yard, and saw, lying close to a bank of earth that ran round the hut, a gaunt, beardless man with his shirt tucked into his trousers, as is the custom in Little Russia.[12] The man must have lain down in the shade, but the sun had come round and now shone full on him. Though not asleep, he still lay there. Elisha called to him, and asked for a drink, but the man gave no answer.

'He is either ill or unfriendly,' thought Elisha; and going to the door he heard a child crying in the hut. He took hold of the ring that served as a door handle, and knocked with it.

'Hey, masters!' he called. No answer. He knocked again with his staff.

'Hey, Christians!' Nothing stirred.

'Hey, servants of God!' Still no reply.

Elisha was about to turn away, when he thought he heard a groan the other side of the door.

'Dear me, some misfortune must have happened to the people? I had better have a look.'

And Elisha entered the hut.

IV

Elisha turned the ring; the door was not fastened. He opened it and went along up the narrow passage. The door into the dwelling-room was open. To the left was a brick oven; in front against the wall was an icon stand[13] and a table before it; by the table was a bench on which sat an old woman, bareheaded and wearing only a single garment. There she sat with her head resting on the table,

12 *In Great Russia the peasants let their shirt hang outside their trousers.*
13 *An icon (properly ikón) is a representation of God, Christ, an angel, or a saint, usually painted, enamelled or embossed.*

and near her was a thin, wax-coloured boy, with a protruding stomach. He was asking for something, pulling at her sleeve, and crying bitterly. Elisha entered. The air in the hut was very foul. He looked round, and saw a woman lying on the floor behind the oven: she lay flat on the ground with her eyes closed and her throat rattling, now stretching out a leg, now dragging it in, tossing from side to side; and the foul smell came from her. Evidently she could do nothing for herself and no one had been attending to her needs. The old woman lifted her head, and saw the stranger.

'What do you want?' said she. 'What do you want man? We have nothing.'

Elisha understood her, though she spoke in the Little-Russian dialect.

'I came in for a drink of water, servant of God,' he said.

'There's no one – no one – we have nothing to fetch it in. Go your way.'

Then Elisha asked:

'Is there no one among you, then, well enough to attend to that woman?'

'No, we have no one. My son is dying outside, and we are dying in here.'

The little boy had ceased crying when he saw the stranger, but when the old woman began to speak, he began again, and clutching hold of her sleeve cried:

'Bread, Granny, bread.'

Elisha was about to question the old woman, when the man staggered into the hut. He came along the passage, clinging to the wall, but as he was entering the dwelling-room he fell in the corner near the threshold, and without trying to get up again to reach the bench, he began to speak in broken words. He brought out a word at a time, stopping to draw breath, and gasping.

'Illness has seized us ... ,' said he, 'and famine. He is dying ... of hunger.'

And he motioned towards the boy, and began to sob.

Elisha jerked up the sack behind his shoulder and, pulling the straps off his arms, put it on the floor. Then he lifted it on to the bench, and untied the strings. Having opened the sack, he took out a loaf of bread, and, cutting off a piece with his knife, handed it to the man. The man would not take it, but pointed to the little boy and to a little girl crouching behind the oven, as if to say:

'Give it to them.'

Elisha held it out to the boy. When the boy smelt bread, he stretched out his arms, and seizing the slice with both his little hands, bit into it so that his nose disappeared in the chunk. The little girl came out from behind the oven and fixed her eyes on the bread. Elisha gave her also a slice. Then he cut off another piece and gave it to the old woman, and she too began munching it.

'If only some water could be brought,' she said, 'their mouths are parched. I tried to fetch some water yesterday – or was it today – I can't remember, but I fell down and could go no further, and the pail has remained there, unless someone has taken it.'

Elisha asked where the well was. The old woman told him. Elisha went out, found the pail, brought some water, and gave the people a drink. The children and the old woman ate some more bread with the water, but the man would not eat.

'I cannot eat,' he said.

All this time the younger woman did not show any consciousness, but continued to toss from side to side. Presently Elisha went to the village shop and bought some millet, salt, flour and oil. He found an axe, chopped some wood, and made a fire. The little girl came and helped him. Then he boiled some soup, and gave the starving people a meal.

V

The man ate a little, the old woman had some too, and the little girl and boy licked the bowl clean, and then curled up and fell fast asleep in one another's arms.

The man and the old woman then began telling Elisha how they had sunk to their present state.

'We were poor enough before?' said they, 'but when the crops failed, what we gathered hardly lasted us through the autumn. We had nothing left by the time winter came, and had to beg from the neighbours and from anyone we could. At first they gave, then they began to refuse. Some would have been glad enough to help us, but had nothing to give. And we were ashamed of asking: we were in debt all round, and owed money, and flour, and bread.'

'I went to look for work,' the man said, 'but could find none. Everywhere people were offering to work merely for their own keep. One day you'd get a short job, and then you might spend two days looking for work. Then the old woman and the girl went begging, further away. But they got very little; bread was so scarce. Still we scraped food together somehow, and hoped to struggle through till next harvest, but towards spring people ceased to give anything. And then this illness seized us. Things became worse and worse. One day we might have something to eat, and then nothing for two days. We began eating grass. Whether it was the grass, or what, made my wife ill, I don't know. She could not keep on her legs, and I had no strength left, and there was nothing to help us to recovery.'

'I struggled on alone for a while,' said the old woman, 'but at last I broke down too for want of food, and grew quite weak. The girl also grew weak and timid. I told her to go to the neighbours – she would not leave the hut, but crept into a corner and sat there. The day before yesterday a neighbour looked in, but seeing that we were ill and hungry she turned away and left us. Her husband has had to go away, and she has nothing for her own little ones to eat. And so we lay, waiting for death.'

Having heard their story, Elisha gave up the thought of overtaking his comrade that day, and remained with them all night. In the morning he got up and began doing the housework, just as if it were his own home. He kneaded the bread with the old woman's help, and lit the fire. Then he went with the little girl to the neighbours to get the most necessary things; for there was nothing in the hut: everything had been sold for bread – cooking utensils, clothing, and all. So Elisha began replacing what was necessary, making some things himself, and buying some. He remained there one day, then another, and then a third. The little boy picked up strength and, whenever Elisha sat down, crept along the bench and nestled up to him. The little girl brightened up and helped in all the work, running after Elisha and calling,

'Daddy, daddy.'

The old woman grew stronger, and managed to go out to see a neighbour. The man too improved, and was able to get about, holding on to the wall. Only the wife could not get up, but even she regained consciousness on the third day, and asked for food.

'Well,' thought Elisha, 'I never expected to waste so much time on the way. Now I must be getting on.'

VI

The fourth day was the feast day after the summer fast, and Elisha thought:

'I will stay and break the fast with these people. I'll go and buy them something, and keep the feast with them, and tomorrow evening I will start.'

So Elisha went into the village, bought milk, wheat flour and dripping, and helped the old woman to boil and bake for the morrow. On the feast day Elisha went to church, and then broke the fast with his friends at the hut. That day the wife got up, and managed to move about a bit. The husband had shaved and put on a clean shirt, which the old woman had washed for him; and he went to beg for mercy of a rich peasant in the village to whom his ploughland and meadow were mortgaged. He went to beg the rich peasant to grant him the use of the meadow and field till after the harvest; but in the evening he came back very sad, and began to weep. The rich peasant had shown no mercy, but had said: 'Bring me the money.'

Elisha again grew thoughtful. 'How are they to live now?' thought he to himself. 'Other people will go haymaking, but there will be nothing for these to mow, their grassland is mortgaged. The rye will ripen. Others will reap (and what a fine crop Mother Earth is giving this year), but they have nothing to look forward to. Their three acres are pledged to the rich peasant. When I am gone, they'll drift back into the state I found them in.'

Elisha was in two minds, but finally decided not to leave that evening, but to wait until the morrow. He went out into the yard to sleep. He said his prayers, and lay down; but he could not sleep. On the one hand he felt he ought to be going, for he had spent too much time and money as it was; on the other hand he felt sorry for the people.

'There seems to be no end to it, he said. 'First I only meant to bring them a little water and give them each a slice of bread: and just see where it has landed me. It's a case of redeeming the meadow and the cornfield. And when I have done that, I shall have to buy a cow for them, and a horse for the man to cart his sheaves. A nice coil you've got yourself into, brother Elisha! You've slipped your cables and lost your reckoning!'

Elisha got up, lifted his coat which he had been using for a pillow, unfolded it, got out his snuff box and took a pinch, thinking that it might perhaps clear his thoughts.

But no! He thought and thought, and came to no conclusion. He ought to be going; and yet pity held him back. He did not know what to do. He refolded his coat and put it under his head again. He lay thus for a long time, till the cocks had already crowed once: then he was quite drowsy. And suddenly it seemed as if someone had roused him. He saw that he was dressed for the journey, with the sack on his back and the staff in his hand, and the gate stood ajar so that he could just squeeze through. He was about to pass out, when his sack caught against the fence on one side: he tried to free it, but then his leg band caught on the other side and came undone. He pulled at the sack, and saw that it had not caught on the fence, but that the little girl was holding it and crying,

'Bread, daddy, bread!'

He looked at his foot, and there was the tiny boy holding him by the leg-band, while the master of the hut and the old woman were looking at him through the window.

Elisha awoke, and said to himself in an audible voice:

'Tomorrow I will redeem their cornfield, and will buy them a horse, and flour to last till the harvest, and a cow for the little ones; or else while I go to seek the Lord beyond the sea, I may lose Him in myself.'

Then Elisha fell asleep, and slept till morning. He awoke early, and going to the rich peasant, redeemed both the cornfield and the meadow land. He bought a scythe (for that also had been sold) and brought it back with him. Then he sent the man to mow, and himself went into the village. He heard that there was a horse and cart for sale at the public house, and he struck a bargain with the owner, and bought them. Then he bought a sack of flour, put it in the cart, and went to see about a cow. As he was going along he overtook two women talking as they went. Though they spake the Little-Russian dialect, he understood what they were saying.

'At first, it seems, they did not know him; they thought he was just an ordinary man. He came in to ask for a drink of water, and then he remained. Just think of the things he has bought for them! Why they say he bought a horse and cart for them at the publican's, only this morning! There are not many such men in the world. It's worth while going to have a look at him.'

Elisha heard and understood that he was being praised, and he did not go to buy the cow, but returned to the inn, paid for the horse, harnessed it, drove up to the hut, and got out. The people in the hut were astonished when they saw the horse. They thought it might be for them, but dared not ask. The man came out to open the gate.

'Where did you get a horse from, grandfather,' he asked.

'Why, I bought it,' said Elisha. 'It was going cheap. Go and cut some grass and put it in the manger for it to eat during the night. And take in the sack.'

The man unharnessed the horse, and carried the sack into the barn. Then he mowed some grass and put it in the manger. Everybody lay down to sleep. Elisha went outside and lay by the roadside. That evening he took his bag out with him. When everyone was asleep, he got up, packed and fastened his bag, wrapped the linen bands round his legs, put on his shoes and coat, and set off to follow Efím.

VII

When Elisha had walked rather more than three miles it began to grow light. He sat down under a tree, opened his bag, counted his money, and found he had only seventeen roubles and twenty kopeks left.

'Well,' thought he, 'it is no use trying to cross the sea with this. If I beg my way it may be worse than not going at all. Friend Efím will get to Jerusalem without me, and will place a candle at the shrines in my name. As for me, I'm afraid I shall never fulfil my vow in this life. I must be thankful it was made to a merciful Master, and to one who pardons sinners.'

Elisha rose, jerked his bag well up on his shoulders, and turned back. Not wishing to be recognized by anyone, he made a circuit to avoid the village, and walked briskly homeward. Coming from home the way had seemed difficult to him, and he had found it hard to keep up with Efím, but now on his return journey, God helped him to get over the ground so that he hardly felt fatigue. Walking seemed like child's play. He went along swinging his staff, and did his forty to fifty miles a day.

When Elisha reached home the harvest was over. His family

were delighted to see him again, and all wanted to know what had happened: Why and how he had been left behind? And why he had returned without reaching Jerusalem? But Elisha did not tell them.

'It was not God's will that I should get there,' said he. 'I lost my money on the way, and lagged behind my companion. Forgive me, for the Lord's sake!'

Elisha gave his old wife what money he had left. Then he questioned them about home affairs. Everything was going on well; all the work had been done, nothing neglected, and all were living in peace and concord.

Efím's family heard of his return the same day, and came for news of their old man; and to them Elisha gave the same answers.

'Efím is a fast walker. We parted three days before St. Peter's day, and I meant to catch him up again, but all sorts of things happened. I lost my money, and had no means to get any further, so I turned back.'

The folks were astonished that so sensible a man should have acted so foolishly: should have started and not got to his destination, and should have squandered all his money. They wondered at it for a while, and then forgot all about it; and Elisha forgot it too. He set to work again on his homestead. With his son's help he cut wood for fuel for the winter. He and the women threshed the corn. Then he mended the thatch on the outhouses, put the bees under cover, and handed over to his neighbour the ten hives he had sold him in spring, and all the swarms that had come from them. His wife tried not to tell how many swarms there had been from these hives, but Elisha knew well enough from which there had been swarms and from which not. And instead of ten, he handed over seventeen swarms to his neighbour. Having got everything ready for the winter, Elisha sent his son away to find work, while he himself took to platting shoes of bark, and hollowing out logs for hives.

VIII

All that day while Elisha stopped behind in the hut with the sick people, Efím waited for him. He only went on a little way before he sat down. He waited and waited, had a nap, woke up again, and again sat waiting; but his comrade did not come. He gazed till his eyes ached. The sun was already sinking behind a tree, and still no Elisha was to be seen.

'Perhaps he has passed me,' thought Efím, 'or perhaps someone gave him a lift and he drove by while I slept, and did not see me. But how could he help seeing me? One can see so far here in the steppe. Shall I go back? Suppose he is on in front, we shall then miss each other completely and it will be still worse. I had better go on, and we shall be sure to meet where we put up for the night.'

He came to a village, and told the watchman, if an old man of a certain description came along, to bring him to the hut where Efím stopped. But Elisha did not turn up that night. Efím went on, asking all he met whether they had not seen a little, bald-headed, old man? No one had seen such a traveller. Efím wondered, but went on alone, saying:

'We shall be sure to meet in Odessa, or on board the ship,' and he did not trouble more about it.

On the way, he came across a pilgrim wearing a priest's coat, with long hair and a skull cap such as priests wear. This pilgrim had been to Mount Athos, and was now going to Jerusalem for the second time. They both stopped at the same place one night, and, having met, they travelled on together.

They got safely to Odessa, and there had to wait three days for a ship. Many pilgrims from many different parts were in the same case. Again Efím asked about Elisha, but no one had seen him.

Efím got himself a foreign passport, which cost him five roubles. He paid forty roubles for a return ticket to Jerusalem, and bought a supply of bread and herrings for the voyage.

The pilgrim began explaining to Efím how he might get on to the ship without paying his fare; but Efím would not listen. 'No, I came prepared to pay, and I shall pay,' said he.

The ship was freighted, and the pilgrims went on board, Efím and his new comrade among them. The anchors were weighed, and the ship put out to sea.

All day they sailed smoothly, but towards night a wind arose, rain came on, and the vessel tossed about and shipped water. The people were frightened: the women wailed and screamed, and some of the weaker men ran about the ship looking for shelter. Efím too was frightened, but he would not show it, and remained at the place on deck where he had settled down when first he came on board, beside some old men from Tambóf. There they sat silent, all night and all next day, holding on to their sacks. On the third day it grew calm, and on the fifth day they anchored at Constantinople. Some of the pilgrims went on shore to visit the Church of St. Sophia, now held by the Turks. Efím remained on the ship, and only bought some white bread. They lay there for twenty-four hours, and then put to sea again. At Smyrna they stopped again; and at Alexandria; but at last they arrived safely at Jaffa, where all the pilgrims had to disembark. From there still it was more than forty miles by road to Jerusalem. When disembarking the people were again much frightened. The ship was high, and the people were dropped into boats, which rocked so much that it was easy to miss them and fall into the water. A couple of men did get a wetting, but at last all were safely landed.

They went on on foot, and at noon on the third day reached Jerusalem. They stopped outside the town, at the Russian inn, where their passports were indorsed. Then, after dinner, Efím visited the Holy Places with his companion, the pilgrim. It was not the time when they could be admitted to the Holy Sepulchre, but they went to the Patriarchate. All the pilgrims assembled there. The women were separated from the men, who were all told to sit in a circle, barefoot. Then a monk came in with a towel to wash their feet. He washed, wiped, and then kissed their feet, and did this to everyone in the circle. Efím's feet were washed and kissed, with the rest. He stood through vespers and matins, prayed, placed candles at the shrines, and handed in booklets inscribed with his parents' names, that they might be mentioned in the church prayers. Here at the Patriarchate food and wine were given them. Next morning they went to the cell of Mary of Egypt, where she had lived doing penance. Here too they placed candles and had prayers read. From there they went to Abraham's Monastery, and saw the place where Abraham intended to slay his son as an offering to God. Then they visited the spot where Christ appeared to Mary Magdalene, and the Church of James, the Lord's brother. The pilgrim showed Efím all these places, and told him how much money to give at each place. At midday they returned to the inn and had dinner. As they were preparing to lie down and rest, the pilgrim cried out, and began to search his clothes, feeling them all over.

'My purse has been stolen, there were twenty-three roubles in it,' said he, 'two ten-rouble notes and the rest in change.'

He sighed and lamented a great deal, but as there was no help for it, they lay down to sleep.

IX

As Efím lay there, he was assailed by temptation.

'No one has stolen any money from this pilgrim,' thought he, 'I do not believe he had any. He gave none away anywhere, though he made me give, and even borrowed a rouble of me.'

This thought had no sooner crossed his mind, than Efím rebuked himself, saying: 'What right have I to judge a man? It is a sin. I will think no more about it.' But as soon as his thoughts began to wander, they turned again to the pilgrim: how interested he seemed to be in money, and how unlikely it sounded when he declared that his purse had been stolen.

'He never had any money,' thought Efím. 'It's all an invention.'

Towards evening they got up, and went to midnight Mass at

the great Church of the Resurrection, where the Lord's Sepulchre is. The pilgrim kept close to Efím and went with him everywhere. They came to the Church; a great many pilgrims were there; some Russians and some of other nationalities: Greeks, Armenians, Turks and Syrians. Efím entered the Holy Gates with the crowd. A monk led them past the Turkish sentinels, to the place where the Saviour was taken down from the cross and anointed, and where candles were burning in nine great candlesticks. The monk showed and explained everything. Efím offered a candle there. Then the monk led Efím to the right, up the steps to Golgotha, to the place where the cross had stood. Efím prayed there. Then they showed him the cleft where the ground had been rent asunder to its nethermost depths; then the place where Christ's hands and feet were nailed to the cross; then Adam's tomb, where the blood of Christ had dripped on to Adam's bones. Then they showed him the stone on which Christ sat when the crown of thorns was placed on His head; then the post to which Christ was bound when He was scourged. Then Efím saw the stone with two holes for Christ's feet. They were going to show him something else, but there was a stir in the crowd, and the people all hurried to the church of the Lord's Sepulchre itself. The Latin Mass had just finished there, and the Russian Mass was beginning. And Efím went with the crowd to the tomb cut in the rock.

He tried to get rid of the pilgrim, against whom he was still sinning in his mind, but the pilgrim would not leave him, but went with him to the Mass at the Holy Sepulchre. They tried to get to the front, but were too late. There was such a crowd that it was impossible to move either backwards or forwards. Efím stood looking in front of him, praying, and every now and then feeling for his purse. He was in two minds: sometimes he thought that the pilgrim was deceiving him, and then again he thought that if the pilgrim spoke the truth and his purse had really been stolen, the same thing might happen to himself.

X

Efím stood there gazing into the little chapel in which was the
Holy Sepulchre itself with thirty-six lamps burning above it. As
he stood looking over the people's heads, he saw something that
surprised him. Just beneath the lamps in which the sacred fire
burns, and in front of everyone, Efím saw an old man in a grey
coat, whose bald, shining head was just like Elisha Bódrof.

'It is like him,' thought Efím, 'but it cannot be Elisha. He
could not have got ahead of me. The ship before ours started a
week sooner. He could not have caught that; and he was not on
ours, for I saw every pilgrim on board.'

Hardly had Efím thought this, when the little old man began
to pray, and bowed three times: once forwards to God, then once
on each side – to the brethren. And as he turned his head to the
right, Efím recognized him. It was Elisha Bódrof himself, with
his dark, curly beard turning grey at the cheeks, with his brows,
his eyes and nose, and his expression of face. Yes, it was he!

Efím was very pleased to have found his comrade again, and
wondered how Elisha had got ahead of him.

'Well done, Elisha!' thought he. 'See how he has pushed ahead.
He must have come across someone who showed him the way.
When we get out, I will find him, get rid of this fellow in the
skull cap, and keep to Elisha. Perhaps he will show me how to
get to the front also.'

Efím kept looking out, so as not to lose sight of Elisha. But
when the Mass was over, the crowd began to sway, pushing forward
to kiss the tomb, and pushed Efím aside. He was again seized
with fear lest his purse should be stolen. Pressing it with his hand,
he began elbowing through the crowd, anxious only to get out.
When he reached the open, he went about for a long time
searching for Elisha both outside and in the Church itself. In the
cells of the Church he saw many people of all kinds, eating, and
drinking wine, and reading and sleeping there. But Elisha was
nowhere to be seen. So Efím returned to the inn without having

found his comrade. That evening the pilgrim in the skull cap did not turn up. He had gone off without repaying the rouble, and Efím was left alone.

The next day Efím went to the Holy Sepulchre again, with an old man from Tambóf, whom he had met on the ship. He tried to get to the front, but was again pressed back; so he stood by a pillar and prayed. He looked before him, and there in the foremost place under the lamps, close to the very Sepulchre of the Lord, stood Elisha, with his arms spread out like a priest at the altar, and with his bald head all shining.

'Well, now,' thought Efím, 'I won't lose him!'

He pushed forward to the front, but when he got there, there was no Elisha: he had evidently gone away.

Again on the third day Efím looked, and saw at the Sepulchre, in the holiest place, Elisha standing in the sight of all men, his arms outspread, and his eyes gazing upwards as if he saw something above. And his bald head was all shining.

'Well, this time,' thought Efím, 'he shall not escape me! I will go and stand at the door, then we can't miss one another!'

Efím went out and stood by the door till past noon. Everyone had passed out, but still Elisha did not appear.

Efím remained six weeks in Jerusalem, and went everywhere: to Bethlehem, and to Bethany, and to the Jordan. He had a new shirt sealed at the Holy Sepulchre for his burial, and he took a bottle of water from the Jordan, and some holy earth, and bought candles that had been lit at the sacred flame. In eight places he inscribed names to be prayed for, and he spent all his money, except just enough to get home with. Then he started homeward. He walked to Jaffa, sailed thence to Odessa, and walked home from there on foot.

XI

Efím travelled the same road he had come by; and as he drew nearer home his former anxiety returned as to how affairs were getting on in his absence. 'Much water flows away in a year,' the proverb says. It takes a lifetime to build up a homestead, but not long to ruin it, thought he. And he wondered how his son had managed without him, what sort of spring they were having, how the cattle had wintered, and whether the cottage was well finished. When Efím came to the district where he had parted from Elisha the summer before, he could hardly believe that the people living there were the same. The year before they had been starving, but now they were living in comfort. The harvest had been good, and the people had recovered, and had forgotten their former misery.

One evening Efím reached the very place where Elisha had remained behind; and as he entered the village, a little girl in a white smock ran out of a hut.

'Daddy, daddy, come to our house!'

Efím meant to pass on, but the little girl would not let him. She took hold of his coat, laughing, and pulled him towards the hut, where a woman with a small boy came out into the porch and beckoned to him.

'Come in, grandfather,' she said. 'Have supper and spend the night with us.'

So Efím went in.

'I may as well ask about Elisha,' he thought. 'I fancy this is the very hut he went to for a drink of water.'

The woman helped him off with the bag he carried, and gave him water to wash his face. Then she made him sit down to table, and set milk, curd-cakes and porridge before him. Efím thanked her, and praised her for her kindness to a pilgrim. The woman shook her head.

'We have good reason to welcome pilgrims,' she said. 'It was a pilgrim who showed us what life is. We were living forgetful of God, and God punished us almost to death. We reached such a pass last summer, that we all lay ill and helpless with nothing to eat. And we should have died, but that God sent an old man to help us – just such a one as you. He came in one day to ask for a drink of water, saw the state we were in, took pity on us, and remained with us. He gave us food and drink, and set us on our feet again; and he redeemed our land, and bought a cart and horse and gave them to us.'

Here the old woman entering the hut, interrupted the younger one and said:

'We don't know whether it was a man, or an angel from God. He loved us all, pitied us all, and went away without telling us his name, so that we don't even know whom to pray for. I can see it all before me now! There I lay waiting for death, when in comes a bald-headed old man. He was not anything much to look at, and he asked for a drink of water. I, sinner that I am, thought to myself: "What does he come prowling about here for?" And just think what he did! As soon as he saw us, he let down his bag, on this very spot, and untied it.'

Here the little girl joined in.

'No, Granny,' said she, 'first he put it down here in the middle of the hut, and then he lifted it on to the bench.'

And they began discussing and recalling all he had said and done, where he sat and slept, and what he had said to each of them.

At night the peasant himself came home on his horse, and he too began to tell about Elisha and how he had lived with them.

'Had he not come we should all have died in our sins. We were dying in despair, murmuring against God and man. But he set us on our feet again; and through him we learned to know God, and to believe that there is good in man. May the Lord bless him! We used to live like animals; he made human beings of us.'

After giving Efím food and drink, they showed him where he was to sleep; and lay down to sleep themselves.

But though Efím lay down, he could not sleep. He could not get Elisha out of his mind, but remembered how he had seen him three times at Jerusalem, standing in the foremost place.

'So that is how he got ahead of me,' thought Efím. 'God may or may not have accepted my pilgrimage, but He has certainly accepted his!'

Next morning Efím bade farewell to the people, who put some patties in his sack before they went to their work, and he continued his journey.

XII

Efím had been away just a year, and it was spring again when he reached home one evening. His son was not at home, but had gone to the public house, and when he came back, he had had a drop too much. Efím began questioning him. Everything showed that the young fellow had been unsteady during his father's absence. The money had all been wrongly spent, and the work had been neglected. The father began to upbraid the son; and the son answered rudely.

'Why didn't you stay and look after it yourself?' he said. 'You go off, taking the money with you, and now you demand it of me!'

The old man grew angry, and struck his son.

In the morning Efím went to the village Elder to complain of his son's conduct. As he was passing Elisha's house, his friend's wife greeted him from the porch.

'How do you do, neighbour,' she said. 'How do you do, dear friend? Did you get to Jerusalem safely?'

Efím stopped.

'Yes, thank God,' he said. 'I have been there. I lost sight of your old man, but I hear he got home safely.'

The old woman was fond of talking:

'Yes, neighbour, he has come back,' said she. 'He's been back a long time. Soon after Assumption, I think it was, he returned. And we were glad the Lord had sent him back to us! We were dull without him. We can't expect much work from him any more, his years for work are past; but still he is the head of the household and it's more cheerful when he's at home. And how glad our lad was! He said, "It's like being without sunlight, when father's away!" It was dull without him, dear friend. We're fond of him, and take good care of him.'

'Is he at home now?'

'He is, dear friend. He is with his bees. He is hiving the swarms. He says they are swarming well this year. The Lord has given such strength to the bees that my husband doesn't remember the like. "The Lord is not rewarding us according to our sins," he says. Come in, dear neighbour, he will be so glad to see you again.'

Efím passed through the passage into the yard and to the apiary, to see Elisha. There was Elisha in his grey coat, without any face-net or gloves, standing under the birch trees, looking upwards, his arms stretched out and his bald head shining, as Efím had seen him at the Holy Sepulchre in Jerusalem: and above him the sunlight shone through the birches as the flames of fire had done in the holy place, and the golden bees flew round his head like a halo and did not sting him.

Efím stopped. The old woman called to her husband.

'Here's your friend come,' she cried.

Elisha looked round with a pleased face, and came towards Efím, gently picking bees out of his own beard.

'Good day, neighbour, good day, dear friend. Did you get there safely?'

'My feet walked there, and I have brought you some water from the river Jordan. You must come to my house for it. But whether the Lord accepted my efforts...'

'Well the Lord be thanked! May Christ bless you!' said Elisha.

Efím was silent for a while, and then added:

'My feet have been there, but whether my soul, or another's, has been there more truly ...'

'That's God's business, neighbour, God's business,' interrupted Elisha.

'On my return journey I stopped at the hut where you remained behind...'

Elisha was alarmed, and said hurriedly:

'God's business, neighbour, God's business! Come into the cottage, I'll give you some of our honey.' And Elisha changed the conversation, and talked of home affairs.

Efím sighed, and did not speak to Elisha of the people in the hut, nor of how he had seen him in Jerusalem. But he now understood that the best way to keep one's vows to God and to do His will, is for each man while he lives to show love and do good to others.

WHERE LOVE IS, GOD IS

In a certain town there lived a cobbler, Martin Avdéitch by name. He had a tiny room in a basement, the one window of which looked out on to the street. Through it one could only see the feet of those who passed by, but Martin recognized the people by their boots. He had lived long in the place and had many acquaintances. There was hardly a pair of boots in the neighbourhood that had not been once or twice through his hands, so he often saw his own handiwork through the window. Some he had re-soled, some patched, some stitched up, and to some he had even put fresh uppers. He had plenty to do, for he worked well, used good material, did not charge too much, and could be relied on. If he could do a job by the day required, he undertook it; if not, he told the truth and gave no false promises; so he was well known and never short of work.

Martin had always been a good man; but in his old age he began to think more about his soul and to draw nearer to God. While he still worked for a master, before he set up on his own account, his wife had died, leaving him with a three-year old son. None of his elder children had lived – they had all died in infancy. At first Martin thought of sending his little son to his sister's in the country, but then he felt sorry to part with the boy, thinking: 'It would be hard for my little Kapitón to have to grow up in a strange family; I will keep him with me.'

Martin left his master and went into lodgings with his little son. But he had no luck with his children. No sooner had the boy reached an age when he could help his father and be a support as well as a joy to him, than he fell ill and, after being laid up for a week with a burning fever, died. Martin buried his son, and gave way to despair so great and overwhelming that he murmured against God. In his sorrow he prayed again and again that he too might die, reproaching God for having taken the son he loved, his only son, while he, old as he was, remained alive. After that Martin left off going to church.

One day an old man from Martin's native village, who had been a pilgrim for the last eight years, called in on his way from Tróitsa Monastery. Martin opened his heart to him, and told him of his sorrow.

'I no longer even wish to live, holy man,' he said. 'All I ask of God is that I soon may die. I am now quite without hope in the world.'

The old man replied: 'You have no right to say such things, Martin. We cannot judge God's ways. Not our reasoning, but God's will, decides. If God willed that your son should die and you should live, it must be best so. As to your despair – that comes because you wish to live for your own happiness.'

'What else should one live for?' asked Martin.

'For God, Martin,' said the old man. 'He gives you life, and you must live for Him. When you have learnt to live for Him, you will grieve no more, and all will seem easy to you.'

Martin was silent awhile, and then asked: 'But how is one to live for God?'

The old man answered: 'How one may live for God has been shown us by Christ. Can you read? Then buy the Gospels, and read them: there you will see how God would have you live. You have it all there.'

These words sank deep into Martin's heart, and that same day he went and bought himself a Testament in large print, and began to read.

At first he meant only to read on holidays, but having once begun he found it made his heart so light that he read every day. Sometimes he was so absorbed in his reading that the oil in his lamp burnt out before he could tear himself away from the book. He continued to read every night, and the more he read the more clearly he understood what God required of him, and how he might live for God. And his heart grew lighter and lighter. Before, when he went to bed he used to lie with a heavy heart, moaning as he thought of his little Kapitón; but now he only repeated again and again: 'Glory to Thee, glory to Thee, O Lord! Thy will be done!'

From that time Martin's whole life changed. Formerly, on holidays he used to go and have tea at the public house, and did not even refuse a glass or two of vódka. Sometimes, after having had a drop with a friend, he left the public house not drunk, but rather merry, and would say foolish things: shout at a man, or abuse him. Now, all that sort of thing passed away from him. His life became peaceful and joyful. He sat down to his work in the morning, and when he had finished his day's work he took the lamp down from the wall, stood it on the table, fetched his book from the shelf, opened it, and sat down to read. The more he read the better he understood, and the clearer and happier he felt in his mind.

It happened once that Martin sat up late, absorbed in his book. He was reading Luke's Gospel; and in the sixth chapter he came upon the verses:

'To him that smiteth thee on the one cheek offer also the other; and from him that taketh away thy cloke withhold not thy coat also. Give to every man that asketh thee; and of him that taketh away thy goods ask them not again. And as ye would that men should do to you, do ye also to them likewise.'

He also read the verses where our Lord says:

'And why call ye me, "Lord, Lord," and do not the things which I say? Whosoever cometh to me, and heareth my sayings, and doeth them, I will shew you to whom he is like: He is like a man which built an house, and digged deep, and laid the foundation on a rock: and when the flood arose, the stream beat vehemently upon that house, and could not shake it: for it was founded upon a rock. But he that heareth and doeth not, is like a man that without a foundation built an house upon the earth, against which the stream did beat vehemently, and immediately it fell; and the ruin of that house was great.'

When Martin read these words his soul was glad within him. He took off his spectacles and laid them on the book, and leaning his elbows on the table pondered over what he had read. He tried his own life by the standard of those words, asking himself:

'Is my house built on the rock, or on sand? If it stands on the rock, it is well. It seems easy enough while one sits here alone, and one thinks one has done all that God commands; but as soon as I cease to be on my guard, I sin again. Still I will persevere. It brings such joy. Help me, O Lord!'

He thought all this, and was about to go to bed, but was loath to leave his book. So he went on reading the seventh chapter – about the centurion, the widow's son, and the answer to John's disciples – and he came to the part where a rich Pharisee invited the Lord to his house; and he read how the woman who was a sinner, anointed his feet and washed them with her tears, and how he justified her. Coming to the forty-fourth verse, he read:

'And turning to the woman, he said unto Simon, "Seest thou this woman? I entered into thine house, thou gavest me no water for my feet: but she hath wetted my feet with her tears, and wiped them with her hair. Thou gavest me no kiss; but she, since the time I came in, hath not ceased to kiss my feet. My head with oil thou didst not anoint: but she hath anointed my feet with ointment."'

He read these verses and thought: 'He gave no water for his feet, gave no kiss, his head with oil he did not anoint...' And Martin took off his spectacles once more, laid them on his book, and pondered.

'He must have been like me, that Pharisee. He too thought only of himself – how to get a cup of tea, how to keep warm and comfortable; never a thought of his guest. He took care of himself, but for his guest he cared nothing at all. Yet who was the guest? The Lord himself! If he came to me, should I behave like that?'

Then Martin laid his head upon both his arms and, before he was aware of it, he fell asleep.

'Martin!' he suddenly heard a voice, as if someone had breathed the word above his ear.

He started from his sleep. 'Who's there?' he asked.

He turned round and looked at the door; no one was there. He called again. Then he heard quite distinctly: 'Martin, Martin! Look out into the street tomorrow, for I shall come.'

Martin roused himself, rose from his chair and rubbed his eyes, but did not know whether he had heard these words in a dream or awake. He put out the lamp and lay down to sleep.

Next morning he rose before daylight, and after saying his prayers he lit the fire and prepared his cabbage soup and buck-wheat porridge. Then he lit the samovár, put on his apron, and sat down by the window to his work. As he sat working Martin thought over what had happened the night before. At times it seemed to him like a dream, and at times he thought that he had really heard the voice. 'Such things have happened before now,' thought he.

So he sat by the window, looking out into the street more than he worked, and whenever anyone passed in unfamiliar boots he would stoop and look up, so as to see not the feet only but the face of the passer-by as well. A house porter passed in new felt boots; then a water-carrier. Presently an old soldier of Nicholas' reign came near the window, spade in hand. Martin knew him by his boots, which were shabby old felt ones, goloshed with leather. The old man was called Stepánitch: a neighbouring tradesman kept him in his house for charity, and his duty was to help the house porter. He began to clear away the snow before

Martin's window. Martin glanced at him and then went on with his work.

'I must be growing crazy with age,' said Martin, laughing at his fancy. 'Stepánitch comes to clear away the snow, and I must needs imagine it's Christ coming to visit me. Old dotard that I am!'

Yet after he had made a dozen stitches he felt drawn to look out of the window again. He saw that Stepánitch had leaned his spade against the wall, and was either resting himself or trying to get warm. The man was old and broken down, and had evidently not enough strength even to clear away the snow.

'What if I called him in and gave him some tea?' thought Martin. 'The samovár is just on the boil.'

He stuck his awl in its place, and rose; and putting the samovár on the table, made tea. Then he tapped the window with his fingers. Stepánitch turned and came to the window. Martin beckoned to him to come in, and went himself to open the door.

'Come in,' he said, 'and warm yourself a bit. I'm sure you must be cold.'

'May God bless you!' Stepánitch answered. 'My bones do ache to be sure.' He came in, first shaking off the snow, and lest he should leave marks on the floor he began wiping his feet; but as he did so he tottered and nearly fell.

'Don't trouble to wipe your feet,' said Martin; 'I'll wipe up the floor – it's all in the day's work. Come, friend, sit down and have some tea.'

Filling two tumblers, he passed one to his visitor, and pouring his own out into the saucer, began to blow on it.

Stepánitch emptied his glass, and, turning it upside down, put the remains of his piece of sugar on the top. He began to express his thanks, but it was plain that he would be glad of some more.

'Have another glass,' said Martin, refilling the visitor's tumbler and his own. But while he drank his tea Martin kept looking out into the street.

'Are you expecting anyone?' asked the visitor.

'Am I expecting anyone? Well, now, I'm ashamed to tell you. It isn't that I really expect anyone; but I heard something last night which I can't get out of my mind. Whether it was a vision, or only a fancy, I can't tell. You see, friend, last night I was reading the Gospel, about Christ the Lord, how he suffered, and how he walked on earth. You have heard tell of it, I dare say.'

'I have heard tell of it,' answered Stepánitch; 'but I'm an ignorant man and not able to read.'

'Well, you see, I was reading of how he walked on earth. I came to that part, you know, where he went to a Pharisee who did not receive him well. Well, friend, as I read about it, I thought how that man did not receive Christ the Lord with proper honour. Suppose such a thing could happen to such a man as myself, I thought, what would I not do to receive him! But that man gave him no reception at all. Well, friend, as I was thinking of this, I began to doze, and as I dozed I heard someone call me by name. I got up, and thought I heard someone whispering, "Expect me; I will come tomorrow." This happened twice over. And to tell you the truth, it sank so into my mind that, though I am ashamed of it myself, I keep on expecting him, the dear Lord!'

Stepánitch shook his head in silence, finished his tumbler and laid it on its side; but Martin stood it up again and refilled it for him.

'Here drink another glass, bless you! And I was thinking, too, how he walked on earth and despised no one, but went mostly among common folk. He went with plain people, and chose his disciples from among the likes of us, from workmen like us, sinners that we are. "He who raises himself," he said, "shall be humbled and he who humbles himself shall be raised." "You call me Lord," he said, "and I will wash your feet." "He who would be first," he said, "let him be the servant of all; because," he said, "blessed are the poor, the humble, the meek, and the merciful."'

Stepánitch forgot his tea. He was an old man, easily moved to tears, and as he sat and listened the tears ran down his cheeks.

'Come, drink some more,' said Martin. But Stepánitch crossed himself, thanked him, moved away his tumbler, and rose.

'Thank you, Martin Avdéitch,' he said, 'you have given me food and comfort both for soul and body.'

'You're very welcome. Come again another time. I am glad to have a guest,' said Martin.

Stepánitch went away; and Martin poured out the last of the tea and drank it up. Then he put away the tea things and sat down to his work, stitching the back seam of a boot. And as he stitched he kept looking out of the window, waiting for Christ, and thinking about him and his doings. And his head was full of Christ's sayings.

Two soldiers went by: one in Government boots, the other in boots of his own; then the master of a neighbouring house, in shining goloshes; then a baker carrying a basket. All these passed on. Then a woman came up in worsted stockings and peasant-made shoes. She passed the window, but stopped by the wall. Martin glanced up at her through the window, and saw that she was a stranger, poorly dressed, and with a baby in her arms. She stopped by the wall with her back to the wind, trying to wrap the baby up though she had hardly anything to wrap it in. The woman had only summer clothes on, and even they were shabby and worn. Through the window Martin heard the baby crying, and the woman trying to soothe it, but unable to do so. Martin rose, and going out of the door and up the steps he called to her.

'My dear, I say, my dear!'

The woman heard, and turned round.

'Why do you stand out there with the baby in the cold? Come inside. You can wrap him up better in a warm place. Come this way!'

The woman was surprised to see an old man in an apron, with spectacles on his nose, calling to her, but she followed him in.

They went down the steps, entered the little room, and the old man led her to the bed.

'There, sit down, my dear, near the stove. Warm yourself, and feed the baby.'

'Haven't any milk. I have eaten nothing myself since early morning,' said the woman, but still she took the baby to her breast.

Martin shook his head. He brought out a basin and some bread. Then he opened the oven door and poured some cabbage soup into the basin. He took out the porridge pot also, but the porridge was not yet ready, so he spread a cloth on the table and served only the soup and bread.

'Sit down and eat, my dear, and I'll mind the baby. Why, bless me, I've had children of my own; I know how to manage them.'

The woman crossed herself, and sitting down at the table began to eat, while Martin put the baby on the bed and sat down by it. He chucked and chucked, but having no teeth he could not do it well and the baby continued to cry. Then Martin tried poking at him with his finger; he drove his finger straight at the baby's mouth and then quickly drew it back, and did this again and again. He did not let the baby take his finger in its mouth, because it was all black with cobbler's wax. But the baby first grew quiet watching the finger, and then began to laugh. And Martin felt quite pleased.

The woman sat eating and talking, and told him who she was, and where she had been.

'I'm a soldier's wife,' said she. 'They sent my husband somewhere, far away, eight months ago, and I have heard nothing of him since. I had a place as cook till my baby was born, but then they would not keep me with a child. For three months now I have been struggling, unable to find a place, and I've had to sell all I had for food. I tried to go as a wet-nurse, but no one would have me; they said I was too starved-looking and thin. Now I have just been to see a tradesman's wife (a woman from our village is in service with her) and she has promised to take me. I thought it was all settled at last, but she tells me not to come till next week. It is far to her place, and I am fagged out, and baby is quite starved, poor mite. Fortunately our landlady has pity on us, and lets us lodge free, else I don't know what we should do.'

Martin sighed. 'Haven't you any warmer clothing?' he asked.

'How could I get warm clothing?' said she. 'Why, I pawned my last shawl for sixpence yesterday.'

Then the woman came and took the child, and Martin got up. He went and looked among some things that were hanging on the wall, and brought back an old cloak.

'Here,' he said, 'though it's a worn-out old thing, it will do to wrap him up in.'

The woman looked at the cloak, then at the old man, and taking it, burst into tears. Martin turned away, and groping under the bed brought out a small trunk. He fumbled about in it, and again sat down opposite the woman. And the woman said:

'The Lord bless you, friend. Surely Christ must have sent me to your window, else the child would have frozen. It was mild when I started, but now see how cold it has turned. Surely it must have been Christ who made you look out of your window and take pity on me, poor wretch!'

Martin smiled and said; 'It is quite true; it was he made me do it. It was no mere chance made me look out.'

And he told the woman his dream, and how he had heard the Lord's voice promising to visit him that day.

'Who knows? All things are possible,' said the woman. And she got up and threw the cloak over her shoulders, wrapping it round herself and round the baby. Then she bowed, and thanked Martin once more.

'Take this for Christ's sake,' said Martin, and gave her sixpence to get her shawl out of pawn. The woman crossed herself, and Martin did the same, and then he saw her out.

After the woman had gone, Martin ate some cabbage soup, cleared the things away, and sat down to work again. He sat and worked, but did not forget the window, and every time a shadow fell on it he looked up at once to see who was passing.

People he knew and strangers passed by, but no one remarkable.

After a while Martin saw an apple-woman stop just in front of his window. She had a large basket, but there did not seem to be many apples left in it; she had evidently sold most of her stock. On her back she had a sack full of chips, which she was taking home. No doubt she had gathered them at some place where building was going on. The sack evidently hurt her, and she wanted to shift it from one shoulder to the other, so she put it down on the footpath and, placing her basket on a post, began to shake down the chips in the sack. While she was doing this a boy in a tattered cap ran up, snatched an apple out of the basket, and tried to slip away; but the old woman noticed it, and turning, caught the boy by his sleeve. He began to struggle, trying to free himself, but the old woman held on with both hands, knocked his cap off his head, and seized hold of his hair. The boy screamed and the old woman scolded. Martin dropped his awl, not waiting to stick it in its place, and rushed out of the door. Stumbling up the steps, and dropping his spectacles in his hurry, he ran out into the street. The old woman was pulling the boy's hair and scolding him, and threatening to take him to the police. The lad was struggling and protesting, saying, 'I did not take it. What are you beating me for? Let me go!'

Martin separated them. He took the boy by the hand and said, 'Let him go, Granny. Forgive him for Christ's sake.'

'I'll pay him out, so that he won't forget it for a year! I'll take the rascal to the police!'

Martin began entreating the old woman.

'Let him go, Granny. He won't do it again. Let him go for Christ's sake!'

The old woman let go, and the boy wished to run away, but Martin stopped him.

'Ask the Granny's forgiveness!' said he. 'And don't do it another time. I saw you take the apple.'

The boy began to cry and to beg pardon.

'That's right. And now here's an apple for you,' and Martin took an apple from the basket and gave it to the boy, saying, 'I will pay you, Granny.'

'You will spoil them that way, the young rascals,' said the old woman. 'He ought to be whipped so that he should remember it for a week.'

'Oh, Granny, Granny,' said Martin, 'that's our way – but it's not God's way. If he should be whipped for stealing an apple, what should be done to us for our sins?'

The old woman was silent.

And Martin told her the parable of the lord who forgave his servant a large debt, and how the servant went out and seized his debtor by the throat. The old woman listened to it all, and the boy, too, stood by and listened.

'God bids us forgive,' said Martin, 'or else we shall not be forgiven. Forgive everyone; and a thoughtless youngster most of all.'

The old woman wagged her head and sighed.

'It's true enough,' said she, 'but they are getting terribly spoilt.'

'Then we old ones must show them better ways,' Martin replied.

'That's just what I say,' said the old woman. 'I have had seven of them myself, and only one daughter is left.' And the old woman began to tell how and where she was living with her daughter, and how many grandchildren she had. 'There now,' she said, 'I have but little strength left, yet I work hard for the sake of my grandchildren; and nice children they are, too. No one comes out to meet me but the children. Little Annie, now, won't leave me for anyone. "It's grandmother, dear grandmother, darling grandmother."' And the old woman completely softened at the thought.

'Of course, it was only his childishness, God help him,' said she, referring to the boy.

As the old woman was about to hoist her sack on her back, the lad sprang forward to her, saying, 'Let me carry it for you, Granny. I'm going that way.'

The old woman nodded her head, and put the sack on the boy's back, and they went down the street together, the old woman quite forgetting to ask Martin to pay for the apple. Martin stood and watched them as they went along talking to each other.

When they were out of sight Martin went back to the house. Having found his spectacles unbroken on the steps, he picked up his awl and sat down again to work. He worked a little, but could soon not see to pass the bristle through the holes in the leather; and presently he noticed the lamplighter passing on his way to light the street lamps.

'Seems it's time to light up,' thought he. So he trimmed his lamp, hung it up, and sat down again to work. He finished off one boot and, turning it about, examined it. It was all right. Then he gathered his tools together, swept up the cuttings, put away the bristles and the thread and the awls, and, taking down the lamp, placed it on the table. Then he took the Gospels from the shelf. He meant to open them at the place he had marked the day before with a bit of morocco, but the book opened at another place. As Martin opened it, his yesterday's dream came back to his mind, and no sooner had he thought of it than he seemed to hear footsteps, as though someone were moving behind him. Martin turned round, and it seemed to him as if people were standing in the dark corner, but he could not make out who they were. And a voice whispered in his ear: 'Martin, Martin, don't you know me?'

'Who is it?' muttered Martin.

'It is I,' said the voice. And out of the dark corner stepped Stepánitch, who smiled and vanishing like a cloud was seen no more.

'It is I,' said the voice again. And out of the darkness stepped the woman with the baby in her arms, and the woman smiled and the baby laughed, and they too vanished.

'It is I,' said the voice once more. And the old woman and the boy with the apple stepped out and both smiled, and then they too vanished.

And Martin's soul grew glad. He crossed himself, put on his

spectacles, and began reading the Gospel just where it had opened; and at the top of the page he read:

'I was an hungred, and ye gave me meat: I was thirsty, and ye gave me drink: I was a stranger, and ye took me in.'

And at the bottom of the page he read:

'Inasmuch as ye did it unto one of these my brethren, even these least, ye did it unto me' (Matthew 25:40).

And Martin understood that his dream had come true; and that the Saviour had really come to him that day, and he had welcomed him.

THE STORY OF IVAN THE FOOL

...and of his two brothers, Simon the Soldier and Tarás the Stout; and of his dumb sister Martha, and of the old devil and the three little imps.

I

Once upon a time, in a certain province of a certain country, there lived a rich peasant, who had three sons: Simon the Soldier, Tarás the Stout, and Iván the Fool, besides an unmarried daughter, Martha, who was deaf and dumb. Simon the Soldier went to the wars to serve the king; Tarás the Stout went to a merchant's in town to trade, and Iván the Fool stayed at home with the lass, to till the ground till his back bent.

Simon the Soldier obtained high rank and an estate, and married a nobleman's daughter. His pay was large and his estate was large, but yet he could not make ends meet. What the husband earned his lady wife squandered, and they never had money enough.

So Simon the Soldier went to his estate to collect the income, but his steward said, 'where is any income to come from? We have neither cattle, nor tools, nor horse, nor plough, nor harrow. We must first get all these, and then the money will come.'

Then Simon the Soldier went to his father and said: 'You,

father, are rich, but have given me nothing. Divide what you have, and give me a third part, that I may improve my estate.'

But the old man said: 'You brought nothing into my house; why should I give you a third part? It would be unfair to Iván and to the girl.'

But Simon answered, 'He is a fool; and she is an old maid, and deaf and dumb besides; what's the good of property to them?'

The old man said, 'We will see what Iván says about it.'

And Iván said, 'Let him take what he wants.'

So Simon the Soldier took his share of his father's goods and removed them to his estate, and went off again to serve the king.

Tarás the Stout also gathered much money, and married into a merchant's family, but still he wanted more. So he, also, came to his father and said, 'Give me my portion.'

But the old man did not wish to give Tarás a share either, and said, 'You brought nothing here. Iván has earned all we have in the house, and why should we wrong him and the girl?'

But Tarás said, 'What does he need? He is a fool! He cannot marry, no one would have him; and the dumb lass does not need anything either. Look here, Iván!' said he, 'give me half the corn; I don't want the tools, and of the livestock I will take only the grey stallion, which is of no use to you for the plough.'

Iván laughed and said, 'Take what you want. I will work to earn some more.'

So they gave a share to Tarás also; and he carted the corn away to town, and took the grey stallion. And Iván was left with one old mare, to lead his peasant life as before, and to support his father and mother.

II

Now the old Devil was vexed that the brothers had not quarrelled over the division, but had parted peacefully; and he summoned three imps.

'Look here,' said he, 'there are three brothers: Simon the

Soldier, Tarás the Stout and Iván the Fool. They should have quarrelled, but are living peaceably and meet on friendly terms. The fool Iván has spoilt the whole business for me. Now you three go and tackle those three brothers, and worry them till they scratch each other's eyes out! Do you think you can do it?'

'Yes, we'll do it,' said they.

'How will you set about it?'

'Why,' said they, 'first we'll ruin them. And when they haven't a crust to eat we'll tie them up together, and then they'll fight each other, sure enough!'

'That's capital; I see you understand your business. Go, and don't come back till you've set them by the ears, or I'll skin you alive!'

The imps went off into a swamp, and began to consider how they should set to work. They disputed and disputed, each wanting the lightest job; but at last they decided to cast lots which of the brothers each imp should tackle. If one imp finished his task before the others, he was to come and help them. So the imps cast lots, and appointed a time to meet again in the swamp to learn who had succeeded and who needed help.

The appointed time came round, and the imps met again in the swamp as agreed. And each began to tell how matters stood. The first, who had undertaken Simon the Soldier, began: 'My business is going on well. Tomorrow Simon will return to his father's house.'

His comrades asked, 'How did you manage it?'

'First,' says he, 'I made Simon so bold that he offered to conquer the whole world for his king; and the king made him his general and sent him to fight the King of India. They met for battle, but the night before, I damped all the powder in Simon's camp, and made more straw soldiers for the Indian King than you could count. And when Simon's soldiers saw the straw soldiers surrounding them, they grew frightened. Simon ordered them to fire; but their cannons and guns would not go off. Then Simon's soldiers were quite frightened, and ran like sheep, and the Indian

King slaughtered them. Simon was disgraced. He has been deprived of his estate, and tomorrow they intend to execute him. There is only one day's work left for me to do; I have just to let him out of prison that he may escape home. Tomorrow I shall be ready to help whichever of you needs me.'

Then the second imp, who had Tarás in hand, began to tell how he had fared. 'I don't want any help,' said he, 'my job is going all right. Tarás can't hold out for more than a week. First I caused him to grow greedy and fat. His covetousness became so great that whatever he saw he wanted to buy. He has spent all his money in buying immense lots of goods, and still continues to buy. Already he has begun to use borrowed money. His debts hang like a weight round his neck, and he is so involved that he can never get clear. In a week his bills come due, and before then I will spoil all his stock. He will be unable to pay and will have to go home to his father.'

Then they asked the third imp (Iván's), 'And how are you getting on?'

'Well,' said he, 'my affair goes badly. First I spat into his drink to make his stomach ache, and then I went into his field and hammered the ground hard as a stone that he should not be able to till it. I thought he wouldn't plough it, but like the fool that he is, he came with his plough and began to make a furrow. He groaned with the pain in his stomach, but went on ploughing. I broke his plough for him, but he went home, got out another, and again started ploughing. I crept under the earth and caught hold of the ploughshares, but there was no holding them; he leant heavily upon the plough, and the ploughshare was sharp and cut my hands. He has all but finished ploughing the field, only one little strip is left. Come, brothers, and help me; for if we don't get the better of him, all our labour is lost. If the fool holds out and keeps on working the land, his brothers will never know want, for he will feed them both.'

Simon the Soldier's imp promised to come next day to help, and so they parted.

III

Iván had ploughed up the whole fallow, all but one little strip. He came to finish it. Though his stomach ached, the ploughing must be done. He freed the harness ropes, turned the plough, and began to work. He drove one furrow, but coming back the plough began to drag as if it had caught in a root. It was the imp, who had twisted his legs round the ploughshare and was holding it back.

'What a strange thing!' thought Iván. 'There were no roots here at all, and yet here's a root.'

Iván pushed his hand deep into the furrow, groped about, and, feeling something soft, seized hold of it and pulled it out. It was black like a root, but it wriggled. Why, it was a live imp!

'What a nasty thing!' said Iván, and he lifted his hand to dash it against the plough, but the imp squealed out:

'Don't hurt me, and I'll do anything you tell me to.'

'What can you do?'

'Anything you tell me to.'

Iván scratched his head.

'My stomach aches,' said he; 'can you cure that?'

'Certainly I can.'

'Well then, do so.'

The imp went down into the furrow, searched about, scratched with his claws, and pulled out a bunch of three little roots, which he handed to Iván.

'Here,' says he, 'whoever swallows one of these will be cured of any illness.'

Iván took the roots, separated them, and swallowed one. The pain in his stomach was cured at once. The imp again begged to be let off; 'I will jump right into the earth, and never come back,' said he.

'All right,' said Iván; 'begone, and God be with you!'

And as soon as Iván mentioned God, the imp plunged into the earth like a stone thrown into the water. Only a hole was left.

Iván put the other two pieces of root into his cap and went on with his ploughing. He ploughed the strip to the end, turned his plough over, and went home. He unharnessed the horse, entered the hut, and there he saw his elder brother, Simon the Soldier and his wife, sitting at supper. Simon's estate had been confiscated, he himself had barely managed to escape from prison, and he had come back to live in his father's house.

Simon saw Iván, and said: 'I have come to live with you. Feed me and my wife till I get another appointment.'

'All right,' said Iván, 'you can stay with us.'

But when Iván was about to sit down on the bench, the lady disliked the smell, and said to her husband: 'I cannot sup with a dirty peasant.'

So Simon the Soldier said, 'My lady says you don't smell nice. You'd better go and eat outside.'

'All right,' said Iván; 'anyway I must spend the night outside, for I have to pasture the mare.'

So he took some bread, and his coat, and went with the mare into the fields.

IV

Having finished his work that night, Simon's imp came, as agreed, to find Iván's imp and help him to subdue the fool. He came to the field and searched and searched; but instead of his comrade he found only a hole.

'Clearly,' thought he, 'some evil has befallen my comrade. I must take his place. The field is ploughed up, so the fool must be tackled in the meadow.'

So the imp went to the meadows and flooded Iván's hayfield with water, which left the grass all covered with mud.

Iván returned from the pasture at dawn, sharpened his scythe, and went to mow the hayfield. He began to mow, but had only swung the scythe once or twice when the edge turned so that it would not cut at all, but needed resharpening. Iván struggled on for awhile, and then said: 'It's no good. I must go home and bring a tool to straighten the scythe, and I'll get a chunk of bread at the same time. If I have to spend a week here, I won't leave till the mowing's done.'

The imp heard this and thought to himself, 'This fool is a tough 'un; I can't get round him this way. I must try some other dodge.'

Iván returned, sharpened his scythe, and began to mow. The imp crept into the grass and began to catch the scythe by the heel, sending the point into the earth. Iván found the work very hard, but he mowed the whole meadow, except one little bit which was in the swamp. The imp crept into the swamp and, thought he to himself, 'Though I cut my paws I will not let him mow.'

Iván reached the swamp. The grass didn't seem thick, but yet it resisted the scythe. Iván grew angry and began to swing the scythe with all his might. The imp had to give in; he could not keep up with the scythe, and, seeing it was a bad business, he scrambled into a bush. Iván swung the scythe, caught the bush, and cut off half the imp's tail. Then he finished mowing the grass, told his sister to rake it up, and went himself to mow the rye. He went with the scythe, but the dock-tailed imp was there first, and entangled the rye so that the scythe was of no use. But Iván went home and got his sickle, and began to reap with that and he reaped the whole of the rye.

'Now it's time,' said he, 'to start on the oats.'

The dock-tailed imp heard this, and thought, 'I couldn't get the better of him on the rye, but I shall on the oats. Only wait till the morning.'

In the morning the imp hurried to the oat field, but the oats were already mowed down! Iván had mowed them by night, in order that less grain should shake out. The imp grew angry.

'He has cut me all over and tired me out – the fool. It is worse than war. The accursed fool never sleeps; one can't keep up with him. I will get into his stacks now and rot them.'

So the imp entered the rye, and crept among the sheaves, and they began to rot. He heated them, grew warm himself, and fell asleep.

Iván harnessed the mare, and went with the lass to cart the rye. He came to the heaps, and began to pitch the rye into the cart. He tossed two sheaves and again thrust his fork – right into the imp's back. He lifts the fork and sees on the prongs a live imp; dock-tailed, struggling, wriggling, and trying to jump.

'What, you nasty thing, are you here again?'

'I'm another,' said the imp. 'The first was my brother. I've been with your brother Simon.'

'Well,' said Iván, 'whoever you are, you've met the same fate!'

He was about to dash him against the cart, but the imp cried out: 'Let me off, and I will not only let you alone, but I'll do anything you tell me to do.'

'What can you do?'

'I can make soldiers out of anything you like.'

'But what use are they?'

'You can turn them to any use; they can do anything you please.'

'Can they sing?'

'Yes, if you want them to.'

'All right; you may make me some.'

And the imp said, 'Here, take a sheaf of rye, then bump it upright on the ground, and simply say:

'O sheaf! my slave
This order gave:
Where a straw has been
Let a soldier be seen!'

Iván took the sheaf, struck it on the ground, and said what the imp had told him to. The sheaf fell asunder, and all the straws changed into soldiers, with a trumpeter and a drummer playing in front, so that there was a whole regiment.

Iván laughed.

'How clever!' said he. 'This is fine! How pleased the girls will be!'

'Now let me go,' said the imp.

'No,' said Iván, 'I must make my soldiers of thrashed straw, otherwise good grain will be wasted. Teach me how to change them back again into the sheaf. I want to thrash it.'

And the imp said, 'Repeat:

'Let each be a straw
Who was soldier before,
For my true slave
This order gave!"

Iván said this, and the sheaf reappeared.

Again the imp began to beg, 'Now let me go!'

'All right.' And Iván pressed him against the side of the cart, held him down with his hand, and pulled him off the fork.

'God be with you,' said he.

And as soon as he mentioned God, the imp plunged into the earth like a stone into water. Only a hole was left.

Iván returned home, and there was his other brother, Tarás with his wife, sitting at supper.

Tarás the Stout had failed to pay his debts, had run away from his creditors, and had come home to his father's house. When he saw Iván, 'Look here', said he, 'till I can start in business again, I want you to keep me and my wife.'

'All right,' said Iván, 'you can live here, if you like.'

Iván took off his coat and sat down to table, but the merchant's wife said: 'I cannot sit at table with this clown, he smells of perspiration.'

Then Tarás the Stout said, 'Iván, you smell too strong. Go and eat outside.'

'All right,' said Iván, taking some bread and going into the yard. 'It is time, anyhow, for me to go and pasture the mare.'

V

Tarás's imp, being also free that night, came, as agreed, to help his comrades subdue Iván the Fool. He came to the cornfield, looked and looked for his comrades – no one was there. He only found a hole. He went to the meadow, and there he found an imp's tail in the swamp, and another hole in the rye stubble.

'Evidently, some ill-luck has befallen my comrades,' thought he. 'I must take their place and tackle the fool.'

So the imp went to look for Iván, who had already stacked the corn and was cutting trees in the wood. The two brothers had begun to feel crowded, living together, and had told Iván to cut down trees to build new houses for them.

The imp ran to the wood, climbed among the branches, and began to hinder Iván from felling the trees. Iván undercut one tree so that it should fall clear, but in falling it turned askew and caught among some branches. Iván cut a pole with which to lever it aside, and with difficulty contrived to bring it to the ground. He set to work to fell another tree – again the same thing occurred; and with all his efforts he could hardly get the tree clear. He began on a third tree, and again the same thing happened.

Iván had hoped to cut down half a hundred small trees, but had not felled even half a score, and now the night was come and he was tired out. The steam from him spread like a mist through the wood, but still he stuck to his work. He undercut another tree, but his back began to ache so that he could not stand. He drove his axe into the tree and sat down to rest.

The imp, noticing that Iván had stopped work, grew cheerful.

'At last,' thought he, 'he is tired out! He will give it up. Now I can take a rest myself.'

He seated himself astride a branch and chuckled. But soon Iván got up, pulled the axe out, swung it, and smote the tree from the opposite side with such force that the tree gave way at once and came crashing down. The imp had not expected this, and had no time to get his feet clear, and the tree in breaking, gripped his paw. Iván began to lop off the branches, when he noticed a live imp hanging in the tree! Iván was surprised.

'What, you nasty thing,' says he, 'so you are here again!'

'I am another one,' says the imp. 'I have been with your brother Tarás.'

'Whoever you are, you have met your fate,' said Iván, and swinging his axe he was about to strike him with the haft, but the imp begged for mercy: 'Don't strike me,' said he, 'and I will do anything you tell me to.'

'What can you do?'

'I can make money for you, as much as you want.'

'All right, make some.' So the imp showed him how to do it.

'Take,' said he, 'some leaves from this oak and rub them in your hands, and gold will fall out on the ground.'

Iván took some leaves and rubbed them, and gold ran down from his hands.

'This stuff will do fine,' said he, 'for the fellows to play with on their holidays.'

'Now let me go.' said the imp.

'All right,' said Iván, and taking a lever he set the imp free. 'Now begone! And God be with you,' says he.

And as soon as he mentioned God, the imp plunged into the earth, like a stone into water. Only a hole was left.

VI

So the brothers built houses, and began to live apart; and Iván finished the harvest work, brewed beer, and invited his brothers to spend the next holiday with him. His brothers would not come.

'We don't care about peasant feasts,' said they.

So Iván entertained the peasants and their wives, and drank until he was rather tipsy. Then he went into the street to a ring of dancers; and going up to them he told the women to sing a song in his honour; 'for,' said he, 'I will give you something you never saw in your lives before!'

The women laughed and sang his praises, and when they had finished they said, 'Now let us have your gift.'

'I will bring it directly,' said he.

He took a seed-basket and ran into the woods. The women laughed. 'He is a fool!' said they, and they began to talk of something else.

But soon Iván came running back, carrying the basket full of something heavy.

'Shall I give it you?'

'Yes! give it to us.'

Iván took a handful of gold and threw it to the women. You should have seen them throw themselves upon it to pick it up! And the men around scrambled for it, and snatched it from one another. One old woman was nearly crushed to death. Iván laughed.

'Oh, you fools!' says he. 'Why did you crush the old grandmother? Be quiet, and I will give you some more,' and he threw them some more. The people all crowded round, and Iván threw them all the gold he had. They asked for more, but Iván said, 'I have no more just now. Another time I'll give you some more. Now let us dance, and you can sing me your songs.'

The women began to sing.

'Your songs are no good,' says he.

'Where will you find better ones?' say they.

'I'll soon show you,' says he.

He went to the barn, took a sheaf, thrashed it, stood it up, and bumped it on the ground.

'Now,' said he:

'O sheaf! my slave
This order gave:
Where a straw has been
Let a soldier be seen!'

And the sheaf fell asunder and became so many soldiers. The drums and trumpets began to play. Iván ordered the soldiers to play and sing. He led them out into the street, and the people were amazed. The soldiers played and sang, and then Iván (forbidding anyone to follow him) led them back to the thrashing ground, changed them into a sheaf again, and threw it in its place.

He then went home and lay down in the stables to sleep.

VII

Simon the Soldier heard of all these things next morning, and went to his brother.

'Tell me,' says he, 'where you got those soldiers from, and where you have taken them to?'

'What does it matter to you?' said Iván.

'What does it matter? Why, with soldiers one can do anything. One can win a kingdom.'

Iván wondered.

'Really!' said he; 'Why didn't you say so before? I'll make you as many as you like. It's well the lass and I have thrashed so much straw.'

Iván took his brother to the barn and said:

'Look here; if I make you some soldiers, you must take them away at once, for if we have to feed them, they will eat up the whole village in a day.'

Simon the Soldier promised to lead the soldiers away; and Iván began to make them. He bumped a sheaf on the thrashing floor – a company appeared. He bumped another sheaf, and there was a second company. He made so many that they covered the field.

'Will that do?' he asked.

Simon was overjoyed, and said: 'That will do! Thank you, Iván!'

'All right,' said Iván. 'If you want more, come back, and I'll make them. There is plenty of straw this season.'

Simon the Soldier at once took command of his army, collected and organized it, and went off to make war.

Hardly had Simon the Soldier gone, when Tarás the Stout came along. He, too, had heard of yesterday's affair, and he said to his brother:

'Show me where you get gold money! If I only had some to start with, I could make it bring me in money from all over the world.'

Iván was astonished.

'Really!' said he. 'You should have told me sooner. I will make you as much as you like.'

His brother was delighted.

'Give me three basketfuls to begin with.'

'All right,' said Iván. 'Come into the forest; or better still, let us harness the mare, for you won't be able to carry it all.'

They drove to the forest, and Iván began to rub the oak leaves. He made a great heap of gold.

'Will that do?'

Tarás was overjoyed.

'It will do for the present,' said he. 'Thank you, Iván!'

'All right,' says Iván, 'if you want more, come back for it. There are plenty of leaves left.'

Tarás the Stout gathered up a whole cartload of money, and went off to trade.

So the two brothers went away: Simon to fight, and Tarás to buy and sell. And Simon the Soldier conquered a kingdom for himself; and Tarás the Stout made much money in trade.

When the two brothers met, each told the other: Simon how he got the soldiers, and Tarás how he got the money. And Simon the Soldier said to his brother, I have conquered a kingdom and live in grand style, but I have not money enough to keep my soldiers.'

And Tarás the Stout said, 'And I have made much money, but the trouble is, I have no one to guard it.'

Then said Simon the Soldier, 'Let us go to our brother. I will tell him to make more soldiers, and will give them to you to guard your money, and you can tell him to make money for me to feed my men.'

And they drove away to Iván; and Simon said, 'Dear brother, I have not enough soldiers; make me another couple of ricks or so.'

Iván shook his head.

'No!' says he, 'I will not make any more soldiers.'

'But you promised you would.'

'I know I promised, but I won't make any more.'

'But why not, fool?'

'Because your soldiers killed a man. I was ploughing the other day near the road, and I saw a woman taking a coffin along in a cart, and crying. I asked her who was dead. She said, "Simon's soldiers have killed my husband in the war." I thought the soldiers would only play tunes, but they have killed a man. I won't give you any more.'

And he stuck to it, and would not make any more soldiers.

Tarás the Stout, too, began to beg Iván to make him more gold money. But Iván shook his head.

'No, I won't make any more,' said he.

'Didn't you promise?'

'I did, but I'll make no more,' said he.

'Why not, fool?'

'Because your gold coins took away the cow from Michael's daughter.'

'How?'

'Simply took it away! Michael's daughter had a cow. Her children used to drink the milk. But the other day her children came to me to ask for milk. I said, "Where's your cow?" They answered, "The steward of Tarás the Stout came and gave mother three bits of gold, and she gave him the cow, so we have nothing to drink." I thought you were only going to play with the gold pieces, but you have taken the children's cow away. I will not give you any more.'

And Iván stuck to it and would not give him any more. So the brothers went away. And as they went they discussed how they could meet their difficulties. And Simon said:

'Look here, I tell you what to do. You give me money to feed my soldiers, and I will give you half my kingdom with soldiers enough to guard your money.' Tarás agreed. So the brothers divided what they possessed, and both became kings, and both were rich.

VIII

Iván lived at home, supporting his father and mother and working in the fields with his dumb sister. Now it happened that Iván's yard dog fell sick, grew mangy, and was near dying. Iván, pitying it, got some bread from his sister, put it in his cap, carried it out, and threw it to the dog. But the cap was torn, and together with the bread one of the little roots fell to the ground. The old dog ate it up with the bread, and as soon as she had swallowed it she jumped up and began to play, bark, and wag her tail – in short became quite well again.

The father and mother saw it and were amazed.

'How did you cure the dog?' asked they.

Iván answered: 'I had two little roots to cure any pain, and she swallowed one.'

Now about that time it happened that the King's daughter fell ill, and the King proclaimed in every town and village, that he would reward anyone who could heal her, and if any unmarried man could heal the King's daughter he should have her for his wife. This was proclaimed in Iván's village as well as everywhere else.

His father and mother called Iván, and said to him: 'Have you heard what the King has proclaimed? You said you had a root that would cure any sickness. Go and heal the King's daughter, and you will be made happy for life.'

'All right,' said he.

And Iván prepared to go, and they dressed him in his best. But as he went out of the door he met a beggar woman with a crippled hand.

'I have heard,' said she, 'that you can heal people. I pray you cure my arm, for I cannot even put on my boots myself.'

'All right,' said Iván, and giving the little root to the beggar woman he told her to swallow it. She swallowed it, and was cured. She was at once able to move her arm freely.

His father and mother came out to accompany Iván to the King, but when they heard that he had given away the root, and that he had nothing left to cure the King's daughter with, they began to scold him.

'You pity a beggar woman, but are not sorry for the King's daughter!' said they. But Iván felt sorry for the King's daughter also. So he harnessed the horse, put straw in the cart to sit on, and sat down to drive away.

'Where are you going, fool?'

'To cure the King's daughter.'

'But you've nothing left to cure her with?'

'Never mind,' said he, and drove off.

He drove to the King's palace, and as soon as he stepped on the threshold the King's daughter got well.

The King was delighted, and had Iván brought to him, and had him dressed in fine robes.

'Be my son-in-law,' said he.

'All right,' said Iván.

And Iván married the Princess. Her father died soon after, and Iván became King. So all three brothers were now kings.

IX

The three brothers lived and reigned. The eldest brother, Simon the Soldier, prospered. With his straw soldiers he levied real soldiers. He ordered throughout his whole kingdom a levy of one soldier from every ten houses, and each soldier had to be tall, and clean in body and in face. He gathered many such soldiers and trained them; and when anyone opposed him, he sent these soldiers at once, and got his own way, so that everyone began to fear him, and his life was a comfortable one. Whatever he cast his eyes on and wished for, was his. He sent soldiers, and they brought him all he desired.

Tarás the Stout also lived comfortably. He did not waste the money he got from Iván, but increased it largely. He introduced law and order into his kingdom. He kept his money in coffers, and taxed the people. He instituted a poll tax, tolls for walking and driving, and a tax on shoes and stockings and dress trimmings. And whatever he wished for he got. For the sake of money, people brought him everything, and they offered to work for him – for everyone wanted money.

Iván the Fool, also, did not live badly. As soon as he had buried his father-in-law, he took off all his royal robes and gave them to his wife to put away in a chest; and he again donned his hempen shirt, his breeches and peasant shoes, and started again to work.

'It's dull for me,' said he. 'I'm getting fat and have lost my appetite and my sleep.' So he brought his father and mother and his dumb sister to live with him, and worked as before.

People said, 'But you are a king!'

'Yes,' said he, 'but even a king must eat.'

One of his ministers came to him and said, 'We have no money to pay salaries.'

'All right,' says he, 'then don't pay them.'

'Then no one will serve.'

'All right; let them not serve. They will have more time to work; let them cart manure. There is plenty of scavenging to be done.'

And people came to Iván to be tried. One said, 'He stole my money.' And Iván said, 'All right, that shows that he wanted it.'

And they all got to know that Iván was a fool. And his wife said to him, 'People say that you are a fool.'

'All right,' said Iván.

His wife thought and thought about it, but she also was a fool. 'Shall I go against my husband? Where the needle goes the thread follows,' said she.

So she took off her royal dress, put it away in a chest, and went to the dumb girl to learn to work. And she learned to work and began to help her husband.

And all the wise men left Iván's kingdom; only the fools remained.

Nobody had money. They lived and worked. They fed themselves; and they fed others.

X

The old Devil waited and waited for news from the imps of their having ruined the three brothers. But no news came. So he went himself to inquire about it. He searched and searched, but instead of finding the three imps he found only the three holes.

'Evidently they have failed,' thought he. 'I shall have to tackle it myself.'

So he went to look for the brothers, but they were no longer in their old places. He found them in three different kingdoms. All three were living and reigning. This annoyed the old Devil very much.

'Well,' said he, 'I must try my own hand at the job.'

First he went to King Simon. He did not go to him in his own shape, but disguised himself as a general, and drove to Simon's palace.

'I hear, King Simon,' said he, 'that you are a great warrior, and as I know that business well, I desire to serve you.'

King Simon questioned him, and seeing that he was a wise man, took him into his service.

The new commander began to teach King Simon how to form a strong army.

'First,' said he, 'we must levy more soldiers, for there are in your kingdom many people unemployed. We must recruit all the young men without exception. Then you will have five times as many soldiers as formerly. Secondly, we must get new rifles and cannons. I will introduce rifles that will fire a hundred balls at once; they will fly out like peas. And I will get cannons that will consume with fire either man, or horse, or wall. They will burn up everything!'

Simon the King listened to the new commander, ordered all young men without exception to be enrolled as soldiers, and had new factories built in which he manufactured large quantities of improved rifles and cannons. Then he made haste to declare war against a neighbouring king. As soon as he met the other army, King Simon ordered his soldiers to rain balls against it and shoot fire from the cannons, and at one blow he burned and crippled half the enemy's army. The neighbouring king was so thoroughly frightened that he gave way and surrendered his kingdom. King Simon was delighted.

'Now,' said he, 'I will conquer the King of India.'

But the Indian King had heard about King Simon, and had adopted all his inventions, and added more of his own. The Indian King enlisted not only all the young men, but all the single women also, and got together a greater army even than King Simon's. And he copied all King Simon's rifles and cannons, and invented a way of flying through the air to throw explosive bombs from above.

King Simon set out to fight the Indian King, expecting to beat him as he had beaten the other king; but the scythe that had cut so well had lost its edge. The King of India did not let Simon's army come within gunshot, but sent his women through the air to hurl down explosive bombs on to Simon's army. The women began to rain down bombs on to the army like borax upon cockroaches. The army ran away, and Simon the King was left alone. So the Indian King took Simon's kingdom, and Simon the Soldier fled as best he might.

Having finished with this brother, the old Devil went to King Tarás. Changing himself into a merchant, he settled in Tarás's kingdom, started a house of business, and began spending money. He paid high prices for everything, and everybody hurried to the new merchant's to get money. And so much money spread among the people that they began to pay all their taxes promptly, and paid up all their arrears, and King Tarás rejoiced.

'Thanks to the new merchant,' thought he, 'I shall have more money than ever; and my life will be yet more comfortable.'

And Tarás the King began to form fresh plans, and began to build a new palace. He gave notice that people should bring him wood and stone, and come to work, and he fixed high prices for everything. King Tarás thought people would come in crowds to work as before, but to his surprise all the wood and stone was taken to the merchant's, and all the workmen went there too. King Tarás increased his price, but the merchant bid yet more. King Tarás had much money, but the merchant had still more, and outbid the King at every point.

The King's palace was at a standstill; the building did not get on.

King Tarás planned a garden, and when autumn came he called for the people to come and plant the garden, but nobody came. All the people were engaged digging a pond for the merchant. Winter came, and King Tarás wanted to buy sable furs for a new overcoat. He sent to buy them, but the messengers returned and said, 'There are no sables left. The merchant has all the furs. He gave the best price, and made carpets of the skins.'

King Tarás wanted to buy some stallions. He sent to buy them, but the messengers returned saying, 'The merchant has all the good stallions; they are carrying water to fill his pond.'

All the King's affairs came to a standstill. Nobody would work for him, for everyone was busy working for the merchant; and they only brought King Tarás the merchant's money to pay their taxes.

And the King collected so much money that he had nowhere to store it, and his life became wretched. He ceased to form plans, and would have been glad enough simply to live, but he was hardly able even to do that. He ran short of everything. One after another his cooks, coachmen and servants left him to go to the merchant. Soon he lacked even food. When he sent to the market to buy anything, there was nothing to be got – the merchant had bought up everything, and people only brought the King money to pay their taxes.

Tarás the King got angry and banished the merchant from the country. But the merchant settled just across the frontier, and went on as before. For the sake of the merchant's money, people took everything to him instead of to the King.

Things went badly with King Tarás. For days together he had nothing to eat, and a rumour even got about that the merchant was boasting that he would buy up the King himself! King Tarás got frightened, and did not know what to do.

At this time Simon the Soldier came to him, saying, 'Help me, for the King of India has conquered me.'

But King Tarás himself was over head and ears in difficulties. 'I myself,' said he, 'have had nothing to eat for two days.'

XI

Having done with the two brothers, the old Devil went to Iván. He changed himself into a General, and coming to Iván began to persuade him that he ought to have an army.

'It does not become a king,' said he, 'to be without an army. Only give me the order, and I will collect soldiers from among your people and form one.'

Iván listened to him. 'All right,' said Iván, 'form an army, and teach them to sing songs well. I like to hear them do that.'

So the old Devil went through Iván's kingdom to enlist men. He told them to go and be entered as soldiers, and each should have a quart of spirits and a fine red cap.

The people laughed.

'We have plenty of spirits,' said they. 'We make it ourselves; and as for caps, the women make all kinds of them, even striped ones with tassels.'

So nobody would enlist.

The old Devil came to Iván and said: 'Your fools won't enlist of their own free will. We shall have to make them.'

'All right,' said Iván, 'you can try.'

So the old Devil gave notice that all the people were to enlist, and that Iván would put to death anyone who refused.

The people came to the General and said, 'You say that if we do not go as soldiers the King will put us to death, but you don't say what will happen if we do enlist. We have heard say that soldiers get killed!'

'Yes, that happens sometimes.'

When the people heard this they became obstinate.

'We won't go,' said they. 'Better meet death at home. Either way we must die.'

'Fools! You are fools!' said the old Devil. 'A soldier may be killed or he may not, but if you don't go, King Iván will have you killed for certain.'

The people were puzzled, and went to Iván the Fool to consult him.

'A General has come,' said they, 'who says we must all become soldiers. "If you go as soldiers," says he, "you may be killed or you may not, but if you don't go, King Iván will certainly kill you." Is this true?'

Iván laughed and said, 'How can I, alone, put all you to death? If I were not a fool I would explain it to you, but as it is, I don't understand it myself.'

'Then,' said they, 'we will not serve.'

'All right,' says he, 'don't.'

So the people went to the General and refused to enlist. And the old Devil saw that this game was up, and he went off and ingratiated himself with the King of Tarakán.

'Let us make war,' says he, 'and conquer King Iván's country. It is true there is no money, but there is plenty of corn and cattle and everything else.'

So the King of Tarakán prepared to make war. He mustered a

great army, provided rifles and cannons, marched to the frontier, and entered Iván's kingdom.

And people came to Iván and said, 'The King of Tarakán is coming to make war on us.'

'All right,' said Iván, 'let him come.'

Having crossed the frontier, the King of Tarakán sent scouts to look for Iván's army. They looked and looked, but there was no army! They waited and waited for one to appear somewhere, but there were no signs of an army, and nobody to fight with. The King of Tarakán then sent to seize the villages. The soldiers came to a village, and the people, both men and women, rushed out in astonishment to stare at the soldiers. The soldiers began to take their corn and cattle; the people let them have it, and did not resist. The soldiers went on to another village; the same thing happened again. The soldiers went on for one day, and for two days, and everywhere the same thing happened. The people let them have everything, and no one resisted, but only invited the soldiers to live with them.

'Poor fellows,' said they, 'if you have a hard life in your own land, why don't you come and stay with us altogether?'

The soldiers marched and marched: still no army, only people living and feeding themselves and others, and not resisting, but inviting the soldiers to stay and live with them. The soldiers found it dull work, and they came to the King of Tarakán and said, 'We cannot fight here, lead us elsewhere. War is all right, but what is this? It is like cutting pea-soup! We will not make war here any more.'

The King of Tarakán grew angry, and ordered his soldiers to overrun the whole kingdom, to destroy the villages, to burn the grain and the houses, and to slaughter the cattle. 'And if you do not obey my orders,' said he, 'I will execute you all.'

The soldiers were frightened, and began to act according to the King's orders. They began to burn houses and corn, and to kill cattle. But the fools still offered no resistance, and only wept. The old men wept, and the old women wept, and the young people wept.

'Why do you harm us?' they said. 'Why do you waste good things? If you need them, why do you not take them for yourselves?'

At last the soldiers could stand it no longer. They refused to go any further, and the army disbanded and fled.

XII

The old Devil had to give it up. He could not get the better of Iván with soldiers. So he changed himself into a fine gentleman, and settled down in Iván's kingdom. He meant to overcome him by means of money, as he had overcome Tarás the Stout.

'I wish,' says he, 'to do you a good turn, to teach you sense and reason. I will build a house among you and organize a trade.'

'All right,' said Iván, 'come and live among us if you like.'

Next morning the fine gentleman went out into the public square with a big sack of gold and a sheet of paper, and said, 'You all live like swine. I wish to teach you how to live properly. Build me a house according to this plan. You shall work, I will tell you how, and I will pay you with gold coins.' And he showed them the gold.

The fools were astonished; there was no money in use among them; they bartered their goods, and paid one another with labour. They looked at the gold coins with surprise.

'What nice little things they are!' said they.

And they began to exchange their goods and labour for the gentleman's gold pieces. And the old Devil began, as in Tarás's kingdom, to be free with his gold, and the people began to exchange everything for gold and to do all sorts of work for it.

The old Devil was delighted, and thought he to himself, 'Things are going right this time. Now I shall ruin the Fool as I did Tarás, and I shall buy him up body and soul.'

But as soon as the fools had provided themselves with gold pieces they gave them to the women for necklaces. The lasses plaited them into their tresses, and at last the children in the street began to play with the little pieces. Everybody had plenty of them, and they stopped taking them. But the fine gentleman's mansion was not yet half-built, and the grain and cattle for the year were not yet provided. So he gave notice that he wished people to come and work for him, and that he wanted cattle and grain; for each thing, and for each service, he was ready to give many more pieces of gold.

But nobody came to work and nothing was brought. Only sometimes a boy or a little girl would run up to exchange an egg for a gold coin, but nobody else came, and he had nothing to eat. And being hungry, the fine gentleman went through the village to try to buy something for dinner. He tried at one house, and offered a gold piece for a fowl, but the housewife wouldn't take it.

'I have a lot already,' said she.

He tried at a widow's house to buy a herring, and offered a gold piece.

'I don't want it, my good sir,' said she. 'I have no children to play with it, and I myself already have three coins as curiosities.'

He tried at a peasant's house to get bread, but neither would the peasant take money.

'I don't need it,' said he, 'but if you are begging "for Christ's sake[14]," wait a bit and I'll tell the housewife to cut you a piece of bread.'

At that the Devil spat, and ran away. To hear Christ's name mentioned, let alone receiving anything for Christ's sake, hurt him more than sticking a knife into him.

And so he got no bread. Everyone had gold, and no matter where the old Devil went, nobody would give anything for money, but everyone said, 'Either bring something else, or come and work, or receive what you want in charity for Christ's sake.'

But the old Devil had nothing but money; for work he had no liking, and as for taking anything 'for Christ's sake' he could not do that. The old Devil grew very angry.

14 *'For Christ's sake' is the usual appeal of Russian beggars or poor pilgrims.*

'What more do you want, when I give you money?' said he. 'You can buy everything with gold, and hire any kind of labourer.' But the fools did not heed him.

'No, we do not want money,' said they. 'We have no payments to make, and no taxes, so what should we do with it?'

The old Devil lay down to sleep – supperless.

The affair was told to Iván the Fool. People came and asked him, 'What are we to do? A fine gentleman has turned up, who likes to eat and drink and dress well, but he does not like to work, does not beg in "Christ's name", but only offers gold pieces to everyone. At first people gave him all he wanted, until they had plenty of gold pieces, but now no one gives him anything. What's to be done with him? He will die of hunger before long.'

Iván listened.

'All right,' says he, 'we must feed him. Let him live by turn at each house as a shepherd[15] does.'

There was no help for it. The old Devil had to begin making the round.

In due course the turn came for him to go to Iván's house. The old Devil came in to dinner, and the dumb girl was getting it ready.

She had often been deceived by lazy folk who came early to dinner – without having done their share of work – and ate up all the porridge, so it had occurred to her to find out the sluggards by their hands. Those who had horny hands, she put at the table, but the others got only the scraps that were left over.

The old Devil sat down at the table, but the dumb girl seized him by the hands and looked at them – there were no hard places there: the hands were clean and smooth, with long nails. The dumb girl gave a grunt and pulled the Devil away from the table.

---

15 It is often arranged that the shepherd who looks after the cattle of a Russian village Commune should get his board and lodging at the houses of the villagers, passing from one to another in turn.

And Iván's wife said to him, 'Don't be offended, fine gentleman. My sister-in-law does not allow anyone to come to table who hasn't horny hands. But wait awhile, after the folk have eaten you shall have what is left.'

The old Devil was offended that in the King's house they wished him to feed like a pig. He said to Iván, 'It is a foolish law you have in your kingdom that everyone must work with his hands. It's your stupidity that invented it. Do people work only with their hands? What do you think wise men work with?'

And Iván said, 'How are we fools to know? We do most of our work with our hands and our backs.'

'That is because you are fools! But I will teach you how to work with the head. Then you will know that it is more profitable to work with the head than with the hands.'

Iván was surprised.

'If that is so,' said he, 'then there is some sense in calling us fools!'

And the old Devil went on. 'Only it is not easy to work with one's head. You give me nothing to eat, because I have no hard places on my hands, but you do not know that it is a hundred times more difficult to work with the head. Sometimes one's head quite splits.'

Iván became thoughtful.

'Why, then, friend, do you torture yourself so? Is it pleasant when the head splits? Would it not be better to do easier work with your hands and your back?'

But the Devil said, 'I do it all out of pity for you fools. If I didn't torture myself you would remain fools for ever. But, having worked with my head, I can now teach you.'

Iván was surprised.

'Do teach us!' said he, 'so that when our hands get cramped we may use our heads for a change.'

And the Devil promised to teach the people. So Iván gave notice throughout the kingdom that a fine gentleman had come who would teach everybody how to work with their heads; that with the head more could be done than with the hands; and that the people ought all to come and learn.

Now there was in Iván's kingdom a high tower, with many steps leading up to a lantern on the top. And Iván took the gentleman up there that everyone might see him.

So the gentleman took his place on the top of the tower and began to speak, and the people came together to see him. They thought the gentleman would really show them how to work with the head without using the hands. But the old Devil only taught them in many words how they might live without working. The people could make nothing of it. They looked and considered, and at last went off to attend to their affairs.

The old Devil stood on the tower a whole day, and after that a second day, talking all the time. But standing there so long he grew hungry, and the fools never thought of taking food to him up in the tower. They thought that if he could work with his head better than with his hands, he could at any rate easily provide himself with bread.

The old Devil stood on the top of the tower yet another day, talking away. People came near, looked on for awhile, and then went away.

And Iván asked, 'Well, has the gentleman begun to work with his head yet?'

'Not yet,' said the people; 'he's still spouting away.'

The old Devil stood on the tower one day more, but he began to grow weak, so that he staggered and hit his head against one of the pillars of the lantern. One of the people noticed it and told Iván's wife, and she ran to her husband, who was in the field.

'Come and look,' said she. 'They say the gentleman is beginning to work with his head.'

Iván was surprised.

'Really?' says he, and he turned his horse round, and went to the tower. And by the time he reached the tower the old Devil was quite exhausted with hunger, and was staggering and knocking his head against the pillars. And just as Iván arrived at the tower, the Devil stumbled, fell, and came bump, bump, bump, straight down the stairs to the bottom, counting each step with a knock of his head!

'Well!' says Iván, 'the fine gentleman told the truth when he said that "sometimes one's head quite splits". This is worse than blisters; after such work there will be swellings on the head.'

The old Devil tumbled out at the foot of the stairs, and struck his head against the ground. Iván was about to go up to him to see how much work he had done – when suddenly the earth opened and the old Devil fell through. Only a hole was left.

Iván scratched his head.

'What a nasty thing,' says he. 'It's one of those devils again! What a whopper! He must be the father of them all.'

Iván is still living, and people crowd to his kingdom. His own brothers have come to live with him, and he feeds them, too. To everyone who comes and says, 'Give me food!' Iván says, 'All right. You can stay with us; we have plenty of everything.'

Only there is one special custom in his kingdom; whoever has horny hands comes to table, but whoever has not, must eat what the others leave.

LITTLE GIRLS WISER THAN MEN

It was an early Easter. Sledging was only just over; snow still lay in the yards; and water ran in streams down the village street.

Two little girls from different houses happened to meet in a lane between two homesteads, where the dirty water after running through the farmyards had formed a large puddle. One girl was very small, the other a little bigger. Their mothers had dressed them both in new frocks. The little one wore a blue frock, the other a yellow print, and both had red kerchiefs on their heads. They had just come from church when they met, and first they showed each other their finery, and then they began to play. Soon the fancy took them to splash about in the water, and the smaller one was going to step into the puddle, shoes and all, when the elder checked her:

'Don't go in so, Malásha,' said she, 'your mother will scold you. I will take off my shoes and stockings, and you take off yours.'

They did so; and then, picking up their skirts, began walking towards each other through the puddle. The water came up to Malásha's ankles, and she said:

'It is deep, Akoúlya, I'm afraid!'

'Come on,' replied the other. 'Don't be frightened. It won't get any deeper.'

When they got near one another, Akoúlya said:

'Mind, Malásha, don't splash. Walk carefully!'

She had hardly said this, when Malásha plumped down her foot so that the water splashed right on to Akoúlya's frock. The frock was splashed, and so were Akoúlya's eyes and nose. When she saw the stains on her frock, she was angry and ran after Malásha to strike her. Malásha was frightened, and seeing that she had got herself into trouble, she scrambled out of the puddle, and prepared to run home. Just then Akoúlya's mother happened to be passing, and seeing that her daughter's skirt was splashed, and her sleeves dirty, she said:

'You naughty, dirty girl, what have you been doing?'

'Malásha did it on purpose,' replied the girl.

At this Akoúlya's mother seized Malásha, and struck her on the back of her neck. Malásha began to howl so that she could be heard all down the street. Her mother came out.

'What are you beating my girl for?' said she; and began scolding her neighbour. One word led to another and they had an angry quarrel. The men came out, and a crowd collected in the street, everyone shouting and no one listening. They all went on quarrelling, till one gave another a push, and the affair had very nearly come to blows, when Akoúlya's old grandmother, stepping in among them, tried to calm them.

'What are you thinking of, friends? Is it right to behave so? On a day like this, too! It is a time for rejoicing, and not for such folly as this.'

They would not listen to the old woman, and nearly knocked her off her feet. And she would not have been able to quiet the crowd, if it had not been for Akoúlya and Malásha themselves. While the women were abusing each other, Akoúlya had wiped the mud off her frock, and gone back to the puddle. She took a stone and began scraping away the earth in front of the puddle to make a channel through which the water could run out into the street. Presently Malásha joined her, and with a chip of wood helped her dig the channel. Just as the men were beginning to fight, the water from the little girls' channel ran streaming into the street towards the very place where the old woman was trying to pacify the men. The girls followed it; one running each side of the little stream.

'Catch it, Malásha! Catch it!' shouted Akoúlya; while Malásha could not speak for laughing.

Highly delighted, and watching the chip float along on their stream, the little girls ran straight into the group of men; and the old woman, seeing them, said to the men:

'Are you not ashamed of yourselves? To go fighting on account of these lassies, when they themselves have forgotten all about it, and are playing happily together. Dear little souls! They are wiser than you!'

The men looked at the little girls, and were ashamed, and, laughing at themselves, went back each to his own home.

'Except ye turn, and become as little children, ye shall in no wise enter into the kingdom of heaven.'

ILYÁS

There once lived, in the Government of Oufá, a Bashkír named Ilyás. His father, who died a year after he had found his son a wife, did not leave him much property. Ilyás then had only seven mares, two cows, and about a score of sheep. He was a good manager, however, and soon began to acquire more. He and his wife worked from morn till night; rising earlier than others and going later to bed; and his possessions increased year by year. Living in this way, Ilyás little by little acquired great wealth. At the end of thirty-five years he had 200 horses, 150 head of cattle, and 1,200 sheep. Hired labourers tended his flocks and herds, and hired women milked his mares and cows, and made kumiss[16], butter and cheese. Ilyás had abundance of everything, and everyone in the district envied him. They said of him:

'Ilyás is a fortunate man: he has plenty of everything. This world must be a pleasant place for him.'

People of position heard of Ilyás and sought his acquaintance. Visitors came to him from afar; and he welcomed everyone, and gave them food and drink. Whoever might come, there was always kumiss, tea, sherbet and mutton to set before them. Whenever visitors arrived a sheep would be killed, or sometimes two; and if many guests came he would even slaughter a mare for them.

16 Kumiss (or more properly koumýs) is a fermented drink prepared from mare's milk.

Ilyás had three children: two sons and a daughter; and he married them all off. While he was poor, his sons worked with him, and looked after the flocks and herds themselves; but when he grew rich they got spoiled, and one of them took to drink. The eldest was killed in a brawl; and the younger, who had married a self-willed woman, ceased to obey his father, and they could not live together any more.

So they parted, and Ilyás gave his son a house and some of the cattle; and this diminished his wealth. Soon after that, a disease broke out among Ilyás's sheep, and many died. Then followed a bad harvest, and the hay crop failed; and many cattle died that winter. Then the Kirghíz captured his best herd of horses; and Ilyás's property dwindled away. It became smaller and smaller, while at the same time his strength grew less; till, by the time he was seventy years old, he had begun to sell his furs, carpets, saddles and tents. At last he had to part with his remaining cattle, and found himself face to face with want. Before he knew how it had happened, he had lost everything, and in their old age he and his wife had to go into service. Ilyás had nothing left, except the clothes on his back, a fur cloak, a cup, his indoor shoes and over-shoes, and his wife, Sham-Shemagi, who also was old by this time. The son who had parted from him had gone into a far country, and his daughter was dead, so that there was no one to help the old couple.

Their neighbour, Muhammad-Shah, took pity on them. Muhammad-Shah was neither rich nor poor, but lived comfortably, and was a good man. He remembered Ilyás's hospitality, and pitying him, said:

'Come and live with me, Ilyás, you and your old woman. In summer you can work in my melon garden as much as your strength allows, and in winter feed my cattle; and Sham-Shemagi shall milk my mares and make kumiss. I will feed and clothe you both. When you need anything, tell me, and you shall have it.'

Ilyás thanked his neighbour, and he and his wife took service with Muhammad-Shah as labourers. At first the position seemed hard to them, but they got used to it, and lived on, working as much as their strength allowed.

Muhammad-Shah found it was to his advantage to keep such people, because, having been masters themselves, they knew how to manage and were not lazy, but did all the work they could. Yet it grieved Muhammad-Shah to see people brought so low who had been of such high standing.

It happened once that some of Muhammad-Shah's relatives came from a great distance to visit him, and a Mullah came too. Muhammad-Shah told Ilyás to catch a sheep and kill it. Ilyás skinned the sheep, and boiled it, and sent it in to the guests. The guests ate the mutton, had some tea, and then began drinking kumiss. As they were sitting with their host on down cushions on a carpet, conversing and sipping kumiss from their cups, Ilyás, having finished his work, passed by the open door. Muhammad-Shah, seeing him pass, said to one of the guests:

'Did you notice that old man who passed just now?'

'Yes,' said the visitor, 'what is there remarkable about him?'

'Only this – that he was once the richest man among us,' replied the host. 'His name is Ilyás. You may have heard of him.'

'Of course I have heard of him,' the guest answered, 'I never saw him before, but his fame has spread far and wide.'

'Yes, and now he has nothing left,' said Muhammad-Shah, 'and he lives with me as my labourer, and his old woman is here too – she milks the mares.'

The guest was astonished: he clicked with his tongue, shook his head, and said:

'Fortune turns like a wheel. One man it lifts, another it sets down! Does not the old man grieve over all he has lost?'

'Who can tell. He lives quietly and peacefully, and works well.'

'May I speak to him?' asked the guest. 'I should like to ask him about his life.'

'Why not?' replied the master, and he called from the kibitka[17] in which they were sitting:

'Babay;' (which in the Bashkir tongue means 'Grandfather') 'come in and have a cup of kumiss with us, and call your wife here also.'

Ilyás entered with his wife; and after exchanging greetings with his master and the guests, he repeated a prayer, and seated himself near the door. His wife passed in behind the curtain and sat down with her mistress.

A cup of kumiss was handed to Ilyás; he wished the guests and his master good health, bowed, drank a little, and put down the cup.

'Well, Daddy,' said the guest who had wished to speak to him, 'I suppose you feel rather sad at the sight of us. It must remind you of your former prosperity, and of your present sorrows.'

Ilyás smiled, and said:

'If I were to tell you what is happiness and what is misfortune, you would not believe me. You had better ask my wife. She is a woman, and what is in her heart is on her tongue. She will tell you the whole truth.'

The guest turned towards the curtain.

'Well, Granny,' he cried, 'tell me how your former happiness compares with your present misfortune.'

And Sham-Shemagi answered from behind the curtain:

'This is what I think about it: My old man and I lived for fifty years seeking happiness and not finding it; and it is only now, these last two years, since we had nothing left and have lived as labourers, that we have found real happiness, and we wish for nothing better than our present lot.'

The guests were astonished, and so was the master; he even rose and drew the curtain back, so as to see the old woman's face. There she stood with her arms folded, looking at her old husband, and smiling; and he smiled back at her. The old woman went on:

17 *A kibitka is a movable dwelling, made up of detachable wooden frames, forming a round, and covered over with felt.*

'I speak the truth and do not jest. For half a century we sought for happiness, and as long as we were rich we never found it. Now that we have nothing left, and have taken service as labourers, we have found such happiness that we want nothing better.'

'But in what does your happiness consist?' asked the guest.

'Why, in this,' she replied, 'when we were rich, my husband and I had so many cares that we had no time to talk to one another, or to think of our souls, or to pray to God. Now we had visitors, and had to consider what food to set before them, and what presents to give them, lest they should speak ill of us. When they left, we had to look after our labourers, who were always trying to shirk work and get the best food, while we wanted to get all we could out of them. So we sinned. Then we were in fear lest a wolf should kill a foal or a calf, or thieves steal our horses. We lay awake at night, worrying lest the ewes should overlie their lambs, and we got up again and again to see that all was well. One thing attended to, another care would spring up: how, for instance, to get enough fodder for the winter. And besides that, my old man and I used to disagree. He would say we must do so and so, and I would differ from him; and then we disputed – sinning again. So we passed from one trouble to another, from one sin to another, and found no happiness.'

'Well, and now?'

'Now, when my husband and I wake in the morning, we always have a loving word for one another, and we live peacefully, having nothing to quarrel about. We have no care but how best to serve our master. We work as much as our strength allows, and do it with a will, that our master may not lose, but profit by us. When we come in, dinner or supper is ready and there is kumiss to drink. We have fuel to burn when it is cold, and we have our fur cloak. And we have time to talk, time to think of our souls, and time to pray. For fifty years we sought happiness, but only now at last have we found it.'

The guests laughed.

But Ilyás said:

'Do not laugh, friends. It is not a matter for jesting – it is the truth of life. We also were foolish at first, and wept at the loss of our wealth; but now God has shown us the truth, and we tell it, not for our own consolation, but for your good.'

And the Mullah said:

'That is a wise speech. Ilyás has spoken the exact truth. The same is said in Holy Writ.'

And the guests ceased laughing and became thoughtful.

THE DEATH OF IVAN ILYCH

I

During an interval in the Melvinski trial in the large building of the Law Courts the members and public prosecutor met in Ivan Egorovich Shebek's private room, where the conversation turned on the celebrated Krasovski case. Fedor Vasilievich warmly maintained that it was not subject to their jurisdiction, Ivan Egorovich maintained the contrary, while Peter Ivanovich, not having entered into the discussion at the start, took no part in it but looked through the *Gazette* which had just been handed in.

'Gentlemen,' he said, 'Ivan Ilych has died!'

'You don't say so!'

'Here, read it yourself,' replied Peter Ivanovich, handing Fedor Vasilievich the paper still damp from the press. Surrounded by a black border were the words: 'Praskovya Fedorovna Golovina, with profound sorrow, informs relatives and friends of the demise of her beloved husband Ivan Ilych Golovin, Member of the Court of Justice, which occurred on February the 4th of this year 1882. The funeral will take place on Friday at one o'clock in the afternoon.'

Ivan Ilych had been a colleague of the gentlemen present and was liked by them all. He had been ill for some weeks with an illness said to be incurable. His post had been kept open for him, but there had been conjectures that in case of his death Alexeev might receive his appointment, and that either Vinnikov or Shtabel would succeed Alexeev. So on receiving the news of Ivan Ilych's death the first thought of each of the gentlemen in that private room was of the changes and promotions it might occasion among themselves or their acquaintances.

'I shall be sure to get Shtabel's place or Vinnikov's,' thought Fedor Vasilievich. 'I was promised that long ago, and the promotion means an extra eight hundred rubles a year for me besides the allowance.'

'Now I must apply for my brother-in-law's transfer from Kaluga,' thought Peter Ivanovich. 'My wife will be very glad, and then she won't be able to say that I never do anything for her relations.' 'I thought he would never leave his bed again,' said Peter Ivanovich aloud. 'It's very sad.' 'But what really was the matter with him?'

'The doctors couldn't say – at least they could, but each of them said something different. When last I saw him I though he was getting better.'

'And I haven't been to see him since the holidays. I always meant to go.' 'Had he any property?'

'I think his wife had a little – but something quite trifling.'

'We shall have to go to see her, but they live so terribly far away.'

'Far away from you, you mean. Everything's far away from your place.'

'You see, he never can forgive my living on the other side of the river,' said Peter Ivanovich, smiling at Shebek. Then, still talking of the distances between different parts of the city, they returned to the Court.

Besides considerations as to the possible transfers and promotions likely to result from Ivan Ilych's death, the mere fact of the death of a near acquaintance aroused, as usual, in all who heard of it the complacent feeling that, 'it is he who is dead and not I.'

Each one thought or felt, 'Well, he's dead but I'm alive!' But the more intimate of Ivan Ilych's acquaintances, his so-called friends, could not help thinking also that they would now have to fulfil the very tiresome demands of propriety by attending the funeral service and paying a visit of condolence to the widow.

Fedor Vasilievich and Peter Ivanovich had been his nearest acquaintances. Peter Ivanovich had studied law with Ivan Ilych and had considered himself to be under obligations to him. Having told his wife at dinner-time of Ivan Ilych's death, and of his conjecture that it might be possible to get her brother transferred to their circuit, Peter Ivanovich sacrificed his usual nap, put on his evening clothes and drove to Ivan Ilych's house.

At the entrance stood a carriage and two cabs. Leaning against the wall in the hall downstairs near the cloakstand was a coffin lid covered with cloth of gold, ornamented with gold cord and tassels, that had been polished up with metal powder. Two ladies in black were taking off their fur cloaks. Peter Ivanovich recognized one of them as Ivan Ilych's sister, but the other was a stranger to him. His colleague Schwartz was just coming downstairs, but on seeing Peter Ivanovich enter he stopped and winked at him, as if to say: 'Ivan Ilych has made a mess of things – not like you and me.'

Schwartz's face with his Piccadilly whiskers, and his slim figure in evening dress, had as usual an air of elegant solemnity which contrasted with the playfulness of his character and had a special piquancy here, or so it seemed to Peter Ivanovich.

Peter Ivanovich allowed the ladies to precede him and slowly followed them upstairs. Schwartz did not come down but remained where he was, and Peter Ivanovich understood that he wanted to arrange where they should play bridge that evening. The ladies went upstairs to the widow's room, and Schwartz with seriously compressed lips but a playful look in his eyes, indicated by a twist of his eyebrows the room to the right where the body lay.

Peter Ivanovich, like everyone else on such occasions, entered feeling uncertain what he would have to do. All he knew was that at such times it is always safe to cross oneself. But he was not quite sure whether one should make obeisances while doing so. He therefore adopted a middle course. On entering the room he began crossing himself and made a slight movement resembling a bow. At the same time, as far as the motion of his head and arm allowed, he surveyed the room. Two young men – apparently nephews, one of whom was a high-school pupil – were leaving the room, crossing themselves as they did so. An old woman was standing motionless, and a lady with strangely arched eyebrows was saying something to her in a whisper. A vigorous, resolute Church Reader in a frock coat was reading something in a loud voice with an expression that precluded any contradiction. The butler's assistant, Gerasim, stepping lightly in front of Peter Ivanovich, was strewing something on the floor. Noticing this, Peter Ivanovich was immediately aware of a faint odour of a decomposing body.

The last time he had called on Ivan Ilych, Peter Ivanovich had seen Gerasim in the study. Ivan Ilych had been particularly fond of him and he was performing the duty of a sick nurse. Peter Ivanovich continued to make the sign of the cross slightly inclining his head in an intermediate direction between the coffin, the Reader, and the icons on the table in a corner of the room. Afterwards, when it seemed to him that this movement of his arm in crossing himself had gone on too long, he stopped and began to look at the corpse.

The dead man lay, as dead men always lie, in a specially heavy way, his rigid limbs sunk in the soft cushions of the coffin, with the head forever bowed on the pillow. His yellow waxen brow with bald patches over his sunken temples was thrust up in the way peculiar to the dead, the protruding nose seeming to press on the upper lip. He was much changed and grown even thinner since Peter Ivanovich had last seen him, but, as is always the case with the dead, his face was handsomer and above all more dignified than when he was alive. The expression on the face said that what was necessary had been accomplished, and accomplished rightly. Besides this there was in that expression a reproach and a warning to the living. This warning seemed to Peter Ivanovich out of place, or at least not applicable to him. He felt a certain discomfort and so he hurriedly crossed himself once more and turned and went out of the door – too hurriedly and too regardless of propriety, as he himself was aware.

Schwartz was waiting for him in the adjoining room with legs spread wide apart and both hands toying with his top hat behind his back. The mere sight of that playful, well-groomed, and elegant figure refreshed Peter Ivanovich. He felt that Schwartz was above all these happenings and would not surrender to any depressing influences. His very look said that this incident of a church service for Ivan Ilych could not be a sufficient reason for infringing the order of the session – in other words, that it would certainly not prevent his unwrapping a new pack of cards and shuffling them that evening while a footman placed fresh candles on the table: in fact, that there was no reason for supposing that this incident would hinder their spending the evening agreeably. Indeed he said this in a whisper as Peter Ivanovich passed him, proposing that they should meet for a game at Fedor Vasilievich's. But apparently Peter Ivanovich was not destined to play bridge that evening. Praskovya Fedorovna (a short, fat woman who despite all efforts to the contrary had continued to broaden steadily from her shoulders downwards and who had the same extraordinarily arched eyebrows as the lady who had been standing by the coffin), dressed all in black, her head covered with lace, came out of her own room with some other ladies, conducted them to the room where the dead body lay, and said: 'The service will begin immediately. Please go in.'

Schwartz, making an indefinite bow, stood still, evidently neither accepting nor declining this invitation. Praskovya Fedorovna recognizing Peter Ivanovich, sighed, went close up to him, took his hand, and said: 'I know you were a true friend to Ivan Ilych...' and looked at him awaiting some suitable response. And Peter Ivanovich knew that, just as it had been the right thing to cross himself in that room, so what he had to do here was to press her hand, sigh, and say, 'Believe me...' So he did all this and as he did it felt that the desired result had been achieved: that both he and she were touched.

'Come with me. I want to speak to you before it begins,' said the widow. 'Give me your arm.' Peter Ivanovich gave her his arm and they went to the inner rooms, passing Schwartz who winked at Peter Ivanovich compassionately.

'That does for our bridge! Don't object if we find another player. Perhaps you can cut in when you do escape,' said his playful look.

Peter Ivanovich sighed still more deeply and despondently, and Praskovya Fedorovna pressed his arm gratefully. When they reached the drawing room, upholstered in pink cretonne and lighted by a dim lamp, they sat down at the table – she on a sofa and Peter Ivanovich on a low pouffe, the springs of which yielded spasmodically under his weight. Praskovya Fedorovna had been on the point of warning him to take another seat, but felt that such a warning was out of keeping with her present condition and so changed her mind. As he sat down on the pouffe Peter Ivanovich recalled how Ivan Ilych had arranged this room and had consulted him regarding this pink cretonne with green leaves. The whole room was full of furniture and knick-knacks, and on her way to the sofa the lace of the widow's black shawl caught on the edge of the table. Peter Ivanovich rose to detach it, and the springs of the pouffe, relieved of his weight, rose also and gave him a push. The widow began detaching her shawl herself, and Peter Ivanovich again sat down, suppressing the rebellious springs of the pouffe under him. But the widow had not quite freed herself and Peter Ivanovich got up again, and again the pouffe rebelled and even creaked. When this was all over she took out a clean cambric handkerchief and began to weep. The episode with the shawl and the struggle with the pouffe had cooled Peter Ivanovich's emotions and he sat there with a sullen look on his face. This awkward situation was interrupted by Sokolov, Ivan Ilych's butler, who came to report that the plot in the cemetery that Praskovya Fedorovna had chosen would cost two hundred rubles. She stopped weeping and, looking at Peter Ivanovich with the air of a victim, remarked in French that it was very hard for her. Peter Ivanovich made a silent gesture signifying his full conviction that it must indeed be so. 'Please smoke,' she said in a magnanimous yet crushed voice, and turned to discuss with Sokolov the price of the plot for the grave.

Peter Ivanovich while lighting his cigarette heard her inquiring very circumstantially into the prices of different plots in the cemetery and finally decide which she would take. When that was done she gave instructions about engaging the choir. Sokolov then left the room. 'I look after everything myself,' she told Peter Ivanovich, shifting the albums that lay on the table; and noticing that the table was endangered by his cigarette ash, she immediately passed him an ashtray, saying as she did so: 'I consider it an affectation to say that my grief prevents my attending to practical affairs. On the contrary, if anything can – I won't say console me, but – distract me, it is seeing to everything concerning him.' She again took out her handkerchief as if preparing to cry, but suddenly, as if mastering her feeling, she shook herself and began to speak calmly. 'But there is something I want to talk to you about.'

Peter Ivanovich bowed, keeping control of the springs of the pouffe, which immediately began quivering under him.

'He suffered terribly the last few days.'

'Did he?' said Peter Ivanovich.

'Oh, terribly! He screamed unceasingly, not for minutes but for hours. For the last three days he screamed incessantly. It was unendurable. I cannot understand how I bore it; you could hear him three rooms off. Oh, what I have suffered!'

'Is it possible that he was conscious all that time?' asked Peter Ivanovich.

'Yes,' she whispered. 'To the last moment. He took leave of us a quarter of an hour before he died, and asked us to take Vasya away.'

The thought of the suffering of this man he had known so intimately, first as a merry little boy, then as a schoolmate, and later as a grown-up colleague, suddenly struck Peter Ivanovich with horror, despite an unpleasant consciousness of his own and this woman's dissimulation. He again saw that brow, and that nose pressing down on the lip, and felt afraid for himself.

'Three days of frightful suffering and the death! Why, that might suddenly, at any time, happen to me,' he thought, and for a moment felt terrified. But – he did not himself know how – the customary reflection at once occurred to him that this had happened to Ivan Ilych and not to him, and that it should not and could not happen to him, and that to think that it could would be yielding to depression which he ought not to do, as Schwartz's expression plainly showed. After which reflection Peter Ivanovich felt reassured, and began to ask with interest about the details of Ivan Ilych's death, as though death was an accident natural to Ivan Ilych but certainly not to himself. After many details of the really dreadful physical sufferings Ivan Ilych had endured (which details he learnt only from the effect those sufferings had produced on Praskovya Fedorovna's nerves) the widow apparently found it necessary to get to business.

'Oh, Peter Ivanovich, how hard it is! How terribly, terribly hard!' and she again began to weep. Peter Ivanovich sighed and waited for her to finish blowing her nose. When she had done so he said, 'Believe me...' and she again began talking and brought out what was evidently her chief concern with him – namely, to question him as to how she could obtain a grant of money from the government on the occasion of her husband's death. She made it appear that she was asking Peter Ivanovich's advice about her pension, but he soon saw that she already knew about that to the minutest detail, more even than he did himself. She knew how much could be got out of the government in consequence of her husband's death, but wanted to find out whether she could not possibly extract something more. Peter Ivanovich tried to think of some means of doing so, but after reflecting for a while and, out of propriety, condemning the government for its niggardliness, he said he thought that nothing more could be got. Then she sighed and evidently began to devise means of getting rid of her visitor. Noticing this, he put out his cigarette, rose, pressed her hand, and went out into the anteroom.

In the dining room where the clock stood that Ivan Ilych had liked so much and had bought at an antique shop, Peter Ivanovich met a priest and a few acquaintances who had come to attend the service, and he recognized Ivan Ilych's daughter, a handsome young woman. She was in black and her slim figure appeared slimmer than ever. She had a gloomy, determined, almost angry expression, and bowed to Peter Ivanovich as though he were in some way to blame. Behind her, with the same offended look, stood a wealthy young man, an examining magistrate, whom Peter Ivanovich also knew and who was her fiance, as he had heard. He bowed mournfully to them and was about to pass into the death chamber, when from under the stairs appeared the figure of Ivan Ilych's schoolboy son, who was extremely like his father. He seemed a little Ivan Ilych, such as Peter Ivanovich remembered when they studied law together. His tear-stained eyes had in them the look that is seen in the eyes of boys of thirteen or fourteen who are not pure-minded. When he saw Peter Ivanovich he scowled morosely and shamefacedly. Peter Ivanovich nodded to him and entered the death chamber. The service began: candles, groans, incense, tears and sobs. Peter Ivanovich stood looking gloomily down at his feet. He did not look once at the dead man, did not yield to any depressing influence, and was one of the first to leave the room. There was no one in the anteroom, but Gerasim darted out of the dead man's room, rummaged with his strong hands among the fur coats to find Peter Ivanovich's and helped him on with it.

'Well, friend Gerasim,' said Peter Ivanovich, so as to say something. 'It's a sad affair, isn't it?'

'It's God will. We shall all come to it some day,' said Gerasim, displaying his teeth – the even white teeth of a healthy peasant – and, like a man in the thick of urgent work, he briskly opened the front door, called the coachman, helped Peter Ivanovich into the sledge, and sprang back to the porch as if in readiness for what he had to do next. Peter Ivanovich found the fresh air particularly pleasant after the smell of incense, the dead body and carbolic acid.

'Where to sir?' asked the coachman.

'It's not too late even now... I'll call round on Fedor Vasilievich.'

He accordingly drove there and found them just finishing the first rubber, so that it was quite convenient for him to cut in.

II

Ivan Ilych's life had been most simple and most ordinary and therefore most terrible. He had been a member of the Court of Justice, and died at the age of forty-five. His father had been an official who, after serving in various ministries and departments in Petersburg, had made the sort of career which brings men to positions from which by reason of their long service they cannot be dismissed, though they are obviously unfit to hold any responsible position, and for whom therefore posts are specially created, which though fictitious carry salaries of from six to ten thousand rubles that are not fictitious, and in receipt of which they live on to a great age. Such was the Privy Councillor and superfluous member of various superfluous institutions, Ilya Epimovich Golovin.

He had three sons, of whom Ivan Ilych was the second. The eldest son was following in his father's footsteps only in another department, and was already approaching that stage in the service at which a similar sinecure would be reached. The third son was a failure. He had ruined his prospects in a number of positions and was now serving in the railway department. His father and brothers, and still more their wives, not merely disliked meeting him, but avoided remembering his existence unless compelled to do so. His sister had married Baron Greff, a Petersburg official of her father's type. Ivan Ilych was *le phénix de la famille* as people said. He was neither as cold and formal as his elder brother nor as wild as the younger, but was a happy mean between them – an intelligent, polished, lively and agreeable man. He had studied with his younger brother at the School of Law, but the latter had failed to complete the course and was expelled when he was in the fifth class. Ivan Ilych finished the course well. Even when he was at the School of Law he was just what he remained for the rest of his life: a capable, cheerful, good-natured and sociable man, though strict in the fulfilment of what he considered to be his duty: and he considered his duty to be what was so considered by those in authority. Neither as a boy nor as a man was he a toady, but from early youth was by nature attracted to people of high station as a fly is drawn to the light, assimilating their ways and views of life and establishing friendly relations with them. All the enthusiasms of childhood and youth passed without leaving much trace on him; he succumbed to sensuality, to vanity, and latterly among the highest classes to liberalism, but always within limits which his instinct unfailingly indicated to him as correct.

At school he had done things which had formerly seemed to him very horrid and made him feel disgusted with himself when he did them; but when later on he saw that such actions were done by people of good position and that they did not regard them as wrong, he was able not exactly to regard them as right, but to forget about them entirely or not be at all troubled at remembering them. Having graduated from the School of Law and qualified for the tenth rank of the civil service, and having received money from his father for his equipment, Ivan Ilych ordered himself clothes at Scharmer's, the fashionable tailor, hung a medallion inscribed *respice finem* on his watch chain, took leave of his professor and the prince who was patron of the school, had a farewell dinner with his comrades at Donon's first-class restaurant, and with his new and fashionable portmanteau, linen, clothes, shaving and other toilet appliances, and a travelling rug, all purchased at the best shops, he set off for one of the provinces where, through his father's influence, he had been attached to the governor as an official for special service.

In the province Ivan Ilych soon arranged as easy and agreeable a position for himself as he had had at the School of Law. He performed his official task, made his career, and at the same time amused himself pleasantly and decorously. Occasionally he paid official visits to country districts where he behaved with dignity both to his superiors and inferiors, and performed the duties entrusted to him, which related chiefly to the sectarians, with an exactness and incorruptible honesty of which he could not but feel proud.

In official matters, despite his youth and taste for frivolous gaiety, he was exceedingly reserved, punctilious, and even severe; but in society he was often amusing and witty, and always good-natured, correct in his manner, and *bon enfant*, as the governor and his wife – with whom he was like one of the family – used to say of him.

In the province he had an affair with a lady who made advances to the elegant young lawyer, and there was also a milliner; and there were carousals with aides-de-camp who visited the district, and after-supper visits to a certain outlying street of doubtful reputation; and there was, too, some obsequiousness to his chief and even to his chief's wife, but all this was done with such a tone of good breeding that no hard names could be applied to it. It all came under the heading of the French saying: '*Il faut que jeunesse se passe.*' It was all done with clean hands, in clean linen, with French phrases, and above all among people of the best society and consequently with the approval of people of rank.

So Ivan Ilych served for five years and then came a change in his official life. The new and reformed judicial institutions were introduced, and new men were needed. Ivan Ilych became such a new man. He was offered the post of examining magistrate, and he accepted it though the post was in another province and obliged him to give up the connections he had formed and to make new ones. His friends met to give him a send-off; they had a group photograph taken and presented him with a silver cigarette case, and he set off to his new post.

As examining magistrate Ivan Ilych was just as *comme il faut* and decorous a man, inspiring general respect and capable of separating his official duties from his private life, as he had been when acting as an official on special service. His duties now as examining magistrate were far more interesting and attractive than before. In his former position it had been pleasant to wear an undress uniform made by Scharmer, and to pass through the crowd of petitioners and officials who were timorously awaiting an audience with the governor, and who envied him as with free and easy gait he went straight into his chief's private room to have a cup of tea and a cigarette with him. But not many people had then been directly dependent on him – only police officials and the sectarians when he went on special missions – and he liked to treat them politely, almost as comrades, as if he were letting them feel that he who had the power to crush them was treating them in this simple, friendly way. There were then but few such people. But now, as an examining magistrate, Ivan Ilych felt that everyone without exception, even the most important and self-satisfied, was in his power, and that he need only write a few words on a sheet of paper with a certain heading, and this or that important, self-satisfied person would be brought before him in the role of an accused person or a witness, and if he did not choose to allow him to sit down, would have to stand before him and answer his questions. Ivan Ilych never abused his power; he tried on the contrary to soften its expression, but the consciousness of it and the possibility of softening its effect, supplied the chief interest and attraction of his office. In his work itself, especially in his examinations, he very soon acquired a method of eliminating all considerations irrelevant to the legal aspect of the case, and reducing even the most complicated case to a form in which it would be presented on paper only in its externals, completely excluding his personal opinion of the matter, while above all observing every prescribed formality. The work was new and Ivan Ilych was one of the first men to apply the new Code of 1864.

On taking up the post of examining magistrate in a new town, he made new acquaintances and connections, placed himself on a new footing and assumed a somewhat different tone. He took up an attitude of rather dignified aloofness towards the provincial authorities, but picked out the best circle of legal gentlemen and wealthy gentry living in the town and assumed a tone of slight dissatisfaction with the government, of moderate liberalism, and of enlightened citizenship. At the same time, without at all altering the elegance of his toilet, he ceased shaving his chin and allowed his beard to grow as it pleased.

Ivan Ilych settled down very pleasantly in this new town. The society there, which inclined towards opposition to the governor, was friendly, his salary was larger, and he began to play *vint*, which he found added not a little to the pleasure of life, for he had a capacity for cards, played good-humouredly, and calculated rapidly and astutely, so that he usually won.

After living there for two years he met his future wife, Praskovya Fedorovna Mikhel, who was the most attractive, clever and brilliant girl of the set in which he moved, and among other amusements and relaxations from his labours as examining magistrate, Ivan Ilych established light and playful relations with her.

While he had been an official on special service he had been accustomed to dance, but now as an examining magistrate it was exceptional for him to do so. If he danced now, he did it as if to show that though he served under the reformed order of things, and had reached the fifth official rank, yet when it came to dancing he could do it better than most people. So at the end of an evening he sometimes danced with Praskovya Fedorovna, and it was chiefly during these dances that he captivated her. She fell in love with him. Ivan Ilych had at first no definite intention of marrying, but when the girl fell in love with him he said to himself: 'Really, why shouldn't I marry?'

Praskovya Fedorovna came of a good family, was not bad looking, and had some little property. Ivan Ilych might have aspired to a more brilliant match, but even this was good. He had his salary, and she, he hoped, would have an equal income. She was well connected, and was a sweet, pretty and thoroughly correct young woman. To say that Ivan Ilych married because he fell in love with Praskovya Fedorovna and found that she sympathized with his views of life would be as incorrect as to say that he married because his social circle approved of the match. He was swayed by both these considerations: the marriage gave him personal satisfaction, and at the same time it was considered the right thing by the most highly placed of his associates. So Ivan Ilych got married.

The preparations for marriage and the beginning of married life, with its conjugal caresses, the new furniture, new crockery, and new linen, were very pleasant until his wife became pregnant – so that Ivan Ilych had begun to think that marriage would not impair the easy, agreeable, gay and always decorous character of his life, approved of by society and regarded by himself as natural, but would even improve it. But from the first months of his wife's pregnancy, something new, unpleasant, depressing and unseemly, and from which there was no way of escape, unexpectedly showed itself. His wife, without any reason – *de gaiete de coeur* as Ivan Ilych expressed it to himself – began to disturb the pleasure and propriety of their life. She began to be jealous without any cause, expected him to devote his whole attention to her, found fault with everything, and made coarse and ill-mannered scenes.

At first Ivan Ilych hoped to escape from the unpleasantness of this state of affairs by the same easy and decorous relation to life that had served him heretofore: he tried to ignore his wife's disa- greeable moods, continued to live in his usual easy and pleasant way, invited friends to his house for a game of cards, and also tried going out to his club or spending his evenings with friends. But one day his wife began upbraiding him so vigorously, using such coarse words, and continued to abuse him every time he did not fulfil her demands, so resolutely and with such evident determination not to give way till he submitted – that is, till he stayed at home and was bored just as she was – that he became alarmed. He now realized that matrimony – at any rate with Praskovya Fedorovna – was not always conducive to the pleasures and amenities of life, but on the contrary often infringed both comfort and propriety, and that he must therefore entrench himself against such infringement. And Ivan Ilych began to seek for means of doing so. His official duties were the one thing that imposed upon Praskovya Fedorovna, and by means of his official work and the duties attached to it he began struggling with his wife to secure his own independence.

With the birth of their child, the attempts to feed it and the various failures in doing so, and with the real and imaginary illnesses of mother and child, in which Ivan Ilych's sympathy was demanded but about which he understood nothing, the need of securing for himself an existence outside his family life became still more imperative.

As his wife grew more irritable and exacting and Ivan Ilych transferred the centre of gravity of his life more and more to his official work, so did he grow to like his work better and became more ambitious than before.

Very soon, within a year of his wedding, Ivan Ilych had realized that marriage, though it may add some comforts to life, is in fact a very intricate and difficult affair towards which in order to perform one's duty, that is, to lead a decorous life approved of by society, one must adopt a definite attitude just as towards one's official duties.

And Ivan Ilych evolved such an attitude towards married life. He only required of it those conveniences – dinner at home, housewife and bed – which it could give him, and above all that propriety of external forms required by public opinion. For the rest he looked for lighthearted pleasure and propriety, and was very thankful when he found them, but if he met with antagonism and querulousness he at once retired into his separate fenced-off world of official duties, where he found satisfaction.

Ivan Ilych was esteemed a good official, and after three years was made Assistant Public Prosecutor. His new duties, their importance, the possibility of indicting and imprisoning anyone he chose, the publicity his speeches received, and the success he had in all these things, made his work still more attractive.

More children came. His wife became more and more querulous and ill-tempered, but the attitude Ivan Ilych had adopted towards his home life rendered him almost impervious to her grumbling. After seven years' service in that town he was transferred to another province as Public Prosecutor. They moved, but were short of money and his wife did not like the place they moved to. Though the salary was higher, the cost of living was greater, besides which two of their children died and family life became still more unpleasant for him.

Praskovya Fedorovna blamed her husband for every inconvenience they encountered in their new home. Most of the conversations between husband and wife, especially as to the children's education, led to topics which recalled former disputes, and these disputes were apt to flare up again at any moment. There remained only those rare periods of amorousness which still came to them at times but did not last long. These were islets at which they anchored for a while and then again set out upon that ocean of veiled hostility which showed itself in their aloofness from one another. This aloofness might have grieved Ivan Ilych had he considered that it ought not to exist, but he now regarded the position as normal, and even made it the goal at which he aimed in family life. His aim was to free himself more and more from those unpleasantnesses and to give them a semblance of harmlessness and propriety. He attained this by spending less and less time with his family, and when obliged to be at home he tried to safeguard his position by the presence of outsiders. The chief thing however was that he had his official duties. The whole interest of his life now centred in the official world and that interest absorbed him. The consciousness of his power, being able to ruin anybody he wished to ruin, the importance, even the external dignity of his entry into court, or meetings with his subordinates, his success with superiors and inferiors, and above all his masterly handling of cases, of which he was conscious – all this gave him pleasure and filled his life, together with chats with his colleagues, dinners and bridge. So that on the whole Ivan Ilych's life continued to flow as he considered it should do – pleasantly and properly.

So things continued for another seven years. His eldest daughter was already sixteen, another child had died, and only one son was left, a schoolboy and a subject of dissension. Ivan Ilych wanted to put him in the School of Law, but to spite him Praskovya Fedorovna entered him at the High School. The daughter had been educated at home and had turned out well: the boy did not learn badly either.

III

So Ivan Ilych lived for seventeen years after his marriage. He was already a Public Prosecutor of long standing, and had declined several proposed transfers while awaiting a more desirable post, when an unanticipated and unpleasant occurrence quite upset the peaceful course of his life. He was expecting to be offered the post of presiding judge in a University town, but Happe somehow came to the front and obtained the appointment instead. Ivan Ilych became irritable, reproached Happe, and quarrelled both with him and with his immediate superiors – who became colder to him and again passed him over when other appointments were made.

This was in 1880, the hardest year of Ivan Ilych's life. It was then that it became evident on the one hand that his salary was insufficient for them to live on, and on the other that he had been forgotten, and not only this, but that what was for him the greatest and most cruel injustice appeared to others a quite ordinary occurrence. Even his father did not consider it his duty to help him. Ivan Ilych felt himself abandoned by everyone, and that they regarded his position with a salary of 3,500 rubles as quite normal and even fortunate. He alone knew that with the consciousness of the injustices done him, with his wife's incessant nagging, and with the debts he had contracted by living beyond his means, his position was far from normal.

In order to save money that summer he obtained leave of absence and went with his wife to live in the country at her brother's place. In the country, without his work, he experienced *ennui* for the first time in his life, and not only *ennui* but intolerable depression, and he decided that it was impossible to go on living like that, and that it was necessary to take energetic measures. Having passed a sleepless night pacing up and down the veranda, he decided to go to Petersburg and bestir himself, in order to punish those who had failed to appreciate him and to get transferred to another ministry.

Next day, despite many protests from his wife and her brother, he started for Petersburg with the sole object of obtaining a post with a salary of five thousand rubles a year. He was no longer bent on any particular department, or tendency, or kind of activity. All he now wanted was an appointment to another post with a salary of five thousand rubles, perhaps in the administration, in the banks, with the railways, in one of the Empress Marya's Institutions, or even in the customs – but it had to carry with it a salary of five thousand rubles and be in a ministry other than that in which they had failed to appreciate him.

And this quest of Ivan Ilych's was crowned with remarkable and unexpected success. At Kursk an acquaintance of his, F. I. Ilyin, got into the first-class carriage, sat down beside Ivan Ilych, and told him of a telegram just received by the governor of Kursk announcing that a change was about to take place in the ministry: Peter Ivanovich was to be superseded by Ivan Semonovich.

The proposed change, apart from its significance for Russia, had a special significance for Ivan Ilych, because by bringing forward a new man, Peter Petrovich, and consequently his friend Zachar Ivanovich, it was highly favourable for Ivan Ilych, since

Zachar Ivanovich was a friend and colleague of his.

In Moscow this news was confirmed, and on reaching Petersburg Ivan Ilych found Zachar Ivanovich and received a definite promise of an appointment in his former Department of Justice. A week later he telegraphed to his wife: 'Zachar in Miller's place. I shall receive appointment on presentation of report.'

Thanks to this change of personnel, Ivan Ilych had unexpectedly obtained an appointment in his former ministry which placed him two states above his former colleagues besides giving him five thousand rubles salary and three thousand five hundred rubles for expenses connected with his removal. All his ill humour towards his former enemies and the whole department vanished, and Ivan Ilych was completely happy.

He returned to the country more cheerful and contented than he had been for a long time. Praskovya Fedorovna also cheered up and a truce was arranged between them. Ivan Ilych told of how he had been feted by everybody in Petersburg, how all those who had been his enemies were put to shame and now fawned on him, how envious they were of his appointment, and how much everybody in Petersburg had liked him.

Praskovya Fedorovna listened to all this and appeared to believe it. She did not contradict anything, but only made plans for their life in the town to which they were going. Ivan Ilych saw with delight that these plans were his plans, that he and his wife agreed, and that, after a stumble, his life was regaining its due and natural character of pleasant lightheartedness and decorum.

Ivan Ilych had come back for a short time only, for he had to take up his new duties on the 10th of September. Moreover, he needed time to settle into the new place, to move all his belongings from the province, and to buy and order many additional things: in a word, to make such arrangements as he had resolved on, which were almost exactly what Praskovya Fedorovna too had decided on.

Now that everything had happened so fortunately, and that he and his wife were at one in their aims and moreover saw so little of one another, they got on together better than they had done since the first years of marriage. Ivan Ilych had thought of taking his family away with him at once, but the insistence of his wife's brother and her sister-in-law, who had suddenly become particularly amiable and friendly to him and his family, induced him to depart alone.

So he departed, and the cheerful state of mind induced by his success and by the harmony between his wife and himself, the one intensifying the other, did not leave him. He found a delightful house, just the thing both he and his wife had dreamt of. Spacious, lofty reception rooms in the old style, a convenient and dignified study, rooms for his wife and daughter, a study for his son – it might have been specially built for them. Ivan Ilych himself superintended the arrangements, chose the wallpapers, supplemented the furniture (preferably with antiques which he considered particularly *comme il faut*), and supervised the upholstering. Everything progressed and progressed and approached the ideal he had set himself: even when things were only half completed they exceeded his expectations. He saw what a refined and elegant character, free from vulgarity, it would all have when it was ready. On falling asleep he pictured to himself how the reception room would look. Looking at the yet unfinished drawing room he could see the fireplace, the screen, the what-not, the little chairs dotted here and there, the dishes and plates on the walls, and the bronzes, as they would be when everything was in place. He was pleased by the thought of how his wife and daughter, who shared his taste in this matter, would be impressed by it. They were certainly not expecting as much. He had been particularly successful in finding, and buying cheaply, antiques which gave a particularly aristocratic character to the whole place. But in his letters he intentionally understated everything in order to be able to surprise them. All this so absorbed him that his new duties – though he liked his official work – interested him less than he had expected. Sometimes he even had moments of absent-mindedness during the court sessions and would consider whether he should have straight or curved cornices for his curtains. He was so interested in it all that he often did things himself, rearranging the furniture, or rehanging the curtains. Once when mounting a step ladder to show the upholsterer, who did not understand, how he wanted the hangings draped, he made a false step and slipped, but being a strong and agile man he clung on and only knocked his side against the knob of the window frame. The bruised place was painful but the pain soon passed, and he felt particularly bright and well just then. He wrote: 'I feel fifteen years younger.' He thought he would have everything ready by September, but it dragged on till mid-October. But the result was charming not only in his eyes but to everyone who saw it.

In reality it was just what is usually seen in the houses of people of moderate means who want to appear rich, and therefore succeed only in resembling others like themselves: there are damasks, dark wood, plants, rugs, and dull and polished bronzes – all the things people of a certain class have in order to resemble other people of that class. His house was so like the others that it would never have been noticed, but to him it all seemed to be quite exceptional. He was very happy when he met his family at the station and brought them to the newly furnished house all lit up, where a footman in a white tie opened the door into the hall decorated with plants, and when they went on into the drawing room and the study uttering exclamations of delight. He conducted them everywhere, drank in their praises eagerly, and beamed with pleasure. At tea that evening, when Praskovya Fedorovna among other things asked him about his fall, he laughed, and showed them how he had gone flying and had frightened the upholsterer.

'It's a good thing I'm a bit of an athlete. Another man might have been killed, but I merely knocked myself, just here; it hurts when it's touched, but it's passing off already – it's only a bruise.' So they began living in their new home – in which, as always happens, when they got thoroughly settled in they found they were just one room short – and with the increased income, which as always was just a little (some five hundred rubles) too little, but it was all very nice.

Things went particularly well at first, before everything was finally arranged and while something had still to be done: this thing bought, that thing ordered, another thing moved and something else adjusted. Though there were some disputes between husband and wife, they were both so well satisfied and had so much to do that it all passed off without any serious quarrels. When nothing was left to arrange it became rather dull and something seemed to be lacking, but they were then making acquaintances, forming habits, and life was growing fuller.

Ivan Ilych spent his mornings at the law court and came home to diner, and at first he was generally in a good humour, though he occasionally became irritable just on account of his house. (Every spot on the tablecloth or the upholstery, and every broken window-blind string, irritated him. He had devoted so much trouble to arranging it all that every disturbance of it distressed him.) But on the whole his life ran its course as he believed life should do: easily, pleasantly and decorously. He got up at nine, drank his coffee, read the paper, and then put on his undress uniform and went to the law courts. There the harness in which he worked had already been stretched to fit him and he donned it without a hitch: petitioners, inquiries at the chancery, the chancery itself, and the sittings public and administrative. In all this the thing was to exclude everything fresh and vital, which always disturbs the regular course of official business, and to admit only official relations with people, and then only on official grounds. A man would come, for instance, wanting some information. Ivan Ilych, as one in whose sphere the matter did not lie, would have nothing to do with him: but if the man had some business with him in his official capacity, something that could be expressed on officially stamped paper, he would do everything, positively everything he could within the limits of such relations, and in doing so would maintain the semblance of friendly human relations, that is, would observe the courtesies of life. As soon as the official relations ended, so did everything else.

Ivan Ilych possessed this capacity to separate his real life from the official side of affairs and not mix the two, in the highest degree, and by long practice and natural aptitude had brought it to such a pitch that sometimes, in the manner of a virtuoso, he would even allow himself to let the human and official relations mingle. He let himself do this just because he felt that he could at any time he chose resume the strictly official attitude again and drop the human relation, and he did it all easily, pleasantly, correctly and even artistically.

In the intervals between the sessions he smoked, drank tea, chatted a little about politics, a little about general topics, a little about cards, but most of all about official appointments. Tired, but with the feelings of a virtuoso – one of the first violins who has played his part in an orchestra with precision – he would return home to find that his wife and daughter had been out paying calls, or had a visitor, and that his son had been to school, had done his homework with his tutor, and was surely learning what is taught at High Schools. Everything was as it should be. After dinner, if they had no visitors, Ivan Ilych sometimes read a book that was being much discussed at the time, and in the evening settled down to work, that is, read official papers, compared the depositions of witnesses, and noted paragraphs of the Code applying to them. This was neither dull nor amusing. It was dull when he might have been playing bridge, but if no bridge was available it was at any rate better than doing nothing or sitting with his wife.

Ivan Ilych's chief pleasure was giving little dinners to which he invited men and women of good social position, and just as his drawing room resembled all other drawing rooms so did his enjoyable little parties resemble all other such parties. Once they even gave a dance. Ivan Ilych enjoyed it and everything went off well, except that it led to a violent quarrel with his wife about the cakes and sweets. Praskovya Fedorovna had made her own plans, but Ivan Ilych insisted on getting everything from an expensive confectioner and ordered too many cakes, and the quarrel occurred because some of those cakes were left over and the confectioner's bill came to forty-five rubles. It was a great and disagreeable quarrel. Praskovya Fedorovna called him 'a fool and an imbecile', and he clutched at his head and made angry allusions to divorce.

But the dance itself had been enjoyable. The best people were there, and Ivan Ilych had danced with Princess Trufonova, a sister of the distinguished founder of the Society 'Bear My Burden'. The pleasures connected with his work were pleasures of ambition; his social pleasures were those of vanity; but Ivan Ilych's greatest pleasure was playing bridge. He acknowledged that whatever disagreeable incident happened in his life, the pleasure that beamed like a ray of light above everything else was to sit down to bridge with good players, not noisy partners, and of course to four-handed bridge (with five players it was annoying to have to stand out, though one pretended not to mind), to play a clever and serious game (when the cards allowed it) and then to have supper and drink a glass of wine. After a game of bridge, especially if he had won a little (to win a large sum was unpleasant), Ivan Ilych went to bed in a specially good humour.

So they lived. They formed a circle of acquaintances among the best people and were visited by people of importance and by young folk. In their views as to their acquaintances, husband, wife and daughter were entirely agreed, and tacitly and unanimously kept at arm's length and shook off the various shabby friends and relations who, with much show of affection, gushed into the drawing room with its Japanese plates on the walls. Soon these shabby friends ceased to obtrude themselves and only the best people remained in the Golovins' set.

Young men made up to Lisa, and Petrishchev, an examining magistrate and Dmitri Ivanovich Petrishchev's son and sole heir, began to be so attentive to her that Ivan Ilych had already spoken to Praskovya Fedorovna about it, and considered whether they should not arrange a party for them, or get up some private theatricals.

So they lived, and all went well, without change, and life flowed pleasantly.

IV

They were all in good health. It could not be called ill health if
Ivan Ilych sometimes said that he had a queer taste in his mouth
and felt some discomfort in his left side. But this discomfort
increased and, though not exactly painful, grew into a sense of
pressure in his side accompanied by ill humour. And his irritability
became worse and worse and began to mar the agreeable, easy
and correct life that had established itself in the Golovin family.
Quarrels between husband and wife became more and more
frequent, and soon the ease and amenity disappeared and even
the decorum was barely maintained. Scenes again became frequent,
and very few of those islets remained on which husband and wife
could meet without an explosion. Praskovya Fedorovna now had
good reason to say that her husband's temper was trying. With
characteristic exaggeration she said he had always had a dreadful
temper, and that it had needed all her good nature to put up with
it for twenty years. It was true that now the quarrels were started
by him. His bursts of temper always came just before dinner, often
just as he began to eat his soup. Sometimes he noticed that a plate
or dish was chipped, or the food was not right, or his son put his
elbow on the table, or his daughter's hair was not done as he liked
it, and for all this he blamed Praskovya Fedorovna. At first she
retorted and said disagreeable things to him, but once or twice
he fell into such a rage at the beginning of dinner that she realized it was due to some physical derangement brought on by
taking food, and so she restrained herself and did not answer, but
only hurried to get the dinner over. She regarded this self-restraint
as highly praiseworthy. Having come to the conclusion that her
husband had a dreadful temper and made her life miserable, she
began to feel sorry for herself, and the more she pitied herself
the more she hated her husband. She began to wish he would die;
yet she did not want him to die because then his salary would
cease. And this irritated her against him still more. She considered
herself dreadfully unhappy just because not even his death could

save her, and though she concealed her exasperation, that hidden exasperation of hers increased his irritation also. After one scene in which Ivan Ilych had been particularly unfair and after which he had said in explanation that he certainly was irritable but that it was due to his not being well, she said that if he was ill it should be attended to, and insisted on his going to see a celebrated doctor. He went. Everything took place as he had expected and as it always does. There was the usual waiting and the important air assumed by the doctor, with which he was so familiar (resembling that which he himself assumed in court), and the sounding and listening, and the questions which called for answers that were foregone conclusions and were evidently unnecessary, and the look of importance which implied that 'if only you put yourself in our hands we will arrange everything – we know indubitably how it has to be done, always in the same way for everybody alike.' It was all just as it was in the law courts. The doctor put on just the same air towards him as he himself put on towards an accused person.

The doctor said that so-and-so indicated that there was so-and-so inside the patient, but if the investigation of so-and-so did not confirm this, then he must assume that and that. If he assumed that and that, then...and so on. To Ivan Ilych only one question was important: was his case serious or not? But the doctor ignored that inappropriate question. From his point of view it was not the one under consideration, the real question was to decide between a floating kidney, chronic catarrh, or appendicitis. It was not a question of Ivan Ilyich's life or death, but one between a floating kidney and appendicitis. And that the doctor solved brilliantly, as it seemed to Ivan Ilych, in favour of the appendix, with the reservation that should an examination of the urine give fresh indications the matter would be reconsidered. All this was just what Ivan Ilych had himself brilliantly accomplished a thousand times in dealing with men on trial. The doctor summed up just as brilliantly, looking over his spectacles triumphantly and even gaily at the accused. From the doctor's summing up Ivan

Ilych concluded that things were bad, but that for the doctor, and perhaps for everybody else, it was a matter of indifference, though for him it was bad. And this conclusion struck him painfully, arousing in him a great feeling of pity for himself and of bitterness towards the doctor's indifference to a matter of such importance.

He said nothing of this, but rose, placed the doctor's fee on the table, and remarked with a sigh: 'We sick people probably often put inappropriate questions. But tell me, in general, is this complaint dangerous, or not?...'

The doctor looked at him sternly over his spectacles with one eye, as if to say: 'Prisoner, if you will not keep to the questions put to you, I shall be obliged to have you removed from the court.' 'I have already told you what I consider necessary and proper. The analysis may show something more.' And the doctor bowed.

Ivan Ilych went out slowly, seated himself disconsolately in his sledge, and drove home. All the way home he was going over what the doctor had said, trying to translate those complicated, obscure, scientific phrases into plain language and find in them an answer to the question: 'Is my condition bad? Is it very bad? Or is there as yet nothing much wrong?' And it seemed to him that the meaning of what the doctor had said was that it was very bad. Everything in the streets seemed depressing. The cabmen, the houses, the passers-by, and the shops were dismal. His ache, this dull gnawing ache that never ceased for a moment, seemed to have acquired a new and more serious significance from the doctor's dubious remarks. Ivan Ilych now watched it with a new and oppressive feeling.

He reached home and began to tell his wife about it. She listened, but in the middle of his account his daughter came in with her hat on, ready to go out with her mother. She sat down reluctantly to listen to this tedious story, but could not stand it long, and her mother too did not hear him to the end.

'Well, I am very glad,' she said. 'Mind now to take your medicine regularly. Give me the prescription and I'll send Gerasim to the chemist's.' And she went to get ready to go out. While she was in the room Ivan Ilych had hardly taken time to breathe, but he sighed deeply when she left it.

'Well,' he thought, 'perhaps it isn't so bad after all.'

He began taking his medicine and following the doctor's directions, which had been altered after the examination of the urine, but then it happened that there was a contradiction between the indications drawn from the examination of the urine and the symptoms that showed themselves. It turned out that what was happening differed from what the doctor had told him, and that he had either forgotten or blundered, or hidden something from him. He could not, however, be blamed for that, and Ivan Ilych still obeyed his orders implicitly and at first derived some comfort from doing so.

From the time of his visit to the doctor, Ivan Ilych's chief occupation was the exact fulfilment of the doctor's instructions regarding hygiene and the taking of medicine, and the observation of his pain and his excretions. His chief interest came to be people's ailments and people's health. When sickness, deaths or recoveries were mentioned in his presence, especially when the illness resembled his own, he listened with agitation which he tried to hide, asked questions, and applied what he heard to his own case.

The pain did not grow less, but Ivan Ilych made efforts to force himself to think that he was better. And he could do this so long as nothing agitated him. But as soon as he had any unpleasantness with his wife, any lack of success in his official work, or held bad cards at bridge, he was at once acutely sensible of his disease. He had formerly borne such mischances, hoping soon to adjust what was wrong, to master it and attain success, or make a grand slam. But now every mischance upset him and plunged him into despair. He would say to himself: 'There now, just as I was beginning to get better and the medicine had begun to take effect, comes this accursed misfortune, or unpleasantness...' And he was furious with the mishap, or with the people who were causing the unpleasantness and killing him, for he felt that this fury was killing him but he could not restrain it. One would have thought that it should have been clear to him that this exasperation with circumstances and people aggravated his illness, and that he ought therefore to ignore unpleasant occurrences. But he drew the very opposite conclusion: he said that he needed peace, and he watched for everything that might disturb it and became irritable at the slightest infringement of it. His condition was rendered worse by the fact that he read medical books and consulted doctors. The progress of his disease was so gradual that he could deceive himself when comparing one day with another – the difference was so slight. But when he consulted the doctors it seemed to him that he was getting worse, and even very rapidly. Yet despite this he was continually consulting them.

That month he went to see another celebrity, who told him almost the same as the first had done but put his questions rather differently, and the interview with this celebrity only increased Ivan Ilych's doubts and fears. A friend of a friend of his, a very good doctor, diagnosed his illness again quite differently from the others, and though he predicted recovery, his questions and suppositions bewildered Ivan Ilych still more and increased his doubts. A homeopathist diagnosed the disease in yet another way, and prescribed medicine which Ivan Ilych took secretly for a week. But after a week, not feeling any improvement and having lost confidence both in the former doctor's treatment and in this one's, he became still more despondent. One day a lady acquaintance mentioned a cure effected by a wonder-working icon. Ivan Ilych caught himself listening attentively and beginning to believe that it had occurred. This incident alarmed him. 'Has my mind really weakened to such an extent?' he asked himself. 'Nonsense! It's all rubbish. I mustn't give way to nervous fears but having chosen a doctor must keep strictly to his treatment. That is what I will do. Now it's all settled. I won't think about it, but will follow the treatment seriously till summer, and then we shall see. From now there must be no more of this wavering!' This was easy to say but impossible to carry out. The pain in his side oppressed him and seemed to grow worse and more incessant, while the taste in his mouth grew stranger and stranger. It seemed to him that his breath had a disgusting smell, and he was conscious of a loss of appetite and strength. There was no deceiving himself: something terrible, new, and more important than anything before in his life, was taking place within him of which he alone was aware. Those about him did not understand or would not understand it, but thought everything in the world was going on as usual. That tormented Ivan Ilych more than anything. He saw that his household, especially his wife and daughter who were in a perfect whirl of visiting, did not understand anything of it and were annoyed that he was so depressed and so exacting, as if he were to blame for it. Though they tried to disguise it he saw that he was an obstacle in their path, and that his wife had adopted a definite line in regard to his illness and kept to it regardless of anything he said or did. Her attitude was this: 'You know,' she would say to her friends, 'Ivan Ilych can't do as other people do, and keep to the treatment prescribed for him. One day he'll take his drops and keep strictly to his diet and go to bed in good time, but the next day unless I watch him he'll suddenly forget his medicine, eat sturgeon – which is forbidden – and sit up playing cards till one o'clock in the morning.'

'Oh, come, when was that?' Ivan Ilych would ask in vexation. 'Only once at Peter Ivanovich's.'

'And yesterday with Shebek.'

'Well, even if I hadn't stayed up, this pain would have kept me awake.'

'Be that as it may, you'll never get well like that, but will always make us wretched.'

Praskovya Fedorovna's attitude to Ivan Ilych's illness, as she expressed it both to others and to him, was that it was his own fault and was another of the annoyances he caused her. Ivan Ilych felt that this opinion escaped her involuntarily – but that did not make it easier for him.

At the law courts too, Ivan Ilych noticed, or thought he noticed, a strange attitude towards himself. It sometimes seemed to him that people were watching him inquisitively as a man whose place might soon be vacant. Then again, his friends would suddenly begin to chaff him in a friendly way about his low spirits, as if the awful, horrible and unheard-of thing that was going on within him, incessantly gnawing at him and irresistibly drawing him away, was a very agreeable subject for jests. Schwartz in particular irritated him by his jocularity, vivacity and savoir-faire, which reminded him of what he himself had been ten years ago.

Friends came to make up a set and they sat down to cards. They dealt, bending the new cards to soften them, and he sorted the diamonds in his hand and found he had seven. His partner said 'No trumps' and supported him with two diamonds. What more could be wished for? It ought to be jolly and lively. They would make a grand slam. But suddenly Ivan Ilych was conscious of that gnawing pain, that taste in his mouth, and it seemed ridiculous that in such circumstances he should be pleased to make a grand slam.

He looked at his partner Mikhail Mikhaylovich, who rapped the table with his strong hand and instead of snatching up the tricks pushed the cards courteously and indulgently towards Ivan Ilych that he might have the pleasure of gathering them up without the trouble of stretching out his hand for them. 'Does he think I am too weak to stretch out my arm?' thought Ivan Ilych, and forgetting what he was doing he over-trumped his partner, missing the grand slam by three tricks. And what was most awful of all was that he saw how upset Mikhail Mikhaylovich was about it but did not himself care. And it was dreadful to realize why he did not care.

They all saw that he was suffering, and said: 'We can stop if you are tired. Take a rest.' Lie down? No, he was not at all tired, and he finished the rubber. All were gloomy and silent. Ivan Ilych felt that he had diffused this gloom over them and could not dispel it. They had supper and went away, and Ivan Ilych was left alone with the consciousness that his life was poisoned and was poisoning the lives of others, and that this poison did not weaken but penetrated more and more deeply into his whole being.

With this consciousness, and with physical pain besides the terror, he must go to bed, often to lie awake the greater part of the night. Next morning he had to get up again, dress, go to the law courts, speak and write; or if he did not go out, spend at home those twenty-four hours a day each of which was a torture. And he had to live thus all alone on the brink of an abyss, with no one who understood or pitied him.

V

So one month passed and then another. Just before the New Year his brother-in-law came to town and stayed at their house. Ivan Ilych was at the law courts and Praskovya Fedorovna had gone shopping. When Ivan Ilych came home and entered his study he found his brother-in-law there – a healthy, florid man – unpacking his portmanteau himself. He raised his head on hearing Ivan Ilych's footsteps and looked up at him for a moment without a word. That stare told Ivan Ilych everything. His brother-in-law opened his mouth to utter an exclamation of surprise but checked himself, and that action confirmed it all.

'I have changed, eh?'

'Yes, there is a change.'

And after that, try as he would to get his brother-in-law to return to the subject of his looks, the latter would say nothing about it. Praskovya Fedorovna came home and her brother went out to her. Ivan Ilych locked the door and began to examine himself in the glass, first full face, then in profile. He took up a portrait of himself taken with his wife, and compared it with what he saw in the glass. The change in him was immense. Then he bared his arms to the elbow, looked at them, drew the sleeves down again, sat down on an ottoman, and grew blacker than night.

'No, no, this won't do!' he said to himself, and jumped up, went to the table, took up some law papers and began to read them, but could not continue. He unlocked the door and went into the reception room. The door leading to the drawing room was shut. He approached it on tiptoe and listened.

'No, you are exaggerating!' Praskovya Fedorovna was saying.

'Exaggerating! Don't you see it? Why, he's a dead man! Look at his eyes – there's no life in them. But what is it that is wrong with him?'

'No one knows. Nikolaevich said something, but I don't know what. And Leshchetitsky said quite the contrary...'

Ivan Ilych walked away, went to his own room, lay down and began musing; 'The kidney, a floating kidney.' He recalled all the doctors had told him of how it detached itself and swayed about. And by an effort of imagination he tried to catch that kidney and arrest it and support it. So little was needed for this, it seemed to him. 'No, I'll go to see Peter Ivanovich again.' He rang, ordered the carriage, and got ready to go.

'Where are you going, Jean?' asked his wife with a specially sad and exceptionally kind look. This exceptionally kind look irritated him. He looked morosely at her.

'I must go to see Peter Ivanovich.'

He went to see Peter Ivanovich, and together they went to see his friend, the doctor. He was in, and Ivan Ilych had a long talk with him.

Reviewing the anatomical and physiological details of what in the doctor's opinion was going on inside him, he understood it all.

There was something, a small thing, in the vermiform appendix. It might all come right. Only stimulate the energy of one organ and check the activity of another, then absorption would take place and everything would come right. He got home rather late for dinner, ate his dinner and conversed cheerfully, but could not for a long time bring himself to go back to work in his room. At last, however, he went to his study and did what was necessary, but the consciousness that he had put something aside – an important, intimate matter which he would revert to when his work was done

– never left him. When he had finished his work he remembered that this intimate matter was the thought of his vermiform appendix. But he did not give himself up to it, and went to the drawing room for tea.

There were callers there, including the examining magistrate who was a desirable match for his daughter, and they were conversing, playing the piano and singing. Ivan Ilych, as Praskovya Fedorovna remarked, spent that evening more cheerfully than usual, but he never for a moment forgot that he had postponed the important matter of the appendix.

At eleven o'clock he said goodnight and went to his bedroom. Since his illness he had slept alone in a small room next to his study. He undressed and took up a novel by Zola, but instead of reading it he fell into thought, and in his imagination that desired improvement in the vermiform appendix occurred. There were the absorption and evacuation and the re-establishment of normal activity. 'Yes, that's it!' he said to himself. 'One need only assist nature, that's all.' He remembered his medicine, rose, took it, and lay down on his back watching for the beneficent action of the medicine and for it to lessen the pain. 'I need only take it regularly and avoid all injurious influences. I am already feeling better, much better.' He began touching his side: it was not painful to the touch. 'There, I really don't feel it. It's much better already.' He put out the light and turned on his side ... 'The appendix is getting better, absorption is occurring.' Suddenly he felt the old, familiar, dull, gnawing pain, stubborn and serious. There was the same familiar loathsome taste in his mouth. His heart sank and he felt dazed. 'My God! My God!' he muttered. 'Again, again! And it will never cease.' And suddenly the matter presented itself in a quite different aspect. 'Vermiform appendix! Kidney!' he said to himself. 'It's not a question of appendix or kidney, but of life and...death. Yes, life was there and now it is going, going and I cannot stop it. Yes. Why deceive myself? Isn't it obvious to everyone but me that I'm dying, and that it's only a question of weeks, days...it may happen this moment. There was light and now there is darkness. I was here and now I'm going there! Where?' A chill came over him, his breathing ceased, and he felt only the throbbing of his heart. 'When I am not, what will there be? There will be nothing. Then where shall I be when I am no more? Can this be dying? No, I don't want to!' He jumped up and tried to light the candle, felt for it with trembling hands, dropped candle and candlestick on the floor, and fell back on his pillow.

'What's the use? It makes no difference,' he said to himself, staring with wide-open eyes into the darkness. 'Death. Yes, death. And none of them knows or wishes to know it, and they have no pity for me. Now they are playing.' (He heard through the door the distant sound of a song and its accompaniment.) 'It's all the same to them, but they will die too! Fools! I first, and they later, but it will be the same for them. And now they are merry... the beasts!'

Anger choked him and he was agonizingly, unbearably miserable. 'It is impossible that all men have been doomed to suffer this awful horror!' He raised himself.

'Something must be wrong. I must calm myself – must think it all over from the beginning.' And he again began thinking. 'Yes, the beginning of my illness: I knocked my side, but I was still quite well that day and the next. It hurt a little, then rather more. I saw the doctors, then followed despondency and anguish, more doctors, and I drew nearer to the abyss. My strength grew less and I kept coming nearer and nearer, and now I have wasted away and there is no light in my eyes. I think of the appendix – but this is death! I think of mending the appendix, and all the while here is death! Can it really be death?' Again terror seized him and he gasped for breath. He leant down and began feeling for the matches, pressing with his elbow on the stand beside the bed. It was in his way and hurt him, he grew furious with it, pressed on it still harder, and upset it. Breathless and in despair he fell on his back, expecting death to come immediately.

Meanwhile the visitors were leaving. Praskovya Fedorovna was seeing them off. She heard something fall and came in.

'What has happened?'

'Nothing. I knocked it over accidentally.'

She went out and returned with a candle. He lay there panting heavily, like a man who has run a thousand yards, and stared upwards at her with a fixed look.

'What is it, Jean?'

'No... no... thing. I upset it.' ('Why speak of it? She won't understand,' he thought.) And in truth she did not understand. She picked up the stand, lit his candle, and hurried away to see another visitor off. When she came back he still lay on his back, looking upwards.

'What is it? Do you feel worse?'

'Yes.'

She shook her head and sat down. 'Do you know, Jean, I think we must ask Leshchetitsky to come and see you here.' This meant calling in the famous specialist, regardless of expense.

He smiled malignantly and said 'No.' She remained a little longer and then went up to him and kissed his forehead. While she was kissing him he hated her from the bottom of his soul and with difficulty refrained from pushing her away.

'Good night. Please God you'll sleep.'

'Yes.'

VI

Ivan Ilych saw that he was dying, and he was in continual despair. In the depth of his heart he knew he was dying, but not only was he not accustomed to the thought, he simply did not and could not grasp it.

The syllogism he had learnt from Kiesewetter's Logic: 'Caius is a man, men are mortal, therefore Caius is mortal,' had always seemed to him correct as applied to Caius, but certainly not as applied to himself. That Caius – man in the abstract – was mortal, was perfectly correct, but he was not Caius, not an abstract man, but a creature quite, quite separate from all others. He had been little Vanya, with a mamma and a papa, with Mitya and Volodya, with the toys, a coachman and a nurse, afterwards with Katenka and will all the joys, griefs, and delights of childhood, boyhood, and youth. What did Caius know of the smell of that striped leather ball Vanya had been so fond of? Had Caius kissed his mother's hand like that, and did the silk of her dress rustle so for Caius? Had he rioted like that at school when the pastry was bad? Had Caius been in love like that? Could Caius preside at a session as he did? 'Caius really was mortal, and it was right for him to die; but for me, little Vanya, Ivan Ilych, with all my thoughts and emotions, it's altogether a different matter. It cannot be that I ought to die. That would be too terrible.'

Such was his feeling.

'If I had to die like Caius I would have known it was so. An inner voice would have told me so, but there was nothing of the sort in me and I and all my friends felt that our case was quite different from that of Caius. And now here it is!' he said to himself. 'It can't be. It's impossible! But here it is. How is this? How is one to understand it?'

He could not understand it, and tried to drive this false, incorrect, morbid thought away and to replace it by other proper and healthy thoughts. But that thought, and not the thought only but the reality itself, seemed to come and confront him.

And to replace that thought he called up a succession of others, hoping to find in them some support. He tried to get back into the former current of thoughts that had once screened the thought of death from him. But strange to say, all that had formerly shut off, hidden and destroyed his consciousness of death, no longer had that effect. Ivan Ilych now spent most of his time in attempting to re-establish that old current. He would say to himself: 'I will take up my duties again – after all I used to live by them.' And banishing all doubts he would go to the law courts, enter into conversation with his colleagues, and sit carelessly as was his wont, scanning the crowd with a thoughtful look and leaning both his emaciated arms on the arms of his oak chair; bending over as usual to a colleague and drawing his papers nearer he would interchange whispers with him, and then suddenly raising his eyes and sitting erect would pronounce certain words and open the proceedings. But suddenly in the midst of those proceedings the pain in his side, regardless of the stage the proceedings had reached, would begin its own gnawing work. Ivan Ilych would turn his attention to it and try to drive the thought of it away, but without success. It would come and stand before him and look at him, and he would be petrified and the light would die out of his eyes, and he would again begin asking himself whether It alone was true. And his colleagues and subordinates would see with surprise and distress that he, the brilliant and subtle judge, was becoming confused and making mistakes. He would shake himself, try to pull himself together, manage somehow to bring the sitting to a close, and return home with the sorrowful consciousness that his judicial labours could not as formerly hide from him what he wanted them to hide, and could not deliver him from It. And what was worst of all was that It drew his attention to itself not in order to make him take some action but only that he should look at It, look It straight in the face: look at It and without doing anything, suffer inexpressibly.

And to save himself from this condition Ivan Ilych looked for consolations – new screens – and new screens were found and for a while seemed to save him, but then they immediately fell to pieces or rather became transparent, as if It penetrated them and nothing could veil It.

In these latter days he would go into the drawing room he had arranged – that drawing room where he had fallen and for the sake of which (how bitterly ridiculous it seemed) he had sacrificed his life – for he knew that his illness originated with that knock. He would enter and see that something had scratched the polished table. He would look for the cause of this and find that it was the bronze ornamentation of an album, that had got bent. He would take up the expensive album which he had lovingly arranged, and feel vexed with his daughter and her friends for their untidiness – for the album was torn here and there and some of the photographs turned upside down. He would put it carefully in order and bend the ornamentation back into position. Then it would occur to him to place all those things in another corner of the room, near the plants. He would call the footman, but his daughter or wife would come to help him. They would not agree, and his wife would contradict him, and he would dispute and grow angry. But that was all right, for then he did not think about It. It was invisible.

But then, when he was moving something himself, his wife would say: 'Let the servants do it. You will hurt yourself again.' And suddenly It would flash through the screen and he would see it. It was just a flash, and he hoped it would disappear, but he would involuntarily pay attention to his side. 'It sits there as before, gnawing just the same!' And he could no longer forget It, but could distinctly see It looking at him from behind the flowers. 'What is it all for?' 'It really is so! I lost my life over that curtain as I might have done when storming a fort. Is that possible? How terrible and how stupid. It can't be true! It can't, but it is.' He would go to his study, lie down, and again be alone with It: face to face with It. And nothing could be done with It except to look at it and shudder.

VII

How it happened it is impossible to say because it came about step by step, unnoticed, but in the third month of Ivan Ilych's illness, his wife, his daughter, his son, his acquaintances, the doctors, the servants, and above all he himself, were aware that the whole interest he had for other people was whether he would soon vacate his place, and at last release the living from the discomfort caused by his presence and be himself released from his sufferings. He slept less and less. He was given opium and hypodermic injections of morphine, but this did not relieve him. The dull depression he experienced in a somnolent condition at first gave him a little relief, but only as something new; afterwards it became as distressing as the pain itself or even more so.

Special foods were prepared for him by the doctors' orders, but all those foods became increasingly distasteful and disgusting to him. For his excretions also special arrangements had to be made, and this was a torment to him every time – a torment from the uncleanliness, the unseemliness, and the smell, and from knowing that another person had to take part in it.

But just through his most unpleasant matter, Ivan Ilych obtained comfort. Gerasim, the butler's young assistant, always came in to carry the things out. Gerasim was a clean, fresh peasant lad, grown stout on town food and always cheerful and bright. At first the sight of him, in his clean Russian peasant costume, engaged on that disgusting task embarrassed Ivan Ilych.

Once when he got up from the commode too weak to draw up his trousers, he dropped into a soft armchair and looked with horror at his bare, enfeebled thighs with the muscles so sharply marked on them. Gerasim with a firm light tread, his heavy boots emitting a pleasant smell of tar and fresh winter air, came in wearing a clean Hessian apron, the sleeves of his print shirt tucked up over his strong bare young arms; and refraining from looking at his sick master out of consideration for his feelings, and restraining the joy of life that beamed from his face, he went up to the commode.

'Gerasim!' said Ivan Ilych in a weak voice.

'Gerasim started, evidently afraid he might have committed some blunder, and with a rapid movement turned his fresh, kind, simple young face which just showed the first downy signs of a beard.

'Yes, sir?'

'That must be very unpleasant for you. You must forgive me. I am helpless.'

'Oh, why, sir,' and Gerasim's eyes beamed and he showed his glistening white teeth, 'what's a little trouble? It's a case of illness with you, sir.'

And his deft strong hands did their accustomed task, and he went out of the room stepping lightly. Five minutes later he as lightly returned. Ivan Ilych was still sitting in the same position in the armchair. 'Gerasim,' he said when the latter had replaced the freshly washed utensil. 'Please come here and help me.' Gerasim went up to him. 'Lift me up. It is hard for me to get up, and I have sent Dmitri away.'

Gerasim went up to him, grasped his master with his strong arms deftly but gently, in the same way that he stepped – lifted him, supported him with one hand, and with the other drew up his trousers and would have set him down again, but Ivan Ilych asked to be led to the sofa. Gerasim, without an effort and without apparent pressure, led him, almost lifting him, to the sofa and placed him on it. 'Thank you. How easily and well you do it all!'

Gerasim smiled again and turned to leave the room. But Ivan Ilych felt his presence such a comfort that he did not want to let him go.

'One thing more, please move up that chair. No, the other one – under my feet. It is easier for me when my feet are raised.'

Gerasim brought the chair, set it down gently in place, and raised Ivan Ilych's legs on it. It seemed to Ivan Ilych that he felt better while Gerasim was holding up his legs.

'It's better when my legs are higher,' he said. 'Place that cushion under them.'

Gerasim did so. He again lifted the legs and placed them, and again Ivan Ilych felt better while Gerasim held his legs. When he set them down Ivan Ilych fancied he felt worse.

'Gerasim,' he said. 'Are you busy now?'

'Not at all, sir,' said Gerasim, who had learnt from the towns-folk how to speak to gentlefolk.

'What have you still to do?'

'What have I to do? I've done everything except chopping the logs for tomorrow.'

'Then hold my legs up a bit higher, can you?'

'Of course I can. Why not?' and Gerasim raised his master's legs higher and Ivan Ilych thought that in that position he did not feel any pain at all.

'And how about the logs?'

'Don't trouble about that, sir. There's plenty of time.'

Ivan Ilych told Gerasim to sit down and hold his legs, and began to talk to him. And strange to say it seemed to him that he felt better while Gerasim held his legs up.

After that Ivan Ilych would sometimes call Gerasim and get him to hold his legs on his shoulders, and he liked talking to him. Gerasim did it all easily, willingly, simply and with a good nature that touched Ivan Ilych. Health, strength and vitality in other people were offensive to him, but Gerasim's strength and vitality did not mortify but soothed him.

What tormented Ivan Ilych most was the deception, the lie, which for some reason they all accepted, that he was not dying but was simply ill, and that he only need keep quiet and undergo a treatment and then something very good would result. He however knew that do what they would nothing would come of it, only still more agonizing suffering and death. This deception tortured him – their not wishing to admit what they all knew and what he knew, but wanting to lie to him concerning his terrible condition, and wishing and forcing him to participate in that lie. Those lies – lies enacted over him on the eve of his death and destined to degrade this awful, solemn act to the level of their visitings, their curtains, their sturgeon for dinner – were a terrible agony for Ivan Ilych. And strangely enough, many times when they were going through their antics over him he had been within a hairbreadth of calling out to them: 'Stop lying! You know and I know that I am dying. Then at least stop lying about it!' But he had never had the spirit to do it. The awful, terrible act of his dying was, he could see, reduced by those about him to the level of a casual, unpleasant and almost indecorous incident (as if someone entered a drawing room defusing an unpleasant odour) and this was done by that very decorum which he had served all his life long. He saw that no one felt for him, because no one even wished to grasp his position. Only Gerasim recognized it and pitied him. And so Ivan Ilych felt at ease only with him. He felt comforted when Gerasim supported his legs (sometimes all night long) and refused to go to bed, saying: 'Don't you worry, Ivan Ilych. I'll get sleep enough later on,' or when he suddenly became familiar and exclaimed: 'If you weren't sick it would be another matter, but as it is, why should I grudge a little trouble?' Gerasim alone did not lie; everything showed that he alone understood the facts of the case and did not consider it necessary to disguise them, but simply felt sorry for his emaciated and enfeebled master. Once when Ivan Ilych was sending him away he even said straight out: 'We shall all of us die, so why should I grudge a little trouble?' – expressing the fact that he did not think his work burdensome, because he was doing it for a dying man and hoped someone would do the same for him when his time came.

Apart from this lying, or because of it, what most tormented Ivan Ilych was that no one pitied him as he wished to be pitied. At certain moments after prolonged suffering he wished most of all (though he would have been ashamed to confess it) for someone to pity him as a sick child is pitied. He longed to be petted and comforted. He knew he was an important functionary, that he had a beard turning grey, and that therefore what he longed for was impossible, but still he longed for it. And in Gerasim's attitude towards him there was something akin to what he wished for, and so that attitude comforted him. Ivan Ilych wanted to weep, wanted to be petted and cried over, and then his colleague Shebek would come, and instead of weeping and being petted, Ivan Ilych would assume a serious, severe and profound air, and by force of habit would express his opinion on a decision of the Court of Cassation and would stubbornly insist on that view. This falsity around him and within him did more than anything else to poison his last days.

VIII

It was morning. He knew it was morning because Gerasim had gone, and Peter the footman had come and put out the candles, drawn back one of the curtains and begun quietly to tidy up. Whether it was morning or evening, Friday or Sunday, made no difference, it was all just the same: the gnawing, unmitigated, agonizing pain, never ceasing for an instant, the consciousness of life inexorably waning but not yet extinguished, the approach of that ever dreaded and hateful Death which was the only reality, and always the same falsity. What were days, weeks, hours, in such a case?

'Will you have some tea, sir?'

'He wants things to be regular, and wishes the gentlefolk to drink tea in the morning,' thought Ivan Ilych, and only said 'No.'

'Wouldn't you like to move onto the sofa, sir?'

'He wants to tidy up the room, and I'm in the way. I am uncleanliness and disorder,' he thought, and said only:

'No, leave me alone.'

The man went on bustling about. Ivan Ilych stretched out his hand. Peter came up, ready to help.

'What is it, sir?'

'My watch.'

Peter took the watch which was close at hand and gave it to his master.

'Half-past eight. Are they up?'

'No sir, except Vladimir Ivanovich, who has gone to school. Praskovya Fedorovna ordered me to wake her if you asked for her. Shall I do so?'

'No, there's no need to.' 'Perhaps I'd better have some tea,' he thought, and added aloud: 'Yes, bring me some tea.'

Peter went to the door, but Ivan Ilych dreaded being left alone. 'How can I keep him here? Oh yes, my medicine.' 'Peter, give me my medicine.' 'Why not? Perhaps it may still do some good.' He took a spoonful and swallowed it. 'No, it won't help. It's all tomfoolery, all deception,' he decided as soon as he became aware of the familiar, sickly, hopeless taste. 'No, I can't believe in it any longer. But the pain, why this pain? If it would only cease just for a moment!' And he moaned. Peter turned towards him. 'It's all right. Go and fetch me some tea.'

Peter went out. Left alone Ivan Ilych groaned not so much with pain, terrible though that was, as from mental anguish. Always and forever the same, always these endless days and nights. If only it would come quicker! If only what would come quicker? Death, darkness?... No, no! anything rather than death!

When Peter returned with the tea on a tray, Ivan Ilych stared at him for a time in perplexity, not realizing who and what he was. Peter was disconcerted by that look and his embarrassment brought Ivan Ilych to himself.

'Oh, tea! All right, put it down. Only help me to wash and put on a clean shirt.'

And Ivan Ilych began to wash. With pauses for rest, he washed his hands and then his face, cleaned his teeth, brushed his hair, looked in the glass. He was terrified by what he saw, especially by the limp way in which his hair clung to his pallid forehead.

While his shirt was being changed he knew that he would be still more frightened at the sight of his body, so he avoided looking at it. Finally he was ready. He drew on a dressing gown, wrapped himself in a plaid, and sat down in the armchair to take his tea. For a moment he felt refreshed, but as soon as he began to drink the tea he was again aware of the same taste, and the pain also returned. He finished it with an effort, and then lay down stretching out his legs, and dismissed Peter. Always the same. Now a spark of hope flashes up, then a sea of despair rages, and always pain; always pain, always despair, and always the same. When alone he had a dreadful and distressing desire to call someone, but he knew beforehand that with others present it would be still worse. 'Another dose of morphine – to lose consciousness. I will tell him, the doctor, that he must think of something else. It's impossible, impossible, to go on like this.'

An hour and another pass like that. But now there is a ring at the door bell. Perhaps it's the doctor? It is. He comes in fresh, hearty, plump and cheerful, with that look on his face that seems to say: 'There now, you're in a panic about something, but we'll arrange it all for you directly!' The doctor knows this expression is out of place here, but he has put it on once for all and can't take it off – like a man who has put on a frock coat in the morning to pay a round of calls. The doctor rubs his hands vigorously and reassuringly.

'Brr! How cold it is! There's such a sharp frost; just let me warm myself!' he says, as if it were only a matter of waiting till he was warm, and then he would put everything right.

'Well now, how are you?'

Ivan Ilych feels that the doctor would like to say: 'Well, how are our affairs?' but that even he feels that this would not do, and says instead: 'What sort of a night have you had?' Ivan Ilych looks at him as much as to say: 'Are you really never ashamed of lying?' But the doctor does not wish to understand this question, and Ivan Ilych says: 'Just as terrible as ever. The pain never leaves me and never subsides. If only something ...'

'Yes, you sick people are always like that... There, now I think I am warm enough. Even Praskovya Fedorovna, who is so particular, could find no fault with my temperature. Well, now I can say good morning,' and the doctor presses his patient's hand.

Then dropping his former playfulness, he begins with a most serious face to examine the patient, feeling his pulse and taking his temperature, and then begins the sounding and auscultation. Ivan Ilych knows quite well and definitely that all this is nonsense and pure deception, but when the doctor, getting down on his knee, leans over him, putting his ear first higher then lower, and performs various gymnastic movements over him with a significant expression on his face, Ivan Ilych submits to it all as he used to submit to the speeches of the lawyers, though he knew very well that they were all lying and why they were lying.

The doctor, kneeling on the sofa, is still sounding him when Praskovya Fedorovna's silk dress rustles at the door and she is heard scolding Peter for not having let her know of the doctor's arrival.

She comes in, kisses her husband, and at once proceeds to prove that she has been up a long time already, and only owing to a misunderstanding failed to be there when the doctor arrived. Ivan Ilych looks at her, scans her all over, sets against her the whiteness and plumpness and cleanness of her hands and neck, the gloss of her hair, and the sparkle of her vivacious eyes. He hates her with his whole soul. And the thrill of hatred he feels for her makes him suffer from her touch.

Her attitude towards him and his diseases is still the same. Just as the doctor had adopted a certain relation to his patient which he could not abandon, so had she formed one towards him – that he was not doing something he ought to do and was himself to blame, and that she reproached him lovingly for this – and she could not now change that attitude.

'You see he doesn't listen to me and doesn't take his medicine at the proper time. And above all he lies in a position that is no doubt bad for him – with his legs up.'

She described how he made Gerasim hold his legs up.

The doctor smiled with a contemptuous affability that said: 'What's to be done? These sick people do have foolish fancies of that kind, but we must forgive them.'

When the examination was over the doctor looked at his watch, and then Praskovya Fedorovna announced to Ivan Ilych that it was of course as he pleased, but she had sent today for a celebrated specialist who would examine him and have a consultation with Michael Danilovich.

'Please don't raise any objections. I am doing this for my own sake,' she said ironically, letting it be felt that she was doing it all for his sake and only said this to leave him no right to refuse. He remained silent, knitting his brows. He felt that he was surrounded and involved in such a mesh of falsity that it was hard to unravel anything.

Everything she did for him was entirely for her own sake, and she told him she was doing for herself what she actually was doing for herself, as if that was so incredible that he must understand the opposite.

At half-past eleven the celebrated specialist arrived. Again the sounding began and the significant conversations in his presence and in another room, about the kidneys and the appendix, and the questions and answers, with such an air of importance that again, instead of the real question of life and death which now alone confronted him, the question arose of the kidney and appendix which were not behaving as they ought to and would now be attacked by Michael Danilovich and the specialist and forced to amend their ways.

The celebrated specialist took leave of him with a serious though not hopeless look, and in reply to the timid question Ivan Ilych, with eyes glistening with fear and hope, put to him as to whether there was a chance of recovery, said that he could not vouch for it but there was a possibility. The look of hope with which Ivan Ilych watched the doctor out was so pathetic that Praskovya Fedorovna, seeing it, even wept as she left the room to hand the doctor his fee.

The gleam of hope kindled by the doctor's encouragement did not last long. The same room, the same pictures, curtains, wall-paper, medicine bottles, were all there, and the same aching suffering body, and Ivan Ilych began to moan. They gave him a subcutaneous injection and he sank into oblivion.

It was twilight when he came to. They brought him his dinner and he swallowed some beef tea with difficulty, and then everything was the same again and night was coming on.

After dinner, at seven o'clock, Praskovya Fedorovna came into the room in evening dress, her full bosom pushed up by her corset, and with traces of powder on her face. She had reminded him in the morning that they were going to the theatre. Sarah Bernhardt was visiting the town and they had a box, which he had insisted on their taking. Now he had forgotten about it and her toilet offended him, but he concealed his vexation when he remembered that he had himself insisted on their securing a box and going because it would be an instructive and aesthetic pleasure for the children.

Praskovya Fedorovna came in, self-satisfied but yet with a rather guilty air. She sat down and asked how he was, but, as he saw, only for the sake of asking and not in order to learn about it, knowing that there was nothing to learn – and then went on to what she really wanted to say: that she would not on any account have gone but that the box had been taken and Helen and their daughter were going, as well as Petrishchev (the examining magistrate, their daughter's fiancé) and that it was out of the question to let them go alone; but that she would have much preferred to sit with him for a while; and he must be sure to follow the doctor's orders while she was away.

'Oh, and Fedor Petrovich' (the fiancé) 'would like to come in. May he? And Lisa?'

'All right.'

Their daughter came in in full evening dress, her fresh young flesh exposed (making a show of that very flesh which in his own case caused so much suffering), strong, healthy, evidently in love, and impatient with illness, suffering and death because they interfered with her happiness.

Fedor Petrovich came in too, in evening dress, his hair curled à la Capoul, a tight stiff collar round his long sinewy neck, an enormous white shirt front and narrow black trousers tightly stretched over his strong thighs. He had one white glove tightly drawn on, and was holding his opera hat in his hand.

Following him the schoolboy crept in unnoticed, in a new uniform, poor little fellow, and wearing gloves. Terribly dark shadows showed under his eyes, the meaning of which Ivan Ilych knew well. His son had always seemed pathetic to him, and now it was dreadful to see the boy's frightened look of pity. It seemed to Ivan Ilych that Vasya was the only one besides Gerasim who understood and pitied him.

They all sat down and again asked how he was. A silence followed. Lisa asked her mother about the opera glasses, and there was an altercation between mother and daughter as to who had taken them and where they had been put. This occasioned some unpleasantness.

Fedor Petrovich inquired of Ivan Ilych whether he had ever seen Sarah Bernhardt. Ivan Ilych did not at first catch the question, but then replied: 'No, have you seen her before?'

'Yes, in *Adrienne Lecouvreur*.'

Praskovya Fedorovna mentioned some roles in which Sarah Bernhardt was particularly good. Her daughter disagreed. Conversation sprang up as to the elegance and realism of her acting – the sort of conversation that is always repeated and is always the same.

In the midst of the conversation Fedor Petrovich glanced at Ivan Ilych and became silent. The others also looked at him and grew silent. Ivan Ilych was staring with glittering eyes straight before him, evidently indignant with them. This had to be rectified, but it was impossible to do so. The silence had to be broken, but for a time no one dared to break it and they all became afraid that the conventional deception would suddenly become obvious and the truth become plain to all. Lisa was the first to pluck up courage and break that silence, but by trying to hide what everybody was feeling, she betrayed it.

'Well, if we are going it's time to start,' she said, looking at her watch, a present from her father, and with a faint and significant smile at Fedor Petrovich relating to something known only to them. She got up with a rustle of her dress. They all rose, said good night, and went away.

When they had gone it seemed to Ivan Ilych that he felt better; the falsity had gone with them. But the pain remained – that same pain and that same fear that made everything monotonously alike, nothing harder and nothing easier. Everything was worse.

Again minute followed minute and hour followed hour. Everything remained the same and there was no cessation. And the inevitable end of it all became more and more terrible. 'Yes, send Gerasim here,' he replied to a question Peter asked.

IX

His wife returned late at night. She came in on tiptoe, but he heard her, opened his eyes, and made haste to close them again. She wished to send Gerasim away and to sit with him herself, but he opened his eyes and said: 'No, go away.'

'Are you in great pain?'

'Always the same.'

'Take some opium.'

He agreed and took some. She went away.

Till about three in the morning he was in a state of stupefied misery. It seemed to him that he and his pain were being thrust into a narrow, deep black sack, but though they were pushed further and further in they could not be pushed to the bottom. And this, terrible enough in itself, was accompanied by suffering. He was frightened yet wanted to fall through the sack, he struggled but yet co-operated. And suddenly he broke through, fell, and regained consciousness. Gerasim was sitting at the foot of the bed dozing quietly and patiently, while he himself lay with his emaciated stockinged legs resting on Gerasim's shoulders; the same shaded candle was there and the same unceasing pain.

'Go away, Gerasim,' he whispered.

'It's all right, sir. I'll stay a while.'

'No. Go away.'

He removed his legs from Gerasim's shoulders, turned sideways onto his arm, and felt sorry for himself. He only waited till Gerasim had gone into the next room and then restrained himself no longer but wept like a child. He wept on account of his helplessness, his terrible loneliness, the cruelty of man, the cruelty of God, and the absence of God. 'Why hast Thou done all this? Why hast Thou brought me here? Why, why dost Thou torment me so terribly?'

He did not expect an answer and yet wept because there was no answer and could be none. The pain again grew more acute, but he did not stir and did not call. He said to himself: 'Go on!

Strike me! But what is it for? What have I done to Thee? What is it for?'

Then he grew quiet and not only ceased weeping but even held his breath and became all attention. It was as though he were listening not to an audible voice but to the voice of his soul, to the current of thoughts arising within him.

'What is it you want?' was the first clear conception capable of expression in words, that he heard. 'What do you want? What do you want?' he repeated to himself.

'What do I want? To live and not to suffer,' he answered.

And again he listened with such concentrated attention that even his pain did not distract him. 'To live? How?' asked his inner voice.

'Why, to live as I used to – well and pleasantly.'

'As you lived before, well and pleasantly?' the voice repeated.

And in imagination he began to recall the best moments of his pleasant life. But strange to say none of those best moments of his pleasant life now seemed at all what they had then seemed – none of them except the first recollections of childhood. There, in childhood, there had been something really pleasant with which it would be possible to live if it could return. But the child who had experienced that happiness existed no longer, it was like a reminiscence of somebody else.

As soon as the period began which had produced the present Ivan Ilych, all that had then seemed joys now melted before his sight and turned into something trivial and often nasty.

And the further he departed from childhood and the nearer he came to the present the more worthless and doubtful were the joys. This began with the School of Law. A little that was really good was still found there – there was light-heartedness, friendship and hope. But in the upper classes there had already been fewer of such good moments. Then during the first years of his official career, when he was in the service of the governor, some pleasant moments again occurred: they were the memories of love for a woman. Then all became confused and there was still less of what was good; later on again there was still less that was good, and the further he went the less there was. His marriage, a mere accident, then the disenchantment that followed it, his wife's bad breath and the sensuality and hypocrisy: then that deadly official life and those preoccupations about money, a year of it, and two, and ten, and twenty, and always the same thing. And the longer it lasted the more deadly it became. 'It is as if I had been going downhill while I imagined I was going up. And that is really what it was. I was going up in public opinion, but to the same extent life was ebbing away from me. And now it is all done and there is only death.

'Then what does it mean? Why? It can't be that life is so senseless and horrible. But if it really has been so horrible and senseless, why must I die, and die in agony? There is something wrong! 'Maybe I did not live as I ought to have done,' it suddenly occurred to him. 'But how could that be, when I did everything properly?' he replied, and immediately dismissed from his mind this, the sole solution of all the riddles of life and death, as something quite impossible.

'Then what do you want now? To live? Live how? Live as you lived in the law courts when the usher proclaimed "The judge is coming!" The judge is coming, the judge!' he repeated to himself. 'Here he is, the judge. But I am not guilty!' he exclaimed angrily. 'What is it for?' And he ceased crying, but turning his face to the wall continued to ponder on the same question: Why, and for what purpose, is there all this horror? But however much he pondered he found no answer. And whenever the thought occurred to him, as it often did, that it all resulted from his not having lived as he ought to have done, he at once recalled the correctness of his whole life and dismissed so strange an idea.

X

Another fortnight passed. Ivan Ilych now no longer left his sofa. He would not lie in bed but lay on the sofa, facing the wall nearly all the time. He suffered ever the same unceasing agonies and in his loneliness pondered always on the same insoluble question: 'What is this? Can it be that it is Death?' And the inner voice answered: 'Yes, it is Death.'

'Why these sufferings?' And the voice answered, 'For no reason – they just are so.' Beyond and besides this there was nothing.

From the very beginning of his illness, ever since he had first been to see the doctor, Ivan Ilych's life had been divided between two contrary and alternating moods: now it was despair and the expectation of this uncomprehended and terrible death, and now hope and an intently interested observation of the functioning of his organs. Now before his eyes there was only a kidney or an intestine that temporarily evaded its duty, and now only that incomprehensible and dreadful death from which it was impossible to escape.

These two states of mind had alternated from the very beginning of his illness, but the further it progressed the more doubtful and fantastic became the conception of the kidney, and the more real the sense of impending death.

He had but to call to mind what he had been three months before and what he was now, to call to mind with what regularity he had been going downhill, for every possibility of hope to be shattered. Latterly during the loneliness in which he found himself as he lay facing the back of the sofa, a loneliness in the midst of a populous town and surrounded by numerous acquaintances and relations but that yet could not have been more complete anywhere – either at the bottom of the sea or under the earth – during that terrible loneliness Ivan Ilych had lived only in memories of the past. Pictures of his past rose before him one after another. They always began with what was nearest in time and then went back to what was most remote – to his childhood – and rested there. If he thought of the stewed prunes that had been offered him that day, his mind went back to the raw shrivelled French plums of his childhood, their peculiar flavour and the flow of saliva when he sucked their stones, and along with the memory of that taste came a whole series of memories of those days: his nurse, his brother, and their toys. 'No, I mustn't think of that... It is too painful,' Ivan Ilych said to himself, and brought himself back to the present – to the button on the back of the sofa and the creases in its morocco. 'Morocco is expensive, but it does not wear well: there had been a quarrel about it. It was a different kind of quarrel and a different kind of morocco that time when we tore father's portfolio and were punished, and mamma brought us some tarts...' And again his thoughts dwelt on his childhood, and again it was painful and he tried to banish them and fix his mind on something else.

Then again, together with that chain of memories another series passed through his mind – of how his illness had progressed and grown worse. There also the further back he looked the more life there had been. There had been more of what was good in life and more of life itself. The two merged together. 'Just as the pain went on getting worse and worse, so my life grew worse and worse,' he thought. 'There is one bright spot there at the back, at the beginning of life, and afterwards all becomes blacker and blacker and proceeds more and more rapidly – in inverse ratio to the square of the distance from death,' thought Ivan Ilych. And the example of a stone falling downwards with increasing velocity entered his mind. Life, a series of increasing sufferings, flies further and further towards its end – the most terrible suffering. 'I am flying...' He shuddered, shifted himself, and tried to resist, but was already aware that resistance was impossible, and again with eyes weary of gazing but unable to cease seeing what was before them, he stared at the back of the sofa and waited – awaiting that dreadful fall and shock and destruction.

'Resistance is impossible!' he said to himself. 'If I could only understand what it is all for! But that too is impossible. An explanation would be possible if it could be said that I have not lived as I ought to. But it is impossible to say that,' and he remembered all the legality, correctitude and propriety of his life. 'That at any rate can certainly not be admitted,' he thought, and his lips smiled ironically as if someone could see that smile and be taken in by it. 'There is no explanation! Agony, death... What for?'

XI

Another two weeks went by in this way and during that fortnight an event occurred that Ivan Ilych and his wife had desired. Petrishchev formally proposed. It happened in the evening. The next day Praskovya Fedorovna came into her husband's room considering how best to inform him of it, but that very night there had been a fresh change for the worse in his condition. She found him still lying on the sofa but in a different position. He lay on his back, groaning and staring fixedly straight in front of him.

She began to remind him of his medicines, but he turned his eyes towards her with such a look that she did not finish what she was saying; so great an animosity, to her in particular, did that look express.

'For Christ's sake let me die in peace!' he said.

She would have gone away, but just then their daughter came in and went up to say good morning. He looked at her as he had done at his wife, and in reply to her inquiry about his health said dryly that he would soon free them all of himself. They were both silent and after sitting with him for a while went away.

'Is it our fault?' Lisa asked her mother. 'It's as if we were to blame! I am sorry for papa, but why should we be tortured?'

The doctor came at his usual time. Ivan Ilych answered 'Yes' and 'No,' never taking his angry eyes from him, and at last said: 'You know you can do nothing for me, so leave me alone.'

'We can ease your sufferings.'

'You can't even do that. Let me be.'

The doctor went into the drawing room and told Praskovya Fedorovna that the case was very serious and that the only resource left was opium to allay her husband's sufferings, which must be terrible. It was true, as the doctor said, that Ivan Ilych's physical sufferings were terrible, but worse than the physical sufferings were his mental sufferings which were his chief torture.

His mental sufferings were due to the fact that that night, as he looked at Gerasim's sleepy, good-natured face with its prominent cheekbones, the question suddenly occurred to him: 'What if my whole life has been wrong?'

It occurred to him that what had appeared perfectly impossible before, namely that he had not spent his life as he should have done, might after all be true. It occurred to him that his scarcely perceptible attempts to struggle against what was considered good by the most highly placed people, those scarcely noticeable impulses which he had immediately suppressed, might have been the real thing, and all the rest false. And his professional duties and the whole arrangement of his life and of his family, and all his social and official interests, might all have been false. He tried to defend all those things to himself and suddenly felt the weakness of what he was defending. There was nothing to defend.

'But if that is so,' he said to himself, 'and I am leaving this life with the consciousness that I have lost all that was given me and it is impossible to rectify it – what then?' He lay on his back and began to pass his life in review in quite a new way. In the morning when he saw first his footman, then his wife, then his daughter, and then the doctor, their every word and movement confirmed to him the awful truth that had been revealed to him during the night. In them he saw himself – all that for which he had lived – and saw clearly that it was not real at all, but a terrible and huge deception which had hidden both life and death. This consciousness intensified his physical suffering tenfold. He groaned and tossed about, and pulled at his clothing which choked and stifled him. And he hated them on that account.

He was given a large dose of opium and became unconscious, but at noon his sufferings began again. He drove everybody away and tossed from side to side. His wife came to him and said:

'Jean, my dear, do this for me. It can't do any harm and often helps. Healthy people often do it.' He opened his eyes wide.

'What? Take communion? Why? It's unnecessary! However...' She began to cry.

'Yes, do, my dear. I'll send for our priest. He is such a nice man.'

'All right. Very well,' he muttered.

When the priest came and heard his confession, Ivan Ilych was softened and seemed to feel a relief from his doubts and consequently from his sufferings, and for a moment there came a ray of hope. He again began to think of the vermiform appendix and the possibility of correcting it. He received the sacrament with tears in his eyes.

When they laid him down again afterwards he felt a moment's ease, and the hope that he might live awoke in him again. He began to think of the operation that had been suggested to him. 'To live! I want to live!' he said to himself.

His wife came in to congratulate him after his communion, and when uttering the usual conventional words she added:

'You feel better, don't you?'

Without looking at her he said 'Yes.'

Her dress, her figure, the expression of her face, the tone of her voice, all revealed the same thing. 'This is wrong, it is not as it should be. All you have lived for and still live for is falsehood and deception, hiding life and death from you.' And as soon as he admitted that thought, his hatred and his agonizing physical suffering again sprang up, and with that suffering a consciousness of the unavoidable, approaching end. And to this was added a new sensation of grinding shooting pain and a feeling of suffocation.

The expression of his face when he uttered that 'Yes' was dreadful. Having uttered it, he looked her straight in the eyes, turned on his face with a rapidity extraordinary in his weak state and shouted:

'Go away! Go away and leave me alone!'

XII

From that moment the screaming began that continued for three days, and was so terrible that one could not hear it through two closed doors without horror. At the moment he answered his wife he realized that he was lost, that there was no return, that the end had come, the very end, and his doubts were still unsolved and remained doubts.

'Oh! Oh! Oh!' he cried in various intonations. He had begun by screaming 'I won't!' and continued screaming on the letter 'O'.

For three whole days, during which time did not exist for him, he struggled in that black sack into which he was being thrust by an invisible, resistless force. He struggled as a man condemned to death struggles in the hands of the executioner, knowing that he cannot save himself. And every moment he felt that despite all his efforts he was drawing nearer and nearer to what terrified him. He felt that his agony was due to his being thrust into that black hole and still more to his not being able to get right into it. He was hindered from getting into it by his conviction that his life had been a good one. That very justification of his life held him fast and prevented his moving forward, and it caused him most torment of all.

Suddenly some force struck him in the chest and side, making it still harder to breathe, and he fell through the hole and there at the bottom was a light. What had happened to him was like the sensation one sometimes experiences in a railway carriage when one thinks one is going backwards while one is really going forwards and suddenly becomes aware of the real direction.

'Yes, it was not the right thing,' he said to himself, 'but that's no matter. It can be done. But what is the right thing? he asked himself, and suddenly grew quiet.

This occurred at the end of the third day, two hours before his death. Just then his schoolboy son had crept softly in and gone up to the bedside. The dying man was still screaming desperately and waving his arms. His hand fell on the boy's head, and the boy caught it, pressed it to his lips, and began to cry.

At that very moment Ivan Ilych fell through and caught sight of the light, and it was revealed to him that though his life had not been what it should have been, this could still be rectified. He asked himself, 'What is the right thing?' and grew still, listening. Then he felt that someone was kissing his hand. He opened his eyes, looked at his son, and felt sorry for him. His wife came up to him and he glanced at her. She was gazing at him open-mouthed, with undried tears on her nose and cheek and a despairing look on her face. He felt sorry for her too.

'Yes, I am making them wretched,' he thought. 'They are sorry, but it will be better for them when I die.' He wished to say this but had not the strength to utter it. 'Besides, why speak? I must act,' he thought. with a look at his wife he indicated his son and said: 'Take him away... sorry for him... sorry for you too...' He tried to add, 'Forgive me,' but said 'Forego' and waved his hand, knowing that He whose understanding mattered would understand.

And suddenly it grew clear to him that what had been oppressing him and would not leave him was all dropping away at once from two sides, from ten sides, and from all sides. He was sorry for them, he must act so as not to hurt them: release them and free himself from these sufferings. 'How good and how simple!' he thought. 'And the pain?' he asked himself. 'What has become of it? Where are you, pain?'

He turned his attention to it.

'Yes, here it is. Well, what of it? Let the pain be.'

'And death... Where is it?'

He sought his former accustomed fear of death and did not find it. 'Where is it? What death?' There was no fear because there was no death.

In place of death there was light.

'So that's what it is!' he suddenly exclaimed aloud. 'What joy!'

To him all this happened in a single instant, and the meaning of that instant did not change. For those present his agony continued for another two hours. Something rattled in his throat, his emaciated body twitched, then the gasping and rattle became less and less frequent.

'It is finished!' said someone near him. He heard these words and repeated them in his soul.

'Death is finished,' he said to himself. 'It is no more!'

He drew in a breath, stopped in the midst of a sigh, stretched out, and died.

THE THREE HERMITS

AN OLD LEGEND CURRENT IN THE
VOLGA DISTRICT

'And in praying use not vain repetitions, as the Gentiles do:
for they think that they shall be heard for their much
speaking. Be not therefore like unto them: for your Father
knoweth what things ye have need of, before ye ask Him.'
(Matthew 6: 7–8).

A bishop was sailing from Archangel to the Solovetsky
Monastery; and on the same vessel were a number of pilgrims
on their way to visit the shrines at that place. The voyage was
a smooth one. The wind favourable, and the weather fair. The
pilgrims lay on deck, eating, or sat in groups talking to one
another. The Bishop, too, came on deck, and as he was pacing
up and down, he noticed a group of men standing near the
prow and listening to a fisherman, who was pointing to the
sea and telling them something. The Bishop stopped, and
looked in the direction in which the man was pointing. He
could see nothing, however, but the sea glistening in the
sunshine. He drew nearer to listen, but when the man saw
him, he took off his cap and was silent. The rest of the people
also took off their caps, and bowed.

'Do not let me disturb you, friends,' said the Bishop. 'I came
to hear what this good man was saying.'

'The fisherman was telling us about the hermits,' replied one, a tradesman, rather bolder than the rest.

'What hermits?' asked the Bishop, going to the side of the vessel and seating himself on a box. 'Tell me about them. I should like to hear. What were you pointing at?'

'Why, that little island you can just see over there,' answered the man, pointing to a spot ahead and a little to the right. 'That is the island where the hermits live for the salvation of their souls.'

'Where is the island?' asked the Bishop. 'I see nothing.'

'There, in the distance, if you will please look along my hand. Do you see that little cloud? Below it, and a bit to the left, there is just a faint streak. That is the island.'

The Bishop looked carefully, but his unaccustomed eyes could make out nothing but the water shimmering in the sun.

'I cannot see it,' he said. 'But who are the hermits that live there?'

'They are holy men,' answered the fisherman. 'I had long heard tell of them, but never chanced to see them myself till the year before last.'

And the fisherman related how once, when he was out fishing, he had been stranded at night upon that island, not knowing where he was. In the morning, as he wandered about the island, he came across an earth hut, and met an old man standing near it. Presently two others came out, and after having fed him, and dried his things, they helped him mend his boat.

'And what are they like?' asked the Bishop.

'One is a small man and his back is bent. He wears a priest's cassock and is very old; he must be more than a hundred, I should say. He is so old that the white of his beard is taking a greenish tinge, but he is always smiling, and his face is as bright as an angel's from heaven. The second is taller, but he also is very old. He wears a tattered peasant coat. His beard is broad, and of a yellowish grey colour. He is a strong man. Before I had time to help him, he turned my boat over as if it were only a pail. He too, is kindly and cheerful. The third is tall, and has a beard as white as snow and reaching to his knees. He is stern, with over-hanging eyebrows; and he wears nothing but a mat tied round his waist.'

'And did they speak to you?' asked the Bishop.

'For the most part they did everything in silence, and spoke but little even to one another. One of them would just give a glance, and the others would understand him. I asked the tallest whether they had lived there long. He frowned, and muttered something as if he were angry; but the oldest one took his hand and smiled, and then the tall one was quiet. The oldest one only said: "Have mercy upon us," and smiled.'

While the fisherman was talking, the ship had drawn nearer to the island.

'There, now you can see it plainly, if your Grace will please to look,' said the tradesman, pointing with his hand.

The Bishop looked, and now he really saw a dark streak – which was the island. Having looked at it a while, he left the prow of the vessel, and going to the stern, asked the helmsman:

'What island is that?'

'That one,' replied the man, 'has no name. There are many such in this sea.'

'Is it true that there are hermits who live there for the salvation of their souls?'

'So it is said, your Grace, but I don't know if it's true. Fishermen say they have seen them; but of course they may only be spinning yarns.'

'I should like to land on the island and see these men,' said the Bishop. 'How could I manage it?'

'The ship cannot get close to the island,' replied the helmsman, 'but you might be rowed there in a boat. You had better speak to the captain.'

The captain was sent for and came.

'I should like to see these hermits,' said the Bishop. 'Could I not be rowed ashore?'

The captain tried to dissuade him.

'Of course it could be done,' said he, 'but we should lose much time. And if I might venture to say so to your Grace, the old men are not worth your pains. I have heard say that they are foolish old fellows, who understand nothing, and never speak a word, any more than the fish in the sea.'

'I wish to see them,' said the Bishop, 'and I will pay you for your trouble and loss of time. Please let me have a boat.'

There was no help for it; so the order was given. The sailors trimmed the sails, the steersman put up the helm, and the ship's course was set for the island. A chair was placed at the prow for the Bishop, and he sat there, looking ahead. The passengers all collected at the prow, and gazed at the island. Those who had the sharpest eyes could presently make out the rocks on it, and then a mud hut was seen. At last one man saw the hermits themselves. The captain brought a telescope and, after looking through it, handed it to the Bishop.

'It's right enough. There are three men standing on the shore. There, a little to the right of that big rock.'

The Bishop took the telescope, got it into position, and he saw the three men: a tall one, a shorter one, and one very small and bent, standing on the shore and holding each other by the hand.

The captain turned to the Bishop.

'The vessel can get no nearer in than this, your Grace. If you wish to go ashore, we must ask you to go in the boat, while we anchor here.'

The cable was quickly let out, the anchor cast, and the sails furled. There was a jerk, and the vessel shook. Then a boat having been lowered, the oarsmen jumped in, and the Bishop descended the ladder and took his seat. The men pulled at their oars, and the boat moved rapidly towards the island. When they came within a stone's throw, they saw three old men: a tall one with only a mat tied round his waist: a shorter one in a tattered peasant coat, and a very old one bent with age and wearing an old cassock – all three standing hand in hand.

The oarsmen pulled in to the shore, and held on with the boathook while the Bishop got out.

The old men bowed to him, and he gave them his benediction, at which they bowed still lower. Then the Bishop began to speak to them.

'I have heard,' he said, 'that you, godly men, live here saving your own souls, and praying to our Lord Christ for your fellow men. I, an unworthy servant of Christ, am called, by God's mercy, to keep and teach His flock. I wished to see you, servants of God, and to do what I can to teach you, also.'

The old men looked at each other smiling, but remained silent.

'Tell me,' said the Bishop, 'what you are doing to save your souls, and how you serve God on this island.'

The second hermit sighed, and looked at the oldest, the very ancient one. The latter smiled, and said:

'We do not know how to serve God. We only serve and support ourselves, servant of God.'

'But how do you pray to God?' asked the Bishop.

'We pray in this way,' replied the hermit. 'Three are ye, three are we, have mercy upon us.'

And when the old man said this, all three raised their eyes to heaven, and repeated:

'Three are ye, three are we, have mercy upon us!'

The Bishop smiled.

'You have evidently heard something about the Holy Trinity,' said he. 'But you do not pray aright. You have won my affection, godly men. I see you wish to please the Lord, but you do not know how to serve Him. That is not the way to pray; but listen to me, and I will teach you. I will teach you, not a way of my own, but the way in which God in the Holy Scriptures has commanded all men to pray to Him.'

And the Bishop began explaining to the hermits how God had revealed Himself to men; telling them of God the Father, and God the Son, and God the Holy Ghost.

'God the Son came down on Earth,' said he, 'to save men, and this is how He taught us all to pray. Listen, and repeat after me: "Our Father."'

And the first old man repeated after him, 'Our Father,' and the second said, 'Our Father,' and the third said, 'Our Father.'

'Which art in heaven,' continued the Bishop.

The first hermit repeated, 'Which art in heaven,' but the second blundered over the words, and the tall hermit could not say them properly. His hair had grown over his mouth so that he could not speak plainly. The very old hermit, having no teeth, also mumbled indistinctly.

The Bishop repeated the words again, and the old men repeated them after him. The Bishop sat down on a stone, and the old men stood before him, watching his mouth, and repeating the words as he uttered them. And all day long the Bishop laboured, saying a word twenty, thirty, a hundred times over, and the old men repeated it after him. They blundered, and he corrected them, and made them begin again.

The Bishop did not leave off till he had taught them the whole of the Lord's Prayer so that they could not only repeat it after him, but could say it by themselves. The middle one was the first to know it, and to repeat the whole of it alone. The Bishop made him say it again and again, and at last the others could say it too.

It was getting dark, and the moon was appearing over the water, before the Bishop rose to return to the vessel. When he took leave of the old men, they all bowed down to the ground before him. He raised them, and kissed each of them, telling them to pray as he had taught them. Then he got into the boat and returned to the ship.

And as he sat in the boat and was rowed to the ship he could hear the three voices of the hermits loudly repeating the Lord's Prayer. As the boat drew near the vessel their voices could no longer be heard, but they could still be seen in the moonlight, standing as he had left them on the shore, the shortest in the middle, the tallest on the right, the middle one on the left. As soon as the Bishop had reached the vessel and got on board, the anchor was weighed and the sails unfurled. The wind filled them, and the ship sailed away, and the Bishop took a seat in the stern

and watched the island they had left. For a time he could still see
the hermits, but presently they disappeared from sight, though
the island was still visible. At last it too vanished, and only the
sea was to be seen, rippling in the moonlight.

The pilgrims lay down to sleep, and all was quiet on deck. The
Bishop did not wish to sleep, but sat alone at the stern, gazing at
the sea where the island was no longer visible, and thinking of
the good old men. He thought how pleased they had been to
learn the Lord's Prayer; and he thanked God for having sent him
to teach and help such godly men.

So the Bishop sat, thinking, and gazing at the sea where the
island had disappeared. And the moonlight flickered before his
eyes, sparkling, now here, now there, upon the waves. Suddenly
he saw something white and shining, on the bright path which
the moon cast across the sea. Was it a seagull, or the little gleaming
sail of some small boat? The Bishop fixed his eyes on it, wondering.

'It must be a boat sailing after us,' thought he, 'but it is overtaking us very rapidly. It was far, far away a minute ago, but now
it is much nearer. It cannot be a boat, for I can see no sail; but
whatever it may be, it is following us, and catching us up.'

And he could not make out what it was. Not a boat, nor a bird,
nor a fish! It was too large for a man, and besides a man could
not be out there in the midst of the sea. The Bishop rose, and
said to the helmsman:

'Look there, what is that, my friend? What is it?' the Bishop
repeated, though he could now see plainly what it was – the three
hermits running upon the water, all gleaming white, their grey
beards shining, and approaching the ship as quickly as though it
were not moving.

The steersman looked and let go the helm in terror.

'Oh Lord! The hermits are running after us on the water as
though it were dry land!'

The passengers hearing him, jumped up, and crowded to the
stern. They saw the hermits coming along hand in hand, and the
two outer ones beckoning the ship to stop. All three were gliding

along upon the water without moving their feet. Before the ship could be stopped, the hermits had reached it, and raising their heads, all three as with one voice, began to say:

'We have forgotten your teaching, servant of God. As long as we kept repeating it we remembered, but when we stopped saying it for a time, a word dropped out, and now it has all gone to pieces. We can remember nothing of it. Teach us again.'

The Bishop crossed himself, and leaning over the ship's side, said:

'Your own prayer will reach the Lord, men of God. It is not for me to teach you. Pray for us sinners.'

And the Bishop bowed low before the old men; and they turned and went back across the sea. And a light shone until daybreak on the spot where they were lost to sight.

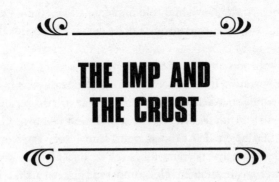

THE IMP AND
THE CRUST

A poor peasant set out early one morning to plough, taking
with him for his breakfast a crust of bread. He got his plough
ready, wrapped the bread in his coat, put it under a bush, and set
to work. After a while, when his horse was tired and he was hungry,
the peasant fixed the plough, let the horse loose to graze, and
went to get his coat and his breakfast.

He lifted the coat, but the bread was gone! He looked and
looked, turned the coat over, shook it out – but the bread was
gone. The peasant could not make this out at all.

'That's strange,' thought he; 'I saw no one, but all the same
someone has been here and has taken the bread!'

It was an imp who had stolen the bread while the peasant was
ploughing, and at that moment he was sitting behind the bush,
waiting to hear the peasant swear and call on the Devil.

The peasant was sorry to lose his breakfast, but 'It can't be
helped,' said he. 'After all, I shan't die of hunger! No doubt
whoever took the bread needed it. May it do him good!'

And he went to the well, had a drink of water, and rested a
bit. Then he caught his horse, harnessed it, and began ploughing
again.

The imp was crestfallen at not having made the peasant sin,
and he went to report what had happened to the Devil, his master.

He came to the Devil and told how he had taken the peasant's bread, and how the peasant instead of cursing had said, 'May it do him good!'

The Devil was angry, and replied: 'If the man got the better of you, it was your own fault – you don't understand your business! If the peasants, and their wives after them, take to that sort of thing, it will be all up with us. The matter can't be left like that! Go back at once,' said he, 'and put things right. If in three years you don't get the better of that peasant, I'll have you ducked in holy water!'

The imp was frightened. He scampered back to earth, thinking how he could redeem his fault. He thought and thought, and at last hit upon a good plan.

He turned himself into a labouring man, and went and took service with the poor peasant. The first year he advised the peasant to sow corn in a marshy place. The peasant took his advice, and sowed in the marsh. The year turned out a very dry one, and the crops of the other peasants were all scorched by the sun, but the poor peasant's corn grew thick and tall and full-eared. Not only had he grain enough to last him for the whole year, but he had much left over besides.

The next year the imp advised the peasant to sow on the hill; and it turned out a wet summer. Other people's corn was beaten down and rotted and the ears did not fill; but the peasant's crop, up on the hill, was a fine one. He had more grain left over than before, so that he did not know what to do with it all.

Then the imp showed the peasant how he could mash the grain and distil spirit from it; and the peasant made strong drink, and began to drink it himself and to give it to his friends.

So the imp went to the Devil, his master, and boasted that he had made up for his failure. The Devil said that he would come and see for himself how the case stood.

He came to the peasant's house, and saw that the peasant had invited his well-to-do neighbours and was treating them to drink. His wife was offering the drink to the guests, and as she handed it round she tumbled against the table and spilt a glassful.

The peasant was angry, and scolded his wife: 'What do you mean, you slut? Do you think it's ditchwater, you cripple, that you must go pouring good stuff like that over the floor?'

The imp nudged the Devil, his master, with his elbow: 'See,' said he, 'that's the man who did not grudge his last crust!'

The peasant, still railing at his wife, began to carry the drink round himself. Just then a poor peasant returning from work came in uninvited. He greeted the company, sat down, and saw that they were drinking. Tired with his day's work, he felt that he too would like a drop. He sat and sat, and his mouth kept watering, but the host instead of offering him any only muttered: 'I can't find drink for everyone who comes along.'

This pleased the Devil; but the imp chuckled and said, 'Wait a bit, there's more to come yet!'

The rich peasants drank, and their host drank too. And they began to make false, oily speeches to one another.

The Devil listened and listened, and praised the imp.

'If,' said he, 'the drink makes them so foxy that they begin to cheat each other, they will soon all be in our hands.'

'Wait for what's coming,' said the imp. 'Let them have another glass all round. Now they are like foxes, wagging their tails and trying to get round one another; but presently you will see them like savage wolves.'

The peasants had another glass each, and their talk became wilder and rougher. Instead of oily speeches, they began to abuse and snarl at one another. Soon they took to fighting, and punched one another's noses. And the host joined in the fight, and he too got well beaten.

The Devil looked on and was much pleased at all this.

'This is first-rate!' said he.

But the imp replied: 'Wait a bit – the best is yet to come. Wait till they have had a third glass. Now they are raging like wolves, but let them have one more glass, and they will be like swine.'

The peasants had their third glass, and became quite like brutes.

They muttered and shouted, not knowing why, and not listening to one another.

Then the party began to break up. Some went alone, some in twos, and some in threes, all staggering down the street. The host went out to speed his guests, but he fell on his nose into a puddle, smeared himself from top to toe, and lay there grunting like a hog.

This pleased the Devil still more.

'Well,' said he, 'you have hit on a first-rate drink, and have quite made up for your blunder about the bread. But now tell me how this drink is made. You must first have put in fox's blood: that was what made the peasants sly as foxes. Then, I suppose, you added wolf's blood: that is what made them fierce like wolves. And you must have finished off with swine's blood, to make them behave like swine.'

'No,' said the imp, 'that was not the way I did it. All I did was to see that the peasant had more corn than he needed. The blood of the beasts is always in man; but as long as he has only enough corn for his needs, it is kept in bounds. While that was the case, the peasant did not grudge his last crust. But when he had corn left over, he looked for ways of getting pleasure out of it. And I showed him a pleasure – drinking! And when he began to turn God's good gifts into spirits for his own pleasure – the fox's, wolf's and swine's blood in him all came out. If only he goes on drinking, he will always be a beast!'

The Devil praised the imp, forgave him for his former blunder, and advanced him to a post of high honour.

HOW MUCH LAND DOES A MAN NEED

I

An elder sister came to visit her younger sister in the country. The elder was married to a tradesman in town, the younger to a peasant in the village. As the sisters sat over their tea talking, the elder began to boast of the advantages of town life: saying how comfortably they lived there, how well they dressed, what fine clothes her children wore, what good things they ate and drank, and how she went to the theatre, promenades and entertainments.

The younger sister was piqued, and in turn disparaged the life of a tradesman, and stood up for that of a peasant.

'I would not change my way of life for yours,' said she. 'We may live roughly, but at least we are free from anxiety. You live in better style than we do, but though you often earn more than you need, you are very likely to lose all you have. You know the proverb, "Loss and gain are brothers twain." It often happens that people who are wealthy one day are begging their bread the next. Our way is safer. Though a peasant's life is not a fat one, it is a long one. We shall never grow rich, but we shall always have enough to eat.'

The elder sister said sneeringly:

'Enough? Yes, if you like to share with the pigs and the calves!

What do you know of elegance or manners! However much your good man may slave, you will die as you are living – on a dung heap – and your children the same.'

'Well, what of that?' replied the younger. 'Of course our work is rough and coarse. But, on the other hand, it is sure; and we need not bow to anyone. But you, in your towns, are surrounded by temptations; today all may be right, but tomorrow the Evil One may tempt your husband with cards, wine or women, and all will go to ruin. Don't such things happen often enough?'

Pahóm, the master of the house, was lying on the top of the oven, and he listened to the women's chatter.

'It is perfectly true,' thought he. 'Busy as we are from childhood tilling mother earth, we peasants have no time to let any nonsense settle in our heads. Our only trouble is that we haven't land enough. If I had plenty of land, I shouldn't fear the Devil himself!'

The women finished their tea, chatted a while about dress, and then cleared away the tea things and lay down to sleep.

But the Devil had been sitting behind the oven, and had heard all that was said. He was pleased that the peasant's wife had led her husband into boasting, and that he had said that if he had plenty of land he would not fear the Devil himself.

'All right,' thought the Devil. 'We will have a tussle. I'll give you land enough; and by means of that land I will get you into my power.'

II

Close to the village there lived a lady, a small landowner, who had an estate of about three hundred acres[18]. She had always lived on good terms with the peasants, until she engaged as her steward an old soldier, who took to burdening the people with fines. However careful Pahóm tried to be, it happened again and again

18 *120 desyatins. The desyatina is properly 2.7 acres; but in this story round numbers are used.*

that now a horse of his got among the lady's oats, now a cow strayed into her garden, now his calves found their way into her meadows – and he always had to pay a fine.

Pahóm paid, but grumbled, and, going home in a temper, was rough with his family. All through that summer, Pahóm had much trouble because of this steward; and he was even glad when winter came and the cattle had to be stabled. Though he grudged the fodder when they could no longer graze on the pastureland, at least he was free from anxiety about them.

In the winter the news got about that the lady was going to sell her land, and that the keeper of the inn on the high road was bargaining for it. When the peasants heard this they were very much alarmed.

'Well,' thought they, 'if the innkeeper gets the land, he will worry us with fines worse than the lady's steward. We all depend on that estate.'

So the peasants went on behalf of their Commune, and asked the lady not to sell the land to the innkeeper; offering her a better price for it themselves. The lady agreed to let them have it. Then the peasants tried to arrange for the Commune to buy the whole estate, so that it might be held by all in common. They met twice to discuss it, but could not settle the matter; the Evil One sowed discord among them, and they could not agree. So they decided to buy the land individually, each according to his means; and the lady agreed to this plan as she had to the other.

Presently Pahóm heard that a neighbour of his was buying fifty acres, and that the lady had consented to accept one half in cash and to wait a year for the other half. Pahóm felt envious.

'Look at that,' thought he, 'the land is all being sold, and I shall get none of it.' So he spoke to his wife.

'Other people are buying,' said he, 'and we must also buy twenty acres or so. Life is becoming impossible. That steward is simply crushing us with his fines.'

So they put their heads together and considered how they could manage to buy it. They had one hundred roubles laid by. They sold a colt, and one half of their bees; hired out one of their sons as a labourer, and took his wages in advance; borrowed the rest from a brother-in-law, and so scraped together half the purchase money.

Having done this, Pahóm chose out a farm of forty acres, some of it wooded, and went to the lady to bargain for it. They came to an agreement, and he shook hands with her upon it, and paid her a deposit in advance. Then they went to town and signed the deeds; he paying half the price down, and undertaking to pay the remainder within two years.

So now Pahóm had land of his own. He borrowed seed, and sowed it on the land he had bought. The harvest was a good one, and within a year he had managed to pay off his debts both to the lady and to his brother-in-law. So he became a landowner, ploughing and sowing his own land, making hay on his own land, cutting his own trees, and feeding his cattle on his own pasture. When he went out to plough his fields, or to look at his growing corn, or at his grass meadows, his heart would fill with joy. The grass that grew and the flowers that bloomed there, seemed to him unlike any that grew elsewhere. Formerly, when he had passed by that land, it had appeared the same as any other land, but now it seemed quite different.

III

So Pahóm was well contented, and everything would have been right if the neighbouring peasants would only not have trespassed on his cornfields and meadows. He appealed to them most civilly, but they still went on: now the Communal herdsmen would let the village cows stray into his meadows; then horses from the night pasture would get among his corn. Pahóm turned them out again and again, and forgave their owners, and for a long time he forbore from prosecuting anyone. But at last he lost patience and complained to the District Court. He knew it was the peasants' want of land, and no evil intent on their part, that caused the trouble; but he thought:

'I cannot go on overlooking it, or they will destroy all I have. They must be taught a lesson.'

So he had them up, gave them one lesson, and then another, and two or three of the peasants were fined. After a time Pahóm's neighbours began to bear him a grudge for this, and would now and then let their cattle on to his land on purpose. One peasant even got into Pahóm's wood at night and cut down five young lime trees for their bark. Pahóm passing through the wood one day noticed something white. He came nearer, and saw the stripped trunks lying on the ground, and close by stood the stumps, where the tree had been. Pahóm was furious.

'If he had only cut one here and there it would have been bad enough,' thought Pahóm, 'but the rascal has actually cut down a whole clump. If I could only find out who did this, I would pay him out.'

He racked his brains as to who it could be. Finally he decided: 'It must be Simon – no one else could have done it.' So he went to Simon's homestead to have a look round, but he found nothing, and only had an angry scene. However, he now felt more certain than ever that Simon had done it, and he lodged a complaint. Simon was summoned. The case was tried, and re-tried, and at the end of it all Simon was acquitted, there being no evidence against him. Pahóm felt still more aggrieved, and let his anger loose upon the Elder and the Judges.

'You let thieves grease your palms,' said he. 'If you were honest folk yourselves, you would not let a thief go free.'

So Pahóm quarrelled with the Judges and with his neighbours. Threats to burn his building began to be uttered. So though Pahóm had more land, his place in the Commune was much worse than before.

About this time a rumour got about that many people were moving to new parts.

'There's no need for me to leave my land,' thought Pahóm. 'But some of the others might leave our village, and then there would be more room for us. I would take over their land myself, and make my estate a bit bigger. I could then live more at ease. As it is, I am still too cramped to be comfortable.'

One day Pahóm was sitting at home, when a peasant passing through the village happened to call in. He was allowed to stay the night, and supper was given him. Pahóm had a talk with this peasant and asked him where he came from. The stranger answered that he came from beyond the Volga, where he had been working. One word led to another, and the man went on to say that many people were settling in those parts. He told how some people from his village had settled there. They had joined the Commune, and had had twenty-five acres per man granted them. The land was so good, he said, that the rye sown on it grew as high as a horse, and so thick that five cuts of a sickle made a sheaf. One peasant, he said, had brought nothing with him but his bare hands, and now he had six horses and two cows of his own.

Pahóm's heart kindled with desire. He thought:

'Why should I suffer in this narrow hole, if one can live so well elsewhere? I will sell my land and my homestead here, and with the money I will start afresh over there and get everything new. In this crowded place one is always having trouble. But I must first go and find out all about it myself.'

Towards summer he got ready and started. He went down the Volga on a steamer to Samára, then walked another three hundred miles on foot, and at last reached the place. It was just as the stranger had said. The peasants had plenty of land: every man had twenty-five acres of Communal land given him for his use, and anyone who had money could buy, besides, at two shillings an acre as much good freehold land as he wanted.

Having found out all he wished to know, Pahóm returned home as autumn came on, and began selling off his belongings. He sold his land at a profit, sold his homestead and all his cattle, and withdrew from membership of the Commune. He only waited till the spring, and then started with his family for the new settlement.

IV

As soon as Pahóm and his family arrived at their new abode, he applied for admission into the Commune of a large village. He stood treat to the Elders, and obtained the necessary documents. Five shares of Communal land were given him for his own and his sons' use: that is to say, 125 acres (not all together, but in different fields) besides the use of the Communal pasture. Pahóm put up the buildings he needed, and bought cattle. Of the Communal land alone he had three times as much as at his former home, and the land was good corn land. He was ten times better off than he had been. He had plenty of arable land and pasturage, and could keep as many head of cattle as he liked.

At first, in the bustle of building and settling down, Pahóm was pleased with it all, but when he got used to it he began to think that even here he had not enough land. The first year, he sowed wheat on his share of the Communal land, and had a good crop. He wanted to go on sowing wheat, but had not enough Communal land for the purpose, and what he had already used was not available; for in those parts wheat is only sown on virgin soil or on fallow land. It is sown for one or two years, and then the land lies fallow till it is again overgrown with prairie grass. There were many who wanted such land, and there was not enough for all; so that people quarrelled about it. Those who were better off, wanted it for growing wheat, and those who were poor, wanted it to let to dealers, so that they might raise money to pay their taxes. Pahóm wanted to sow more wheat; so he rented land from a dealer for a year. He sowed much wheat and had a fine crop, but the land was too far from the village – the wheat had to be carted more than ten miles. After a time Pahóm noticed that some peasant-dealers were living on separate farms, and were growing wealthy; and he thought:

'If I were to buy some freehold land, and have a homestead on it, it would be a different thing, altogether. Then it would all be nice and compact.'

The question of buying freehold land recurred to him again and again.

He went on in the same way for three years: renting land and sowing wheat. The seasons turned out well and the crops were good, so that he began to lay money by. He might have gone on living contentedly, but he grew tired of having to rent other people's land every year, and having to scramble for it. Wherever there was good land to be had, the peasants would rush for it and it was taken up at once, so that unless you were sharp about it you got none. It happened in the third year that he and a dealer together rented a piece of pastureland from some peasants; and they had already ploughed it up, when there was some dispute, and the peasants went to law about it, and things fell out so that the labour was all lost.

'If it were my own land,' thought Pahóm, 'I should be independent, and there would not be all this unpleasantness.'

So Pahóm began looking out for land which he could buy; and he came across a peasant who had bought thirteen hundred acres, but having got into difficulties was willing to sell again cheap. Pahóm bargained and haggled with him, and at last they settled the price at 1,500 roubles, part in cash and part to be paid later. They had all but clinched the matter, when a passing dealer happened to stop at Pahóm's one day to get a feed for his horse. He drank tea with Pahóm, and they had a talk. The dealer said that he was just returning from the land of the Bashkírs, far away, where he had bought thirteen thousand acres of land all for 1,000 roubles. Pahóm questioned him further, and the tradesman said:

'All one need do is to make friends with the chiefs. I gave away about one hundred roubles' worth of dressing gowns and carpets, besides a case of tea, and I gave wine to those who would drink it; and I got the land for less than twopence an acre. And he showed Pahóm the title deeds, saying:

'The land lies near a river, and the whole prairie is virgin soil.'

Pahóm plied him with questions, and the tradesman said:

'There is more land there than you could cover if you walked a year, and it all belongs to the Bashkírs. They are as simple as sheep, and land can be got almost for nothing.'

'There now,' thought Pahóm, 'with my one thousand roubles, why should I get only thirteen hundred acres, and saddle myself with a debt besides? If I take it out there, I can get more than ten times as much for the money.'

V

Pahóm inquired how to get to the place, and as soon as the tradesman had left him, he prepared to go there himself. He left his wife to look after the homestead, and started on his journey, taking his man with him. They stopped at a town on their way, and bought a case of tea, some wine and other presents, as the tradesman had advised. On and on they went until they had gone more than three hundred miles, and on the seventh day they came to a place where the Bashkírs had pitched their tents. It was all just as the tradesman had said. The people lived on the steppes, by a river, in felt-covered tents. They neither tilled the ground, nor ate bread. Their cattle and horses grazed in herds on the steppe. The colts were tethered behind the tents, and the mares were driven to them twice a day. The mares were milked, and from the milk kumiss was made. It was the women who prepared kumiss, and they also made cheese. As far as the men were concerned, drinking kumiss and tea, eating mutton, and playing on their pipes, was all they cared about. They were all stout and merry, and all the summer long they never thought of doing any work. They were quite ignorant, and knew no Russian, but were good natured enough.

As soon as they saw Pahóm, they came out of their tents and gathered round their visitor. An interpreter was found, and Pahóm told them he had come about some land. The Bashkírs seemed very glad; they took Pahóm and led him into one of the best tents, where they made him sit on some down cushions placed on a carpet, while they sat round him. They gave him tea and kumiss, and had a sheep killed, and gave him mutton to eat. Pahóm took presents out of his cart and distributed them among the Bashkírs, and divided amongst them the tea. The Bashkírs were delighted. They talked a great deal among themselves, and then told the interpreter to translate.

'They wish to tell you,' said the interpreter, 'that they like you, and that it is our custom to do all we can to please a guest and to repay him for his gifts. You have given us presents, now tell us which of the things we possess please you best, that we may present them to you.'

'What pleases me best here,' answered Pahóm, 'is your land. Our land is crowded, and the soil is exhausted; but you have plenty of land and it is good land. I never saw the like of it.'

The interpreter translated. The Bashkírs talked among themselves for a while. Pahóm could not understand what they were saying, but saw that they were much amused, and that they shouted and laughed. Then they were silent and looked at Pahóm while the interpreter said:

'They wish me to tell you that in return for your presents they will gladly give you as much land as you want. You have only to point it out with your hand and it is yours.'

The Bashkírs talked again for a while and began to dispute. Pahóm asked what they were disputing about, and the interpreter told him that some of them thought they ought to ask their Chief about the land and not act in his absence, while others thought there was no need to wait for his return.

VI

While the Bashkírs were disputing, a man in a large fox-fur cap appeared on the scene. They all became silent and rose to their feet. The interpreter said, 'This is our Chief himself.'

Pahóm immediately fetched the best dressing gown and five pounds of tea, and offered these to the Chief. The Chief accepted them, and seated himself in the place of honour. The Bashkírs at once began telling him something. The Chief listened for a while, then made a sign with his head for them to be silent, and addressing himself to Pahóm, said in Russian:

'Well, let it be so. Choose whatever piece of land you like; we have plenty of it.'

'How can I take as much as I like?' thought Pahóm. 'I must get a deed to make it secure, or else they may say, "It is yours," and afterwards may take it away again.'

'Thank you for your kind words,' he said aloud. 'You have much land, and I only want a little. But I should like to be sure which bit is mine. Could it not be measured and made over to me? Life and death are in God's hands. You good people give it to me, but your children might wish to take it away again.'

'You are quite right,' said the Chief. 'We will make it over to you.'

'I heard that a dealer had been here,' continued Pahóm, 'and that you gave him a little land, too, and signed title deeds to that effect. I should like to have it done in the same way.'

The Chief understood.

'Yes,' replied he, 'that can be done quite easily. We have a scribe, and we will go to town with you and have the deed properly sealed.'

'And what will be the price?' asked Pahóm.

'Our price is always the same: one thousand roubles a day.'

Pahóm did not understand.

'A day? What measure is that? How many acres would that be?'

'We do not know how to reckon it out,' said the Chief. 'We sell it by the day. As much as you can go round on your feet in a day is yours, and the price is one thousand roubles a day.'

Pahóm was surprised.

'But in a day you can get round a large tract of land,' he said.

The Chief laughed.

'It will all be yours!' said he. 'But there is one condition: If you don't return on the same day to the spot whence you started, your money is lost.'

'But how am I to mark the way that I have gone?'

'Why, we shall go to any spot you like, and stay there. You must start from that spot and make your round, taking a spade with you. Wherever you think necessary, make a mark. At every turning, dig a hole and pile up the turf; then afterwards we will go round with a plough from hole to hole. You may make as large a circuit as you please, but before the sun sets you must return to the place you started from. All the land you cover will be yours.'

Pahóm was delighted. It was decided to start early next morning. They talked a while, and after drinking some more kumiss and eating some more mutton, they had tea again, and then the night came on. They gave Pahóm a feather bed to sleep on, and the Bashkírs dispersed for the night, promising to assemble the next morning at daybreak and ride out before sunrise to the appointed spot.

VII

Pahóm lay on the feather bed, but could not sleep. He kept thinking about the land.

'What a large tract I will mark off!' thought he. 'I can easily do thirty-five miles in a day. The days are long now, and within a circuit of thirty-five miles what a lot of land there will be! I will sell the poorer land, or let it to peasants, but I'll pick out the best and farm it. I will buy two ox-teams, and hire two more labourers. About a hundred and fifty acres shall be plough-land, and I will pasture cattle on the rest.'

Pahóm lay awake all night, and dozed off only just before dawn. Hardly were his eyes closed when he had a dream. He thought he was lying in that same tent, and heard somebody chuckling outside. He wondered who it could be, and rose and went out, and he saw the Bashkír Chief sitting in front of the tent holding his side and rolling about with laughter. Going nearer to the Chief, Pahóm asked: 'What are you laughing at?' But he saw that it was no longer the Chief, but the dealer who had recently stopped at his house and had told him about the land. Just as Pahóm was going to ask, 'Have you been here long?' he saw that it was not the dealer, but the peasant who had come up from the Volga, long ago, to Pahóm's old home. Then he saw that it was not the peasant either, but the Devil himself with hoofs and horns, sitting there and chuckling, and before him lay a man barefoot, prostrate on the ground, with only trousers and a shirt on. And Pahóm dreamt that he looked more attentively to see what sort of a man it was lying there, and he saw that the man was dead, and that it was himself! He awoke horror-struck.

'What things one does dream,' thought he.

Looking round he saw through the open door that the dawn was breaking.

'It's time to wake them up,' thought he. 'We ought to be starting.'

He got up, roused his man (who was sleeping in his cart), bade him harness; and went to call the Bashkírs.

'It's time to go to the steppe to measure the land,' he said.

The Bashkírs rose and assembled, and the Chief came, too. Then they began drinking kumiss again, and offered Pahóm some tea, but he would not wait.

'If we are to go, let us go. It is high time,' said he.

VIII

The Bashkírs got ready and they all started: some mounted on horses, and some in carts. Pahóm drove in his own small cart with his servant, and took a spade with him. When they reached the steppe, the morning red was beginning to kindle. They ascended a hillock (called by the Bashkírs a *shikhan*) and dismounting from their carts and their horses, gathered in one spot. The Chief came up to Pahóm and stretched out his arm towards the plain:

'See,' said he, 'all this, as far as your eye can reach, is ours. You may have any part of it you like.'

Pahóm's eyes glistened: it was all virgin soil, as flat as the palm of your hand, as black as the seed of a poppy, and in the hollows different kinds of grasses grew breast high.

The Chief took off his fox-fur cap, placed it on the ground and said:

'This will be the mark. Start from here, and return here again. All the land you go round shall be yours.'

Pahóm took out his money and put it on the cap. Then he took off his outer coat, remaining in his sleeveless under coat. He unfastened his girdle and tied it tight below his stomach, put a little bag of bread into the breast of his coat, and tying a flask of water to his girdle, he drew up the tops of his boots, took the spade from his man, and stood ready to start. He considered for some moments which way he had better go – it was tempting everywhere.

'No matter,' he concluded, 'I will go towards the rising sun.'

He turned his face to the east, stretched himself, and waited for the sun to appear above the rim.

'I must lose no time,' he thought, 'and it is easier walking while it is still cool.'

The sun's rays had hardly flashed above the horizon, before Pahóm, carrying the spade over his shoulder, went down into the steppe.

Pahóm started walking neither slowly nor quickly. After having gone a thousand yards he stopped, dug a hole, and placed pieces of turf one on another to make it more visible. Then he went on; and now that he had walked off his stiffness he quickened his pace. After a while he dug another hole.

Pahóm looked back. The hillock could be distinctly seen in the sunlight, with the people on it, and the glittering tyres of the cartwheels. At a rough guess Pahóm concluded that he had walked three miles. It was growing warmer; he took off his under coat, flung it across his shoulder, and went on again. It had grown quite warm now; he looked at the sun, it was time to think of breakfast.

'The first shift is done, but there are four in a day, and it is too soon yet to turn. But I will just take off my boots,' said he to himself.

He sat down, took off his boots, stuck them into his girdle, and went on. It was easy walking now.

'I will go on for another three miles,' thought he, 'and then turn to the left. The spot is so fine, that it would be a pity to lose it. The further one goes, the better the land seems.'

He went straight on for a while, and when he looked round, the hillock was scarcely visible and the people on it looked like black ants, and he could just see something glistening there in the sun.

'Ah,' thought Pahóm, 'I have gone far enough in this direction, it is time to turn. Besides I am in a regular sweat, and very thirsty.'

He stopped, dug a large hole, and heaped up pieces of turf. Next he untied his flask, had a drink, and then turned sharply to the left. He went on and on; the grass was high, and it was very hot.

Pahóm began to grow tired: he looked at the sun and saw that it was noon.

'Well,' he thought, 'I must have a rest.'

He sat down, and ate some bread and drank some water; but he did not lie down, thinking that if he did he might fall asleep. After sitting a little while, he went on again. At first he walked easily: the food had strengthened him; but it had become terribly hot, and he felt sleepy; still he went on, thinking: 'An hour to suffer, a lifetime to live.'

He went a long way in this direction also, and was about to turn to the left again, when he perceived a damp hollow: 'It would be a pity to leave that out,' he thought. 'Flax would do well there.' So he went on past the hollow, and dug a hole on the other side of it before he turned the corner. Pahóm looked towards the hillock. The heat made the air hazy: it seemed to be quivering, and through the haze the people on the hillock could scarcely be seen.

'Ah!' thought Pahóm, 'I have made the sides too long; I must make this one shorter.' And he went along the third side, stepping faster. He looked at the sun: it was nearly halfway to the horizon, and he had not yet done two miles of the third side of the square. He was still ten miles from the goal.

'No,' he thought, 'though it will make my land lopsided, I must hurry back in a straight line now. I might go too far, and as it is I have a great deal of land.'

So Pahóm hurriedly dug a hole, and turned straight towards the hillock.

IX

Pahóm went straight towards the hillock, but he now walked with difficulty. He was done up with the heat, his bare feet were cut and bruised, and his legs began to fail. He longed to rest, but it was impossible if he meant to get back before sunset. The sun waits for no man, and it was sinking lower and lower.

'Oh dear,' he thought, 'if only I have not blundered trying for too much! What if I am too late?'

He looked towards the hillock and at the sun. He was still far from his goal, and the sun was already near the rim.

Pahóm walked on and on; it was very hard walking, but he went quicker and quicker. He pressed on, but was still far from the place. He began running, threw away his coat, his boots, his flask and his cap, and kept only the spade which he used as a support.

'What shall I do,' he thought again, 'I have grasped too much, and ruined the whole affair. I can't get there before the sun sets.'

And this fear made him still more breathless. Pahóm went on running, his soaking shirt and trousers stuck to him, and his mouth was parched. His breast was working like a blacksmith's bellows, his heart was beating like a hammer, and his legs were giving way as if they did not belong to him. Pahóm was seized with terror lest he should die of the strain.

Though afraid of death, he could not stop. 'After having run all that way they will call me a fool if I stop now,' thought he. And he ran on and on, and drew near and heard the Bashkírs yelling and shouting to him, and their cries inflamed his heart still more. He gathered his last strength and ran on.

The sun was close to the rim, and cloaked in mist looked large, and red as blood. Now, yes now, it was about to set! The sun was quite low, but he was also quite near his aim. Pahóm could already see the people on the hillock waving their arms to hurry him up. He could see the fox-fur cap on the ground, and the money on it, and the Chief sitting on the ground holding his sides. And Pahóm remembered his dream.

'There is plenty of land,' thought he, 'but will God let me live on it? I have lost my life, I have lost my life! I shall never reach that spot!'

Pahóm looked at the sun, which had reached the earth: one side of it had already disappeared. With all his remaining strength he rushed on, bending his body forward so that his legs could hardly follow fast enough to keep him from falling. Just as he reached the hillock it suddenly grew dark. He looked up – the sun had already set. He gave a cry: 'All my labour has been in vain,' thought he, and was about to stop, but he heard the Bashkírs still shouting, and remembered that though to him, from below, the sun seemed to have set, they on the hillock could still see it. He took a long breath and ran up the hillock. It was still light there. He reached the top and saw the cap. Before it sat the Chief laughing and holding his sides. Again Pahóm remembered his dream, and he uttered a cry: his legs gave way beneath him, he fell forward and reached the cap with his hands.

'Ah, what a fine fellow!' exclaimed the Chief. 'He has gained much land!'

Pahóm's servant came running up and tried to raise him, but he saw that blood was flowing from his mouth. Pahóm was dead!

The Bashkírs clicked their tongues to show their pity.

His servant picked up the spade and dug a grave long enough for Pahóm to lie in, and buried him in it. Six feet from his head to his heels was all he needed.

THE REPENTANT SINNER

'And he said unto Jesus, "Lord, remember me when thou comest into thy Kingdom." And Jesus said unto him, "Verily I say unto thee, today shalt thou be with me in paradise."' (Luke 23: 42, 43).

There was once a man who lived for seventy years in the world, and lived in sin all that time. He fell ill, but even then did not repent. Only at the last moment, as he was dying, he wept and said:

'Lord! forgive me, as Thou forgavest the thief upon the cross.'

And as he said these words, his soul left his body. And the soul of the sinner, feeling love towards God and faith in His mercy, went to the gates of heaven, and knocked, praying to be let into the heavenly kingdom.

Then a voice spoke from within the gate:

'What man is it that knocks at the gates of Paradise, and what deeds did he do during his life?'

And the voice of the Accuser replied, recounting all the man's evil deeds, and not a single good one.

And the voice from within the gates answered:

'Sinners cannot enter into the kingdom of heaven. Go hence!'

Then the man said:

'Lord, I hear thy voice, but cannot see thy face, nor do I know thy name.'

The voice answered:

'I am Peter, the Apostle.'

And the sinner replied:

'Have pity on me, Apostle Peter! Remember man's weakness, and God's mercy. Wert not thou a disciple of Christ? Didst not thou hear his teaching from his own lips, and hadst thou not his example before thee? Remember then how, when he sorrowed and was grieved in spirit, and three times asked thee to keep awake and pray, thou didst sleep, because thine eyes were heavy, and three times he found thee sleeping. So it was with me. Remember, also, how thou didst promise to be faithful unto death, and yet didst thrice deny him, when he was taken before Caiaphas. So it was with me. And remember, too, how when the cock crowed thou didst go out and didst weep bitterly. So it is with me. Thou canst not refuse to let me in.'

And the voice behind the gates was silent.

Then the sinner stood a little while, and again began to knock, and to ask to be let into the kingdom of heaven.

And he heard another voice behind the gates, which said:

'Who is this man, and how did he live on earth?'

And the voice of the Accuser again repeated all the sinner's evil deeds, and not a single good one.

And the voice from behind the gates replied:

'Go hence! Such sinners cannot live with us in Paradise.' Then the sinner said:

'Lord, I hear thy voice, but I see thee not, nor do I know thy name.'

And the voice answered:

'I am David; king and prophet.'

The sinner did not despair, nor did he leave the gates of paradise, but said:

Have pity on me, King David! Remember man's weakness, and

God's mercy. God loved thee and exalted thee among men. Thou hadst all: a kingdom, and honour, and riches, and wives, and children; but thou sawest from thy house-top the wife of a poor man, and sin entered into thee, and thou tookest the wife of Uriah, and didst slay him with the sword of the Ammonites. Thou, a rich man, didst take from the poor man his one ewe lamb, and didst kill him. I have done likewise. Remember, then, how thou didst repent, and how thou saidst, "I acknowledge my transgressions: my sin is ever before me?" I have done the same. Thou canst not refuse to let me in.'

And the voice from within the gates was silent.

The sinner having stood a little while, began knocking again, and asking to be let into the kingdom of heaven. And a third voice was heard within the gates, saying:

'Who is this man, and how has he spent his life on earth?'

And the voice of the Accuser replied for the third time, recounting the sinner's evil deeds, and not mentioning one good deed.

And the voice within the gates said:

'Depart hence! Sinners cannot enter into the kingdom of heaven.'

And the sinner said:

'Thy voice I hear, but thy face I see not, neither do I know thy name.'

Then the voice replied:

'I am John the Divine, the beloved disciple of Christ.'

And the sinner rejoiced and said:

'Now surely I shall be allowed to enter. Peter and David must let me in, because they know man's weakness and God's mercy; and thou wilt let me in, because thou lovest much. Was it not thou, John the Divine, who wrote that God is Love, and that he who loves not, knows not God? And in thine old age didst thou not say unto men: "Brethren, love one another." How, then, canst thou look on me with hatred, and drive me away? Either thou must renounce what thou hast said, or, loving me, must let me enter the kingdom of heaven.'

And the gates of Paradise opened, and John embraced the repentant sinner and took him into the kingdom of heaven.

THE EMPTY DRUM

(A FOLK-TALE LONG CURRENT IN THE REGION
OF THE VOLGA)

Emelyán was a labourer and worked for a master. Crossing
the meadows one day on his way to work, he nearly trod on a
frog that jumped right in front of him, but he just managed to
avoid it. Suddenly he heard someone calling to him from behind.

Emelyán looked round and saw a lovely lassie, who said to him:
'Why don't you get married, Emelyán?'

'How can I marry, my lass?' said he. 'I have but the clothes I
stand up in, nothing more, and no one would have me for a
husband.'

'Take me for a wife,' said she.

Emelyán liked the maid. 'I should be glad to,' said he, 'but
where and how could we live?'

'Why trouble about that?' said the girl. 'One only has to work
more and sleep less, and one can clothe and feed oneself anywhere.'

'Very well then, let us marry,' said Emelyán. 'Where shall we
go to?'

'Let us go to town.'

So Emelyán and the lass went to town, and she took him to a
small hut on the very edge of the town, and they married and
began housekeeping.

One day the King, driving through the town, passed by

Emelyán's hut. Emelyán's wife came out to see the King. The King noticed her and was quite surprised.

'Where did such a beauty come from?' said he, and stopping his carriage he called Emelyán's wife and asked her: 'Who are you?'

'The peasant Emelyán's wife,' said she.

'Why did you, who are such a beauty, marry a peasant?' said the King. 'You ought to be a queen!'

'Thank you for your kind words,' said she, 'but a peasant husband is good enough for me.'

The King talked to her awhile and then drove on. He returned to the palace, but could not get Emelyán's wife out of his head. All night he did not sleep, but kept thinking how to get her for himself. He could think of no way of doing it, so he called his servants and told them they must find a way.

The King's servants said: 'Command Emelyán to come to the palace to work, and we will work him so hard that he will die. His wife will be left a widow, and then you can take her for yourself.'

The King followed their advice. He sent an order that Emelyán should come to the palace as a workman, and that he should live at the palace, and his wife with him.

The messengers came to Emelyán and gave him the King's message. His wife said, 'Go, Emelyán; work all day, but come back home at night.'

So Emelyán went, and when he got to the palace the King's steward asked him, 'Why have you come alone, without your wife?'

'Why should I drag her about?' said Emelyán. 'She has a house to live in.'

At the King's palace they gave Emelyán work enough for two. He began the job not hoping to finish it; but when evening came, lo and behold! it was all done. The steward saw that it was finished, and set him four times as much for the next day.

Emelyán went home. Everything there was swept and tidy; the

oven was heated, his supper was cooked and ready, and his wife sat by the table sewing and waiting for his return. She greeted him, laid the table, gave him something to eat and drink, and then began to ask him about his work.

'Ah!' said he, 'it's a bad business: they give me tasks beyond my strength, and want to kill me with work.'

'Don't fret about the work,' said she, 'don't look either before or behind to see how much you have done or how much there is left to do; only keep on working and all will be right.'

So Emelyán lay down and slept. Next morning he went to work again and worked without once looking round. And, lo and behold! by the evening it was all done, and before dark he came home for the night.

Again and again they increased Emelyán's work, but he always got through it in good time and went back to his hut to sleep. A week passed, and the King's servants saw they could not crush him with rough work, so they tried giving him work that required skill. But this, also, was of no avail. Carpentering and masonry and roofing, whatever they set him to do, Emelyán had it ready in time, and went home to his wife at night. So a second week passed.

Then the King called his servants and said: 'Am I to feed you for nothing? Two weeks have gone, and I don't see that you have done anything. You were going to tire Emelyán out with work, but I see from my windows how he goes home every evening, singing cheerfully! Do you mean to make a fool of me?'

The King's servants began to excuse themselves. 'We tried our best to wear him out with rough work,' they said, 'but nothing was too hard for him; he cleared it all off as though he had swept it away with a broom. There was no tiring him out. Then we set him to tasks needing skill, which we did not think he was clever enough to do, but he managed them all. No matter what one sets him, he does it all, no one knows how. Either he or his wife must know some spell that helps them. We ourselves are sick of him, and wish to find a task he cannot master. We have now thought of setting him to build a cathedral in a single day. Send for Emelyán, and order him to build a cathedral in front of the palace in a single day. Then, if he does not do it, let his head be cut off for disobedience.'

The King sent for Emelyán. 'Listen to my command,' said he: 'build me a new cathedral on the square in front of my palace, and have it ready by tomorrow evening. If you have it ready I will reward you, but if not I will have your head cut off.'

When Emelyán heard the King's command he turned away and went home. 'My end is near,' thought he. And coming to his wife, he said: 'Get ready, wife, we must fly from here, or I shall be lost by no fault of my own.'

'What has frightened you so?' said she, 'and why should we run away?'

'How can I help being frightened? The King has ordered me, tomorrow, in a single day, to build him a cathedral. If I fail he will cut my head off. There is only one thing to be done: we must fly while there is yet time.'

But his wife would not hear of it. 'The King has many soldiers,' said she. 'They would catch us anywhere. We cannot escape from him, but must obey him as long as strength holds out.'

'How can I obey him when the task is beyond my strength?'

'Eh, goodman, don't be downhearted. Eat your supper now, and go to sleep. Rise early in the morning and all will get done.'

So Emelyán lay down and slept. His wife roused him early next day. 'Go quickly,' said she, 'and finish the cathedral. Here are nails and a hammer; there is still enough work there for a day.'

Emelyán went into the town, reached the palace square, and there stood a large cathedral not quite finished. Emelyán set to work to do what was needed, and by the evening all was ready.

When the King awoke he looked out from his palace, and saw the cathedral, and Emelyán going about driving in nails here and there. And the King was not pleased to have the cathedral – he was annoyed at not being able to condemn Emelyán and take his wife. Again he called his servants. 'Emelyán has done this task also,' said the King, 'and there is no excuse for putting him to death. Even this work was not too hard for him. You must find a more cunning plan, or I will cut off your heads as well as his.'

So his servants planned that Emelyán should be ordered to make a river round the palace, with ships sailing on it. And the King sent for Emelyán and set him this new task.

'If,' said he, 'you could build a cathedral in one night, you can also do this. Tomorrow all must be ready. If not, I will have your head off.'

Emelyán was more downcast than before, and returned to his wife sad at heart.

'Why are you so sad?' said his wife. 'Has the King set you a fresh task?'

Emelyán told her about it. 'We must fly,' said he.

But his wife replied: 'There is no escaping the soldiers; they will catch us wherever we go. There is nothing for it but to obey.'

'How can I do it?' groaned Emelyán.

'Eh! eh! goodman,' said she, 'don't be downhearted. Eat your supper now, and go to sleep. Rise early, and all will get done in good time.'

So Emelyán lay down and slept. In the morning his wife woke him. 'Go,' said she, 'to the palace – all is ready. Only, near the wharf in front of the palace, there is a mound left; take a spade and level it.'

When the King awoke he saw a river where there had not been one; ships were sailing up and down, and Emelyán was levelling a mound with a spade. The King wondered, but was pleased neither with the river nor with the ships, so vexed was he at not being able to condemn Emelyán. 'There is no task,' thought he, 'that he cannot manage. What is to be done?' And he called his servants and again asked their advice.

'Find some task,' said he, 'which Emelyán cannot compass. For whatever we plan he fulfils, and I cannot take his wife from him.'

The King's servants thought and thought, and at last devised a plan. They came to the King and said: 'Send for Emelyán and say to him: "Go to there, don't know where," and bring back "that, don't know what." Then he will not be able to escape you. No matter where he goes, you can say that he has not gone to the right place, and no matter what he brings, you can say it is not the right thing. Then you can have him beheaded and can take his wife.'

The King was pleased. "That is well thought of," said he. So the King sent for Emelyán and said to him: 'Go to "there, don't know where," and bring back "that, don't know what." If you fail to bring it, I will have you beheaded.'

Emelyán returned to his wife and told her what the King had said. His wife became thoughtful.

'Well,' said she, 'they have taught the King how to catch you. Now we must act warily.' So she sat and thought, and at last said to her husband: 'You must go far, to our Grandam – the old peasant woman, the mother of soldiers – and you must ask her aid. If she helps you to anything, go straight to the palace with it, I shall be there: I cannot escape them now. They will take me by force, but it will not be for long. If you do everything as Grandam directs, you will soon save me.'

So the wife got her husband ready for the journey. She gave him a wallet, and also a spindle. 'Give her this,' said she. 'By this token she will know that you are my husband.' And his wife showed him his road.

Emelyán set off. He left the town behind, and came to where some soldiers were being drilled. Emelyán stood and watched them. After drill the soldiers sat down to rest. Then Emelyán went up to them and asked: 'Do you know, brothers, the way to "there, don't know where?" and how I can get "that, don't know what?"'

The soldiers listened to him with surprise. 'Who sent you on this errand?' said they.

'The King,' said he.

'We ourselves,' said they, 'from the day we became soldiers, go we "don't know where," and never yet have we got there; and we seek we "don't know what," and cannot find it. We cannot help you.'

Emelyán sat a while with the soldiers and then went on again. He trudged many a mile, and at last came to a wood. In the wood was a hut, and in the hut sat an old, old woman, the mother of peasant soldiers, spinning flax and weeping. And as she spun she did not put her fingers to her mouth to wet them with spittle, but to her eyes to wet them with tears. When the old woman saw Emelyán she cried out at him: 'Why have you come here?' Then Emelyán gave her the spindle, and said his wife had sent it.

The old woman softened at once, and began to question him. And Emelyán told her his whole life: how he married the lass; how they went to live in the town; how he had worked, and what he had done at the palace; how he built the cathedral, and made a river with ships on it, and how the King had now told him to go to 'there, don't know where,' and bring back 'that, don't know what.'

The Grandam listened to the end, and ceased weeping. She muttered to herself: 'The time has surely come,' and said to him: 'All right, my lad. Sit down now, and I will give you something to eat.'

Emelyán ate, and then the Grandam told him what to do. 'Here,' said she, 'is a ball of thread; roll it before you, and follow where it goes. You must go far till you come right to the sea. When you get there, you will see a great city. Enter the city and ask for a night's lodging at the furthest house. There look out for what you are seeking.'

'How shall I know it when I see it, Granny?' said he.

'When you see something men obey more than father or mother, that is it. Seize that, and take it to the King. When you bring it to the King, he will say it is not right, and you must answer: "If it is not the right thing it must be smashed," and you must beat it, and carry it to the river, break it in pieces, and throw it into the water. Then you will get your wife back and my tears will be dried.'

Emelyán bade farewell to the Grandam and began rolling his ball before him. It rolled and rolled until at last it reached the sea. By the sea stood a great city, and at the further end of the city was a big house. There Emelyán begged for a night's lodging, and was granted it. He lay down to sleep, and in the morning awoke and heard a father rousing his son to go and cut wood for the fire. But the son did not obey. 'It is too early,' said he, 'there is time enough.' Then Emelyán heard the mother say, 'Go, my son, your father's bones ache; would you have him go himself? It is time to be up!'

But the son only murmured some words and fell asleep again. Hardly was he asleep when something thundered and rattled in the street. Up jumped the son and quickly putting on his clothes ran out into the street. Up jumped Emelyán, too, and ran after him to see what it was that a son obeys more than father or mother. What he saw was a man walking along the street carrying, tied to his stomach, a thing which he beat with sticks, and *that* it was that rattled and thundered so, and that the son had obeyed. Emelyán ran up and had a look at it. He saw it was round, like a small tub, with a skin stretched over both ends, and he asked what it was called.

He was told, 'A drum.'

'And is it empty?'

'Yes, it is empty.'

Emelyán was surprised. He asked them to give the thing to him, but they would not. So Emelyán left off asking, and followed the drummer. All day he followed, and when the drummer at last lay down to sleep, Emelyán snatched the drum from him and ran away with it.

He ran and ran, till at last he got back to his own town. He went to see his wife, but she was not at home. The day after he went away, the King had taken her. So Emelyán went to the palace, and sent in a message to the King: 'He has returned who went to "there, don't know where," and he has brought with him "that, don't know what."'

They told the King, and the King said he was to come again next day.

But Emelyán said, 'Tell the King I am here today, and have brought what the King wanted. Let him come out to me, or I will go in to him!'

The King came out. 'Where have you been?' said he.

Emelyán told him.

'That's not the right place,' said the King. 'What have you brought?'

Emelyán pointed to the drum, but the King did not look at it. 'That is not it.'

'If it is not the right thing,' said Emelyán, 'it must be smashed, and may the devil take it!'

And Emelyán left the palace, carrying the drum and beating it. And as he beat it all the King's army ran out to follow Emelyán, and they saluted him and waited his commands.

The King, from his window, began to shout at his army telling them not to follow Emelyán. They did not listen to what he said, but all followed Emelyán.

When the King saw that, he gave orders that Emelyán's wife should be taken back to him, and he sent to ask Emelyán to give him the drum.

'It can't be done,' said Emelyán. 'I was told to smash it and to throw the splinters into the river.'

So Emelyán went down to the river carrying the drum, and the soldiers followed him. When he reached the river bank Emelyán smashed the drum to splinters, and threw the splinters into the stream. And then all the soldiers ran away.

Emelyán took his wife and went home with her. And after that the King ceased to trouble him; and so they lived happily ever after.

THE COFFEE HOUSE OF SURAT

(AFTER BERNARDIN DE SAINT-PIERRE.)

In the town of Surat, in India, was a coffee house where many travellers and foreigners from all parts of the world met and conversed.

One day a learned Persian theologian visited this coffee house. He was a man who had spent his life studying the nature of the Deity, and reading and writing books upon the subject. He had thought, read and written so much about God that eventually he lost his wits, became quite confused, and ceased even to believe in the existence of a God. The Shah, hearing of this, had banished him from Persia.

After having argued all his life about the First Cause, this unfortunate theologian had ended by quite perplexing himself, and instead of understanding that he had lost his own reason, he began to think that there was no higher Reason controlling the universe.

This man had an African slave who followed him everywhere. When the theologian entered the coffee house, the slave remained outside, near the door, sitting on a stone in the glare of the sun, and driving away the flies that buzzed around him. The Persian having settled down on a divan in the coffee house, ordered himself a cup of opium. When he had drunk it and the opium had begun to quicken the workings of his brain, he addressed his slave through the open door:

'Tell me, wretched slave,' said he, 'do you think there is a God, or not?'

'Of course there is,' said the slave, and immediately drew from under his girdle a small idol of wood.

'There,' said he, 'that is the God who has guarded me from the day of my birth. Everyone in our country worships the fetish tree, from the wood of which this God was made.'

This conversation between the theologian and his slave was listened to with surprise by the other guests in the coffee house. They were astonished at the master's question, and yet more so at the slave's reply.

One of them, a Brahmin, on hearing the words spoken by the slave, turned to him and said:

'Miserable fool! Is it possible you believe that God can be carried under a man's girdle? There is one God – Brahma, and he is greater than the whole world, for he created it. Brahma is the One, the mighty God, and in His honour are built the temples on the Ganges' banks, where his true priests, the Brahmins, worship him. They know the true God, and none but they. A thousand score of years have passed, and yet through revolution after revolution these priests have held their sway, because Brahma, the one true God, has protected them.'

So spoke the Brahmin, thinking to convince everyone; but a Jewish broker who was present replied to him, and said:

'No! the temple of the true God is not in India. Neither does God protect the Brahmin caste. The true God is not the God of the Brahmins, but of Abraham, Isaac and Jacob. None does He protect but His chosen people, the Israelites. From the commencement of the world, our nation has been beloved of Him, and ours alone. If we are now scattered over the whole earth, it is but to try us; for God has promised that He will one day gather His people together in Jerusalem. Then, with

LEO TOLSTOY

the Temple of Jerusalem – the wonder of the ancient world – restored to its splendour, shall Israel be established a ruler over all nations.'

So spoke the Jew, and burst into tears. He wished to say more, but an Italian missionary who was there interrupted him.

'What you are saying is untrue,' said he to the Jew. 'You attribute injustice to God. He cannot love your nation above the rest. Nay rather, even if it be true that of old He favoured the Israelites, it is now nineteen hundred years since they angered Him, and caused Him to destroy their nation and scatter them over the earth, so that their faith makes no converts and has died out except here and there. God shows preference to no nation, but calls all who wish to be saved to the bosom of the Catholic Church of Rome, the one outside whose borders no salvation can be found.'

So spoke the Italian. But a Protestant minister, who happened to be present, growing pale, turned to the Catholic missionary and exclaimed:

'How can you say that salvation belongs to your religion? Those only will be saved, who serve God according to the Gospel, in spirit and in truth, as bidden by the word of Christ.'

Then a Turk, an office-holder in the custom house at Surat, who was sitting in the coffee house smoking a pipe, turned with an air of superiority to both the Christians.

'Your belief in your Roman religion is vain,' said he. 'It was superseded twelve hundred years ago by the true faith: that of Mohammed! You cannot but observe how the true Mohammedan faith continues to spread both in Europe and Asia, and even in the enlightened country of China. You say yourselves that God has rejected the Jews; and, as a proof, you quote the fact that the Jews are humiliated and their faith does not spread. Confess then the truth of Mohammedanism, for it is triumphant and spreads far and wide. None will be saved but the followers of Mohammed, God's latest prophet; and of them, only the followers of Omar, and not of Ali, for the latter are false to the faith.'

To this the Persian theologian, who was of the sect of Ali, wished to reply; but by this time a great dispute had arisen among all the strangers of different faiths and creeds present. There were Abyssinian Christians, Lamas from Thibet, Ismailians and Fire-Worshippers. They all argued about the nature of God, and how He should be worshipped. Each of them asserted that in his country alone was the true God known and rightly worshipped.

Everyone argued and shouted, except a Chinaman, a student of Confucius, who sat quietly in one corner of the coffee house, not joining in the dispute. He sat there drinking tea and listening to what the others said, but did not speak himself.

The Turk noticed him sitting there, and appealed to him, saying:

'You can confirm what I say, my good Chinaman. You hold your peace, but if you spoke I know you would uphold my opinion. Traders from your country, who come to me for assistance, tell me that though many religions have been introduced into China, you Chinese consider Mohammedanism the best of all, and adopt it willingly. Confirm, then, my words, and tell us your opinion of the true God and of His prophet.'

'Yes, yes,' said the rest, turning to the Chinaman, 'let us hear what you think on the subject.'

The Chinaman, the student of Confucius, closed his eyes, and thought a while. Then he opened them again, and drawing his hands out of the wide sleeves of his garment, and folding them on his breast, he spoke as follows, in a calm and quiet voice.

'Sirs, it seems to me that it is chiefly pride that prevents men agreeing with one another on matters of faith. If you care to listen to me, I will tell you a story which will explain this by an example.

'I came here from China on an English steamer which had

been round the world. We stopped for fresh water, and landed on the east coast of the island of Sumatra. It was midday, and some of us, having landed, sat in the shade of some coconut palms by the seashore, not far from a native village. We were a party of men of different nationalities.

'As we sat there, a blind man approached us. We learnt afterwards that he had gone blind from gazing too long and too persistently at the sun, trying to find out what it is, in order to seize its light.

'He strove a long time to accomplish this, constantly looking at the sun; but the only result was that his eyes were injured by its brightness and he became blind.

'Then he said to himself:

'"The light of the sun is not a liquid; for if it were a liquid it would be possible to pour it from one vessel into another, and it would be moved, like water, by the wind. Neither is it fire; for if it were fire, water would extinguish it. Neither is light a spirit, for it is seen by the eye; nor is it matter, for it cannot be moved. Therefore, as the light of the sun is neither liquid, nor fire, nor spirit, nor matter, it is – nothing!"

'So he argued, and, as a result of always looking at the sun and always thinking about it, he lost both his sight and his reason. And when he went quite blind, he became fully convinced that the sun did not exist.

'With this blind man came a slave, who after placing his master in the shade of a coconut tree, picked up a coconut from the ground and began making it into a nightlight. He twisted a wick from the fibre of the coconut: squeezed oil from the nut into the shell, and soaked the wick in it. As the slave sat doing this, the blind man sighed and said to him:

'"Well, slave, was I not right when I told you there is no sun? Do you not see how dark it is? Yet people say there is a sun. … But if so, what is it?"

'"I do not know what the sun is," said the slave. "That is no business of mine. But I know what light is. Here I have made a nightlight, by the help of which I can serve you and find anything I want in the hut."

'And the slave picked up the coconut shell, saying:

"'This is my sun."

'A lame man with crutches, who was sitting nearby, heard these words, and laughed: "You have evidently been blind all your life," said he to the blind man, "not to know what the sun is. I will tell you what it is. The sun is a ball of fire, which rises every morning out of the sea and goes down again among the mountains of our island each evening. We have all seen this, and if you had had your eyesight you too would have seen it."

'A fisherman, who had been listening to the conversation said: "It is plain enough that you have never been beyond your own island. If you were not lame, and if you had been out as I have in a fishing boat, you would know that the sun does not set among the mountains of our island, but as it rises from the ocean every morning so it sets again in the sea every night. What I am telling you is true, for I see it every day with my own eyes."

'Then an Indian who was of our party, interrupted him by saying: "I am astonished that a reasonable man should talk such nonsense. How can a ball of fire possibly descend into the water and not be extinguished? The sun is not a ball of fire at all, it is the Deity named Deva, who rides forever in a chariot round the golden mountain, Meru. Sometimes the evil serpents Ragu and Ketu attack Deva and swallow him: and then the earth is dark. But our priests pray that the Deity may be released, and then he is set free. Only such ignorant men as you, who have never been beyond their own island, can imagine that the sun shines for their country alone."

'Then the master of an Egyptian vessel, who was present, spoke in his turn. "No," said he, "you also are wrong. The sun is not a Deity, and does not move only round India and its golden mountain. I have sailed much on the Black Sea, and along the coasts of Arabia, and have been to Madagascar and to the Philippines. The sun lights the whole earth, and not India alone. It does not circle round one mountain, but rises far in the East, beyond the Isles of Japan, and sets far, far away in the West, beyond the islands of England. That is why the Japanese call their country 'Nippon,' that is, 'the birth of the sun'. I know this well, for I have myself seen much, and heard more from my grandfather, who sailed to the very ends of the sea."

'He would have gone on, but an English sailor from our ship interrupted him. "There is no country," he said, "where people know so much about the sun's movements as in England. The sun, as everyone in England knows, rises nowhere and sets nowhere. It is always moving round the earth. We can be sure of this for we have just been round the world ourselves, and nowhere knocked up against the sun. Wherever we went, the sun showed itself in the morning and hid itself at night, just as it does here."

'And the Englishman took a stick and, drawing circles on the sand, tried to explain how the sun moves in the heavens and goes round the world. But he was unable to explain it clearly, and pointing to the ship's pilot said: "This man knows more about it than I do. He can explain it properly."

'The pilot, who was an intelligent man, had listened in silence to the talk till he was asked to speak. Now everyone turned to him, and he said: "You are all misleading one another, and are yourselves deceived. The sun does not go round the earth, but the earth goes round the sun, revolving as it goes, and turning towards the sun in the course of each twenty-four hours, not only Japan, and the Philippines, and Sumatra where we now are, but Africa, and Europe, and America, and many lands besides. The sun does not shine for some one mountain, or for some one island, or for some one sea, nor even for one earth alone, but for other planets as well as our earth. If you would only look up at the heavens, instead of at the ground beneath your own feet, you might all understand this, and would then no longer suppose that the sun shines for you, or for your country alone."

'Thus spoke the wise pilot, who had voyaged much about the world, and had gazed much upon the heavens above.

'So on matters of faith,' continued the Chinaman, the student of Confucius, 'it is pride that causes error and discord among men. As with the sun, so it is with God. Each man wants to have a special God of his own, or at least a special God for his native land. Each nation wishes to confine in its own temples Him, whom the world cannot contain.

'Can any temple compare with that which God Himself has built to unite all men in one faith and one religion?

'All human temples are built on the model of this temple, which is God's own world. Every temple has its fonts, its vaulted roof, its lamps, its pictures or sculptures, its inscriptions, its books of the law, its offerings, its altars and its priests. But in what temple is there such a font as the ocean; such a vault as that of the heavens; such lamps as the sun, moon and stars; or any figures to be compared with living, loving, mutually-helpful men? Where are there any records of God's goodness so easy to understand as the blessings which God has strewn abroad for man's happiness? Where is there any book of the law so clear to each man as that written in his heart? What sacrifices equal the self-denials which loving men and women make for one another? And what altar can be compared with the heart of a good man, on which God Himself accepts the sacrifice?

'The higher a man's conception of God, the better will he know Him. And the better he knows God, the nearer will he draw to Him, imitating His goodness, His mercy and His love of man.

'Therefore, let him who sees the sun's whole light filling the world, refrain from blaming or despising the superstitious man, who in his own idol sees one ray of that same light. Let him not despise even the unbeliever who is blind and cannot see the sun at all.'

So spoke the Chinaman, the student of Confucius; and all who were present in the coffee house were silent, and disputed no more as to whose faith was the best.

TOO DEAR!

(TOLSTOY'S ADAPTATION OF A STORY BY GUY DE MAUPASSANT)

Near the borders of France and Italy, on the shore of the Mediterranean Sea, lies a tiny little kingdom called Monaco. Many a small country town can boast more inhabitants than this kingdom, for there are only about seven thousand of them all told, and if all the land in the kingdom were divided there would not be an acre for each inhabitant. But in this toy kingdom there is a real kinglet; and he has a palace, and courtiers, and ministers, and a bishop, and generals, and an army.

It is not a large army, only sixty men in all, but still it is an army. There were also taxes in this kingdom, as elsewhere: a tax on tobacco, and on wine and spirits, and a poll tax. But though the people there drink and smoke as people do in other countries, there are so few of them that the King would have been hard put to it to feed his courtiers and officials and to keep himself, if he had not found a new and special source of revenue. This special revenue comes from a gaming house, where people play roulette. People play, and whether they win or lose the keeper always gets a percentage on the turnover; and out of his profits he pays a large sum to the King. The reason he pays so much is that it is the only such gambling establishment left in Europe. Some of the little German Sovereigns used to keep gaming houses of the same kind, but some years ago they were forbidden to do so. The reason they were stopped was because these gaming houses did so much harm. A man would come and try his luck, then he would risk all he had and lose it, then he would even risk money that did not belong to him and lose that too, and then, in despair, he would drown or shoot himself. So the Germans forbade their rulers to make money in this way; but there was no one to stop the King of Monaco, and he remained with a monopoly of the business.

So now everyone who wants to gamble goes to Monaco. Whether they win or lose, the King gains by it. 'You can't earn stone palaces by honest labour,' as the proverb says; and the Kinglet of Monaco knows it is a dirty business, but what is he to do? He has to live; and to draw a revenue from drink and from tobacco is also not a nice thing. So he lives and reigns, and rakes in the money, and holds his court with all the ceremony of a real king.

He has his coronation, his levées; he rewards, sentences and pardons, and he also has his reviews, councils, laws and courts of justice: just like other kings, only all on a smaller scale.

Now it happened a few years ago that a murder was committed in this toy King's domains. The people of that kingdom are peaceable, and such a thing had not happened before. The judges assembled with much ceremony and tried the case in the most judicial manner. There were judges, and prosecutors, and jurymen, and barristers. They argued and judged, and at last they condemned the criminal to have his head cut off as the law directs. So far so good. Next they submitted the sentence to the King. The King read the sentence and confirmed it. 'If the fellow must be executed, execute him.'

There was only one hitch in the matter; and that was that they had neither a guillotine for cutting heads off, nor an executioner. The Ministers considered the matter, and decided to address an inquiry to the French Government, asking whether the French could not lend them a machine and an expert to cut off the criminal's head; and if so, would the French kindly inform them what the cost would be. The letter was sent. A week later the reply came: a machine and an expert could be supplied, and the cost would be 16,000 francs. This was laid before the King. He thought it over. Sixteen thousand francs! 'The wretch is not worth the money,' said he. 'Can't it be done, somehow, cheaper? Why 16,000 francs is more than two francs a head on the whole population. The people won't stand it, and it may cause a riot!'

So a Council was called to consider what could be done; and it was decided to send a similar inquiry to the King of Italy. The French Government is republican, and has no proper respect for kings; but the King of Italy was a brother monarch, and might be induced to do the thing cheaper. So the letter was written, and a prompt reply was received.

The Italian Government wrote that they would have pleasure in supplying both a machine and an expert; and the whole cost would be 12,000 francs, including travelling expenses. This was cheaper, but still it seemed too much. The rascal was really not worth the money. It would still mean nearly two francs more per head on the taxes. Another Council was called. They discussed and considered how it could be done with less expense. Could not one of the soldiers perhaps be got to do it in a rough and homely fashion? The General was called and was asked: 'Can't you find us a soldier who would cut the man's head off? In war they don't mind killing people. In fact, that is what they are trained for.' So the General talked it over with the soldiers to see whether one of them would not undertake the job. But none of the soldiers would do it.

'No,' they said, 'we don't know how to do it; it is not a thing we have been taught.'

What was to be done? Again the Ministers considered and reconsidered. They assembled a Commission, and a Committee, and a Sub-Committee, and at last they decided that the best thing would be to alter the death sentence to one of imprisonment for life. This would enable the King to show his mercy, and it would come cheaper.

The King agreed to this, and so the matter was arranged. The only hitch now was that there was no suitable prison for a man sentenced for life. There was a small lock-up where people were sometimes kept temporarily, but there was no strong prison fit for permanent use. However, they managed to find a place that would do, and they put the young fellow there and placed a guard over him. The guard had to watch the criminal, and had also to fetch his food from the palace kitchen.

The prisoner remained there month after month till a year had passed. But when a year had passed, the Kinglet, looking over the account of his income and expenditure one day, noticed a new item of expenditure. This was for the keep of the criminal; nor was it a small item either. There was a special guard, and there was also the man's food. It came to more than 600 francs a year. And the worst of it was that the fellow was still young and healthy, and might live for fifty years. When one came to reckon it up, the matter was serious. It would never do. So the King summoned his Ministers and said to them:

'You must find some cheaper way of dealing with this rascal. The present plan is too expensive.' And the Ministers met and considered and reconsidered, till one of them said: 'Gentlemen, in my opinion we must dismiss the guard.'

'But then,' rejoined another Minister, 'the fellow will run away.'

'Well,' said the first speaker, 'let him run away, and be hanged to him!' So they reported the result of their deliberations to the Kinglet, and he agreed with them. The guard was dismissed, and they waited to see what would happen. All that happened was that at dinner-time the criminal came out, and, not finding his guard, he went to the King's kitchen to fetch his own dinner. He took what was given him, returned to the prison, shut the door on himself, and stayed inside. Next day the same thing occurred. He went for his food at the proper time; but as for running away, he did not show the least sign of it! What was to be done? They considered the matter again.

'We shall have to tell him straight out,' said they, 'that we do not want to keep him.' So the Minister of Justice had him brought before him.

'Why do you not run away?' said the Minister. 'There is no guard to keep you. You can go where you like, and the King will not mind.'

'I daresay the King would not mind,' replied the man, 'but I have nowhere to go. What can I do? You have ruined my character by your sentence, and people will turn their backs on me. Besides, I have got out of the way of working. You have treated me badly. It is not fair. In the first place, when once you sentenced me to death you ought to have executed me; but you did not do it. That is one thing. I did not complain about that. Then you sentenced me to imprisonment for life and put a guard to bring me my food; but after a time you took him away again and I had to fetch my own food. Again I did not complain. But now you actually want me to go away! I can't agree to that. You may do as you like, but I won't go away!'

What was to be done? Once more the Council was summoned. What course could they adopt? The man would not go. They reflected and considered. The only way to get rid of him was to offer him a pension. And so they reported to the King. 'There is nothing else for it,' said they; 'we must get rid of him somehow.' The sum fixed was 600 francs, and this was announced to the prisoner.

'Well,' said he, 'I don't mind, so long as you undertake to pay it regularly. On that condition I am willing to go.'

So the matter was settled. He received one-third of his annuity in advance, and left the King's dominions. It was only a quarter of an hour by rail; and he emigrated, and settled just across the frontier, where he bought a bit of land, started market-gardening, and now lives comfortably. He always goes at the proper time to draw his pension. Having received it, he goes to the gaming tables, stakes two or three francs, sometimes wins and sometimes loses, and then returns home. He lives peaceably and well.

It is a good thing that he did not commit his crime in a country where they do not grudge expense to cut a man's head off, or to keeping him in prison for life.

ESARHADDON, KING OF ASSYRIA

The Assyrian King, Esarhaddon[19], had conquered the kingdom of King Lailie, had destroyed and burnt the towns, taken all the inhabitants captive to his own country, slaughtered the warriors, beheaded some chieftains and impaled or flayed others, and had confined King Lailie himself in a cage.

As he lay on his bed one night, King Esarhaddon was thinking how he should execute Lailie, when suddenly he heard a rustling near his bed, and opening his eyes saw an old man with a long grey beard and mild eyes.

19 *In this story Tolstoy has used the names of real people. Esarhaddon (or Assur-akhi-iddina) is mentioned three times in the Bible (2 Kings 19:37; Isaiah 37:38, and Ezra 4:2), and is also alluded to in 2 Chron. 33:11, as, 'the King of Assyria, which took Manasseh in chains, and bound him with fetters, and carried him to Babylon.' His son, Assur-bani-pal, whom he promoted to power before his own death, is once mentioned in the Bible, under the name of Asnapper (Ezra 4:10). Of Lailie history does not tell us much; but in Ernest A. Budge's* History of Esarhaddon *we read: 'A King, called Lailie, asked that the goods which Esarhaddon had captured from him might be restored. His request was granted, and Esarhaddon said, 'I spoke to him of brotherhood, and entrusted to him the sovereignty of the districts of Bazu.'*

'You wish to execute Lailie?' asked the old man.

'Yes,' answered the King. 'But I cannot make up my mind how to do it.'

'But you are Lailie,' said the old man.

'That's not true,' replied the King. 'Lailie is Lailie, and I am I.'

'You and Lailie are one,' said the old man. 'You only imagine you are not Lailie, and that Lailie is not you.'

'What do you mean by that?' said the King. 'Here am I, lying on a soft bed; around me are obedient men-slaves and women-slaves, and tomorrow I shall feast with my friends as I did today; whereas Lailie is sitting like a bird in a cage, and tomorrow he will be impaled, and with his tongue hanging out will struggle till he dies, and his body will be torn in pieces by dogs.'

'You cannot destroy his life,' said the old man.

'And how about the fourteen thousand warriors I killed, with whose bodies I built a mound?' said the King. 'I am alive, but they no longer exist. Does not that prove that I can destroy life?'

'How do you know they no longer exist?'

'Because I no longer see them. And, above all, they were tormented, but I was not. It was ill for them, but well for me.'

'That, also, only seems so to you. You tortured yourself, but not them.'

'I do not understand,' said the King.

'Do you wish to understand?'

'Yes, I do.'

'Then come here,' said the old man, pointing to a large font full of water.

The King rose and approached the font.

'Strip, and enter the font.'

Esarhaddon did as the old man bade him.

'As soon as I begin to pour this water over you,' said the old man, filling a pitcher with the water, 'dip down your head.'

The old man tilted the pitcher over the King's head, and the King bent his head till it was underwater.

And as soon as King Esarhaddon was under the water, he felt that he was no longer Esarhaddon, but someone else. And, feeling himself to be that other man, he saw himself lying on a rich bed, beside a beautiful woman. He had never seen her before, but he knew she was his wife. The woman raised herself and said to him:

'Dear husband, Lailie! You were wearied by yesterday's work and have slept longer than usual, and I have guarded your rest, and have not roused you. But now the Princes await you in the Great Hall. Dress and go out to them.'

And Esarhaddon – understanding from these words that he was Lailie, and not feeling at all surprised at this, but only wondering that he did not know it before – rose, dressed, and went into the Great Hall where the Princes awaited him.

The Princes greeted Lailie, their King, bowing to the ground, and then they rose, and at his word sat down before him; and the eldest of the Princes began to speak, saying that it was impossible longer to endure the insults of the wicked King Esarhaddon, and that they must make war on him. But Lailie disagreed, and gave orders that envoys shall be sent to remonstrate with King Esarhaddon; and he dismissed the Princes from the audience. Afterwards he appointed men of note to act as ambassadors, and impressed on them what they were to say to King Esarhaddon. Having finished this business, Esarhaddon – feeling himself to be Lailie – rode out to hunt wild asses. The hunt was successful. He killed two wild asses himself, and, having returned home, feasted with his friends, and witnessed a dance of slave girls. The next day he went to the Court, where he was awaited by petitioners, suitors, and prisoners brought for trial; and there as usual he decided the cases submitted to him. Having finished this business, he again rode out to his favourite amusement: the hunt. And again he was successful: this time killing with his own hand an old lioness, and capturing her two cubs. After the hunt he again feasted with his friends, and was entertained with music and dances, and the night he spent with the wife whom he loved.

So, dividing his time between kingly duties and pleasures, he lived for days and weeks, awaiting the return of the ambassadors he had sent to that King Esarhaddon who used to be himself. Not till a month had passed did the ambassadors return, and they returned with their noses and ears cut off.

King Esarhaddon had ordered them to tell Lailie that what had been done to them – the ambassadors – would be done to King Lailie himself also, unless he sent immediately a tribute of silver, gold and cypress wood, and came himself to pay homage to King Esarhaddon.

Lailie, formerly Esarhaddon, again assembled the Princes, and took counsel with them as to what he should do. They all with one accord said that war must be made against Esarhaddon, without waiting for him to attack them. The King agreed; and taking his place at the head of the army, started on the campaign. The campaign lasted seven days. Each day the King rode round the army to rouse the courage of his warriors. On the eighth day his army met that of Esarhaddon in a broad valley through which a river flowed. Lailie's army fought bravely, but Lailie, formerly Esarhaddon, saw the enemy swarming down from the mountains like ants, overrunning the valley and overwhelming his army; and, in his chariot, he flung himself into the midst of the battle, hewing and felling the enemy. But the warriors of Lailie were but as hundreds, while those of Esarhaddon were as thousands; and Lailie felt himself wounded and taken prisoner. Nine days he journeyed with other captives, bound, and guarded by the warriors of Esarhaddon.

On the tenth day he reached Nineveh, and was placed in a cage. Lailie suffered not so much from hunger and from his wound as from shame and impotent rage. He felt how powerless he was to avenge himself on his enemy for all he was suffering. All he could do was to deprive his enemies of the pleasure of seeing his sufferings; and he firmly resolved to endure courageously, without a murmur, all they could do to him. For twenty days he sat in his cage, awaiting execution. He saw his relatives and friends led out to death; he heard the groans of those who were executed: some had their hands and feet cut off, others were flayed alive, but he showed neither disquietude, nor pity, nor fear. He saw the wife he loved, bound, and led by two black eunuchs. He knew she was being taken as a slave to Esarhaddon. That, too, he bore without a murmur. But one of the guards placed to watch him said, 'I pity you, Lailie; you were a king, but what are you now?' And hearing these words, Lailie remembered all he had lost. He clutched the bars of his cage, and, wishing to kill himself, beat his head against them. But he had not the strength to do so; and, groaning in despair, he fell upon the floor of his cage.

At last two executioners opened his cage door, and having strapped his arms tight behind him, led him to the place of execution, which was soaked with blood. Lailie saw a sharp stake dripping with blood, from which the corpse of one of his friends had just been torn, and he understood that this had been done that the stake might serve for his own execution. They stripped Lailie of his clothes. He was startled at the leanness of his once strong, handsome body. The two executioners seized that body by its lean thighs; they lifted him up and were about to let him fall upon the stake.

'This is death, destruction!' thought Lailie, and, forgetful of his resolve to remain bravely calm to the end, he sobbed and prayed for mercy. But no one listened to him.

'But this cannot be,' thought he. 'Surely I am asleep. It is a dream.' And he made an effort to rouse himself, and did indeed awake, to find himself neither Esarhaddon nor Lailie, but some kind of an animal. He was astonished that he was an animal, and astonished, also, at not having known this before.

He was grazing in a valley, tearing the tender grass with his teeth, and brushing away flies with his long tail. Around him was frolicking a long-legged, dark-gray ass-colt, striped down its back. Kicking up its hind legs, the colt galloped full speed to Esarhaddon, and poking him under the stomach with its smooth little muzzle, searched for the teat, and, finding it, quieted down, swallowing regularly. Esarhaddon understood that he was a she-ass, the colt's mother, and this neither surprised nor grieved him, but rather gave him pleasure. He experienced a glad feeling of simultaneous life in himself and in his offspring.

But suddenly something flew near with a whistling sound and hit him in the side, and with its sharp point entered his skin and flesh. Feeling a burning pain, Esarhaddon – who was at the same time the ass – tore the udder from the colt's teeth, and laying back his ears galloped to the herd from which he had strayed. The colt kept up with him, galloping by his side. They had already nearly reached the herd, which had started off, when another arrow in full flight struck the colt's neck. It pierced the skin and quivered in its flesh. The colt sobbed piteously and fell upon its knees. Esarhaddon could not abandon it, and remained standing over it. The colt rose, tottered on its long, thin legs, and again fell. A fearful two-legged being – a man – ran up and cut its throat.

'This cannot be; it is still a dream! thought Esarhaddon, and made a last effort to awake. 'Surely I am not Lailie, nor the ass, but Esarhaddon!'

He cried out, and at the same instant lifted his head out of the font... The old man was standing by him, pouring over his head the last drops from the pitcher.

'Oh, how terribly I have suffered! And for how long!' said Esarhaddon.

'Long?' replied the old man, 'you have only dipped your head underwater and lifted it again; see, the water is not yet all out of the pitcher. Do you now understand?'

Esarhaddon did not reply, but only looked at the old man with terror.

'Do you now understand,' continued the old man, 'that Lailie is you, and the warriors you put to death were you also? And not the warriors only, but the animals which you slew when hunting and ate at your feasts, were also you. You thought life dwelt in you alone, but I have drawn aside the veil of delusion, and have let you see that by doing evil to others you have done it to yourself also. Life is one in them all, and yours is but a portion of this same common life. And only in that one part of life that is yours, can you make life better or worse – increasing or decreasing it. You can only improve life in yourself by destroying the barriers that divide your life from that of others, and by considering others as yourself, and loving them. By so doing you increase your share of life. You injure your life when you think of it as the only life, and try to add to its welfare at the expense of other lives. By so doing you only lessen it. To destroy the life that dwells in others is beyond your power. The life of those you have slain has vanished from your eyes, but is not destroyed. You thought to lengthen your own life and to shorten theirs, but you cannot do this. Life knows neither time nor space. The life of a moment, and the life of a thousand years: your life, and the life of all the visible and invisible beings in the world, are equal. To destroy life, or to alter it, is impossible; for life is the one thing that exists. All else, but seems to us to be.'

Having said this the old man vanished.

Next morning King Esarhaddon gave orders that Lailie and all the prisoners should be set at liberty, and that the executions should cease.

On the third day he called his son Assur-bani-pal, and gave the kingdom over into his hands; and he himself went into the desert to think over all he had learnt. Afterwards he went about as a wanderer through the towns and villages, preaching to the people that all life is one, and that when men wish to harm others, they really do evil to themselves.

WORK, DEATH AND SICKNESS

A LEGEND

This is a legend current among the South American Indians. God, say they, at first made men so that they had no need to work: they needed neither houses, nor clothes, nor food, and they all lived till they were a hundred, and did not know what illness was.

When, after some time, God looked to see how people were living, he saw that instead of being happy in their life, they had quarrelled with one another, and, each caring for himself, had brought matters to such a pass that far from enjoying life, they cursed it.

Then God said to himself: 'This comes of their living separately, each for himself.' And to change this state of things, God so arranged matters that it became impossible for people to live without working. To avoid suffering from cold and hunger, they were now obliged to build dwellings, and to dig the ground, and to grow and gather fruits and grain.

'Work will bring them together,' thought God. 'They cannot make their tools, prepare and transport their timber, build their houses, sow and gather their harvests, spin and weave, and make their clothes, each one alone by himself.'

'It will make them understand that the more heartily they work together, the more they will have and the better they will live; and this will unite them.'

Time passed on, and again God came to see how men were living, and whether they were now happy.

But he found them living worse than before. They worked together (that they could not help doing), but not all together, being broken up into little groups. And each group tried to snatch work from other groups, and they hindered one another, wasting time and strength in their struggles, so that things went ill with them all.

Having seen that this, too, was not well, God decided so as to arrange things that man should not know the time of his death, but might die at any moment; and he announced this to them.

'Knowing that each of them may die at any moment,' thought God, 'they will not, by grasping at gains that may last so short a time, spoil the hours of life allotted to them.'

But it turned out otherwise. When God returned to see how people were living, he saw that their life was as bad as ever.

Those who were strongest, availing themselves of the fact that men might die at any time, subdued those who were weaker, killing some and threatening others with death. And it came about that the strongest and their descendants did no work, and suffered from the weariness of idleness, while those who were weaker had to work beyond their strength, and suffered from lack of rest. Each set of men feared and hated the other. And the life of man became yet more unhappy.

Having seen all this, God, to mend matters, decided to make use of one last means; he sent all kinds of sickness among men. God thought that when all men were exposed to sickness they would understand that those who are well should have pity on those who are sick, and should help them, that when they them-selves fall ill, those who are well might in turn help them.

And again God went away; but when He came back to see how men lived now that they were subject to sicknesses, he saw that their life was worse even than before. The very sickness that in God's purpose should have united men, had divided them more than ever. Those men who were strong enough to make others work, forced them also to wait on them in times of sickness; but they did not, in their turn, look after others who were ill. And those who were forced to work for others and to look after them when sick, were so worn with work that they had no time to look after their own sick, but left them without attendance. That the sight of sick folk might not disturb the pleasures of the wealthy, houses were arranged in which these poor people suffered and died, far from those whose sympathy might have cheered them, and in the arms of hired people who nursed them without compassion, or even with disgust. Moreover, people considered many of the illnesses infectious, and, fearing to catch them, not only avoided the sick, but even separated themselves from those who attended the sick.

Then God said to Himself: 'If even this means will not bring men to understand wherein their happiness lies, let them be taught by suffering.' And God left men to themselves.

And, left to themselves, men lived long before they understood that they all ought to, and might be, happy. Only in the very latest times have a few of them begun to understand that work ought not to be a bugbear to some and like galley-slavery for others, but should be a common and happy occupation, uniting all men. They have begun to understand that with death constantly threatening each of us, the only reasonable business of every man is to spend the years, months, hours and minutes allotted him – in unity and love. They have begun to understand that sickness, far from dividing men, should, on the contrary, give opportunity for loving union with one another.

THREE QUESTIONS

It once occurred to a certain king, that if he always knew the right time to begin everything; if he knew who were the right people to listen to, and whom to avoid; and, above all, if he always knew what was the most important thing to do, he would never fail in anything he might undertake.

And this thought having occurred to him, he had it proclaimed throughout his kingdom that he would give a great reward to anyone who would teach him what was the right time for every action, and who were the most necessary people, and how he might know what was the most important thing to do.

And learned men came to the King, but they all answered his questions differently.

In reply to the first question, some said that to know the right time for every action, one must draw up in advance, a table of days, months and years, and must live strictly according to it. Only thus, said they, could everything be done at its proper time. Others declared that it was impossible to decide beforehand the right time for every action; but that, not letting oneself be absorbed in idle pastimes, one should always attend to all that was going on, and then do what was most needful. Others, again, said that however attentive the King might be to what was going on, it was impossible for one man to decide correctly the right time for every action, but that he should have a Council of wise men, who would help him to fix the proper time for everything.

But then again others said there were some things which could not wait to be laid before a Council, but about which one had at once to decide whether to undertake them or not. But in order to decide that, one must know beforehand what was going to happen. It is only magicians who know that; and, therefore, in order to know the right time for every action, one must consult magicians.

Equally various were the answers to the second question. Some said, the people the King most needed were his councillors; others, the priests; others, the doctors; while some said the warriors were the most necessary.

To the third question, as to what was the most important occupation: some replied that the most important thing in the world was science. Others said it was skill in warfare; and others, again, that it was religious worship.

All the answers being different, the King agreed with none of them, and gave the reward to none. But still wishing to find the right answers to his questions, he decided to consult a hermit, widely renowned for his wisdom.

The hermit lived in a wood which he never quitted, and he received none but common folk. So the King put on simple clothes, and before reaching the hermit's cell dismounted from his horse, and, leaving his bodyguard behind, went on alone.

When the King approached, the hermit was digging the ground in front of his hut. Seeing the King, he greeted him and went on digging. The hermit was frail and weak, and each time he stuck his spade into the ground and turned a little earth, he breathed heavily.

The King went up to him and said: 'I have come to you, wise hermit, to ask you to answer three questions: How can I learn to do the right thing at the right time? Who are the people I most need, and to whom should I, therefore, pay more attention than to the rest? And, what affairs are the most important, and need my first attention?'

The hermit listened to the King, but answered nothing. He just spat on his hand and recommenced digging.

'You are tired,' said the King, 'let me take the spade and work awhile for you.'

'Thanks!' said the hermit, and, giving the spade to the King, he sat down on the ground.

When he had dug two beds, the King stopped and repeated his questions. The hermit again gave no answer, but rose, stretched out his hand for the spade, and said:

'Now rest awhile – and let me work a bit.'

But the King did not give him the spade, and continued to dig. One hour passed, and another. The sun began to sink behind the trees, and the King at last stuck the spade into the ground, and said:

'I came to you, wise man, for an answer to my questions. If you can give me none, tell me so, and I will return home.'

'Here comes someone running,' said the hermit, 'let us see who it is.'

The King turned round, and saw a bearded man come running out of the wood. The man held his hands pressed against his stomach, and blood was flowing from under them. When he reached the King, he fell fainting on the ground moaning feebly. The King and the hermit unfastened the man's clothing. There was a large wound in his stomach. The King washed it as best he could, and bandaged it with his handkerchief and with a towel the hermit had. But the blood would not stop flowing, and the King again and again removed the bandage soaked with warm blood, and washed and rebandaged the wound. When at last the blood ceased flowing, the man revived and asked for something to drink. The King brought fresh water and gave it to him. Meanwhile the sun had set, and it had become cool. So the King, with the hermit's help, carried the wounded man into the hut and laid him on the bed. Lying on the bed the man closed his eyes and was quiet; but the King was so tired with his walk and with the work he had done, that he crouched down on the threshold, and also fell asleep – so soundly that he slept all through the short summer night.

When he awoke in the morning, it was long before he could remember where he was, or who was the strange bearded man lying on the bed and gazing intently at him with shining eyes.

'Forgive me!' said the bearded man in a weak voice, when he saw that the King was awake and was looking at him.

'I do not know you, and have nothing to forgive you for,' said the King.

'You do not know me, but I know you. I am that enemy of yours who swore to revenge himself on you, because you executed his brother and seized his property. I knew you had gone alone to see the hermit, and I resolved to kill you on your way back. But the day passed and you did not return. So I came out from my ambush to find you, and I came upon your bodyguard, and they recognized me, and wounded me. I escaped from them, but should have bled to death had you not dressed my wound. I wished to kill you, and you have saved my life. Now, if I live, and if you wish it, I will serve you as your most faithful slave, and will bid my sons do the same. Forgive me!'

The King was very glad to have made peace with his enemy so easily, and to have gained him for a friend, and he not only forgave him, but said he would send his servants and his own physician to attend him, and promised to restore his property.

Having taken leave of the wounded man, the King went out into the porch and looked around for the hermit. Before going away he wished once more to beg an answer to the questions he had put. The hermit was outside, on his knees, sowing seeds in the beds that had been dug the day before.

The King approached him, and said:

'For the last time, I pray you to answer my questions, wise man.'

'You have already been answered!' said the hermit still crouching on his thin legs, and looking up at the King, who stood before him.

'How answered? What do you mean?' asked the King.

'Do you not see,' replied the hermit. 'If you had not pitied my weakness yesterday, and had not dug those beds for me, but had gone your way, that man would have attacked you, and you would have repented of not having stayed with me. So the most important time was when you were digging the beds; and I was the most important man; and to do me good was your most important business. Afterwards when that man ran to us, the most important time was when you were attending to him, for if you had not bound up his wounds he would have died without having made peace with you. So he was the most important man, and what you did for him was your most important business. Remember then: there is only one time that is important – now! It is the most important time because it is the only time when we have any power. The most necessary man is he with whom you are, for no man knows whether he will ever have dealings with anyone else: and the most important affair is, to do him good, because for that purpose alone was man sent into this life!'